"I need your exp[...] crazy alien on my [...]."

"Where's your alien from?" Val asked.

"That's the problem. I don't know. The patient's got no i.d., and isn't very coherent." Joan lowered her voice. "It's a suicide case."

"Why don't you call a mentationist?" Val asked.

"I will, as soon as I know how to describe this patient. Val, this isn't a him or a her."

"A himher?" Val said. That was an easy riddle to solve.

"No," Joan said a little crossly. "I know a Gyne when I see one. This isn't an androgyne. It isn't anything. No sexual characteristics at all—like one of those prudish children's dolls. Have you ever heard of such a thing?"

"I have, but you couldn't have one in your clinic."

"I do," Joan maintained.

"No. What I mean is, there is only one documented case of true, natural asexuals—on Gammadis, the closed planet. No native has ever left it."

HALFWAY HUMAN

CAROLYN IVES GILMAN

AVON · EOS

AVON BOOKS
A division of
The Hearst Corporation
1350 Avenue of the Americas
New York, New York 10019

Copyright © 1998 by Carolyn Ives Gilman
Published by arrangement with the author
Visit our website at **http://www.AvonBooks.com/Eos**
Library of Congress Catalog Card Number: 97-94464
ISBN: 0-380-79799-2

First Avon Eos Printing: February 1998

AVON EOS TRADEMARK REG. U.S. PAT. OFF. AND IN OTHER COUNTRIES, MARCA REGISTRADA, HECHO EN U.S.A.

Printed in the U.S.A.

WCD   10 9 8 7 6 5 4 3 2 1

Prologue

🎵 By night, the enclave of Djenga Shana glittered, and smelled. The palaces of temptation clustered around the waystation, feeding on the nutrient wash of tourists that issued from the wayports, ripe with money and desires. The Worwha Shana, natives of the enclave, made no secret of their wish to eradicate all infidels who didn't share their odd religion; but they had no intention of doing it by violence. Instead, they provided the deadly vices that allowed the infidels to destroy themselves.

It had just rained in Djenga Shana. The streets were smeary with neon rivulets, and a steam-haze rose from hot pavement. Down a dark side street, where the walls were plain gray brick, a door opened for a moment, exhaling a hot breath that smelled of stimsmoke and ambergris. The light from the door silhouetted a figure that slipped out, barefoot and wrapped in a raincoat that was sizes too big. In the dim light it was impossible to tell whether it was a boy made up to look like a woman, or a large-boned woman trying to conceal her sex. Pulling the raincoat tighter and cinching the belt, the figure thrust hard fists into the pockets and headed for the street.

Participarlors, stimulation studios, creep shows, and druggeries showed their wares for the passing crowds. Beneath a patch of translucent pavement, a naked dancer writhed under shifting lights, first scalded red, then skeletal

1

white, jerking like a marionette on piano-wire strings. The wanderer in the raincoat paused to watch, collar turned up high. Then a nearby door opened its moist, fleshy lips, and a feedback buzz of music issued, making the tense body under the coat flinch back. Over the music came a woman's laugh, sharp as a needle, and the wail of a pocket alarm going off. Then the door pursed shut, choking off the noise.

Underfoot, the pavement was strewn with discarded things whose pleasure-value had been used up: a fresh corsage, partly crushed; a tangled wad of shorn hair; a lost endorphin-brooch, the kind made to be pinned direct through skin. The barefoot figure stopped to reach out for the brooch, then thrust the outstretched hand into a pocket instead, where it closed over something hard. For an instant the light from a sign that read Every Wish Fulfilled picked out a glint of touseled golden hair as the wanderer turned down a narrow alley.

The sound of a sharp explosion ricocheted out onto the street. A panhandler paused in midspiel; two drunken students with songbirds tethered to their shoulders peered down the alley. But there was nothing to see, no novelty to lure them, and they turned away. The streetlights cycled through the spectrum, hallucination bright. Their glare hid the trickle of blood mingling with the greasy rain.

Chapter One

෴ When the call came, Valerie Endrada was in the bedroom pawing through a jumble of unpacked containers, looking for her daughter's swimsuit. The mess frustrated her; lately, she had been feeling that her life was full of disorganized corners heaped with things she couldn't find. Moving had only made it worse. When she heard Max talking to the dinery screen, it was a welcome distraction.

He had blanked it by the time she looked in. "Who is it?" she asked.

"For you," he said. "It's Joansie."

That was Max's nickname for his mother when she was on a rampage of good works. Activism ran in his family; at the moment, Max was wearing a Freedom of Information shirt, with a red headband around his forehead. He looked ready to defend the barricades.

"What's she want?" Val said.

Max shrugged. "She's not at home, she's at the clinic."

"Uh-oh," Val said. It was Allday, and they had planned on a picnic with Max's parents. Joan was supposed to be at home fixing food.

"Look, Mama," Dierdre said cheerfully, plucking a red fruit from her breakfast bowl and holding it out.

"That looks good, Deedee," Val said. She had never seen anything like it. It had a vaguely repulsive heart shape, with gaping pores on the surface. To Max she said, "What are you feeding her?"

"It's called a strawberry," Max said, holding out a container of them he was packing for the picnic. "One of those retrogenic things—backbred till it's healthy again, you know." Val took one and bit in cautiously. The inside was white and crunchy; the flavor was tart. She tossed the remainder into the compost. "You didn't pay for them, did you?" she asked.

"Of course not. It was some sort of promotion."

Val went into the studium to take the call.

Joan looked breathless and scattered, as usual. She always tried to keep her graying hair pulled back in a bun, but it was constantly getting loose. The blue lab coat she was wearing meant she was on duty. She had retired from practice five years ago, but still did volunteer work at a charity clinic in Djenga Shana.

"Valerie! Good," she said, all business. "I didn't know who else to call. I've got a very peculiar problem here."

"Joan, why are you at the clinic? I thought we were having a picnic."

"They called me in because they were short-staffed. And I'm calling you in now. I need your expertise."

"Professional or personal?" Val asked.

"Professional. As an exoethnologist. I've got a crazy alien on my hands."

That was not terribly surprising, considering that Djenga Shana attracted some of the most indigent recent arrivals from the Twenty Planets.

"Where's your alien from?" Val asked.

"That's the problem. I don't know. The patient's got no ID, and isn't very coherent." She lowered her voice. "It's a suicide case. It's been twenty years since I've seen one of those, our prevention programs are so good."

"Why don't you call a mentationist?" Val said.

"I will, as soon as I know how to describe this patient. Val, this isn't a him or a her."

"A himher?" Val said. That was an easy riddle to solve.

"No," Joan said a little crossly. "I know a Gyne when I see one. This isn't an androgyne. It isn't anything. No sexual characteristics at all—like one of those prudish children's dolls. Have you ever heard of such a thing?"

Val hesitated a moment. It went against the grain to give away information she could get paid for; but Joansie was family, and it was in a good cause. At last she said, "I have, but you couldn't have one in your clinic."

"I do," Joan maintained.

"No. What I mean is, there is only one documented case of true, natural asexuals—on Gammadis, the closed planet. No native has ever left it, and only about forty Capellans have ever seen it. What you have must be some sort of surgical construct, or a mutation."

"I wish you would come here and look for yourself. I've got a hunch something strange is going on. You'll know what I mean when you get here. If you can make it by 9.50, we'll still have plenty of time to get to the beach."

Val hit the time key to look up the university time. It was 8.90. A little over half an hour to get to the other side of the world. That was just like Joan. She swept people up in her crusades like a small, determined hurricane. "No peripheral vision," Max sometimes said of her. But the fact was, Max had gone and married someone very like his mother.

"I can't, Joan," Val said, even though resistance was futile. "Max would kill me. I promised to be in charge of Deedee today. He's had to do it all week."

"Never mind that," Joan said breezily. "I'll call E.G. and tell him to give Max a hand."

The last time Max's father had baby-sat Dierdre, she had come home calling people she didn't like "infomongers." Max had been more amused than Val.

"I don't know, Joan . . ." Val said.

"Don't try to fool me, you want to come. I'll be expecting you." Joan cut the connection.

Val sat staring at the screen, which had reverted to clock mode. She clicked her thumbnail against her front tooth, a habit that made Max crazy. Actually, Joan had been right; Val *was* curious. She had gone into xenology dreaming of expeditions to new planets; but those days were long gone. No one could afford exploration any more. Magisters minor like herself might spend whole careers just going over dog-eared records from old expeditions, trying to extract from them one more monograph, never seeing any culture but Capella Two's, never discovering anything new. Val was restless for distraction.

"What was it?" Max said when she came out. The dinery table was heaped with picnic food; Dierdre had disappeared into her room.

"Your mother wants me to come to the clinic for a while," Val said. "She's got an interesting case. We'll have to meet you at the beach."

"Does that mean I'm taking Deedee?" Max said, his voice ominously neutral. "Wait until The Boss hears."

Deedee came racing in with a flexup toy in the shape of a fanciful alien. "Look what I'm taking, Mama," she said. "Papa said I could."

Val knelt to be at her level. "Listen, sweetie," she said, "Mama's got to go somewhere for a while. I'll catch up with you later."

"Do I have to go with Papa?" Deedee said, disappointed.

"Yes. Don't eat all the sawberries before I get there."

"Strawberries," Max said.

"I *always* have to go with Papa," Deedee protested. "You never want to take me."

Val wondered if children were genetically programmed to pull their parents' guilt-strings. She hesitated, and all was lost. Deedee brightened at the look on her face.

"Go dress, and maybe you can come," Val said. There had never been a more useless "maybe."

Joyously, Deedee raced off to her room. Max said, "To

the clinic? Val, are you crazy? Have you ever been there?''

"She needs to be exposed to other ways of life," Val rationalized valiantly.

Max looked beseechingly heavenward. "Well, don't blame me if she comes home asking what 'venereal disease' means."

Val kissed him on the cheek and went to the bedroom to find her pack and university scarf.

On the pumice path to the waystation, Val tried to ignore the bite of disappointment at their new, low-rent neighborhood. As Deedee ran ahead down the hill, Val looked out at the bone-gray moonscape, and told herself it wasn't so bad. The subsidized copartment was perched high on the slope of a crater, and the enclave nestled below like some monster bird's nest, a clutch of domed buildings, eggshell white. In the west the huge limb of Gomb spanned half the horizon, its colors bleached to pink by the rising sun. Everything seemed bright and clear-cut in the dry air—all but Val's thoughts. They felt like a messy room, too small for all the piles of neglected problems.

In their student days, she and Max had shared a jaunty contempt for the power structure, because then they could afford it. Val had been succeeding then—honors graduate, scholarship to study under a magister prime—and it had not seemed far-fetched to aim at a career as an independent contractor in the knowledge business. But the years since graduation had brought only frustration. The market was flooded with young magisters, each hawking an obscure expertise. One by one, her friends were giving up and signing life contracts with the big infocompanies, yielding all their future copyrights and patents for secure employment. So far, she had resisted that irrevocable step, hoping she only needed to repackage her knowledge to make it a more appealing commodity.

"Presentation, that's what I need to work on," she would say to Max. He only rolled his eyes. He had supported her loyally, even though it meant staying home with

Deedee because they couldn't afford to send her to school. But Val's enormous education debts were coming due. For a while last month their infoservice had gotten disconnected for nonpayment. Val had grown intensely guilty, knowing it was her fault, for putting independence before responsibility.

The waystation jutted up from among the egg-domes like a shard of broken glass on edge. When Val stopped at the navigator, she found that getting to Djenga Shana was complex; with a twinge of guilt she paid for a printout of the shortest route. The station was crowded with holiday travelers. Holding Deedee's hand, she dodged noisy families in bathing suits and hiking gear, lined up at the ports to the vacation spots. Her own destination port was almost deserted.

Deedee wanted to go through the wayport first, so Val stood and watched as her daughter disappeared in the flash of a lightbeam, leaving only a wisp of steam. The sight always gave her a twinge of panic. Quickly, she paid her own fare, stepped in, felt the familiar tingle, then

stepped out of an identical port in a waystation a thousand miles away. Deedee was there, studying some dried gum on the tile floor. Val took her hand again, then looked around for the next port on their route.

Almost as soon as she stepped from the wayport at Djenga Shana, Val regretted bringing Deedee. She paused to rearrange the scarf that gave her academic immunity here, then took her daughter's hand firmly. It was near noon, and the street was shuttered and empty. The garish signs looked faded and peeling, naked without the glamor of night and light. There was a pervasive smell of spilled beer cooking in the sun.

"Mama," Deedee protested, "don't hold my hand so tight."

"I'm sorry, chick," she said. She dreaded any questions.

Outside a fetish shop, a Worwha Shana gbinja stood,

wrapped in the gray tubular garment he had donned at puberty and would not remove until he died. It was ragged and stained around the hem and sleeves, but the tough fiber looked like it would outlast the man. He glared at Val with loathing from under a mass of unshorn hair, doubtless wishing her to Worwha hell. There was a story in the xenology department at UIC about a researcher who had lived with the Worwha Shana for four years, and when he left, his Worwha family still called him "heathen garbage."

When Val entered the clinic, two wan, barely dressed teenage girls were sleeping in the waiting room. Roused by her entrance, one of them eyed her suspiciously. Val knocked at the battered lexan reception window. The clinic was like an unarmed fort, constantly under siege by drug-seekers.

Joan herself came bustling out to open the locked door. Deedee cried out, "Gramma! We came to visit you."

"Deedee!" Joan said, startled. Then, to Val, a whispered, "Why did you bring her here?"

"Temporary insanity," Val said.

As they passed down the hall, Joan said, "Go on and help yourself to coffee. I'll get Mandy to look after Deedee. Come with me, chickpea."

When Joan returned alone, she poured a cup from the coffee urn and stood sipping it, leaning against the wall as if a little too tired to support her own weight. "It was a pretty standard clientele last night," she said. "A couple of mugged tourists, the usual overdoses and nerve burns, some sexually transmitted diseases. Then about 1.50 Cannie Annie—one of our local characters—came staggering in saying there'd been a murder. You can't trust what she says, so we didn't call the law. I went out to check."

"Joan! You promised us you wouldn't go out of the clinic at night."

"Well, I'm not going to let someone die," Joan said crossly. "Besides, Bart was with me. Annie led us to an alley, and there we found our visitor from another planet, lying in a pool of blood, wearing a raincoat and nothing else. It had tried to blow its brains out with an explosive gun.''

"How horrible," Val said softly.

"It hadn't done a very good job. Not even close. We brought it back, patched it up, checked it over. That's when we found it was an 'it.' I've been checking the medical nets, Val, and I can't find a record of any mutation like this. There could be a surgical explanation—god knows we see some strange body alterations here—but if so they did it without leaving a trace. And why would anyone choose to eradicate their sex?"

"Maybe it wasn't voluntary," Val said. Here, she would believe anything. "Have you been able to ask the patient?"

"Well, that's the problem. Medically, the patient's not in bad shape, aside from being a little low on blood. But mentally—well, at first it was completely unresponsive, almost catatonic. I gave it a standard antidepressant, and it got quite agitated and incoherent. The drugs ought to be wearing off now; maybe we'll have better luck. Let's take a look first."

She led the way into a small observation room. She closed the door, touched the switch, and the wall became a one-way window into the adjoining room.

The patient was crouched in a chair in hospital pajamas, knees drawn up to its chest. Val stared, fascinated. The person beyond the glass fit none of her half-formed expectations. She had pictured something eunuchlike and faintly repulsive, but the neuter's face instead had an androgynous, Greek-sculpture beauty: classic bone structure, long lashes, dark brows under curly golden hair. But now the hair was darkened and matted, the eyes swollen. There was a bandage on the left temple, and the hair around it was singed.

"It used a gun?" she said softly. She was no mentationist, but to her the violence of the method meant something—a particular hatred of the self, a desire to inflict damage and pain. An attempt to match inner violence with outer, perhaps.

"Yes," Joan said. "Good thing its aim was so poor. It could have done real damage to that beautiful face."

Val said, "How old is . . . I feel strange saying 'it'."

"What else can you say? No other word is accurate. If this were one of us, I'd say it's in its mid-twenties."

"Really? That old?" The patient looked younger, but perhaps that was only because Val associated the lack of obvious sexual characteristics with adolescence. "What do you want me to do?"

"First, I'd like you to talk to it and get me some information. You know what a mentationist is going to want. He'll take a scan and want to start altering the patient's mental template. But how can we do that in good conscience when we don't know what's normal for this patient? We need to do a little research before jumping in."

Val felt a little bubble of excitement rising through her chest. Whatever the thing in the next room was, it clearly represented an unstudied aspect of someone's culture. This was an opportunity for discovery, maybe even a profitable one.

In the next room, the figure had moved; now it was pressing its knuckles to its forehead as if to hold in some terrible thought. Val felt a surge of sympathy and alarm invading her scientific detachment. She had never seen a suicidal person before, and the reality dispelled any romantic fantasies she might have had. There was nothing pretty about this. The person in the next room looked to be in almost unendurable pain.

"I'd feel better if there were a mentationist present," she said. "What if I do something wrong?"

"I'll be here, watching. Bart's on standby. Don't worry, Val. You're a trained interviewer. What can you do wrong?"

She didn't dare let Joan know how unprepared she felt.

"You don't mind if we record the interview?" Joan said. "We may need to study it."

Val restrained herself from asking about copyright. The recording was unlikely to be valuable.

Joan opened the door to usher Val into the corridor. She took out an access card and slid it into the slot. The door clicked open; Val took a long breath and stepped through.

As she entered, the patient rose quickly to face her, keeping the chair between them, as suspicious and edgy as a trapped animal. For a moment the two of them stood motionless, staring at each other. Val forced her voice into a friendly tone to say slowly, "Hello. My name is Valerie Endrada. You can call me Val."

"Are you here to drug me?" the neuter asked. Its voice was somewhere between alto and tenor, and full of strain. But what struck Val was the incongruous accent: not just a plain Capellan accent, but the cultivated accent of the intellectual elite, the kind of people you called "magister." She felt a moment of disorientation. Was she talking to someone found half-dead in a squalid alley, or to a colleague?

"No," she said. "I'm not a mentationist."

"Tell them I don't want any more drugs," the neuter said. "I can't think when I'm drugged. I've got to be able to think." One hand rose to its forehead, then flinched away when it touched the bandage. The evidence of what it had done seemed to repulse it.

Val heard her voice drop into the cadence she used with Deedee. "The drugs are only to make you feel better."

"Why do they have to give me drugs at all?" the patient said in a low, agitated voice. "What use is it, forcing me to feel this way? Are they just trying different psychoactives to see how I'll react? Is this an experiment?"

"They're giving you drugs because you tried to kill yourself," Val said.

For a moment it stared at her, as if shocked to hear the news. Then some thought or memory crossed its face and it looked upward, teeth clenched, drawing a ragged breath. Softly, almost to itself, it said, "Why does anyone care about that? What can it matter, one dead bland more or less? Wouldn't it just be simpler to get rid of me?" It turned away then, and with its back to her wiped the tears from its eyes with its hands. After a moment, it looked back and saw Val's dismayed expression; then another emotion swept across its face—guilt, this time. Quickly it said, "I'm sorry, I didn't mean it. Please don't listen. It's the drugs, they make me babble. I barely know what I'm saying."

"That's all right, you can't offend me," Val said. She took a step closer, wishing she could do something. Watching this was agonizing. But the neuter only retreated, hidden behind the wall of paranoia again.

"Are you here to study me, then?" it said. "Are you a xenologist?"

Val hesitated, then decided lying was no way to gain a person's trust. "Yes," she said. "Now you know my name and who I am, and I don't know the first thing about you."

"You Capellans," the alien said softly. "You've always got to *know*."

"If we're going to make you feel better, we have to know something about you."

"Then you're not writing your dissertation about me, or something like that?"

"No."

As if barely daring to hope, it said, "You're not recording this? There are no cameras, or anyone watching?"

Val felt her face giving her away. The alien's expression showed betrayal. Desperately, Val said, "It's not my choice. I'm not in charge. Please believe me, all we want is to help you."

"Then why do you watch me like a peep show?" It was barely a whisper.

"Oh God, what a mess," Val said, mostly to the watching wall. She was in fathoms over her head. "I'm sorry, this is all wrong. Please forgive me." She turned to leave.

"No! Don't leave me!" the neuter cried out. She turned in time to see the desperation on its face, quickly hidden. It began to pace, talking fast, its hands moving nervously, as if it didn't know what to do with them. "I shouldn't be bothered, really. I . . . I'm not naive, like I used to be. You know, once I had the opportunity to use Epco's proprietary database, and I did a search for my own name. There were over two hundred articles written about me, all classified, Epco's property. Two hundred! Even *I* don't know enough about me to write that much. Every step I took, every word I said, was being studied, and had been since I got here. You know, it never even occurred to me why they took all those scans and samples every time I went to the clinic for some virus I had no immunity to. Can you believe that? I didn't even know I was in a zoo. Please don't think I resent it; I just need to get used to the way you Capellans are. It's your nature. You don't mean any harm."

The nervous avalanche of words came to a halt. Val was very curious by now. She didn't want to disturb the alien's train of thought, so she said, "It would drive me crazy."

"Well, you were raised with the expectation of privacy. I don't have that excuse. The way I grew up, we were never alone. We saw everything about each other. There was no ethic of modesty; that is all a product of sexuality. If I were living back on Gammadis, I would be sleeping every night in a roundroom with dozens of other blands, all in a pile, like mice. I would have all that physical closeness, without any taint of sexuality—just plain humanity. I would fall asleep to the sound of their breath, the feel of their skin against mine. Do you realize, I've barely been able to touch another person in innocence for twelve years? On my planet, they believe that neuters need to be with their own kind, or they go crazy. Maybe it's true."

During this speech, Val had drawn a little closer. Now she stood, hands at her sides, and said very quietly, "Would you like me to give you a hug?"

A complex look crossed the alien's face—part fear, part longing. "No," it said, drawing back tensely. "Please don't be offended. It's not you."

"What is it?" she said. She was so close she couldn't help but notice again the alien's striking beauty. In some ways, its vulnerability only heightened the effect. She wanted to hold it as she would Deedee, to lay its head on her shoulder and stroke its hair, to feel the panic subside.

"I'm sorry," the alien said. "You've got to understand how hard it is for me, to live in a gendered world. I have to be so careful. Sexuality is always present, with you. It never leaves your minds. It's as if you exist in a cloud of pheromones I can't sense, but only guess at. I have to be on my guard all the time, thinking of hidden meanings, body language, and innuendoes. I can never assume I understand you, never take anything at face value. It all has to go through a gender-filter in my brain. I wish I could get away from it, just be able to relax, be in a completely nonsexual situation, just for a day. I don't suppose I'll ever be able to, for the rest of my life. . . . You don't want to know all this. These drugs make me babble."

Once more, Val had the disorienting feeling that she was talking to another magister, or at least to someone of formidable—though currently scrambled—intelligence. "I *do* want to know," Val said. "But please tell me something first. You're from Gammadis?"

"Yes. How did you know?" As soon as the words were out of its mouth, the neuter shook its head. "Of course you know. You only have to look at me to know."

"I know because you said so," Val said calmly. "It surprises me, because that planet has been off-limits to Capellans for sixty-three years."

"I came here before that."

Val smiled skeptically. "You don't look that old."

"It's a fifty-one light-year trip."

That, at least, rang true. Any lightbeam traveler would

not have aged during the journey. "You must have been very young when you set out," she said.

"I was seventeen."

"What's your name?"

The alien's eyes fell to the ground, as if in shame. "Tedla Galele," it said indistinctly.

"I'm glad to meet you, Tedla." Val held out her hand. The alien's arms were crossed protectively; it hesitated, then finally held out a hand. They shook formally. After touching her, Tedla turned away and walked numbly across the room till stopped by the wall, then stood leaning against it, cheek resting on the cool ceramoplast.

"Can you get me out of here?" it asked. "I hate this room. It's driving me crazy."

"Not unless you have somewhere to go. Do you have any family, or someone we could contact?"

Tedla stared at its feet. "No. I'm the only one."

"Where have you been living?"

"Out there," the neuter gestured vaguely. "The money's all gone, you know." A current of agitation welled up again, and it said, "I wasn't supposed to have to protect myself, or make decisions, or compete with you. That was the promise. People were going to take care of me. Now I have to act human, but I can never *be* human. If only I could go back! If I were at home I would know exactly what was expected of me. I could live my life surrounded by others of my own kind. Here, I'm nothing . . . Oh god, why can't I shut up?"

Its hands had begun to shake. It clasped them tightly together, making a visible effort to gain control.

On an impulse, Val reached out and took the neuter's hands in hers. She half expected it to pull away, but instead it grasped her hands tightly. Its eyes were closed now. In a whisper, it said, "I feel like there is something I ought to be doing, only I don't know what it is, and I probably wouldn't be able to do it anyway. But if I don't, something terrible is going to happen, but it's hopeless, I can't prevent it. It's already happened, it's who I am. There's nothing I can do, absolutely nothing."

"Shh," Val said, stroking its hands. She could feel the tension in them, the stretched tendons and knotty bones. "It's all right, Tedla. Everything is going to be all right."

"There's nothing out there for me, nothing," Tedla said. "No home, no life that fits me. I'm a piece from a different puzzle. I don't fit anywhere."

"We'll make a place for you," Val said. "Don't worry."

Behind her, the door clicked open. Joan entered, carrying a transdermal.

"No," Tedla whispered.

"Tedla doesn't want any more drugs," Val said.

"It's just a sedative," Joan said to Tedla, "to calm you down. That's all, I promise."

The neuter just looked at her in terror.

"Don't you want to feel a little calmer, Tedla?" Val asked. "Come on, it'll help you think."

Slowly, Tedla held out its arm. With a quick, practiced motion Joan pressed the hypo against the vein. "Why don't you sit down now?" she said in an encouraging, doctor-to-patient voice. She gave Val a significant look, and nodded toward the door.

"I'll be back in a second, Tedla," Val said, and followed Joan out.

In the hall, Joan turned to say, "Good work, Val. All we need now is to find someone looking for a missing Gammadian."

For a brief moment, Val hoped there wasn't anyone. She wanted this find all to herself. Her conscience immediately censored the thought. "Of course," she said. "This shouldn't be hard. There are probably 'missing' notices all over X-O Net."

Joan's office was a tiny cubbyhole cluttered with printouts and mementoes of former patients. Val had to restrain herself from wiping the dust from the screen as she sat down at the terminal.

After tapping into X-O Net, she ran a search for anything posted in the last five days with the key words "Tedla Galele," then sat back to wait. When the terminal beeped, she was surprised to see it had turned up nothing.

"That's odd," she said.

"Expand the search," Joan suggested.

She did, but with no better results.

"What about all those articles in the Epco files?" Joan said.

"If they're proprietary, we'd need to pay a fortune. But some of them must have leaked out into public domain. I'll check." This time, the screen responded with two citations to articles on Gammadian physiology, both ten years old. "Well, at least now we know Tedla really exists," Val said, and hit the key to access the first one. The screen responded, "Classified proprietary: Western Alliance Corporation. Please input access code." Val tried Joan's number, then her own, but both were rejected. She went back and tried the second article, with the same result.

"Did it say WAC?" Joan asked, looking over her shoulder.

"Yes. Not Epco. Maybe Tedla was confused about which infocompany."

"Or maybe they *both* have buckets of classified information."

Val clicked her thumbnail against her teeth, thinking. "Actually, WAC makes more sense than Epco," she said. "I think the original expedition to Gammadis was sponsored by WAC. It would make sense if they were keeping tabs on Tedla."

"Should we ask them?"

Val shook her head. "They don't give out anything cheap. Let's try the public-service sources first. Isn't there some sort of missing persons list?"

So Val embarked on a search. But as time passed, she came to dead end after dead end. No one of Tedla's name or description had been reported missing. Tedla had no listed number or address anywhere on Capella Two. No one of that name had ever registered to vote, or owned taxable property. It had no professional license, no credit history, and no infonet account. They turned up a variety of other Galeles, including one with a criminal record and another who had been expelled from UIC, but no trace of Tedla.

"We've got an invisible person," Val said.

"Or someone who's been hidden," Joan said suspiciously.

Val thought briefly of posting a Found notice, but decided it would violate Tedla's privacy. The fact was, she wasn't entirely disappointed by her failure: The longer it took to track down where the alien belonged, the longer she would have with it.

From down the hall, she heard Deedee's voice raised in play. She checked the time, and groaned. "We were supposed to be at the beach half an hour ago."

"Don't worry, I'll call E.G. and tell him we're hung up. Keep working on it, Val. I can't keep Tedla here much longer. Legally, I have to transfer every client home or to a curatory within twenty-five hours. I'd rather not put this patient at the mercy of the public health system. That's hard enough to negotiate if you know how."

Joan left the room, and Val sat thinking. There was something here that didn't add up. The disastrous end to the Gammadian expedition had happened a dozen years ago. She had been in her teens, but still could remember the near-universal outrage when the explorers had returned from their fifty-one-year trek back, expelled by the rulers of Gammadis for their attempt to interfere in the local culture. Already then, Val had wanted to be an explorer herself. She hadn't been able to imagine how they had squandered the opportunity, the only one in two centuries.

But she could not remember any whisper of a Gammadian having come back with them.

Abruptly, she got up and went back down the hall to Tedla's room.

Tedla was crouched in the chair, the way Val had first seen it; but this time the Gammadian didn't stir at her entrance, merely followed her with its eyes. She sat down facing it.

"Tedla, I need to know more about you," she said.

The neuter looked away indifferently.

The sedative had clearly taken effect—too much effect, perhaps. Val itched to ask outright if Tedla were telling the truth about its name and origins, but something warned her an adversarial approach would only make things worse. She needed to establish an atmosphere of trust.

"All right, let me tell you a little bit about myself," she said. Without much plan, she began to talk at random about the new copartment, and Max, and Deedee, and the picnic they were planning. When she next paused for breath, Tedla was watching her closely.

"You have a child?" it said.

"Yes, Dierdre, but we call her Deedee. She's really a good kid, even though she can be a terrible pain."

"I've never known a Capellan child," Tedla said.

"Would you like to see her picture?"

"Yes." At last, Val thought she saw a flicker of interest in the neuter's face. She went over to the wall screen and accessed her home file, picking out her favorite picture— an impish Deedee looking over her shoulder at the camera. Tedla came to her side, gazing at it in fascination.

"She's a little fiend," Val said.

Tedla looked fixedly at her, obviously uncertain what to say, and somewhat troubled. Choosing its words carefully, it said, "You don't like her, then?"

Val laughed. "Don't be silly, Tedla. Of course I like her."

"But . . . fiend means something horrible."

"I just *know* her, Tedla. Children are nasty little brutes, you know. And we love them anyway."

"I see," Tedla said, as if it didn't.

"You'll understand if you ever . . ." She remembered too late that the person at her side could never have children, and finished, ". . . get to know any children well."

Tedla appeared not to have noticed her slip; in fact, it was preoccupied with some hidden thought. "You love them, even if they do perfectly horrible things? Even if they betray you and hurt you?"

The question was obviously more than theoretical. "Yes," Val said seriously. She watched Tedla's face, and saw the motion of memories across it. She was getting somewhere now.

"Would you like to meet her?" Val said.

"She's here?"

"Yes. Just a second, let me go find her."

When she poked her head out the door, Joan was coming down the hall looking for her. She said, "Joan, go call Deedee. I want Tedla to meet her."

Joan didn't move. "Do you think that's wise?"

"Humor me. I've got a hunch," Val said.

Deedee appeared from a doorway down the hall, saw Val, and came racing toward her, bubbling with news. Val said to Joan, "Make sure the recorder is running." Then, to Deedee, "I want you to meet someone, Dee. Pretend to be good, okay?" Then she ushered her daughter into the mad alien's room.

Deedee stood inside the door, staring at Tedla, who had retreated behind the chair and now stared back, both disconcerted and fascinated.

"This is Tedla, Deedee," Val said. "Tedla comes from another planet—a planet so far away it takes fifty years to make the trip."

Deedee didn't react. She turned to Val and said, "Mama, did you know that people *die* here?"

"No," Val said, startled.

"Mandy showed me. They have a *bin* for *stiffs*."

Good Lord, Val thought, what an introduction. She looked apologetically at Tedla. "I warned you."

Deedee spied the bed, and dashed over to it. "Mama, did you know these beds move?" Before Val could react, she clambered up onto the formable bed and pressed one of the controls. Nothing happened. "Oops," she said, performing now. She pressed another square, and the bed rose to mold itself around her body. She froze it, then scrambled up to look at the impression she had made. Both Val and Tedla moved forward instinctively to catch her as she came close to tumbling backward off the bed. "See?" she said.

"Yes, I see. Now put it back, Deedee. That's Tedla's bed."

Deedee turned around and stared at Tedla again. "Do you know how to play Scratcher?"

"No," Tedla said.

"What will you pay me if I teach you?"

"Not now, Deedee," Val said to her budding infocapitalist. "Come sit down with us."

Deedee allowed Val to lead her to a chair, and all three of them sat. The child was now looking at Tedla fixedly. She said suddenly, "Are you a man or a lady?"

Val was ready to jump in, but Tedla said, "Neither. On the planet I come from, there are three sexes, not just two."

"The polite word is 'asexual', Deedee," Val said.

Val expected more questions, but Deedee was pondering the explanation. Val said awkwardly, "Tedla, which should we call you—'he' or 'she'?"

"Actually, your word 'it' is closest to the pronoun we use on my planet," Tedla said. "We even use the same word to refer to animals and inanimate objects, like you do."

"I don't know. 'It' seems slightly . . . derogatory."

"Well then, that's an accurate translation, too."

Deedee said, "I live with both my mama and papa." She had just been learning that not all children did.

"I never knew my mama or papa," Tedla told her. "No one on my planet does, except the really poor people who live like savages."

"Did you know your gramma?" Deedee asked.

"No. I was brought up in a creche with lots and lots of other children. We had docents and proctors and postulants instead of mamas and papas."

Deedee's nose wrinkled. "I would hate that."

Tedla leaned forward, looking relaxed for the first time. "No, you wouldn't. We had lots of fun. We didn't sleep in beds; we had a roundroom. It's a big, circular room with a domed ceiling. The floor is cushiony, and you can bounce really high on it. All the walls are soft, so no one can get hurt. No grown-ups ever came into our round-room."

"How high could you bounce?" Deedee said.

"Almost to the ceiling."

Deedee stood up on the chair and held up her arms. "This high?"

"No, higher than that."

Deedee bounced on the cushion. "This high?"

Val made her stop. "You're not in a roundroom, Dee-dee. You're in a grown-up place, and you have to act like a grown-up here."

Deedee settled down discontentedly. Val took her hand and said, "Come on, I think it's time for you to go see gramma again."

When Val had taken Deedee out into the hall and re-turned, she found Tedla sitting with its head in its hands, as if in the grip of dejection.

"Tedla? Are you all right?" Val said, a little alarmed.

Tedla looked up at her. Its face was not desperate, as before, but achingly sad. "It's all coming back to me. Things I haven't thought about in years. Seeing her re-minds me of what it was like."

Val sat down facing Tedla. "Are they good memories, or bad?"

"They are all intertwined, good and bad."

"Tell me," Val said softly. "Tell me everything."

Tedla looked down at its hands. Val glanced over at the terminal to make sure it was recording. The red light blinked yes.

Then, very softly, the alien began to speak.

Chapter Two

✢ When I think of home, I see myself as a child, fitting my toes in the bark-crevices of a knotty old aiken tree, trying to climb high enough to look out over the autumn-colored river valley where I grew up. There was a spot on the third tier of branches where I could rest, legs dangling, and see all the broad floodplain, densely wooded with deciduous trees, a calico of gold and umber. The river seemed impossibly far away, a sinuous streak down in the bottomland, sometimes hidden with mist, sometimes shining like metal, sometimes chocolate-colored with mud. On still days I could hear the boat-horns echoing across the valley in the moist air.

Gammadis is a very beautiful planet. Everything there seems old. The plants, the insects, all *fit*. Here on Capella Two, the terraforming seems thin and ill at ease. The trees look like house plants, or museum pieces—on display, aware of their uniqueness. There, you pick up a handful of soil and it smells of eons of germlife permeating the planet. The river valley looks as if it formed of its own accord, not like an invention with vegetation veneered over it. There were even fossils in the limestone cliffs.

We don't call it Gammadis, as you do—we call it Taramond. Once, when I stupidly corrected Magister Galele on this, he laughed and said, ''Yes, and my homeworld is called Earth. The natives of Baker's Knot call their home Eden.'' Only later did I learn what he meant—that every planet is named after the origin world of mankind. As a child, I didn't even know there was such a place. Or I thought my homeworld was it.

I still dream about that river valley where my creche was. But in my dreams the valley has changed. Some transformation has come over it—the water has risen and flooded the valley rim to rim, and it is full of mysterious islands—or all the land is built on, full of drab composite houses like Capella Two. I don't like those dreams. I don't want the valley to change. But there is nothing I can do about it, because it's *me* that has changed, and all I hold in memory has changed with me. Not even in myself does that place exist any more, because the person I was then doesn't exist, and that child was part of the place, as surely as the whiskered mudfish in the river. That child is gone forever.

The creche where I grew up was, of course, underground. The Capellan investigators who came to my planet kept asking why all the civilized societies lived underground, and all we could say was that it is the natural way for people to live. I could not imagine anyone but the poorest vagrant or the bravest frontier sappers living on the surface. When I came here, it took years before I felt easy sleeping in your flimsy houses perched right on the surface. I kept having an irrational feeling that somehow gravity would fail and we would all be flung off into space.

The creche had eight levels, one for every stage of a child's life. We started out as infants on the lowest level, the nursery. When we learned to walk we graduated to the next level, and kept moving up at every developmental phase thereafter. On the highest level lived the protos preparing for matriculation. They were on the threshold of humanity. We feared and envied them at the same time. They seemed more alien than the adults, because they were at the nexus of transformation.

The rooms were all round, like bubbles, which in fact they were: Our buildings are not so much constructed as inflated, like bottles, from lignis, which hardens into a lovely, warm substance like wood, only stronger. Some bubbles were large, like the refectory where we all ate in shifts, or the assembly hall on level three. The rest were classrooms, recreatories, hygiene stations, labs, and offices for the gestagogues. Each level was laid out in a circle, ranged around a central axis. At the center was the round-room for that level. At night the proctors would turn us all loose in our roundroom, the place that was ours alone. We would come pouring in, bouncing as high as we could on the cushiony floor, pushing each other into the soft walls. The only furnishings were pillows, and we had some mighty pillow wars before we would fall asleep, naked bodies all tangled together in the middle of the floor. The roundroom was the center of childhood. It was where we traded secrets, learned songs and stories, and sometimes fought out our rivalries safe from adult intervention.

I say there were eight levels, but in fact there were several below the ones we lived in. Those were grayspace: the territory of the blands. We knew nothing about it. Our food appeared from those levels, as did our linen and all the equipment used to clean our classes and playrooms; but we gave it no more thought than the electrical wiring. I learned later that there was an entire parallel building we never saw, made up of service corridors meant to keep the neuter staff invisible and out of mind. In a creche, that was futile.

The docents and proctors were all human, but as infants we were largely raised by neuters. I can see this surprises you, but it seemed quite natural to us. Blands were perfect for the tedious chores of infant care—nighttime feedings, diaper changes, the constant vigilance against harm. Both parties throve on it. As babies we quieted to a neuter's touch as we never would to a human's, and as toddlers we loved them for their patience and dumb devotion. Then we grew older and learned to despise them for the same reasons.

We have no families on Gammadis, as you do: at least, not ones based on biological relationships. Capellans tend to assume this means that our children lead loveless lives. It isn't true. On the contrary, we cherish our children as if they were human.

🕮 "Just a second," Val interrupted. She had been trying to keep quiet, despite several hundred questions in her mind, but this was too much. "Could you explain? Your children aren't human?"

"No," Tedla said. "We are biologically different from you. Our children are not miniature adults, as yours are. They are born sexually undifferentiated. Our bodies don't change until puberty, when sexual characteristics appear. Until then, there is no way of knowing whether a child will become male or female—or whether it will be one of the minority who never mature, and remain in a childlike, asexual state forever."

"So children are neuters?" Val asked.

Tedla seemed shocked. "No, certainly not. They are proto-humans. They may look like neuters, but they have the potential for humanity."

"I see. You have to forgive my stupidity, Tedla. I don't know much about Gammadis."

Tedla looked at her uneasily. "This probably offends your Cappellan sensibilities. To you, children are already human. On Gammadis, we think of the years before puberty as an extended gestation period. That's why learned people will call a creche a 'gestatory'. The fetal body and mind take that long to mature."

"Unless they never do."

"That's right."

When Tedla resumed the story, it seemed thoughtful.

◀▷ Often I have searched my memories for any clue, any warning, of what I was going to become. I don't know at what point my fate was decided. Perhaps it was at conception, or with some roll of random adrenal dice at puberty. Or—and this is what it's hard not to dwell on—was it something I did? If only I could spot it.

I don't know how I got my nickname, Tedla. Often it was obvious how a child got its nickname, like Moptop or Fidget, because it described the child's looks or temperament. Other times, names are just nonsense words, or some whim of an adult. They don't mean much, as a rule. They are only placeholders, a little better than "You There." We all looked forward to receiving our real names at puberty.

I was a perfectly average child—neither very clever nor remarkably stupid, not especially talented athletically or artistically, but always able to hold my own. The only thing that made me stand out was looks—I was a pretty child. Though the gestagogues tried hard not to have favorites, I got more affection from the adults than the less attractive protos—it was only natural. Good looks counted for less among my peers. I wasn't a natural leader like the brighter and more talented protos, but at least I was never rejected or excluded. When we would form up teams for games, I would be chosen in the very middle.

Virtually none of our learning was competitive, not even the sports. We were never ranked against each other. Often we had to complete assignments in groups, and we were evaluated for cooperation as well as achievement. As a result, I truly have no notion where I stood in my class, as Capellan children do. But I expect I was right in the middle.

Our classes were the usual academic ones—reading, writing, mathematics, science, history, and so on—but we also had sociability training and morality classes, since we had no families to teach us those things. Every day we had meditation to nourish the infant souls growing inside us, and on the seventh day we visited the chapel. The chapel was the only part of the creche that was above ground, and it resembled an indoor garden—glass roof open to the sky, contemplative paths to stroll on, little groves and grottoes where you could sit, with gates to close if you wanted to be private. We never used it, as some sects do, for communal worship. At our creche, religion was a solitary matter, something between a person and his or her own god.

My earliest memories are of the second level. We played in a soft, bubble-shaped room with bright lighting and marvelous, though well-worn, toys: chutes and clamber-frames and ball pools. Many of the toys took more than one to operate, so that we were forced to cooperate with other children, or else enlist one of the blands to help us. I can still see the soft, vein-roped hands of the neuters that used to watch over the playroom. There was one in particular, named Joby, who never tired of playing games, no matter how repetitive or banal. Everyone in the creche thought of Joby as childlike itself, as if its brain had regressed to an infantile state. Later, I learned that all blands have their particular tactics for survival—protective coloration that helps them blend into the background. Joby's sweet, child-like nature was what protected it from harm. The adults taught us to speak to Joby, and others like it, in a firm and gentle tone, slowly, and to use simple words.

One of my most vivid early memories concerns Joby. It happened in the winter of my seventh year. The weather was very severe that year. Drifts of snow nearly buried the chapel and all the familiar landscape around the creche. When we went up for worship, the dome above was covered by a gray layer of snow, and in the odd twilight we could hear the wind pushing against it, trying to get in. Down in the creche, of course, we were quite safe and cozy, a self-sufficient little community, even though cut off from the rest of the world.

We protos were caught up in the preparations for Leastday, our main festival for that time of year. We were decorating the assembly hall for the climactic event of the season, the lighting of the Summer Candle. The candle tree was set up and strung with paper flowers. Fluffweed wreaths and treeshell garlands adorned the hallways. Everything was fragrant with the smell of glue, candle wax, and butterberry cakes cooking in the kitchens down below. Even though the cakes were meant for the celebration, a postulant would sometimes bring one up warm from the oven, and we would crowd around to get a piece, the adults admonishing us to share. On the day before the candle ceremony, the younger proctors got together and made an expedition out into the blizzard to gather evergreen boughs. We thought they were heroes. We hung up the boughs, getting our hands sticky with sap, and then the air was full of the tang of needletrees.

I had spent the day in Crafts, working on my wreath, and by evening my neck was stiff from bending over. When I woke the next morning, I could barely move my head, and I felt lethargic and nauseous. One of the postulants noticed me moping around in the dressing room after all the other excited children had lined up for refectory, and she got me to confess what was wrong. After feeling my temperature, she quickly hurried me off to the clinic.

Ordinarily, being in clinic was no hardship, since you got to miss classes and sleep in a bed of your own, like an adult. But that day there were no classes, and I felt mightily abused to be incarcerated, missing all the fun. But as the day progressed, I began to vomit and developed a headache that felt as if my brain were in a vise. No matter which way I lay, I couldn't get comfortable.

The next morning I realized how worried they were when the Matron came down to see me. She asked me some questions, felt my forehead, then went into the next room to talk to the clinician. At last she came back to my bedside and said, "Tedla, we are calling an aircar to take you to the curatory at Tapis Convergence, so you can get better fast. You'll have to get dressed now. Once you're there, they will take good care of you."

Now I am certain they suspected meningitis, which must strike fear into every gestagogue. The way we children lived gave free rein to any contagion we couldn't be vaccinated against. Fortunately, those were few.

One of the proctors helped me dress in coveralls and coat, then led me up to the top floor. It seemed cold and deserted. In the corridor leading to the entryway, we found Joby waiting, dressed in a coat. It looked terribly anxious. The proctor gave my hand to Joby and said, "Wait in the cloakroom till the aircar arrives. Stay with Joby, Tedla."

As if I were likely to run off. We waited a long time. I lay down on one of the benches, my head pillowed on Joby's lap. The neuter stroked my hair. I had drifted off into an uneasy doze when at last the proctor came in and told us the aircar was here. "They had some trouble getting through," he said. Out in the corridor, blands were carrying in some boxes of medicine, supervised by the clinician. They were tracking wet snow onto the floor, and I felt a groggy surprise that no one was scolding them. When the clinician saw me she squeezed my hand and said, "You'll be all right as soon as you get there."

"Are you coming with me?" I asked.

"No, Joby will go with you in the aircar. Someone will meet you when you get to the curatory."

Outside, the world seemed wild and alien. Every familiar thing was buried under a layer of snow almost as tall as I was. The sky was gray and forbidding; the wind slung a stinging handful of snow into my face as I tried to look around. The blands had cut a path through the drifts to the playfield, where the aircar had landed at an odd angle, its legs sunk deep into snow. Even in the path the snow was deep, and it was exhausting work plowing through it. When Joby saw I was having trouble, it turned and picked me up. I was astonished at the bland's strength; it looked so puny. I laid my head on its shoulder, my arms around its neck, and let it toil through the snow for me.

The pilot—a gruff, bearded man who looked displeased to be out in such weather—lifted me up into one of the two passenger seats and told me how to belt myself in. I looked out the open door to where Joby was still standing in the snow, looking into the aircar. It looked terrified. I said, "Don't be scared, Joby. You'll be all right."

Impatiently, the pilot said, "Get in if you're going to."

Visibly steeling itself, Joby clambered up into the seat beside me, and the pilot slammed the door. I showed Joby how to work the buckles. The engine started with a deafening roar, and Joby clutched my hand. I felt the panic in its body, so I squeezed its hand and leaned against its shoulder.

We rose into the air with a sickening swoop, then banked. Joby's eyes were closed tight. I don't know why I felt so little fear—trust of the adults, perhaps. Or perhaps it was Joby acting like a bland that made me feel the obligation to act more human. At any rate, I stared out the window, trying to keep track of the horizon. Soon we rose into clouds, and there was nothing to see but grayness. Still the turbulent wind buffeted us; the ride was rough as a groundcar on a bad road. Joby and I were flung to either side, or nearly lifted out of our seats when the car dropped into a pocket of air. The pilot was talking to someone on his headset. He said nothing to us.

At last I felt the stomach-numbing sense of falling as we began a steep descent. At the very last moment we broke out of the clouds, and I saw a lighted landing pad below us. The snow was not so deep here, or the wind had swept it away. We settled down with a last bump. Without even stopping the engines, the pilot shoved open the door. Eager to be out, Joby unfastened its straps and clambered down, turning to lift me to the pavement. Then it looked around, trying to figure out what to do. "Where do we go?'' it asked the pilot. He pointed and said, ''Entry's over there. Clear out, I've got another run.''

Joby took my hand and started off across the pad. Behind us the aircar door slammed shut and the engines began to roar. We headed down a ramp that led underground. When we passed through the door into a clean, tubular hallway, the silence was stunning.

No one was there to meet us. We stood looking around, bewildered.

''Maybe we should wait,'' I said.

But there was no place to sit, so Joby steeled itself and chose a direction to go. Presently we came to a more freqented area. People in curatorial tabards were going about their business. Though several times Joby stopped to ask a question, people kept passing us as though we were invisible, and Joby was too timid to stop them.

At last we came to a circular lounge area with a counter in the middle, where a woman sat. Joby went up to her. She ignored us at first, but Joby stood there patiently, and at last she looked up. ''What do you want?''

''Someone was supposed to meet us,'' Joby said in a faint voice.

''What do you mean?'' she said.

Anxiously, Joby said, ''We came from the creche. Tedla's sick. Someone's supposed to tell us what to do.''

''What creche?'' she said.

Joby and I looked at each other. It had never occurred to me that of course there was more than one, and ours must have a name. At last Joby, thinking feverishly, said, ''Cliffside.''

The woman looked at me. ''What's wrong with it?''

''It's sick,'' Joby said.

''I gathered that,'' she said drily. Before Joby could summon the courage to say more, she said, ''Never mind,'' and punched a number on her terminal. When someone answered, she said, ''I've got a proto out here from Cliffside Creche. Do you have any record about this?'' She listened for a while, then turned back to us. "Sit down over there."

"Thank you, ma'am," Joby said, grateful to be told what to do at last.

We settled down to wait on a couch. The excitement of the ride had given me an adrenaline-powered energy that now began to take its toll. I felt uncomfortably hot, and taking my coat off didn't help much. My headache was radiating down my neck, and making me feel sick again, though I had eaten nothing for over a day. I slumped against Joby, and it put an arm around me.

The lounge was very busy; people were constantly coming in, talking to the woman at the desk, sitting down to wait, and being directed into the many halls that radiated out from the hub where we were. Everyone but us seemed to know where they were and what they were doing. I watched them with a growing conviction that we were in the wrong place. We were lost, and no one cared. At last I couldn't sit up any longer, and so I lay down, my head on Joby's lap. It rubbed my back comfortingly. Joby was the only familiar, trustworthy thing in this place; I felt safe as long as it was near, though I knew it was as frightened as I.

After a long time Joby started to get up, and I clutched at it. "Don't go away," I said.

"I'm just going to talk to the lady. I'll be right back," it said.

From the couch I watched another fruitless exchange. Joby turned back to join me, its shoulders slumped in dejection. We didn't say anything to each other, but I hugged it, and it kissed my cheek. "They'll do something soon," Joby promised.

Of course, they didn't. As I drifted in and out of a feverish doze, I noticed that the woman at the desk had changed, and soon Joby had to go over and explain the whole situation again, from the beginning. After that I lost track of time. My mouth was parched, but I didn't even have the energy to ask Joby to fetch me some water. It hurt to move, it hurt even to open my eyes.

I was roused from my torpor by the sound of shouting. The scene I saw then was surreal as a hallucination. Joby was standing at the counter, its face red with anger, its voice raised, the woman looking at it in utter astonishment. "Hours—hours!—that child has been lying there sick, with you ignoring it," Joby shouted passionately. "What are you going to do, wait for it to die before you pay attention?"

The whole room fell silent, shocked to inaction by the sight of a bland stressed beyond its limit, shouting—actually shouting—at a person. Never in my life had I seen such a thing, and even in my condition I felt a pang of fear for Joby. Recovering from her paralysis, the woman at the counter stabbed at her console and said, "Could you send a curator down here immediately?"

"Joby!" I cried out, afraid they would clap it in chains and haul it away, and I would be left all alone. At the sound of my voice, Joby whirled around and came flying back to me. There were tears in its eyes. "Hush, Tedla, it's all right, it's all right," it said, still so distraught its hands shook.

Seconds later, it seemed, a sweet-smelling, gray-haired woman in a curator's tabard was leaning over me, asking questions that Joby stumbled to answer between its tears. Soon a rolling cot arrived, and they lifted me onto it. I wouldn't let go of Joby's hand, though the postulants tried to make me. The curator said, "Let the bland go, too."

Joby stayed by my side through the tests that followed. It stayed when they transferred me to a bed. All through the restless, painful night that followed, every time I woke up, there Joby was, sometimes slumped over asleep but always in sight.

I was very sick for three or four days. When I was finally well enough to sit up and eat something, the curator looked very pleased. "I think you're going to be all right,

Tedla," she said warmly, then added, "now maybe your
bland can get some rest."

I was trying to sort out my memories, so I asked uncertainly, "Why didn't anyone meet us?"

"The pilot delivered you to the wrong curatory."

"Did Joby really make a scene?"

"Oh, yes," she said, laughing, then bent close to whisper, "your bland loves you very much."

When she was gone, I looked over at Joby, who was
standing there like the picture of exhaustion. "I love you
too, Joby," I said shyly.

It came over to my bedside and took my hand. "Hush,
don't say things like that," it said, its eyes downcast.

"Why not?" I said. "It's true."

It put a finger on my lips to silence me. "You're meant
for better things than I," it said.

I didn't understand then what that had to do with love,
but I do now.

For a while after coming back, I enjoyed some romantic
notoriety at the creche as The Proto That Almost Died. I
did not enjoy it. Once my physical stamina started to return, I slid gratefully into anonymity again.

The most lasting result of the episode was my relationship with Joby. Whenever we met in the hallway, Joby's
face would break out in a sunny smile, and I would rush
into its arms. It would twirl me around till my feet left the
floor. I sneaked it treats from refectory, thinking the blands
didn't get treats—though of course they finished up whatever food we didn't eat. This went on for several years,
till the older protos started whispering, "Neuter-lover!"
when I passed, and I learned not to be so open about my
affections.

We kept a great many traditions and holidays in the
creche—more than they do in the outside world. I suppose
it was to give us a sense of cultural identity. My favorite
holiday was Tumbleturn Day, which came in the spring at

a time when the snow was still melting in slushy heaps and the ground was too wet to play on, but spring fever had set in, making us seriously restless. We planned for weeks in advance what we were going to be on Tumbleturn Day, but kept it a secret from all but our truly special friends, so everyone would be surprised—or at least pretend to be.

We always woke early and excited that morning, because it was the one day of the year when confusion reigned, and all roles were reversed. We rushed from the roundroom to our lockers, where we had secreted costumes or insignia to show what we were supposed to be. There were always huge arguments about whether it was better to be a patternist or factor. I generally chose the former.

"Patternists are sly and sneaky," said Bigger, a chunky proto who would have been the bully of our roundroom if anyone had let it get away with such antisocial behavior.

"Well, factors are dumb and greedy," I retorted.

Those were the stereotypes, at any rate. Of course, we all lived up to the stereotypes when we played at being adults. It never occurred to us that our own gestagogues were patternists, since we trusted them implicitly.

In the year I am thinking of, my good friend Litch and I had conspired together to be vestigators, since we could torment the docents by asking them questions. Litch was a small, remarkably ugly proto with protruding teeth and a face that looked like someone had taken it by the ears and pulled out to either side. Litch compensated with comedy. We made such a peculiar-looking pair—me like an angel, Litch like a demon—that people tended to break out laughing just seeing us. Litch had wanted to spend Tumbleturn Day as a beet, since that would *really* be a turnaround; but I balked at being a vegetable.

Our vestigator costumes consisted of long lab coats filched from the dietician and hygienist, notepads, and huge cardboard spectacles. The sleeves of my coat came down several inches over my hands and I kept tripping on the hem, but this only made everyone laugh harder, so I didn't mind.

When we got to refectory, the adults were all eating there as if they were us, dressed not in their gestatorial uniforms but in the bright, color-coded coveralls we always wore, but inside-out and backwards. One middle-aged proctor whom we had never suspected of humor was dressed as an infant in a sleeper, with the diapers on the outside. We shrieked in laughter to see him. The food line was reversed—we had to go through it backwards—and the blands served our food on upside-down plates. Eating got messy, but we knew the blands wouldn't mind cleaning up.

There was a pretense of classes, but of course we all held our books upside down and wrote the words backwards. The docents pretended that this was all perfectly normal, and acted puzzled if anyone said anything the right way. Halfway through the morning, Litch and I set off to do research, as vestigators are supposed to. We had a list of nonsense questions we tried to ask everyone.

There was an older proto named Seldom who was also dressed as a vestigator that day. We didn't know Seldom very well; it hung out with a creative, nonconformist group of protos who had actually written and presented a play the year before. Just before lunch it saw us in the hallway and said, "Do you protes want to discover something really strange?"

Flattered by its attention, we nodded. Seldom's voice got low and mysterious then. "I know where there's something hidden from ancient times. If you want to see it, you're going to have to go on an expedition."

"Okay," Litch said.

"Come on, let's get some supplies," Seldom said, and headed for the refectory.

The blands were instructed never to hand out food except at mealtimes, but everything was so topsy-turvy that day that we managed to wheedle snacks out of them.

"Ready?" Seldom said, viewing us critically. It had a pointer from one of the classrooms that it used as a walking stick.

"Lead on, Chief," Litch said saucily.

We headed down the stairs. On the lower levels things were functioning more normally, since the truly little children didn't know enough about what was normal to appreciate Tumbleturn Day. We passed the toddlers' playroom, running crouched over so the blands wouldn't see us through the window. Then we descended to the infants' level. I hadn't been there in years, and it looked small and low-ceilinged. Through an open door we glimpsed the nursery where the babies' cribs stood, ranged in circles. All but the tiniest babies were off in their exercise room; only a lone bland tended the nursery, slowly gathering laundry.

Seldom stopped by one of the plain gray doors that only blands used, and turned to us. It whispered, "We've got to go through grayspace to get there. Are you ready?"

No one had ever ordered us not to pass through the graydoors. We had learned to avoid them purely through the adults' unspoken example. I was not particularly frightened, but I was repulsed and uneasy. Seldom was watching us appraisingly, so I tried not to show it.

When we passed through the door, the contrast left us in no doubt where we were. Here, the walls were not warm lignis but rough, colorless poured-stone. Bare light fixtures hung from the ceiling, and all around us the pipes and ducts were exposed. It was like seeing the guts of an organism—the parts that make everything run, but no one was meant to know about.

We stood at the top of a metal staircase with open mesh treads. As we descended, our steps echoed loudly against the bare walls, and Seldom warned us to be more quiet. At the bottom, we found ourselves in a long, curving corridor that ran around the circumference of the creche. It looked like it hadn't been cleaned in years. From a door-

way ahead, a loud mechanical humming came. I was relieved when Seldom gestured us away from it. "That's the
laundry," it whispered. "The kitchen's on the other side.
That's why you have to do this at mealtimes. All the
blands are busy preparing the meal."

"What happens if someone finds us down here?" I
asked uneasily.

"Oh, the blands go crazy," Seldom said.

"Really?" Litch said, perking up. "Let's go scare
them."

"Not now," Seldom said. "We've got more important
things to do."

At that moment we heard the sound of a cart approaching down the hall, its wheels rumbling on the cracked
floor. Seldom set off running away from it, and we followed. Our leader skidded to a halt by another graydoor,
and we all dived through. We found ourselves at the head
of another staircase leading down into an even dimmer
level.

The walls in this level were old square blocks of poured
stone with crumbling mortar. There was a dank, musty
smell. "This is where the neuters' roundroom is," Seldom
said. "You want to see it?"

"No," I said.

"Yes," Litch said.

We sneaked down the corridor to an open door. Inside
was a locker room, but not like ours. Where ours was
bright and clean, this one was dim and dingy. The old
metal lockers were scratched and worn. Beyond this room
was a shower room, but instead of shiny ceramic tile there
was a poured-stone floor and walls stained with rust and
hard water deposits. One of the showerheads dripped
loudly as we tiptoed through. We stuck our heads through
the next doorway. The blands' roundroom was threadbare
and dim. There were rips in the cloth covering the walls.

"Look at the neuter-sweat," Litch said with distaste.
The center of the floor, where they slept, was stained with

the mark of decades of bodies resting there. "This is disgusting," Litch said, holding its nose.

We escaped gratefully out into the hall again. Now Seldom led us to another door. This one had been padlocked, but the screws on the hasp had worked loose, so that it only looked secure. Before opening the door, Seldom looked at us and said, "Are you really brave?"

We nodded our heads.

"You've got to go the next part of the way in the dark. Okay?"

Litch and I exchanged a look, but we both nodded. Seldom opened the door and we slipped through. When the older proto came in and closed the door behind it, the darkness was absolute.

"Put your hands on the railing and feel your way down the steps," Seldom whispered. "The light switch is at the bottom."

I groped and found Litch's hand in the dark. Hanging onto each other, we edged our way down the steps. At last my feet touched stone instead of metal, and I said, "Seldom?" For a panicky moment I wondered if the older proto had lured us here in order to escape and leave us in the dark. But I heard Seldom right behind me, feeling for the light switch. At last there was a click, and a sickly yellow light came on—a dusty bulb hanging from a cord. It would have seemed very dim, had our eyes not adjusted to the darkness.

On this level, the walls were not even poured-stone—they were raw limestone, cut from the bedrock itself. Curving away on either side was another corridor heaped with old junk. There were rusty garden tools and filing cabinets, broken furniture, and old machines. Litch and I ventured timidly out into the narrow walkway in the center, feeling dwarfed by the heaps on either side. I stopped to stare at a rusty machine of cast iron with a massive gear on one side. "How old is this stuff?" I said.

"This is the oldest level of the creche," Seldom said. "It was built back in the Machine Age."

We had all learned of the Machine Age, when people had built so many machines, and controlled them so poorly, that they had nearly destroyed life on Taramond. In those days, people had no respect for life or love for their world. To feed the machines' voracious appetites for power, they had poisoned the air and water, altered the climate, leveled the forests, and squandered the soil. In the end, millions had died, and whole species had gone extinct. An aura of evil hung over these machines. They had been used for diabolical purposes. "Is the creche that old?" I asked.

"It wasn't a creche then," Seldom said.

"I bet it was a rocket factory," Litch said. "I bet they built spaceships here." The Machine Age was also when we last had contact with the stars, before what Capellans call the Dire Years.

Seeing how I recoiled from the machines, Seldom said, "Don't worry, these machines couldn't do much harm. They're too little."

The one with the gears was taller than I.

Seldom led us down the hall. It was lit by occasional bulbs, and in between them the shadows gathered. My back was crawling, and I kept looking behind us. Only dust was there.

At last Seldom turned down a passage that led inward like the spoke of a wheel. This hall was lined with cob-webby machines in gray metal casings, full of faded dials calibrated in characters I didn't even recognize. I felt a thousand miles—or a thousand years—away from the creche. Here, everything was alien.

The hall ended in a rough stone archway opening into darkness. A breeze blew in from it, smelling of wet rock. On one wall was a metal box, which Seldom opened. It was full of switches. "Ready?" it said, looking at us. Without waiting for a reply, it pushed one of the switches.

There was a faraway clunk, and the lights beyond the doorway came on, faltered, then came on again.

We edged through. Beyond the door lay a domed cavern carved from the rock. We found ourselves on a balcony that ran around the perimeter, edged with a metal railing. In the center of the space, squatting there like an immense, poisonous toad, was a single machine the size of a house. It was rounded on top, and had a forest of pipes feeding into it.

"This is the kind of machine that poisoned the world," Seldom said in a whisper.

It radiated evil. I backed away, terrified that we would waken it, and it would start up again. "What's it doing here?" I said. "Why didn't they destroy it?"

"I don't know," said Seldom.

"I want to go back," I said.

Litch was braver than I. It crept forward to the railing. "Look," it said with a horrified fascination. "There are ladders to get down."

"Of course," Seldom said. "People had to tend the machine."

I imagined a crew enslaved to the machine, working in chains. In my mind, they were blands. I couldn't imagine people doing it.

"See over there?" Seldom pointed to another opening in the wall opposite the one where we stood. It was pitchy black. "You know where that leads?"

I didn't want to know, but Litch said, "Where?"

"There's a whole nother creche that was abandoned and walled up," Seldom said. "That's the only way into it now. And you know what? The bodies of the protos who were in that creche are still there. They're just skeletons now."

"Let's go back," I pleaded. At last Litch seemed to agree with me. It backed away from the railing. This place was too evil to be in.

We went back into the spoke-corridor and waited while

Seldom opened the box to turn off the lights. It hesitated over the rows of switches. "Maybe I should punch a few others, just to see what they'll do," it said.

"No!" I pleaded, terrified.

Seldom relented and shut off the lights. We hurried back down the hallway to the bottom of the stairs. "Ready?" Seldom said, poised to switch off the lights.

I turned to race up the steps while the lights were still on. I only got about three steps up when Seldom threw the switch. Hanging onto the railing, I made it all the way up, and felt for the door. Suddenly, Seldom was there, blocking the way.

"Listen," it said. "You two have got to swear not to tell anyone you were down here, or what you saw. Not another proto, not a grown-up, not even a bland. If I find you've told anyone, I'll bring you down here and lock you up till you're just another skeleton. Do you swear?"

"I swear," we both said.

Seldom let us out then. We managed to sneak back up without anyone seeing.

I couldn't sleep that night. I kept thinking how, directly below our roundroom, that machine lay in the dark, waiting for someone to start it going again. I kept waking up, heart pounding, thinking I heard it going, feeling imaginary tremors in the floor and a deep-buried growling that would signal the return of an ancient evil. As I would begin to drift off to sleep, I would think how, just above the machine, the blands were sleeping in that dirty roundroom, huddled together naked as we were. Everything horrible seemed like a mirror image of everything good. Nothing was secure any more.

It was a month later that the aliens came out of the sky.

On Gammadis, we joke about how everyone remembers exactly what they were doing when the aliens landed. I am no exception. I was in Language Arts class with my favorite teacher, Docent Mercady. She was young and pretty and gentle, and I worshipped her. We were taking a spelling test when one of the proctors came to the door. He whispered to her, and she stepped out of the room. For a minute we were silent, concentrating on the test. Then, inevitably, Bigger started to make farting noises. Bigger was always doing stupid things to get attention. Some of the other protos started to giggle, then someone else started to burp. Pretty soon, mayhem had spread across the room.

Docent Mercady stepped back in. Her face looked so strained and worried that we instantly became quiet. She said, "Class, I want you to put your pencils down and line up very quietly. We are going to Assembly."

We knew something big was up then.

The Assembly room was awash in whispers, and Litch said in my ear, "Possit says that space aliens have landed." Since Litch was always talking about space and aliens, I said, "Don't be stupid."

We had barely settled down, cross-legged on the floor, when the Matron came to the front of the room. We did not see her often—only on grave occasions. She always looked serious, but never more so than this day. She said, "Children, we have received news of an important event at Magnus Convergence. The mattergraves and electors have been contacted by a delegation from one of our star colonies founded long ago in the Machine Age. We have never known if any of them survived. Now, they have come back across space to visit us."

There was a hum of talk all across the room. I was stunned. So Litch had been right, in a way.

The Matron raised her voice to make us quiet. "Since this is an important event, I want you to learn all about it. We are going to watch some news broadcasts." She gave a signal to one of the proctors, and the screen came on.

We sat there for the next several hours, mesmerized by the viewscreen. The aliens had sent a message from their orbiting ship, politely requesting permission to land. We watched as their atmospheric shuttle came down, not unlike one of our aircars. We waited, breathless, as the vehicle sat there for what seemed like an eternity, motionless. Then at last the door opened, and we saw our first aliens. They looked like little squashed brown people to me. (Please don't be offended; I expect we look strange to you, too.) Across the landing pad, the people sent to meet them waited. They were not electors or mattergraves themselves—that had been deemed too dangerous. Nevertheless, their faces became familiar as those first images were shown over and over. A pair of people—one factor and one patternist—walked forward to greet the approaching aliens. The patternist welcomed the "Members of the Community of Humanity" back to the homeworld. The aliens replied in accented but perfectly comprehensible Argot, saying they came in "brotherhood," an antique term I scarcely recognized, and their purpose was to learn from us. This seemed like either charming humility or deep subterfuge to us, considering that they were the spacefarers. We had no idea at the time that Capellans live to learn, and it was simply the truth.

The delegates ushered the three aliens into a groundcar, and whisked them off. Nothing else happened that day, but that did not stop the commentators from filling the screen with speculation. Why had no one detected the orbiting spaceship? (We later learned that it was specially designed to be invisible to our technology.) How did the aliens know our language? (We learned that they had been studying it, and us, from space for months.) Why were there only three of them? (Magister Galele later told me they were specialists called the First Contact team. The main body of researchers had not even arrived at that time.) What were their true motives in coming here? (No one believed that they had already told us.)

Then, because they had no answers, the commentators began discussing what effect this would have on the delicate balance of power in our own society. As the discussion wore on, I found it boring and irrelevant. How could they talk about politics at a time like this? Couldn't they see that everything had changed?

From where I sat there on the floor of my creche, it seemed as if the world was suddenly vulnerable, like a building with its top blown off, exposed to the sky. We no longer enjoyed the pleasant security of our isolation. No matter what happened, we had lost control. Just weeks before, I had discovered the threats we ourselves had created; now there was an external one. Nothing was safe. I moved closer to Docent Mercady, and she, sensing my fear, put an arm around me. I whispered to her, "Will the aliens start up the machines again?" She kissed me and said, "No. We won't let them do that. Don't worry, Tedla. We won't let anyone hurt you."

For the first time in my life, I wondered if she, or any adult, had the power to make good on such a promise.

In recreation that day, Litch and I played at being aliens. It was our way of robbing the event of strangeness, by acting it out. While most of the others played rocketball, we constructed a spaceship from gym equipment and imagination, and greeted everyone who came by, telling them we came in brotherhood.

After that first day, reports on the aliens became a regular part of our classes. We went on a night expedition outside to look at their home star, Capella Two, through a telescope built by the top roundroom in science class. We learned that their ship had set out hundreds of years ago, but the aliens themselves had only arrived recently by a magically advanced system of transport that made them into lightbeams. Docent Gambrel showed us the spectrum, so we could see the particular frequency of light they had been. Since we were all fascinated by the aliens, and would listen to anything about them, the docents learned to incorporate them in all our lessons. "You'll need to know this if you ever meet an alien," became a frequent refrain.

The strangest thing we learned about them was that they had no childhoods. That is how we interpreted it. They were born adults, fully differentiated, male and female. We would look at each others' naked bodies in the roundroom, and imagine them with sexual organs. It seemed repulsive. The corollary fact that the aliens still had families raised many questions in socialization class, since the docents had always told us that only primitives lived that way, in tribalism, and true civilized amity was impossible as long as the bonds of biology were allowed to coexist with those of community. We discussed it, and I, at least, concluded that the aliens must be more socially primitive than we, despite their technological cleverness. I began to think of them as people who had never outgrown their own Machine Age.

The original sense of community we felt toward them cooled when they claimed not to be descendents of our own colonies. They traced their origin back to a place called Earth, and gently insisted that we had originated there, too, in unspeakably ancient times. Our own questionaries debated this hotly.

However, we soon grew used to seeing the three aliens' gnomish faces on screen. They were endlessly available to answer questions, seemingly quite open with their information, up to a point. Certain questions, especially those about technology, they evaded. They explained that they would share their knowledge when they understood us well enough to know that it would not do us any harm. Having lived on Capella Two, I know this was not strictly true. They would *share* nothing; they intended to *sell* it.

After awhile I grew a little bored with the aliens. I became used to their presence on screen, and on our planet. They became oddities, not threats. I never dreamed that I would become more entangled with them than anyone else on Taramond.

As we grew older, the gestagogues allowed us more freedom to explore the landscape outside the creche on our own.

I loved the outdoors. It seemed as if my senses were more alive there, and I eagerly sampled all the sensations, from the smell of river mud to the stroke of wind on my face. I was feeling everything for the first time; all my emotions were sharp, unblunted by use, like coffee or herbs fresh out of the package. At times I indulged in them so extravagantly that they strained me to the limits. In those days, a melody could pierce to the bone, a sunset could bring tears of painful joy. And an unkindness could gnaw like cancer.

CVP **Tedla broke off suddenly, looking at Val.** "I wonder if humans retain some of that freshness of perception. They told us neuters don't—that everything in a bland's brain becomes blunted and dull, even pain. I know it's true I can't sense things like I did then. It makes me wonder if I'm seeing the world muted, if there is a pitch of sensation closed to me. I wonder if everything I feel is a lesser emotion than humans do."

"I think that's unlikely," Val said, thinking she had hardly ever met a person whose emotions were so close to the surface. Capellans learned to hide their minds much better. "It sounds like they told you a lot of things about neuters that aren't true."

"Yes, but it was all woven in with things that are true."

"If you don't feel the way you did then, it may have more to do with growing up than with being a neuter. I don't feel the way I did as a child, either."

"But how can I tell whether you sense things I don't?"

"I don't know," Val said. "It's the one thing we can never know about each other."

➤¦◄ For you, puberty is a process. To us, it is a precipice. In a single day we pass from the social state of childhood to adulthood. Physically, the transformation takes longer, but it is still abrupt by your standards. At age twelve, we are immature, undifferentiated proto-humans.

At fourteen, we are fully functioning sexual beings.

The gestagogues tried their best to prepare us, but as the metamorphosis came closer, it loomed over all our thoughts, a wall beyond which we could not see. In the roundroom we talked endlessly about whether it was better to be a man or a woman, despite the adults' best efforts to convince us there was no advantage either way. Some protos had strong opinions. Women were better because they could make lots of money having babies. Men were better because they were strong and adventurous. I could never decide. All sexual organs seemed like grotesque deformities to me. In the shower, when I thought no one was looking, I would run my hands over the places on my body where the breasts or the penis would grow. My body, the thing in the world most familiar to me, was about to turn into something alien.

Rumors and legends proliferated in the roundroom, taking up where the instructionaries left off. There were rhymes: Eating beans will produce male genes, the bite of a needletail will make you female. There were diagnostic tests: If you looked at your fingernails palm up rather than palm down, you were sure to be a man. Looking over your shoulder to see the sole of your foot was a sure sign of a woman.

The instructionaries never breathed a hint that there was any third alternative. That knowledge was passed along the way we learned most frightful and unpleasant things, in the whispered roundroom talk at night. One night a group of us was gathered around an older proto named Little Bit, who often knew secrets the rest of us admired it for, even when they were false. This night, it had an especially grave look on its face. We all had to lean close to hear as it whispered, "You know, any one of us could turn into a neuter."

"That's not true!" an argumentative child named Axel said. "They wouldn't be teaching us all this stuff if we were just going to turn into pubers." It was a filthy word.

Axel resented Bit's prestige and was trying to win our admiration by obscenity. It only made most of us uncomfortable.

"They don't know, you see," Bit maintained. "They can't predict who will be a neuter any more than they can predict who will be male or female. So they have to educate everyone, even though some of us will forget it all."

Bit looked at the frightened faces surrounding it. By now everyone in the roundroom had come over to hear. "Any one of us," Bit said in a spooky voice. We all looked around, and most eyes came to rest on Pitter, a fat and sulky proto who was unpopular because it had been a bed wetter, which never gains you points in a roundroom. Someone whispered, "I bet it's Pitter who's the puber."

The phrase sounded so funny that we began to chant it, driving Pitter into a frenzy. Its face got red and it shouted, "Stop it, you creeps! It's not even true. Bit's full of crap."

"You'd better watch out not to touch them too much," Bit said. "Neuter hormones can go right through your skin, and if you touch your eyes or your mouth after touching a neuter, well, that's it."

We were silent, since we had all touched neuters quite unwarily up to that point.

"There's another thing," Bit said. "If you touch yourself down here, you're sure to turn into a neuter."

No one said a word. I expect we had all done that, too.

After that, there was a marked change in our behavior. We became more distant, even hostile and contemptuous, to the blands. Before, we had viewed them with neutrality or pity, since they weren't really our concern—merely unfortunates who could not help what they were. Now, we took them personally. They were reminders of our own vulnerability, the flaw we ourselves might hide, and so we hated them. We were learning to act like humans.

Around that time, my best friend was a proto named Zelly. It was a terribly worried child, afraid and anxious about everything. Zelly found safety in rules— knew them all, obeyed each one to the letter, and was sure to warn the rest of us when we were falling dangerously short. Despite this—or perhaps because of it—I took a perverse pleasure in persuading Zelly to do things that would have terrified it without me—and a few things that should have terrified me.

One midsummer day Zelly and I snuck away from supervised recreation to go exploring in the river bluffs behind the creche. There was a spot where the limestone cliff was eroded in steplike layers, which made for easy scrambling. Zelly followed me a little way, then stopped. "We're not supposed to climb the cliff," it said. "There are rattletails and sucker beetles."

There were hazards everywhere for Zelly. I said, "I'll go first and scare away the rattlers. You know what to do if you hear one?"

Zelly froze in place. "That's right," I said. We were sure the snakes could only see motion, and so we would turn invisible if we kept still.

I led the way up the cliff. Soon we could see over the tops of the aikens, and then we were at the grassy, windswept crest. Below us lay the creche, and the other protos playing on the broad natural terrace. Beyond them the valley fell away in ledges, and off in the blue distance were the river bluffs on the eastern side. To see the creche from outside, in its setting, gave me a feeling of discovery, like seeing a map of a place you knew only from ground level. It gave Zelly a feeling of acrophobia. "Come away from the edge, Tedla!" it pleaded. "You're going to fall."

It sounded like a neuter, and a few months before I would have told it so, teasingly; but now we knew the jibe might be true, and I stayed quiet. All the same, a moment of doubt invaded my day, like the smell of distant poison. I quickly put it out of my mind; I couldn't think such a thing of Zelly. Besides, I told myself, if it were that easy to tell, the adults would have figured it out long ago.

A path ran along the cliff edge, and we followed it single file till we came to a spot where the gray faces of an old ruin stuck up out of the grass.

Gammadis is simply peppered with ruins, mostly of a material we call poured-stone. They are so common that no one pays much attention to any but the most lavish and well preserved. This one was neither—merely a square outline enclosing a depression of hard-packed dirt, where, it was obvious, generations of children from the creche had played. Nevertheless, it looked wondrous in our eyes.

As we explored it, we wove elaborate speculations about what the building had been. We decided it was a fort erected to guard the river valley against invading armies— since we knew from our history lessons that people in the olden days did very little but war with each other and destroy things. Soon it was a place where a pair of freedom fighters had been killed. Since this led to the conclusion that their bones would be buried inside, we got some sticks and began to dig.

"Tedla!" Zelly shrieked, leaping up from its knees. "I found it! I found a skull!"

Eagerly, I came over to look. There it was—a curved, gray-white shard protruding from the soil. One side had a shiny glaze on it. I dug around it with my stick as Zelly peered over my shoulder, and soon wrenched it free.

"It's a piece of a dish!" I said, only a little disappointed it wasn't more macabre. "Maybe it's valuable."

"Maybe it's got a curse on it," Zelly said in a low, thrilling voice.

We looked at each other in fascination and fear. Then we turned back to dig even harder.

Soon we had excavated some bits of rusty metal, a piece of melted red plastic, and a mysterious round glass object with raised marks we imagined to be writing. We laid them out to study.

"You know, you can get diseases from old things in the dirt," Zelly said.

"Then I guess we're going to die," I said.

"We'll die friends, won't we, Tedla?" Zelly said. There was something earnest and anxious in its face, so I took its dirty hand in an improvised secret handshake.

"We'll be friends forever," I said.

We had created quite a satisfactory pile of loose dirt, and Zelly now said, "We ought to make some ammunition to defend ourselves against attack."

There was an old square pit behind the ruins where some scummy water had collected, so now we used it to wet down our dirt and form cannonballs. As we were thus occupied, we heard someone coming up the cliff toward us. Zelly said, "An invader! Quick, Tedla, make more mud-bombs so we can hold them off."

When the invader emerged onto the cliffside path, we saw it was just Joby, walking slowly as if winded by the climb. It came toward us, calling, "Tedla! Zelly! You're supposed to come down."

Obviously, some proctor had noticed our absence and sent Joby to fetch us. At my side, Zelly said in a low, venomous voice, "Filthy puber."

The hatred in Zelly's voice startled and frightened me. The emotion was too virulent for Zelly—cautious Zelly!—but I quickly adjusted. My friend was older, closer to being human, and had to know better than I. Besides, there was something that felt *right* about disobeying Joby. I was going to be human. Humans didn't let neuters order them around. I was different from Joby. I was going to grow up, as it never would. I shouted out, "We don't have to take orders from you!"

Emboldened, Zelly shouted, "Filthy puber! Don't come any closer!"

Joby stopped in its tracks, a complicated expression on its face. I couldn't tell what that expression meant, but my companion recognized it right away. "It's afraid!" Zelly said gleefully, feeling power over another being for the first time.

"Come on, you two," Joby said. "You'll get in trouble.

Proctor Givern wants you to come down now.''

A human would have ordered us, not wheedled. Zelly stood up, a mudball in one hand. "Get away, you defective, or you'll regret it."

Joby hesitated, then said, "Tedla? Are you coming?"

In answer, Zelly let the mudball fly. Joby saw it coming and turned away to shield its face; the bomb hit it on the shoulder with a thunk, spraying dirt into the bland's thinning hair.

"Right on target!" Zelly whooped, then snatched up an armload of mudballs. "Come on, Tedla. We've got it on the run!"

Something had come over my friend. There was a wildness in Zelly's face—a desperate, frightened aggression. I was awed, and caught up in it. I seized a mudball and threw it. When Joby saw that, it turned to flee.

"Sortie!" Zelly called, and leaped past the ruined walls of our fort to chase the retreating bland. I seized up some mudballs and followed. Ahead, Joby started to scramble down the steep cliff path. But the bland was old, and couldn't move fast. We came to the clifftop above it, and began to pelt it with mudballs as it clung to the cliff, slowly trying to move farther down into shelter.

"Mutant! Spado!" Zelly shrieked.

"Puber!" I joined in. In that moment Joby wasn't an individual; it was a symbol for all neuters, all we feared most. And we had power over it.

Zelly finally ran out of mudballs, but didn't want to stop. It picked up a rock from the path and threw it. The rock hit Joby on the side of the head, and its footing slipped. It slid several feet down the cliff before catching a handhold again. We saw blood on its face.

That brought us to our senses. We looked at each other, and suddenly we were ourselves again. Without exchanging a word, we dashed back to the fort.

"What do I care? It's just a bland," Zelly said as we

sat there, debating what to do. "They don't even feel pain like we do."

"Let's go back down now," I said. "Then if Joby tells on us, we can just say it's lying, and we were never even up here."

But Zelly was too afraid of punishment to go back, and I wasn't going to go by myself. Before we could decide anything, we heard someone coming up the cliff. When we crept to the edge, we saw the lanky form of Proctor Givern, with Joby close behind him.

"Let's hide," Zelly said, eyes wide with fear.

But Proctor Givern knew exactly where to look. "Tedla. Zelly. Come out of there," he said in a voice that told us we had never been in trouble like we were in now. When we stood quaking before him, he looked us over with disgust. "Do you think this is funny?" he said, gesturing at Joby. The neuter stood a little behind him. Its face and hair were still crusty with mud, and the trickle of blood from its cut ear was drying on its face. Its coveralls were dirty. Its eyes were cast down—shamed, I thought, for having to fetch a human to defend it from two children.

"We were just playing," Zelly said sulkily.

"Throwing rocks isn't playing," Proctor Givern said harshly. "You could have hurt Joby. Would hurting a bland make you feel proud?" He stared at us, but we couldn't answer. "Only a coward would hurt a bland. They can't fight back; they don't know how. Real humans protect blands. Real humans are kind to them. What do you think that says about you?"

There was a long, horrible silence. At last Proctor Givern said, "Zelly, go down to the creche. Wait in my office till I get there. Tedla, stay here."

Released, Zelly raced away down the path. I watched it go, longing to be with it.

Proctor Givern said, "I really thought better of you, Tedla."

"Zelly started it," I said defensively.

"Zelly never started anything in its life. You're the one I expected to know right from wrong. You've disappointed me."

I stared at the ground, shamed and angry.

"All right. This is your punishment. You are going to spend twenty hours in the chapel in the next ten days, thinking about what you did and why you did it. If you want to talk to me about it, come to my office. Now tell me you're sorry."

I looked up, and the words stuck in my throat. But not because of Proctor Givern. From behind him, Joby was looking at me with the expression of someone watching a child it had cherished mature into a viper. In that moment I hated myself as I had never done before. I had forfeited Joby's love, the only pure and simple love I had ever known, a love without reservations or judgments. I would never know that kind of love again. At the thought, tears sprang into my eyes. I was sorry, so sorry it hurt, but I still couldn't say so, because I wasn't sorry for Proctor Givern—I was sorry for Joby, and Joby was only a bland.

The proctor didn't force the matter. Watching my face, he said, "All right, you can go now."

I climbed recklessly down that cliff, blinded by tears.

Twenty hours is a long time to spend thinking about yourself and why you did something shameful, and I cannot say I used the first ten very profitably. I walked along the quiet, leafy paths, or sat in the grottoes listening to the trickle of water, or watched the fish turn lazily under the lily pads. Whenever I tried to think about myself, as I was supposed to, my mind shied away. By the end of the first day I had constructed a thousand self-justifications and defenses, with corresponding resentments against everyone else. I left the chapel angrier and less repentant than I had walked in. The second day I spent thinking about anyone but myself, cataloging every casual cruelty I had seen adults commit, in order to convince myself that I was being held to a higher standard than humans themselves could meet. By the third day I was miserable again, blaming myself for stupidity, for not thinking ahead, for letting Zelly lead me into trouble.

As I daydreamed on the fourth day, a thought occurred to me: What if there were a drug I could take that would let me live the whole year over again without getting any older? Then, immediately: What if I could just stay twelve forever, and never have to grow up? The thought was so entrancing that I sat there on the stone bench under the ferns, dreaming about it. Then a horrible realization struck me: What I was wishing for was what actually happened to neuters. They never matured. I had been wishing to be like a neuter.

The idea was so horrifying that I stood up, shaking all over, terrified that the mere thought would make it so. I had to talk to someone.

Proctor Givern was in his office. When I came in, he said, "What's wrong, Tedla?"

"Proctor, how can I be sure I'm going to be human?" I said.

"Is that what all this is about?" he asked, as if seeing the light.

"No!" I said. It was so much more complicated. "I don't want to grow up. I don't want to not grow up. I just want to be me. Why do I have to change? It's not fair."

He saw how distressed I was, and said, "Come here, Tedla." When I came, he gave me a long hug. Then he sat me down in a chair facing his, still holding my hands. "Tedla, everyone your age is afraid of growing up," he said. "I was. It's a scary thing. But once it happens, it'll feel like the rightest thing in the world. You'll be really glad you grew up, and you'll never want to go back to being a proto again."

His unquestioning assumption that I was going to grow up calmed me. He obviously saw something about me that I didn't see. Even so, I ventured, "Are blands happy they're blands?"

"Yes," he said, "because that's what they were meant to be. If we tried to make them act like humans, they'd be miserable."

"Can you get neuter hormones by touching them?"

"Who told you that?" he asked, frowning.

"Little Bit did."

"Well, Little Bit's wrong. There is absolutely nothing you can do to determine your sex. It's all a matter of biology. Neuters can't help what they are. They didn't do anything to get that way. The way we show we're human is to treat them kindly and take care of them. It's like a test of how worthy of humanity we are."

Again, that assurance. It was as good as a guarantee to me.

Proctor Givern said, "Now I want you to go back to the chapel and think about what all this has to do with how you acted the other day."

I went back reluctantly. By now I knew that Zelly's punishment had been twenty hours of cleanup work—dirty and humiliating, but at least it was mindless. I had started out thinking my punishment was easier, but now I envied Zelly.

The tenor of my thoughts changed after that. The expression on Joby's face kept coming back to me, and every time it made me more uncomfortable with myself. I was ashamed that I'd hurt Joby, but I was also ashamed to *care* that I'd hurt Joby. It was only a neuter. Why had that look pierced me through? At last I went back to Proctor Givern.

It was hard to frame the question. I sat there a long time, twining my legs under the chair. At last I said, "Proctor, is it wrong to love a neuter?"

He thought about it a long time before answering. "No," he said. "We all get fond of them from time to time. It's only natural. It can even be good, as long as we don't get too attached or possessive. After all, they don't belong to us."

His answer made me feel liberated from a huge weight of shame that had been building up ever since that first taunt of "neuter-lover." I could admit now that I loved Joby, and didn't need to deny it to myself.

After that, thinking became much easier. I realized that I had hated Joby that day on the cliff, because love for it had been such an important part of me as a child—a part I had grown to see as shameful. I wasn't able to simply detach myself and feel nothing toward Joby, as I should have; the feelings were too strong. Joby *was* my childhood, all I had valued and cherished. Now I had to leave all that behind, and didn't want to. I had been throwing those mudballs at myself, at my past.

"I got mixed up," I told Proctor Givern. "I thought I was mad at Joby, but it was really me I was mad at, because I was so scared."

Proctor Givern gave me another big hug. "You're a good kid, Tedla," he said. It made me feel so warm I never wanted to leave his arms.

❦ Val said, "Why do you think your punishment was different from Zelly's?"

"Proctor Givern knew us," Tedla said. "He knew what would be effective for each of us. He made me think about myself, because he knew I would."

"We have an old-fashioned word for that," Val said, smiling. "It's called a conscience."

"Yes, I suppose that's right. He wanted me to have a conscience. It's one of many things that made me think— still does make me think—that they expected me to be human. A conscience is a useless commodity for a bland. Their behavior is too tightly controlled; they don't have to control themselves."

" 'They'? " Val said curiously.

"We."

The word seemed to come hard.

➤¦⟵ Shortly after, there was an event—two events, really—that affected all of us at the creche, but me in particular.

It was justification time, the yearly period when the adults have to review their lives and search their hearts to see if they have made a contribution to nature, culture, or humanity in that year. The air was full of tension and seriousness. The adults were all preoccupied and short with us.

I was struggling with an inner dilemma myself— whether to say anything to Joby. Proctor Givern had given me no advice about it, and I had been afraid to ask. Acknowledging my own emotions in the past had been one thing; acting on them in the present was another.

I kept a watch out for Joby, but though I glimpsed it a few times, there was never any opportunity to talk. Then, mysteriously, Joby seemed to disappear altogether. After five days, I finally asked one of the other blands about it. "Joby's sick," was the answer.

After three days of fretting, I finally went back to Proctor Givern. He was a little more relaxed than the other adults, and wasn't impatient to see me.

"Is Joby sick because of us?" I asked. "Did we really hurt it?"

"No, Tedla." Proctor Givern seemed to debate what to tell me. At last he said, "Joby's been sick a long time. That's why we've been cutting down its duties."

"What's wrong?" I said, trying not to show my alarm.

"It's got cancer. It's probably going to die soon."

He sounded quite matter-of-fact, but to me the news was shattering. I had never known anyone to die before. "Can't you do something?" I said. "Can't you take it to the curatory?"

Proctor Givern put a hand on my shoulder. "That wouldn't be kind, Tedla. We would only prolong its suffering if we tried to cure it. Here, we can keep Joby comfortable in its own familiar surroundings."

"But it wasn't even sick the other day!" I protested.

"Yes, it was. You just couldn't tell."

He saw how troubled I was, and said, "We have to make this kind of decision all the time, Tedla. Blands can't decide when it's right to end their lives, like humans can. We have to decide for them. We'd like to keep Joby around, just like you would. But it wouldn't have a good life, only a sick and feeble one. This way is better."

I had to accept that. But the weight of guilt was crushing. I couldn't bear to think what Joby's last sight of me had been, or that it never would know how sorry I was. I couldn't think of anything else for the rest of the day. In the evening, I crept down to the clinic where we protos went if we were sick, thinking Joby might be there. I tried to peek around, not wanting anyone to know what I was looking for. But Joby wasn't there.

That night in the roundroom I pulled Zelly aside and whispered, "Did you know that Joby's dying?"

A look of shock and fear passed across Zelly's face. "Are they going to blame us?" it whispered.

"No. Joby's got cancer. It's been sick a long time."

Instead of remorse, I saw relief on Zelly's face. "Oh, that's okay then."

Angrily, I said, "Don't you care?"

"Why?" Zelly said defensively. "I didn't do it. What are you blaming me for?"

Disgusted, I turned away. But I knew Zelly's reaction was the safer, righter one. I couldn't let on that I cared. Whatever Proctor Givern might say, the other protos would have made my life a misery of teasing.

I slept apart from the others in the roundroom that night, feeling alienated and unable to face them. The thought of Joby made my throat ache with all the regret I had to swallow. I thought of it till I fell asleep.

The next morning the postulants who oversaw us

seemed grim and upset. When we came into refectory and saw all the younger protos assembled and waiting, we knew something was wrong.

The postulants instructed us to sit down at the tables without any food. All of the gestagogues were there, waiting. It seemed unnaturally quiet. At last the Matron came in.

"I have some important news to tell you," she said. "As you may know, this is the time of justification for all the adults here. Last night, Docent Horst decided to justify himself by making space in the world for another."

The room was perfectly silent. We all knew what she meant. He had ended his own life.

The Matron went on, "Docent Horst's conscience called upon him to take this step, and though we will miss him, we all admire his self-knowledge and support his courageous decision."

It was possibly the nicest thing we had ever heard anyone say about Docent Horst. He had been a heavyset, white-haired man who sweated profusely and often smelled of alcohol. The other docents had treated him with open disrespect. I had only had one class from him, and hadn't learned much.

"Sooner or later, all of us will face the decision Docent Horst faced last night," the Matron said. "I hope that when the time comes, each of us will have the determination he did. This afternoon, we will have an assembly to celebrate his life. The docents and proctors will gather this evening. That is all."

She left, and the blands behind the counter began serving up our breakfasts. There was no weeping or grief; that was inappropriate, since Docent Horst had died the right kind of death, and thus justified any mistakes in his life. To weep would have implied disrespect for his decision. All the same, we were shaken and a little grave, especially those of us on the verge of adulthood. Very soon, the burden of justification would be ours. Every year we would have to decide whether we deserved to continue living.

That afternoon, the blands served up a big butterberry cake in Docent Horst's honor, and we all ate some. There were games for the little ones, and the chorus sang songs.

I watched the blands serving the refreshments and cleaning up. They seemed completely unaffected by Docent Horst's demise, as indifferent to the death of a human as we were to the death of a bland.

No one ever told us when Joby died. Joby simply disappeared, as if it had never existed. I suppose no one thought we would care.

I went through a very emotional time after that. I'm not sure anyone realized I was grieving; I'm not sure I realized it myself. It wasn't just Joby's death. I was grieving for the death of my childhood. I was saying good-bye to the creche and all the places I loved. I was saying good-bye to the person I had been.

I spent a great deal of time outdoors, walking the trails to the river or climbing the bluff. Often I brought along a book to read—mostly sad tales, which suited my mood. I became very interested in religion. The truth was, I desperately needed something to take me out of myself. I was maddeningly aware of my treacherous body and my undeveloped personality. I needed something to give me a nobler persona, whose eyes I could look through—so I could face the world thinking, it's not just me inside here; it's someone else, more worthwhile than me. Otherwise I might have perished of self-awareness.

Now I know, as I didn't then, that emotion is itself a kind of talent not everyone has. A form of intelligence, perhaps—though not much valued by any culture I know of. The intensity of my feelings that fall was a gift—a treacherous gift.

On Gammadis, our religion teaches that all life is suffused with spirit, but that humans, unique among life forms, are able to become aware of it. Each person, they say, has a god inside—an individual emanation of the life force. To search for one's god—to become aware of the aspect of one's self that approaches divinity—is the purpose of worship among us. People approach it in different ways—through dance, song, meditation, even drugs—though the latter, we had been warned, might confuse us with unrealities, not help us touch what is truly real.

That fall, I became absorbed with the idea of searching for my god. The docents would have warned me not to. I was too young, my mind too unformed. But amid the roil of emotions in me I felt one constant: kinship with the landscape I had grown up in. I became convinced that this was the way I had to search: by blending my consciousness with the living things around me.

I spent hours walking down forest paths, my mind excruciatingly attuned to the trees, trying to feel their consciousness around me. I rubbed my cheek against their bark, and listened to the whispering of the leaves. I lay in the grass on top of the bluff, feeling the wind stroking my back.

One day I was coming down a forest path at a time of day when the setting sun reflected off the leaves, giving them a coppery sheen. I discovered that if I unfocused my eyes, the plants all around me seemed to be glowing. My mind filled with exhaltation. I was actually seeing it—seeing the spirit that suffused the world, manifested around me. I felt the glow in myself, as well, coursing through my limbs. The entire world was incandescent with visible spirit. I felt exalted, uplifted, as if I had seen a vision.

I thought I had touched my god. After that, I had no doubt—not a shadow, not a qualm—about my humanity.

I still don't know what it was I experienced. Sometimes I think I was right—that there was a spark of divinity in me, struggling to manifest itself. If so—if that was what I felt—I know I have Joby to thank for it. Without the shock of Joby's death, I might never even have gone searching. If I almost became human in that moment, it was Joby who made me so.

Chapter Three

❧ It was drawing on toward evening, and the clinic hallways were coming alive as the staff geared up for another night's work. Val wandered down the corridor, looking for someone she knew. At last she found Joan talking intently to a woman with heavy eyebrows, heavy shoes, and a Social Services scarf. When Val waved at her, Joan broke off the conversation and came into the hall.

"You're not turning Tedla over to her, are you?" Val asked, a little alarmed.

"No, this is other business," Joan said. Val was surprised at the relief she felt.

"Where is Deedee?" she asked.

"Asleep in one of the detox rooms. We'll have to wake her up soon; we're going to need the bed."

"I guess the picnic's shot," Val said, glancing ruefully at a clock.

"Never mind that," Joan said. "Did you find out anything useful?"

"For me, yes. Very useful. But nothing like a next of kin's address."

"I guess that means we have to find a curatory," Joan said without relish.

"I've got another idea," Val said. She hadn't really thought it out; it just sprang impulsively into her mouth. "I want to take Tedla home with me."

"Oh, no. You can't do that."

"Why not?"

"You don't have any legal relation to this patient, Val. What if something happens? You could be liable."

"Nothing is going to happen overnight."

"How do you know? Tedla needs professional attention."

"I'll take it to a mentationist tomorrow, Joan. This is just temporary. You don't want Tedla to have to spend the night in an institution, do you? I really think a family setting would be better."

"But—"

"Tell you what. Why don't we let Tedla decide?"

When she entered the room again, Tedla was staring pensively at the place where a window would be, if there were one. Its expression was resigned and fatalistic. Val said briskly, "Tedla, we've got a problem about what to do with you. Now, what we *ought* to do is transfer you to a curatory where you can get the care of some trained mentationists."

"Whatever you think is best," Tedla said faintly.

"Well, there's another possibility," Val plunged on. "You could come home with me, and be my guest till you can decide about going to the curatory."

Tedla looked at her as if searching for hidden meanings in her offer. She went on quickly, "The copartment isn't very big, and we'd have to put you on the fold-out in the studium, so you'd have your own room, sort of, but other than that I'm afraid it's not very private. But Max and I would love to have you, and it would be wonderfully educational for Dierdre. If you can put up with us, it would be a real treat." She realized she was babbling and made herself stop.

Slowly, Tedla said, "Do you think you owe me this?"

"No," Val said. "I want to do it."

In the silence that followed, she felt a tug of caution. "There is one thing you would have to promise me," she said. "You must not try to hurt yourself again."

Tedla's eyes fell in shame.

"Do you promise?" Val said.

Tedla nodded, still not looking at her. "I promise."

"You're sure? I can't risk it if you're not."

"Yes. It was stupid and arrogant of me, anyway. I should have known I couldn't succeed. Please let me come with you."

Val smiled and put a hand on the neuter's arm, felt it stiffen at the touch, and pulled back. "Good," she said.

She left the clinic with Deedee on one side and Tedla on the other. The alien wore a fresh bandage and some ill-fitting clothes left by other patients. It walked with eyes cast down. Some of the stimulation shops had begun to open. Val was acutely aware of the curious stares they attracted. She fingered the scarf that indicated her observer status.

"Do you know anyone here, Tedla?" she asked in an undertone.

"No," Tedla said. "But they may know me. I've been around for a couple of months."

"Doing what?"

A pause. "Nothing."

Val glanced over. Tedla wouldn't look at her.

A Skor was watching them strangely from a doorway. His head was completely crusted with cerebs, the bioengineered mollusks that fed on brain tissue. His yellowed eyes followed them eagerly, gleaming with the euphoria of heightened sensory perception the parasites gave.

When they got back to the copartment, Deedee went racing into the dinery shouting, "Papa! Guess what?"

Max came to the bedroom door, a packing box in his arms. He began to say something, but saw Tedla and stopped.

"Max, this is Tedla Galele," Val said. "My husband, Max. I've asked Tedla over for a few nights, till we decide what to do."

"It's a pleasure to meet you," Tedla said nervously.

"Uh . . . hi." Max tried to hold out a hand, but the box in his arms slipped and nearly dropped; he swore. "Sorry," he said. "We're in the middle of unpacking. Let me go put this down. Val?" He disappeared into the bedroom.

"Make yourself at home," Val said to Tedla, and left it standing in the gathering room.

Max closed the bedroom door behind them. "Val, what the hell . . . ?"

"Joan had to get Tedla out of the clinic, and there was no place for it to go," Val said quickly. "We couldn't put it out on the streets."

"So this is the suicidal alien?" Max said. "You've brought home a lunatic?"

"Who told you?"

"Joan called E.G. while we were waiting for you to show up. We were going to have a picnic, remember?"

"I'm sorry, Max. I needed to interview Tedla. Don't worry, it's not dangerous."

"How do you know?"

"Give the poor soul a chance. I'm sorry I didn't check with you first. I swear it's only for a night or two."

"I'll hold you to that," Max said.

When she entered the gathering room again, Tedla was sitting on the couch listening seriously as Deedee explained one of her toys. Seeing Val, the alien rose nervously. "Should I leave?" it whispered.

"No, of course not," Val said. "I just shouldn't have surprised him this way. I should have called first. Come on, I'll show you your room."

Deedee followed them into the studium. "Do you want to play Scratcher?" she said to Tedla.

"Stop being a pest, Dee," Val said as she rummaged in a packing box for some sheets and towels.

Tedla turned to her. "No, really, I'd like to, if you don't mind."

"Suit yourself." Val shrugged. Then, to her daughter, "Tedla's like family, Deedee. You have to share information free."

For the first time in months, Val and Max actually sat down alone together at the dinery table for a glass of wine before dinner. They could hear a constant stream of peremptory instructions coming from the gathering room, punctuated with occasional shrieks of delight. At first Max kept glancing in uneasily.

"Are they okay?" Val asked.

"Deedee is. I'm not sure about your alien. She's bullying it unmercifully."

"She takes after her mother," Val said, looking at him apologetically.

"You can say that again." Max stretched out his legs under the table.

"Am I forgiven?" Val said, rubbing his leg with her stockinged foot.

"Don't push your luck," Max said, but he wasn't serious. "You give new meaning to 'taking your work home with you.' "

They ate picnic food for supper. While they were still at the table, Joan called to see how Tedla was doing. Val felt smugly satisfied at what a harmonious picture of family life they presented to the screen. After a few minutes of small talk, Joan asked to speak to Val privately. Val switched the call into the bedroom and went in there, closing the door.

"Mandy just called me from the clinic," Joan said. She was frowning in puzzlement. "After we left, they got a message from WAC saying they'd noted our inquiries about Tedla Galele. They want to know if we have information on Tedla's whereabouts."

"Did she reply?" Val asked.

"I told her to send back a message asking who wanted to know, and why. No response yet. E.G. is very suspicious. I know it's what we wanted, to find someone that knows Tedla—but it gives me the creeps to think they tracked us down just for asking a question. Isn't that illegal?''

"No, but it was your proprietary information," Val said. "You can charge them for using it."

"Oh, sure. As if I'm going to send WAC a bill."

"You should, Joan. It's what keeps them from doing this more often." Her voice was casual, but in fact, Val couldn't remember ever having tripped off a monitor before. It meant the information was valuable.

"What should I tell them?"

"Nothing, yet. Give me the number. I'll call them in the morning and find out what's up."

Deedee was full of energy and wanted to play again after dinner, but Val insisted she prepare for bed. It devolved into a longer-than-usual ritual, since Deedee had to come out to explain each step to Tedla. When she was finally washed, brushed, and in her sleepers, she crawled up on the sofa beside her new friend. Val noticed that the neuter didn't flinch from Deedee the way it did from adults. She hoped the child was thawing the tension. Then Deedee looked up earnestly at Tedla and said, "If you're not a boy or a girl, how do you pee?"

"Dierdre!" Val said. "That's a rude question."

"That's all right," Tedla said. "Everyone wonders, no one asks. Do you mind if I answer?"

"Only if you want to."

Tedla turned to Deedee. "I pee the same way you do, through a hole called the urethra. Only with me, there's nothing there but the hole."

"I don't have anything else but the hole, either," Deedee said wisely. "Only boys do."

"I think you do," Tedla said. "You have some flaps of skin called labia, and a few other things you'll learn about when you're older."

"Oh," Deedee said, concentrating.

"Oh dear, now I can tell I'll have to do some explaining," Val said. Max was grinning.

"Was that too explicit?" Tedla said apprehensively.

"No, you did just fine," Val said.

"Want to explain the rest of it?" Max said wryly.

"I would be afraid of doing it wrong," Tedla said.

"So are we," said Max.

Later, when everyone else was in bed and she was in her robe, Val went out to the dinery to make sure breakfast was programmed for four. Heading back to the bedroom, she paused at the studium door to listen. There was no sound from inside, so she cracked open the door. Tedla had gone to sleep with the light still on. After a moment's hesitation, Val stepped in.

She looked down on the alien's face. This way, in sleep, it looked very peaceful, and very young. On an impulse, she bent over and kissed the damp forehead, as she would Deedee's. There was no reaction.

"Poor kid," she said. "Poor lost kid."

The persistent chiming of a priority message pulled Val from sleep the next morning. She lay still, waiting for Max to get it, but though his side of the bed was empty, there was no sound from the gathering room. Groaning in exasperation, she rolled out of bed and hit the preview key. When she saw it was only Joan, she answered the call.

Joan was already back at the clinic. She looked brisk and serious. "Did I wake you up? I'm sorry," she said.

"No, that's all right, I should be up anyway." Val stifled a yawn, running her fingers through her thick, rat's-nest hair.

"Well, I thought you'd want to know this. We found some information about Tedla. Mandy did, actually. She's a perfect genius at this sort of thing. Until this year, Tedla was enrolled as a graduate student in exoethnology at the university on C4D, on an Epco scholarship. No wonder we couldn't find any trace of our guest—we were looking on the wrong planet!''

A lot of things made more sense now.

"We sent a query to C4D for some records," Joan said, "but all we could get was lightspeed transmission. It'll take four days. In the meantime, we have to decide what to do. Tedla can't stay at your home."

"Yes. I know, Joan," Val said. "Let me get up and start working this out." Before Joan could cut her off she said, "Oh Joan—I'd like a copy of the recording I made there yesterday. Can you have it downloaded to my cache?"

Joan hesitated. "You know about patient confidentiality, don't you?"

"Of course! I won't use it without Tedla's permission."

"All right."

Val stumbled into the bathroom, then threw some clothes on. No one seemed to be home. When she got to the dinery, she noticed the message light blinking. She hit it.

"Hi there, you lazy bum," Max said. "We couldn't wait around for you to wake up. We're going down to the playground. See you by lunch, if you're not still asleep."

She could only assume "we" meant Tedla, as well. She ordered a cup of coffee and went into the studium to use her console there. The bed was made up, meticulously neat. First, she checked her cache for the interview recording; Tedla's image filled her screen, talking softly. She was so pleased she kissed her fingers and touched them to the screen. Then she stored the recording and set out to get some questions answered.

Her first step was to look up some background information on Gammadis. What came up was oddly scanty. She chose an article labeled "Gammadis—Exploration."

The story started, as most exploration stories did, back in the Second Diaspora, when the scattered offshoots of humanity had reached out across space to locate one another. Capella One had been the motherworld of the questships. Never again, in all likelihood, could any planet afford to make such gloriously elaborate machines, and send them out searching for life on a mere speculation. There had been dozens of questships. At first, discoveries had been common. But as the centuries had passed, and near space was explored, communications from the questships had grown fewer and fewer. Now, no one knew exactly how many were still out there, or where they were bound. They did not communicate until they found something.

The last questship to report a discovery had been targeted at an ordinary G-type star, Gamma Disciplis. When, over a hundred years ago, the monitors on Capella Two had intercepted the message reporting an urban civilization on the third planet, WAC had bid for the right to assemble an expeditionary team, gambling that the monopoly on patents, copyrights, and discoveries would repay the expenses. The explorers made the trip from Capella Two via coherent lightbeam transmission to the wayport on the ship. They spent fifty-one years en route, traveling at the speed of light—which, in fact, they were until reassembled into organics at journey's end. They brought along a state-of-the-art paired-particle communicator, which allowed some limited instantaneous data transmission, but not, alas, instantaneous travel.

Everything had gone smoothly at first. Xenologists, geologists, biologists, economists, and industrial chemists had fanned out across the planet they christened Gammadis, short for Gamma Disciplis. They were welcomed by the inhabitants, who still kept alive traditions of their own spacefaring past and were delighted to be reunited with their kindred in the stars. And yet it soon became apparent that they were only semi-kindred. As with other isolated relics of the human diaspora, the Gammadians had taken their own unique evolutionary path, and had formed their culture around it.

The period of goodwill had lasted only two years. Then, a critical misstep by the researchers had so enraged the Gammadian elites that they had expelled the entire scientific contingent and declared the planet off-limits. Here, the article was irritatingly vague. "Much of the information gathered by the investigators was impounded by Gammadian authorities, and the rest remains proprietary," the article stated in its own defense.

Nowhere was there any mention of Tedla Galele—though an Alair Galele was listed as an ethnographer on the original expedition team. Thinking she might have found a hint, Val sent a query for Alair Galele's current address. The reply came back, "Deceased."

It was time to call in the heavy artillery. She placed a call to Magister Gossup's office. He had been her graduate advisor, and was now her principal ally on the UIC faculty.

Kendra, his assistant, answered. "He's busy right now, Val," she said. "I'll tell him to call you, but it may be a while. Did you hear? He got nominated to the Magisterium."

"Wow. Tell him congratulations." There had been rumors for months, but now Val realized what it meant to her. Members of the Magisterium had little time for chats with magisters minor. With sinking expectations, she said, "Well, let him know I've got some information he'll be interested in." On a hunch she added, "Say it's about Tedla Galele."

"He'll know what that means?" Kendra asked.

"I don't know. See if he does."

She went to get another cup of coffee, but had scarcely poured it when the terminal chimed again. To her utter surprise, Magister Gossup's cultured Vind face filled her screen.

He was the picture of controlled intelligence. Every hair on his head was cut to the same even length. His honey-colored skin was unmarked by either frown or smile lines, despite what had to be an advanced age. There was a half-serious joke in the xenology section at UIC that he had traveled so much, his molecules reconstituted so many times, that he had begun to lose definition. The only culture-specific touch about him was the carnelian caste-stone anchored in his forehead, disconcertingly like a third eye. Perhaps it was; no one but Vinds knew their exact function.

"I was pleased to hear that you called, Valerie," he said quietly. That meant nothing; he did everything quietly, from dressing to dressing down his students. Val instinctively smoothed her hair. He always made her feel helter-skelter.

"Did Kendra give you my message?" she said.

"Yes," he said. "It was . . . intriguing."

That meant there was something valuable about it. Val was very alert by now. "I have an interesting houseguest. From Gammadis."

Anyone who didn't know him well would have thought he had no reaction. Val saw the tiny movement of his eyebrow, and knew what intense pressure he must be under. "Tedla Galele is at your house?" he said.

"Yes." She paused, waiting to see what he would offer for more information. She owed him stunning amounts of money.

"Does WAC know?" he asked.

"Not yet, but they're getting close. I'm giving you first chance at this information."

"I appreciate that, Valerie. The information is very valuable to WAC, and I expect them to be generous. Shall we say, five thousand?"

Val was speechless. It was a windfall beyond her wildest expectations. Five thousand units would send Deedee to school for a year, and free Max to pursue his life again. She caught herself on the verge of accepting gratefully. If the stakes were this high, a gamble might have an even bigger payoff. Glad that Max wasn't listening, she said, "Actually, Magister, I'd prefer an in-kind exchange. You let me in on what's going on, and why WAC's looking for Tedla, and we'll call it square."

From the way he paused, she knew her instincts had been right: She had asked for something more valuable than five thousand units of money.

"I would prefer not to talk over a public connection," he said. "There are some diplomatic problems involved. Can you meet me at the sand fountain outside the Court of Induction?"

If diplomacy was involved, something big had happened. Val said, "I'll be there in twenty-five minutes."

Marep to Overcon to Paratuic—each waynode on the route was a seat of learning, and an enclave of imported culture, in its own right. No other planet thrived on the new like Capella Two. Knowledge was its principal export, and its only major industry. Once, Val had protested the commodification of information along with Max and the rest of the radicals; but she could no longer afford purist principles. Information, as the saying went, was the only truly transportable commodity. It was what had supported the exploration of near space for the past few centuries— and without exploration, what good were xenologists?

The Court of Induction was an indoor plaza in a new section of the university, built from the proceeds of many lucrative research contracts. The stories-high glass ceiling was supported by tracery arches, and the court itself was full of sunlight and varied textures of stone, glass, and metal. Val caught a glimpse of herself in an architectural mirror, and realized that the surroundings made her look underdressed and undergroomed. Her thin, pointed face looked alert, like some small, wily animal's, under her black cap of hair.

She spotted Magister Gossup from across the plaza, waiting at a cafe table near the sand fountain, sipping maté. As she crossed toward him, the bells marking the Twelve Harmonies went off—a courtesy to the Choristers, whose enclave was nearby. She nearly collided with a jingling Chorister who had stopped in midmotion to perform a tuning devolution.

When Val slipped into the seat opposite Magister Gossup, she realized that the background noise of falling sand made it impossible for anyone to eavesdrop. "Thank you for meeting me," Gossup said evenly. He offered her some maté. She shook her head and ordered espresso from the automenu. As if continuing a casual conversation, he said, "I am curious to hear how Tedla came to be at your house."

His face grew very grave as she told the story. At the end, he looked preoccupied. "Suicide," he said. "And I thought this couldn't get more complicated."

"Magister, what is going on? You've got to let me in on it now."

He paused. "How much do you know about the history of our relations with Gammadis?"

"Only what the public can find out," she said.

"Then there are a few things you need to know." He sat back, his normally serene face a map of concentration. "Gammadis is quite a puzzling anomaly. An extremely earthlike ecosystem, genetic stock far too similar to be anything but terraformed; yet the world shows all the evidence of quite ancient settlement, and the inhabitants themselves have no tradition of earth origin. Their social and material technologies have enormous sales potential. All in all, WAC was anticipating a windfall from knowledge acquired there. If the team had imagined how suddenly the Gammadians would turn against them, they might have sent back more information, despite the inconvenience of PPC transmission. But the expulsion took them completely by surprise. Most of their research was confiscated. WAC's losses were enormous. Now we have only the interim reports—enough to tantalize us, not enough to profit by."

His use of "we" when referring to WAC didn't escape Val.

"When we were forced to vacate the planet sixty-three years ago, we naturally left the questship in orbit, tended by its AI. We left the wayport and the paired-particle communicator ready to activate again, in case the mattergraves and electors should change their minds."

"Do you remember this?" Val asked.

"Yes, I was on Capella Two at the time."

No one at UIC knew exactly how old he was; rumors said that he had spoken knowingly about the original colony on Capella One.

He continued, "All the Gammadians had to do was send a radio message to the AI, something well within their technological capabilities. The AI would then transmit the message to us instantaneously via PPC."

"And did they?" Val asked.

"Apparently we underestimated their capabilities, or their tenacity. In the years following our evacuation, they not only communicated with our AI; they found a way to subvert it. Perhaps it malfunctioned. At any rate, they learned a great deal from it without our knowledge. Eventually, they managed to get to the orbiter by mechanical means."

"Rocket technology?" Val asked.

Gossup nodded resignedly. "Once they had access to the ship, of course, they had access to the wayport on it, with lightspeed transport to Capella Two. Twelve years after our evacuation, they sent a two-member delegation to investigate us and demand redress for their grievances. They arrived three days ago. You can imagine our surprise."

There had not been a hint of this news on the nets. "There is a delegation here from Gammadis?" Val said. "Now?" It made her appreciate WAC's powers of information suppression.

"It presents us with a delicate diplomatic situation.

WAC is extremely anxious for a resumption of contact.''

"What about the Gammadians? Do they want contact, as well?''

"I believe so, if they could be assured we will not attempt to meddle in their culture or violate their laws again. The delegates are here to evaluate us. We are on probation, as it were.''

The thought of another expedition to Gammadis made Val's heart fly. She leaned across the table and said intently, "If we go back to Gammadis, Magister, I want to be on the team.''

He evaluated her with an enigmatic smile. "First we must convince them to allow us back.'' His smile faded. "Unfortunately, Tedla's presence here is one of the principal grievances to be ironed out. When they first asked about Tedla's welfare, we had completely lost track of it. We led them to believe—in fact, we thought ourselves— that it was still on C4D. When we found we were mistaken, WAC launched an all-out search.''

"I understand,'' Val said. She also understood why the news of Tedla's mental condition had so upset him. It did not make Capella look good.

"What are you going to tell the Gammadians?'' she asked.

"Nothing, right away,'' he said, looking troubled. "First, we need to find if there is a way to repair Tedla's problem—somehow make up for the damage we have done.''

He seemed to be taking it very personally. Val said gently, "Tedla's problem may not be our fault.''

"I'm afraid I can't be as sanguine as you,'' Gossup said. "Tedla was never supposed to be here in the first place. Its transportation was one of the many breakdowns in our procedures during the debacle of those last few days on Gammadis. Quite a few things went on that never should have happened. From the Gammadians' point of view, Tedla's immigration here was little better than a kidnapping. If Tedla has suffered harm, that can hardly help but be our fault.''

Knowing how carefully planned expeditions were, and how extensively the researchers were trained, Val found it hard to imagine such a total breakdown. "How did it happen?" she said.

"Most of it can be laid at the door of Alair Galele."

"The team's exoethnologist?" Val said.

"Yes. He lost his objectivity about Gammadian society. He formed some sort of idea of bringing them more into line with Capellan values."

"But that's . . . self-defeating," Val said. She had almost said "unprofitable." Every exoethnologist she knew cursed the rapidity with which cultures blended when exposed to one another. The ethnologist's job was often a race against inevitable assimilation. True cultural isolation was vanishingly rare in the information bath of the Twenty Planets—and correspondingly valuable. New variants of culture, like new variants of biology, were rare jewels— which was exactly why WAC wanted them.

"This man had unorthodox professional ethics," Gossup said with a tight-lipped reserve. "He never would have been on the team if they hadn't had so much trouble recruiting. Perhaps I am being too easy on him. He was not just misled; he was evil."

A startled silence followed. Val had never heard Gossup speak so forcefully against someone.

He went on, "But we compounded his corruption by failing to realize what was happening. We failed to protect Tedla from him. In that way, we were culpable. I would prefer the Gammadians not know how badly."

Val was drawing breath to ask a question, but Gossup said, "I'm sorry, I can't be more specific, Valerie. Take my word for it."

"So what do we do now?" Val said.

Gossup appeared relieved to turn away from the past and toward the future, where he could be in control. "The first step is obviously to get Tedla admitted to a curatory, to be thoroughly evaluated by our mentationists. I will speak to Monseigneur Bolduc at the Connuic curatory, and ask him to make a place available. They are very good, and very discreet." He paused, looking carefully at Val. "I need not mention, Valerie, that discretion is essential. What the delegation and the public learn, and when they learn it, must be under our control."

For the first time in her life, she had the heady feeling of controlling some truly valuable information. "I can be very discreet, Magister," she said, "as long as I am part of the team dealing with the situation."

He paused; perhaps, she thought, she hadn't bargained with the proper delicacy. At last he said, "Of course. That goes without saying. We will need your help, Valerie. There is a great deal of research to do."

Research wasn't what she'd had in mind, but she would settle for it. After all, a magister minor couldn't push her luck too far. "I suppose," she said, "if I'm to help with research, that I'll be given access to WAC's proprietary files on Gammadis."

Gossup paused. "I think that can be arranged."

"Good," she said.

"As well as a stipend," he added.

"If you think WAC can afford it," she said wryly.

"I've always enjoyed your honesty, Valerie," Gossup said inscrutably. He pressed his thumb on the menu screen to pay for their drinks. "WAC will want to send someone to fetch Tedla to Connuic. You can come, if you like."

"I would like," Val said. "Besides, I think Tedla might be more comfortable having a friend along." The thought of turning Tedla over gave her a pang, but it was the only moral thing to do. "Give me an hour before you send someone, so I can get Tedla used to the idea."

She saw her family coming up the walk as she was approaching the copartment complex: Max and Tedla on either side, Deedee in the middle, holding Tedla's hand. The neuter was still wearing the scrounged clothes from the clinic: baggy, dilapidated pants and a clashing pullover. Between that and the bandage on its head, Tedla looked like a good candidate to be locked up in a curatory.

Deedee saw her and came racing down the pumice walkway. "Mama! I learned a song! Do you want to hear it?" Without waiting for an answer, Deedee sang out,

> *Inky dinky diddle die*
> *Tell a patternist a lie*
> *She will sell it by and by*
> *Inky dinky diddle die.*

"That's very nice, Deedee," Val said.

Max and Tedla had come up during this performance. Val looked at Tedla and said, "Gammadian, I presume?"

Tedla blushed. "It's not a very polite limerick, I'm afraid."

"I won't tell if you don't."

Deedee pulled on Tedla's hand. "You were going to come see Biff."

"All right," Tedla said.

"We'll join you in a second," Val said. They watched Deedee dragging Tedla to the door. "They're getting inseparable," Val said with some misgivings.

Max looked at her inquiringly. She said, "I've been busy this morning, and found out a lot. Max, you've got to keep this absolutely quiet, but there's a delegation from Gammadis here, negotiating about reopening their planet. WAC has been looking high and low for Tedla. I've managed to wangle myself a contract with them in exchange for letting them know where Tedla is. It could be really profitable."

She had expected him to be overjoyed, but he only said, "What happens to Tedla?"

"It'll be admitted to a curatory for treatment."

"If you want my layman's opinion," he said, "Deedee's better therapy than a whole herd of mentationists."

Val felt a pang of self-doubt.

When they came into the copartment, Max went to order lunch, and Val went into Deedee's room. She found her daughter and the alien both sitting on the floor conferring over a toy.

Val said, "Tedla, I've got to find some better clothes for you. You look like a ghoulnight effigy in those. Come here, I think some of Max's clothes might fit you."

Tedla rose and followed her obediently, but said, "I don't mind these clothes, really."

"Well, you've got an appointment this afternoon at the Connuic curatory. I don't want them to think I dressed you out of the recycle bin." She went to Max's closet and chose some pants that had gotten too tight for him, and a white shirt.

"Nothing too masculine," Tedla said nervously. "I hate it when people treat me as if I were a man."

Surprised, Val said, "Don't worry, we'll be in UIC; it's gender-neutral."

"There's no such thing," Tedla said. "You think so, but laws can't change people's instincts."

She smiled. "I think you overestimate how steeped in sexuality we are. It doesn't dominate our waking thoughts, you know."

"You're not even conscious of it, for the most part, but it's always there. It's very subtle: levels of formality, types of language, deference, rivalry, respect. Even your voices and the way you hold your bodies change, depending on which sex you're with. I don't know why you don't find it oppressive, except that you're so used to it."

This statement would have surprised her before this morning. "So," she said, "you were a student of xenology at C4D."

"Oh. Yes." Tedla looked as if she had reminded it of

something that had happened decades ago, and had long since ceased to be relevant.

"Who did you study with?"

"Magister Delgado."

"He's good. You must have been very good yourself, to get in his program."

Tedla looked away uncomfortably. "No. I wasn't any good. He took me on as an experiment, to see if I could do it."

"And could you?"

"No. I dropped out."

"Why?"

Tedla paused a moment, as if trying to remember. "It wasn't what I expected. It seemed as if we grad students were like a pack wrestling for dominance, determining who was the alpha male through the size of his bibliography."

Val broke out laughing. "Yes, that's right," she said. Seeing Tedla's startled look, she realized it hadn't intended to be funny. She said, "Maybe you analyze too much, Tedla."

The neuter shrugged. "It's what I was taught. I don't have any other skills."

Val chose a different shirt. "Is this non-gendered enough?"

Tedla inspected it. "I suppose so."

Tedla went into the studium to change, and Val sat down at the dinery table. Max said, "Did you tell Tedla?"

"Not the whole story," Val said uncomfortably. "I got a critique of Capellan gender relations. I never know if I'm going to be talking to a child or a visiting xenologist. Why is this so hard, Max?"

In a low voice, Max said, "We could fight them, you know. They've got no right to control Tedla's life. If Tedla wants to stay here, it has a perfect right."

Val looked up in disbelief. "Go up against WAC? Maybe *you* can fight them. I've got a career."

He gave her a long look, but didn't answer.

Soon, lunch arrived, and Max called Deedee in to the table. Since there was no sign of Tedla, Val got up, tapped on the studium door, then looked in. Tedla was dressed, but sitting on the bed looking pensively at the picture of Deedee Val kept on the terminal. She saw at once that the mood had changed. She closed the door behind her. "Tedla?" she said softly.

Tedla wiped its eyes, then glanced at her self-consciously. "I'm sorry," it said. "I was just thinking."

Val sat down beside it. "What of?"

"It's silly."

"No, tell me."

Tedla paused, not looking at her. "They say we're not capable of love. They say all blands can feel is a kind of dumb, animal devotion. But I think of those blands who raised us, and I think of Deedee . . ." It turned to look at her. "What is it you feel for her? What is it like?"

"I don't think I can describe it," Val said. "If you feel it, you just *know* it's love."

"I wish there were some way for me to feel it," Tedla said. "I envy you so much. To be able to give yourself to someone else, to have someone who trusts you like they trust the sun to rise, and to deserve it. It seems like something worth living for, to have a person you would never let down."

Touched, Val took Tedla's hand and squeezed it. This time, Tedla didn't draw away.

"I wish there were some way to protect her," Tedla said softly, "so she would never have to experience ugliness, or malice, or betrayal."

I wish there were some way to protect you, Val thought.

They sat in silence for a while, holding hands.

There was a tap on the door, and Max looked in. "There are some goons from WAC at the door," he whispered.

The moment was gone. But somehow, Val knew her heart had turned.

Briskly, she stood to evaluate the new clothes. "That bandage has to go," she said. "It makes you look deranged." She fetched a scissors and snipped it off, then brushed Tedla's hair over the scab. Then she made Tedla stand up. The effect *was* rather masculine; she found it quite attractive, but was careful not to say so.

"Tedla, you don't mind going to the curatory, do you?" she said.

"No," it said. "I know there's something wrong with me."

A part of her ached as she turned to the door.

They weren't goons, of course—merely two well-dressed young men with security badges. To Val's surprise, one of them was from Epco. Polite and businesslike, the WAC man led the way from the copartment.

As they headed toward the waystation, Tedla whispered to her, "Why are these men here? Do they think I'm dangerous?"

"No, of course not," she said. "It's—well, a professional courtesy."

"I see," Tedla said, as if unconvinced.

It was evening in Connuic and Gomb was high in the sky, but since the curatory functioned on university time, everyone was still on dayshift. They were met in the lobby by a youngish man with a smooth, pale face and a fashionably receding hairline that gave him a large-brained look. He shook Val's hand cordially and introduced himself as Magister Surin, a mentationist. Then he looked past her and said, "And this must be Tedla."

He didn't offer to shake Tedla's hand, a fact Val noted with an irrational surge of resentment. She glanced apologetically at Tedla, but the neuter appeared not to have noticed. Surin said to Tedla, "If you'll come with me . . ." His voice signalled that he was taking over.

Val watched them go off together. The two goons were still at her side, and for a moment she had a ludicrous thought that they had been sent to guard her, not Tedla.

The WAC man said, "I believe Magister Gossup is up-stairs waiting for you, Magister Endrada. I can take you there now, if you like."

"Yes. Please," Val said.

The top floor of the curatory was quiet with private wealth. They passed down a corridor sumptuously furnished in rare antiques: hand-knotted Malvern wall hangings, Gundic roof tiles, a mint-condition Terran hubcap in a theftproof box. When she entered the meeting room, three men and a woman rose from leather seats. Magister Gossup made the introductions: Monseigneur Bolduc was the senior curator—a thin, delicate-looking, white-haired man. Pym and Shankar were capitalists. Pym was from WAC; Shankar, the woman, was from Epco. They had the look of people who could buy the curatory lock, stock, and barrel. The curator had the look of someone who knew that. The strong smell of politics filled the room.

"Thank you for coming," Pym said, holding her hand slightly longer than necessary. He looked in his fifties, but it was probably a surgical youthfulness. He went on, "We are glad that you have signed on to help us, Magister Endrada. WAC will put your expertise to good use."

He spoke like he owned her. Val felt a moment of rebellion, then stifled it. He *did* own her, as long as she needed that stipend.

The capitalist from Epco smiled warmly at her and said something complimentary. Val wondered again how Epco had gotten involved in the short time since she had spoken to Magister Gossup. Things moved fast in the infomarket world.

They all sat around a coffee table by a window looking out on a spangled cityscape of lights, lit twilight pink by the gas giant in the sky. There were the usual polite offers of drink, and comments on how the week had simply flown by. Val was acutely aware that she was on exhibit, being checked over for trustworthiness. At last Shankar said to her, "We are in your debt for your quick action in finding

Tedla for us, Magister Endrada. We had grown quite stumped as to its whereabouts since leaving C4D. There is no telling how long we might have looked if you hadn't been so alert."

At last remembering something Joan had told her, Val said, "Tedla was on an Epco scholarship?"

"Yes. We were extremely pleased with its progress, and were looking forward to giving it a contract. Another month, and it would have had a degree. Yes, Tedla has the best education Capella can offer, purchased at considerable expense."

So that was why they were involved. They didn't want their investment to go to waste. If WAC owned Val, Epco owned Tedla.

"It has occurred to us," Monseigneur Bolduc said with a slight hesitation, "that the education itself might be what unbalanced Tedla's mind. No Gammadian asexual has ever tried to compete in a Capellan-class institute. The stress might have caused harm."

The same argument had once been used to deny an education to unpopular minorities. Val didn't like the sound of it. She quoted the old slogan: "Culturally appropriate education?"

For a moment they all looked startled, and Val wished she had reined in her tongue. Bolduc said, "That's not what I intended to suggest."

Pym said, "No, of course not."

Shankar looked at Val with an implicit wink, as if she were a secret ally.

"We have actually been quite impressed with the Gammadian state of knowledge in certain areas," Pym said conversationally. "You should have heard the delegates talking genetics with the specialists at Paratuic. It was above my head, I can tell you that. It seems they are in the market for methods of artificial gestation. They have difficulty keeping their population up—not exactly a problem on the other worlds!" He chuckled. "Maybe we need to call in Imachinations." It was a company famous for erotic simulations.

A little coldly, Shankar said, "That might be counterproductive."

"That's right," Pym said jocularly. "Synthetic experiences aren't what they need. They need the real thing."

Val decided it was time to change the subject. "Do you think the delegation is well disposed toward us so far?"

"Oh, yes," Pym said. "The key was our offer of reparations. They saw we were serious then. No hurt so deep a little money can't cure it, eh?"

It was clear he was boasting for Shankar's benefit, needling her. Val wondered what the Gammadians made of Pym.

"Now," he said, "all we have to do is make sure nothing interferes with their good impression. We paid too much to throw it away." There was a hardness in his voice that made Val look at his eyes, and she saw in them a ruthlessness that made her blood run cold.

Barely half an hour of uncomfortable conversation had passed when Magister Surin, the mentationist, showed up at the door. No one introduced him; apparently they all were acquainted. Val noticed the smoothness and assurance in Surin's manner, as if this were an audience he was at home with.

The mentationist sat down on the couch by the coffee table, and with a few deft movements activated a hidden control console in the table surface. A 3-D display vitrine rose from it. Surin dimmed the lights, then called up a colored diagram. It was roughly spherical, but formed from a myriad of branching lines radiating from the center.

"This is a graph of the brain function scan we just performed on Tedla," he said.

"That was fast work," Val said.

"The scan doesn't take long," Surin said, as if to an amateur; "interpreting it does." He then called up a second diagram. It was similar, but less complex. "This is the scan that was done when Tedla first arrived on Capella Two twelve years ago, which Mr. Pym has kindly made available to us.''

Pym acknowledged the credit with an ''it was nothing'' gesture. Val wanted to gag.

''For comparison,'' Surin said, ''here is the benchmark 'normal' Capellan scan.'' The third diagram was very different from the first two—much more concentric and symmetrical. ''Of course, we don't have a benchmark Gammadian scan,'' Surin said.

''What about our visitors? Could we get one from them?'' Val asked.

Surin looked at her in disbelief, as if she truly hadn't gotten the point. She felt herself turning red. Of course— she had been thinking as if the point were to cure Tedla, not to hide its condition from the delegation.

''I am not an expert at this,'' Shankar said. ''What can you tell from these scans?''

Surin said, ''Well, obviously the subject's mental development has been very uneven. You can see how overdeveloped the chart is on this side, and how little has taken place in the obverse quadrant. That in itself leads to unbalance. Of course, there is no way for us to add complexity where it's lacking—only life experience and learning can do that. But we can reduce complexity in the sector where it's gotten out of control. That ought to help.''

''Good,'' Pym said, as if it were all settled. ''I knew I could count on you.''

Alarmed, Val said, ''What are we talking about, besides branches on a diagram? What do these 'overdeveloped sectors' represent?''

''Hard to say, without more research,'' Surin said. ''In Capellans, alterations in this right anterior sector can affect abstract thought, language, certain memories. Without a Gammadian scan, we'd be working in the dark, more or less. The safest thing would be to bring the chart back into line with what it was twelve years ago.''

"How would you do that?''

"The basic options in brain alteration are always electrical, chemical, and biological. Biological is most reliable, but takes the longest.''

"We don't have much time,'' Pym said.

Val pressed on, "What effect would brain alterations have on the patient?''

The mentationist glanced at her as if she were a traitor to question him in front of the capitalists—as if playing the game right meant presenting a united front. "Tedla would become closer to the person it was when it arrived here.''

"Would it lose memories? Skills?''

"Both. Mental alteration always affects memory and personality. It will also flatten affect—a desirable result in this case, from what I can see.''

"Yes, yes. We can trust you specialists to work things out,'' Pym said.

Shankar seemed less willing to cut off discussion. "We would have difficulty supporting any solution that jeopardized our investment,'' she said.

"Unfortunately,'' Surin said, "it's quite possible that your investment has jeopardized itself. Comparing the two charts, it's clear that Tedla's education has resulted in an unstable pattern of mental development, the upshot being self-destruction. I don't know how to get around that.''

It was quite a sweeping diagnosis, Val thought, on the basis of half an hour's observation. Almost as if it had been decided in advance.

"Have you consulted Tedla about this?'' she said. "Surely the main question is what Tedla wants.''

They all looked at her coldly. Bolduc was the one who answered. "Do you think Tedla is in a state of mind to make a rational decision?''

Val had to restrain herself from sarcasm. "I think so,''

she said. She looked at Gossup, wondering why he was so silent. He was watching her intently. She suddenly wondered if he had set her up to fight this battle for him. Why?

Surin said, "Personally, I think it's inhumane not to act promptly. The subject is clearly suffering."

"We're not talking about a *subject*," Val said. "We're talking about a human being." She could feel herself losing objectivity. She had to pull back, or she wouldn't be credible. Emotion was never credible. Altering her voice, she said, "As a xenologist, I feel that Tedla's memories constitute a resource we shouldn't squander. Tedla is a potentially valuable informant. It has a unique viewpoint."

"Not in its present state of mind," Surin said. "We're dealing with a very sick human being who deserves the best treatment we can give."

"We need Tedla's information and advice about Gammadis," Val argued.

Surin shot back, "We also need a functioning neuter to present to the delegation."

Finally, they had gotten to the bottom line.

At last Magister Gossup spoke up. "How long would you need to make these alterations, Magister Surin?"

The young man said promptly, "If we go the electro route, I can have the patient functioning well enough to present a normal aspect to the world in three days. A true cure takes longer, of course."

"Then we have some time," Gossup said. "We can keep the delegation otherwise occupied for at least a week. Perhaps the thing to do is to allow Magister Endrada to conduct some interviews, and preserve the most valuable of Tedla's memories, if that's possible. We can reevaluate in five days."

No one seemed terribly satisfied with this, but no one contradicted it, either. The perfect compromise, Val thought. How useful to have a Vind diplomat in the room. And yet, she could not shake the feeling that Gossup would never have had a chance to solve the disagreement if he hadn't set it up in the first place.

After some strained cordialities, Bolduc and Surin left, discussing technical details. Gossup rose; Val realized that was her signal, and stood to take her leave.

"I know we can trust you to make this work," Pym said pointedly, shaking both Gossup's and Val's hands. When Shankar's eyes met Val's there was a conspiratorial congratulation in them.

"I need oxygen," Val said when she and Gossup escaped from the room.

Without a shadow of expression, Gossup said, "Valerie, I need to point out that in this situation, tact is absolutely vital."

"I'm sorry, Magister," Val said contritely.

"Surin is very good," Gossup said. "I have no doubt he can effect a cure."

"He's damned eager to tamper with Tedla's memories," Val said. "You'd think Tedla knew something the delegation shouldn't find out."

Gossup stopped walking and stood stock still. "That is a rather ugly accusation, Valerie. I wouldn't make it lightly, if I were you."

"I didn't mean anything, Magister," she said. "I was just talking."

"Please don't 'just talk' in this situation."

They had come to the elevator, and as Gossup pushed the button, Val said, "I'd like to see Tedla before I leave."

"Yes, that's where we're going."

They descended to the seventh floor. Here, the corridors were bright, antiseptic, and very quiet. From time to time staff ghosted past, but most functions seemed to be on automatic. Magister Gossup, silent in his soft-soled shoes, led the way to a desk where a security officer sat, surrounded by monitors. Gossup instructed the man to add Val to the list of authorized visitors. Impassively the man took her thumb scan and picture, then handed her a slate to sign. "This is a nondisclosure agreement," he said.

She hesitated a moment, but it looked like a standard patient confidentiality form, so she signed. The security man took it back and noticed her name. "Endrada," he said. "I've got something else here for you." He punched a code into a small safe and took out a plain envelope, handing it to Val. It had a magnetically coded card in it.

"It will get you into the relevant WAC files," Gossup explained.

"Thank you," Val said. The security man was holding out another slate for her to sign. This nondisclosure agreement was six pages long and full of whereases, so she just signed without reading. Then she followed Gossup down the corridor to a nondescript set of doors she took at first for another elevator. He pressed the button with his thumb and keyed in a code.

When the doors opened, Val was startled to realize it was a wayport. Gossup gestured her in.

She stepped in

and out again into a windowless, anonymous corridor that could have been in the same building, or a thousand miles away. There was absolutely no way of telling. When Gossup stepped into the corridor beside her, he said, "The port is the only way in and out, and it's programmed only to admit certain people."

"Why all the security?" Val said.

"The networks would love this story," Gossup said. "We don't want the delegation to hear about it that way."

They passed another desk where a guard sat watching a bank of monitors, all blank but one. Gossup ushered her into an observation room that reminded her of the one in the clinic where she had first seen Tedla. When Gossup hit the switch and the window into the next room turned transparent, it was as if she had stepped back in time. "My god!" she said.

Tedla was huddled in a chair, just as it had been at the clinic. The clothes she had chosen were gone; it was dressed in a brief hospital smock. The look of desperate agitation was back.

"What have they done?" she said. "Tedla was much better than this when I brought it in. They've traumatized it somehow."

Gossup was looking into the next room with a curious expression of regret. "Its mental state is very fragile, Valerie. What seemed like improvement to you must have been tenuous. We need to make it stronger."

She knew he was right, but couldn't help her anger. "It seems so inhumane, this way. Locking it up like a prisoner, erasing its personality."

"I wish there were another way," he said. "I wish we had all the time in the world. We don't." His voice was softer and more sympathetic than she had ever heard it. A revelation struck her: this was where Magister Gossup's emotional life lay—with his aliens, his research subjects. He felt a bond to them he never felt to his own kind.

Gossup became aware of Val watching him, and his expression turned neutral again. "Would you like to speak to it?"

"Yes," Val said.

He ushered her into the hallway and to an adjoining door. When she paused for him to unlock it, he said, "Go ahead, it's a sensitive knob. It will open for anyone but Tedla." He turned back to the observation room.

When she entered, Tedla turned listlessly to see who it was; then, recognizing her, it sprang up with a desperate look of hope. "Val! Can we go home now?"

"What happened? Where are your clothes?" Val said.

Tedla looked down self-consciously. "They took them away." In a low, intense voice it said, "Please get me out of here. They're running tests, scanning me a thousand ways. They gave me two injections and wouldn't tell me what they were. They took samples of everything—tissue, blood, urine, stool. I can't stand this. Please take me home."

It was breathing very fast, and its fists were clenched tight. "Shhh," Val said, and put a hand on its arm; it flinched away as if her touch burned. "Calm down, Tedla," she said.

The neuter put its hands over its face, struggling visibly to regain control. "I'm sorry, I'm sorry," it said. "It just reminds me too much—I'll tell you when we get home."

"Sit down," Val said, and pulled up a chair. Tedla crouched edgily in the chair, watching her intently. "Has anyone explained to you what's going on?" she said.

Tedla shook its head.

Val tried to make her voice very calm. "Well, to begin with, they want you to stay here for a while."

"No!" Tedla pleaded.

"They want to make you better, Tedla, and there's no way to do that without tests and observation." She drew a long breath, aware that her words were being overheard. "The problem is, we don't know what's normal for you. The mentationist you met wants to do a procedure that could help you very fast, but the price is, you might lose some memories. You would become much more like you were when you first arrived."

She had expected a panicky response, but there was none. Tedla simply sat watching her, very quiet.

"Do you understand?" Val probed.

"Yes," it said.

"You need to think about it. The treatments will change you. How old were you when you came here?"

"Seventeen," it said.

"And you're what now?"

"Twenty-nine."

"That's a lot of years to lose." Val knew she would fight fiercely if anyone were offering to do it to her. But she was not the suicidal one.

Tedla said, "They just erase parts of my life?"

"It's one side effect."

"Which parts?" it said.

"The painful ones, hopefully."

Tedla closed its eyes, as if to look inside. "That's everything," it said softly.

Val felt a terrible misgiving. For a moment she tried to stay properly detached, but it was useless. She had to throw caution away. "If you don't want this, Tedla, all you have to do is say so. We're still under UIC law here; I don't think they can treat you against your will without taking you to court, and they're not going to do that. So if you feel strongly, you can demand to leave. You've got to stand up for yourself; I can't do it for you."

Softly, it said, "They are distinguished magisters, aren't they, the ones who want to cure me? They must know what's best for me."

"Oh, please!" Val said. "You're nearly a magister yourself. You know it doesn't confer any godlike wisdom."

"That's not true!" Tedla clutched the chair arm tight. "I'm not even close to being a magister. Ask anyone; I wasn't making it at C4D. I couldn't have graduated. I've got to trust people with more learning."

Val would have liked to repeat Shankar's glowing description of Tedla's record, but the neuter gave her no chance. "They're right," it said. "I've become something that's not natural, something I was never meant to be. You Capellans have taken me and stuffed all this useless complexity into my brain. I'm not authentic any more. Before coming here, I couldn't have described myself or my home to you, I was too much a part of it. You've made me step outside it all, so I can look back and observe it. Now I can analyze anything—I can't *stop* analyzing—but I can't *be* anything. I'm not Gammadian, I'm not even a bland any more. I can't ever be unself-conscious again, unless you take that away."

Appalled, Val said, "Tedla, stop. Listen to yourself. You want us to take away your self-awareness?"

"Yes!" it said earnestly.

"You think that will make you content?"

"That's what blands are like!" Tedla said. "They're complacent, placid creatures, like cattle. They can endure the most horrible privations, degradations, things you can't imagine, and still they're happy. Nothing can shake them. That's how I was meant to be. That's how I was, once. If you can just turn back time, and take away this self-awareness, then I won't feel this way. Or at least I won't know it." It looked at her with eager anxiety. "How soon can they do it?"

"Five days," she said heavily.

"Can't they do it now, today, so I can go home?"

"No! You need to think about this, Tedla. The change will be permanent."

"You shouldn't let me think about it." There was a haunted look in its eyes. "I'll just have time to get scared. You shouldn't have told me."

A thousand alarms were going off in Val's mind. She forced herself to say calmly, "This is entirely your decision, Tedla. I just want to say one thing. I value you just the way you are, self-awareness and all."

Tedla looked at her in frozen agitation. "You think I'm wrong?"

If she said yes, she knew Tedla would simply surrender to her judgment. For a moment she was tempted—but only for a moment. "I think you're the only one who can tell if you're right or wrong. Whatever you decide, I'll support you."

Tedla looked as if her words were distilled essence of treachery. "I'm not supposed to have to make decisions," it said. "Only humans are supposed to make decisions."

"Then I've got bad news for you, kiddo," Val said. "As far as I'm concerned, you're as human as they come."

Tedla closed its eyes and leaned back with an expression of utter misery on its face. Val sat waiting, but the neuter said no more. At last she rose.

"Where are you going?" Tedla's eyes snapped open.

"To get your clothes," Val said.

"Don't leave me here alone. Please. Come back."

"I will."

When she entered the observation room, Magister Gossup was sitting there, staring through the window, a terribly pensive look on his face. When Val sat down beside him, he said slowly, "This is much more complicated than I anticipated."

"You're telling me," Val said.

She called Max to let him know she wouldn't be home any time soon. He wanted to know what was going on. "I can't tell you now," she said.

"You mean *can't*," he probed, "or *don't want to*?"

"Can't," she said.

He understood. "Joansie called," he said. "I told her what I knew."

"Be careful," she said, not wanting to get into it.

When Val returned to Tedla's room, the neuter was dressed again, but still looked horribly uneasy. "It's this place, this room," it whispered. "It reminds me of things."

"What sort of things?" Val said, but Tedla wouldn't answer.

If they were still in Connuic, Val thought, it would be near dawn outside; but in this windowless place, there was no telling. The lights in the corridor were beginning to dim for evening shift. There was a screen and terminal in the room, so she asked if Tedla wanted to watch a show, but it shook its head. She sat down at the terminal anyway and accessed her home console. "Would you like to talk to Deedee?" she said.

"Not from here," Tedla said.

Val set the terminal to record and transmit a copy to her home. The red light blinked; she cleared the screen and went to sit in the chair beside Tedla's.

"What does it remind you of?" she said quietly.

Hesitantly, Tedla said, "I've never told anyone this, not even Magister Galele. But if the treatment is going to make me forget it, someone needs to know."

"I think you're right," Val said.

Leaning forward so Val could hear, Tedla began to tell her.

Chapter Four

✦✦ The last year I spent at the creche was very different from the previous twelve. My age mates and I moved to the top floor and began the intensive training that would lead to our matriculation, and finally to humanity.

Our curriculum changed. Social responsibility classes took up more time. We learned about the hormonal changes that would soon be transforming our bodies. But most of all we learned things to prepare us for life as spiritual beings.

One day an invigilator came from the matriculatory, dressed in the teal tabard of her order. She talked to us about the terrible burden of guilt humans bear for their past, when they caused a holocaust among other lifeforms on the planet. Because they thought that life and procreation were their rights, the ancients overburdened the world with their numbers and their greedy use of resources. In their blind rapaciousness, they nearly brought about the end of all life. Only because mutations arose to limit their numbers did they and the planet survive.

"Humankind is the worst disaster ever to befall this planet," the invigilator told us. "With everything we do, we continue to destroy it, a little bit every day. In order to justify our presence here, and our use of space and resources, we must continually earn the favor of existence.''

Life, we learned, was a privilege, not a right. After matriculation, we would inherit the duty of justification. Every year we would be obliged to search our hearts to see if we had made a contribution to nature, culture, or humanity. If so, we could grant ourselves another year. If not—if we had truly become a burden on the world—it was our responsibility to end our unproductive lives. It was the only honorable course open to us.

We were terribly frightened by this, but the invigilator assured us that there were many ways of making a contribution. Merely doing well at our jobs, learning something useful, or planting a garden were sufficient to justify life. Even so, that night in the roundroom we looked at each other grimly, wondering if any of us had ever done anything to justify our existence. It made us look back on our blameless, irresponsible life as protos with new eyes. None of us had dreamed that being a human would be so hard.

Perhaps I took the invigilator's strictures too seriously. The others in my roundroom certainly thought so; that winter they teased me for having grown too grave and quiet. My mind was already dwelling on the future, when life would be nothing but choices and responsibilities. I would have to be the actor, not the acted-upon. More than ever, I wanted time to freeze in its tracks.

But of course, it didn't. Like it or not, the spring of our matriculation grew nearer. The snowdrifts melted, and the chapel dome became beaded with water instead of frost. The smell of mud and leaves rose from the ground, and the chatter of geese filled the valley again. Soon the day was upon us.

The night before we left the creche forever, all the gestagogues gathered to eat butterberry buns and say good-bye to us. It was supposed to be a joyous time, but over all of us hung the thought of never seeing those loving, devoted people again. Other children would take our places in their lives. When I went to shake Proctor Givern's hand like the adult I was going to become, he gave me a bear hug, and before I knew it I was crying on his shoulder. "Don't worry, Tedla," he said. "The world is full of good people and exciting places. You'll never want to come back."

"Yes, I will," I said. And I was right.

We were supposed to spend our last night in the round-room seriously, thinking about the past and future, but instead we were wild and rowdy, trying to enjoy our last moment of childhood before the great change. We all joined in a bouncing dance and shouted out the dirtiest songs we knew, afraid to sleep. There was panic in our gaiety.

The next morning we were not wakened by our own familiar proctors, but by an invigilator, his face masklike as he passed out the blue uniforms we would wear for the next two days. Each uniform had a number stencilled on it; we were supposed to memorize our numbers and answer to them. Once out of our own creche, we would no longer have names.

We filed out into the predawn chill. The river bluffs and grass were covered with a coating of frost, and the air seemed hushed and expectant. A huge gray aircar was waiting on the playing field. Zelly, Litch, and I gravitated together. We clambered into the aircar and crowded onto the same bench seat. Bigger was right behind us, but had to sit somewhere else. We didn't want Bigger near us; for several months it had begun to have an abnormally male look, as if it were differentiating early. There was even a suspicious bulge at its crotch. We were repulsed by it; no one had wanted to sleep next to it in the roundroom, so it had become a kind of pariah.

As the aircar took off, I pressed my forehead to the cold window to see the last of the creche. It looked very small and vulnerable, surrounded by the hugeness of the world. I looked off over the river valley, and as we rose I saw the landscape spread out in muted, misty colors, fields and roads and forest, a larger view than I'd ever seen before.

Then we entered the clouds, and I saw no more.

It seemed like a long flight. The sun had risen and the clouds cleared away by the time we began to descend, and as the aircar circled we could see the matriculatory below us. It was an immense, aboveground edifice shaped like a six-armed star. Litch, Zelly, and I crowded at the window to catch a glimpse of the birthpool, where our matriculation would culminate in two days. It lay at the center of the building, blue and open to the sky. Soon, we knew, we would enter that pool as protos and emerge as human beings.

The aircar set down on a pad at the tip of one of the building's arms, and we disembarked into a scene of noisy mayhem. Mobs of protos were disgorging from the vehicles of a hundred different gestatories, milling around in colored uniforms. The invigilators were trying to control the crowd and move it forward into the building in an orderly flow. My friends and I were determined to stick together, but when the tide of protos pushed us to the front of the line, the invigilator brought his staff down between us and directed us to different entrances. I found myself in a crowd of protos I had never seen before.

The first day was taken up by tests to determine our suitability for humanity. We moved like a noisy river from the tip of the star-arm toward the center. First we were free to flow forward, then we would be dammed into a pool, then allowed to spill over in little rivulets or a great cascade. At each stage we passed a new hurdle.

First they took our numbers, prints, and pictures, then passed us along swiftly to the curators who took our blood and urine samples, looked in our eyes, ears, and mouths, listened to our hearts and lungs, then gave us each an injection and stamped our hands with a clean bill of health. A few of the protos were weeded out and sent off for more elaborate tests. I had had a touch of asthma and worried that they would discover it, but they noticed nothing.

After our bodies, they turned attention to our minds. We

entered a part of the building that was divided up like a maze, into chains of small testing rooms; as we completed each test they directed us to different rooms depending on the results. No one told us how we were doing. They tested dozens of different types of aptitude: memory, logic, music, creativity, speed reasoning. Some of the tests were like games; others were terribly hard. As we passed through, we accumulated codes that indicated our aptitudes, though what they meant we didn't know. I was an E6-Yellow.

Once they had exhausted our minds, they still kept testing: physical aptitudes, this time. We performed tasks to quantify coordination, strength, endurance, dexterity. My excitement of that morning had drained off, and I was so tired I could barely pay attention any more.

At the end of the day we all gathered to eat in a huge refectory halfway down the star-arm. I wandered down lines of tables, looking for someone I knew, and finally spotted Bigger sitting by itself. I didn't want it to see me, so I turned away.

"Tedla!" I heard. It was Axel, waving at me. Grateful to see a familiar face, I went over to sit with it.

"Have you seen anyone else from the creche?" I asked.

"Bigger's over there."

"I know. What about Zelly or Litch?"

Axel shook its head. "Some of the protes say they're weeding the group. This can't be everyone that came in this morning."

I looked around the room; it still seemed like a huge crowd to me. "They can't be weeding, or Bigger wouldn't be here," I said. "There must be another refectory."

That night we all slept in a huge roundroom. It wasn't the great sleep, the one that would end our childhood, but it still seemed significant. Too tired and keyed up to settle down, we gathered in groups to talk. I found Zelly in one group; we greeted each other as if we'd been parted for years.

Some of the other protos seemed to know more about

what was going on than I did. Three of them were talking about the ruby drink we would be offered the next night to help us sleep. "I won't take it," one said. "I want to know what's going on."

"You can't feel it," another said. "You don't turn human overnight, you know. It takes months."

"Then how do they gender-type you?"

"Blood tests. They can tell if it's estrogens or androgens in your bloodstream."

"You know what Gimmy said?" one proto whispered. "It said those shots they gave us this morning were the hormones that stimulate the pineal to start secretions. It takes two days. We're already turning."

This news made me horribly uneasy. Something alien was inside me, transforming me, like a secret parasite. I couldn't trust my body any more.

I slept fitfully that night. Once, I was wakened by a grotesque dream: I got up to go to the birthpool and found I had huge dangling breasts and a penis that dragged on the ground so that I could barely walk, and had to carry it in front of me. I lay awake, sweaty and tense, wishing nature could have found a less disfiguring way to make us into adults.

The next day we entered a new phase of matriculation. The architecture of the building changed. The first day, we had seen only the familiar, modern curves of blown lignis. Now, after hygiene and breakfast, we filed into a hall made from stone, on a monumental scale. The place had obviously been erected at a time when hundreds of thousands of protos had made their journeys to humanity at once; our group, which had seemed so populous the day before, was dwarfed by the spaces we passed through. Our voices and footsteps echoed harshly off the hard, square walls, and the ceiling loomed high above us. It was as if the ancients were there, watching. All their other monuments were mere rubble by now; only the matriculatory survived, unspeakably old.

This day, all the testers and curators were gone, along with the busy hubbub of activity. We were under the sway of the mysterious Order of Matriculators now. It was more than our bodies and minds under scrutiny this day: it was our souls.

The morning was taken up by tests of psychostability, social adaptation, and moral development. At every step, the tests were interwoven with instruction on the duties and privileges of humanity. As the day went on, the spiritual began to overshadow the intellectual. Our groups grew smaller and smaller, till at the end of the day I was ushered alone into a room with a robed invigilator who told me to sit down and tell her anything about my childhood I wanted to leave behind me, so that I could enter my new life unburdened. I thought of telling her about Joby, but guilt stopped me. Instead, I mentioned some less damning things. For each confession she gave me a flower, and told me to drop it in the chapel pool, and the memory of my guilt with it.

When I entered the chapel I found it was night outside, and the dome above was dark; but all the pathways were lit by candles. It was a huge chapel, with a whole landscape of trails and streams and pools in it, so that we could wander quite privately, praying and thinking of our futures. I dropped my flowers into a mossy stream just above a waterfall, and watched them drift over the edge, then down the channel till they reached the quiet of the central pool.

Out of the stillness a sweet bell rang, summoning us to the center. There, invigilators holding torches stood on either side of a cave mouth gated with an ornate wrought-iron grill. It was the entrance to the matrix hall. We stood silently as a matriculator spoke in a soft but penetrating voice.

"Birth is a natural process," she said. "Learn to accept it. Cling neither to the past nor to some imagined future. Your childhood is now behind you; let it stay there, and not hinder your passage. Hoarding the past is the most self-destructive form of covetousness. Do not burden yourself with any memories or ambitions as you enter life. Strive to be born as clean as rainwater or falling snow.''

Another bell rang, and the gates to the matrix hall opened. As we filed in—no longer protos, but applicants for humanity now—the invigilators gave us our cups of ruby drink. No one turned it down.

The matrix hall was round, and far larger than our group. We passed through rows of pillars and saw the concentric circles of beds ranged at the very center, where we were to spend the great sleep. We took our places silently, subdued. The invigilators passed around the circle, taking a vial of blood from each of us. I was quiet as I watched my blood run into the clear tube, wondering which hormones they would find in it. My invigilator patted me on the shoulder when she was done. That little kindness in the midst of all the strangeness of the day made tears start to my eyes. I laid back against the pillow and fell almost at once into a deep sleep.

I was wakened by someone shaking my shoulder. At first, sleep tugged at my brain, trying to pull me back down. Then it came to me: It was the most important morning of my life, the morning of my birth. I sat up, struggling to make myself alert. This of all mornings I wanted to experience to the full.

The sun was coming through a skylight at the center of the hall. There were empty beds all around me, where protos had already been led out to the birthpool; in other beds, protos still slumbered. Silent invigilators with electronic slates were passing along the rows, matching our numbers to their records. I waited till one came by. Seeing I was awake, he punched my number in, then gestured for me to follow him. He didn't smile or speak.

He led me through a raw-wood door and down a stone hallway to a small room where a clerk was working at a desk. The clerk asked for my number, then called up my records. He scanned my thumbprint, then opened a drawer and took out a metal tag on a chain. "Put that around your neck and keep it there," he said. Puzzled, I obeyed. To the invigilator who had brought me in, he said, "I thought the rate was supposed to be going down."

"Not today it isn't," the invigilator said.

The clerk jerked his thumb at a door. "Through there," he said to me.

Their casual attitude clashed with my mood of anticipation. Didn't they know how magical this day was for me? Had the miracle of birth grown so stale for them they couldn't even pretend a joyous attitude?

I went through the door. As I had expected, a dressing room lay beyond. I had heard that they gave you a white robe to leave at the edge of the birthpool; once you emerged they dressed you in red and gave you your real name. There were no other candidates in the room, just a fat older woman at a desk, looking annoyed at her assignment. She told me to clean up and throw my uniform in a laundry chute. I followed her instructions, then came back, shivering a little with excitement as well as cold. She was working on her slate, and didn't look up at first, so I said, "Do I get a robe to go to the birthpool?"

She looked up at me, then gave a short laugh. "You're not going to the birthpool," she said. She reached into a bin beside her and shoved a folded garment across the desk toward me. I was reaching out to pick it up when I realized it was the gray uniform of a bland.

I pulled my hand back. "What's that?" I said, revolted.

"Put it on," she said. "It's yours."

It was as if she had reached inside me and twisted my stomach around. "No!" I cried out. "That's some filthy neuter's clothes. I'm not putting it on. What do you think I am?"

"It doesn't matter what I think," the woman said. There was a note of disgust in her voice.

Now I really felt fear. "You made a mistake!" I said. "I'm not a bland. I'm human."

She rolled her eyes as if she'd heard it a hundred times. "Just be good and put it on."

"No!" I shrieked. I had to escape, and find someone who would set this all straight. I bolted for the door I'd come in through, but it was locked. There was another door on the other end of the room. I ran to it, and pulled it open. Beyond it was a poured-stone corridor with exposed lights. Grayspace. Terrified, I slammed the door and backed away from it. It was the only way out. I was trapped.

The woman at the desk was placing a call, asking someone else to come to the room. "Bring a tranquilizer," she said.

I looked around, desperate for some alternative. The locked door back into the world opened, and an invigilator came through. I ran to her. "This is wrong," I pleaded. "They've made a mistake. Ask Proctor Givern. I'm not a bland."

Her voice was calm and authoritative. "There isn't any mistake, child. No one is forcing this on you. Your own body made the decision. It's your nature; you can't be any other way."

The air was pressing in around me; I could barely breathe. The full horror of my situation was coming clear. Everything was constricting: the world, my life, the future. I began to cry. "It's someone else who's the bland," I said. "It's not me. I'm a person."

She said gently, "You'll be happier this way. We'll find a place where they'll take care of you. You'll be with others of your own kind."

"I don't want to be with neuters!" I shrieked.

She took out a hypodermic needle and said to the other woman, "Come help me."

"No! I'll be good," I said. But the other woman had already come up behind me. She took me in a lock-hold from behind, pinning my arms at my sides while the invigilator gave me the injection. They both walked away then, indifferent. The invigilator left. The other woman tossed the uniform across the room at me. "Put it on," she said. It fell at my feet.

I stood there naked, with no alternative. It came to me then: My life was over. I was shut off from the world forever, behind a locked door of gender. I sank to the floor and began to cry bitterly.

But gradually, as the drug took effect, my thoughts stopped whirling, and my panic dulled. I looked down at the uniform and thought there was no help for it, I might as well put it on. I didn't feel sleepy or dizzy, just indifferent. I could still think, but somehow the thoughts seemed sluggish and calm. This is how blands feel all the time, I thought. I am thinking like a bland.

I pulled the uniform on and went to the door. As I stepped into grayspace I knew that somewhere, back in my real mind, I was screaming in protest—but it was like a faraway voice I could barely hear. It simply didn't matter.

The corridor turned a corner, then led into a large waiting room with stained, peeling walls and a scuffed tile floor. It was crowded with protos in gray uniforms, all sitting on the floor or leaning against the walls. Some of them were crying; others looked frightened, or simply stunned and indifferent, like me. The room smelled of fear. I chose a spot as far away from any others as I could get. They were blands. I wanted nothing to do with them.

We all waited there for several hours as more neuters joined us. The room became so crowded we couldn't help but touch one another. Across the room there was some scuffling where one neuter refused to let any others get near it; it had cleared a space around it with its fists, and was threatening anyone who got too close. "Filthy pubers," it kept saying. "Touch me and you'll regret it." I finally stood to stretch my legs, and was shocked to see that the pugnacious bland was Bigger. I couldn't imagine

Bigger as a neuter—it had been so obviously male. As I watched, Bigger seized the hand of someone who had gotten too near it, and bent back the fingers till the victim screamed in pain. Everyone else surged away like a frightened flock of animals, and I was crushed back against the wall by bodies.

A door opened and two adults appeared. Bigger began to yell obscenities at them. With quick, practiced movements they seized its arms and shoved its face against the wall, then checked its number. "Let's take it straight to surgery," one of them said. As Bigger struggled and swore at them, they dragged it out and closed the door.

There was a silence after they left. I felt chilled even through the drug-haze. There was only one conclusion I could draw: Some neuters might be natural, but others were created. Someone had spotted Bigger's abnormality, and had decided it could not be allowed to reproduce.

Presently the door opened again, and two men in the uniform of bland supervisors began calling out numbers. "Come to the door when you hear your number," they said loudly. The blands around me listened eagerly, hoping to hear their numbers called. I was indifferent. All that could possibly lie ahead was a life of mindless labor. Waiting in this room was not so much worse than that.

However, my number was one of the early ones called. I pushed forward through the press of unsexed bodies, feeling dirtied by them but unable to be revolted. When I got to the door, the supervisor directed a group of six of us down a hallway to where another supervisor met us and checked us off one by one on a list. This time he asked for our names, and entered them beside our numbers. I realized then that I would never have a real name. I would always be just Tedla.

"You're lucky blands," the supervisor said. "You'll be going to Brice's."

A plain freight aircar waited to ferry us to our new home. It had no seats or windows, since we were just cargo now. I didn't mind. A window might have given me a view of the birthpool, where my crechemates would be celebrating their new humanity. I hoped they wouldn't be looking for me, or even remember my name. I wanted no one to guess what had happened to me.

It was a very long flight. When at last we landed and the metal door rumbled back on its tracks, a chill, humid air gusted in along with the dull, gray light of late day. Outside, our new supervisor was waiting: a massive man with an egg-shaped head, broad on the bottom and narrow on the top, with a brush of black hair and eyebrows that made a straight horizontal line across his face. He directed us down a path toward a stand of tall pine trees, their tops hidden in mist. We walked, saying nothing to each other, till we came to a ramp that led down into the ground. When we passed through the door at the bottom we found ourselves in a large, poured-stone room stacked with crates and boxes of supplies. In the center was a cleared space where a group of about twenty neuters our age already waited.

The supervisor came in after us, walking in a brisk, authoritative way that contrasted with our own uncertain amble. Immediately the room focused on him. He climbed onto a wooden pallet with a slate, and began to call our names, scrutinizing us one by one as if to memorize our faces. When he looked at me, I felt completely naked, as if there were no secrets he couldn't uncover.

When he had accounted for everyone, he began to talk in a voice that wasn't raised, but still carried through the room. ''All right, you blands. I know what's in every one of your minds, so let's get it out of the way right now. You all think there's been some mistake, that you're not really a neuter. Maybe some of you think the matriculators are going to find out their mistake and come get you. Every neuter that's ever come here has thought the same. Well, let me tell you, they don't make mistakes. I've seen thousands of you come and go, every one of you thinking

you were really human, and not once has it been true."
He turned to someone in the front row. "You. Tell me
what you really are."

The bland didn't know what he wanted, so it just stared
at him. He said, "Come on, say it."

"I'm a neuter?" the child stammered.

"Shout it," the supervisor ordered.

"I'm a neuter!"

"You." He turned to the next one.

"I'm a neuter!"

He went through the group, one by one, and we all
shouted the hated words. I'm lying, I thought inside, even
as I said it.

"All right," he said. "Now, you're all really lucky to
have been sent here. We're going to train you to do jobs
most blands never get a chance to do. People all over the
world have heard of Brice's Blands, and they compete to
get 'em. Some day it'll be a real feather in your cap, to
be able to say to the other blands, 'I'm from Brice's.'
We'll treat you well here. You'll get plenty to eat, and the
work isn't dangerous. But let me tell you something. If
you goof off, we'll ship you out of here so fast you won't
know what happened till you wake up working in a trap
mine somewhere. What do I mean by goofing off?" He
began to raise thick fingers. "Laziness. Disrespect for your
supervisors. Disobedience. Uncooperativeness. You stay
away from those things, and you'll do just fine here.
Okay?" He scanned all our faces again. "My name's Motivator Jockety. If your supervisors have any trouble with
you, I'm the one you'll get sent to. You don't want that
to happen, do you?"

"No, sir," several blands mumbled.

"All right. Now you go eat and sleep, and you'll start
your training in the morning."

He exited the room through a raw-wood door. When he
opened it, I glimpsed through it the soft curves of a lignis
hallway decorated with woven hangings. Human space.

There was a clunk, and a bland opened a gray metal door for us, leading into a cinderblock hallway. We crowded through it and soon came to a refectory like the one in the creche, except that there was not a color in it and the tables were all bare metal. It seemed big enough to seat only about sixty at once. Either there weren't many blands here, or they ate in shifts.

I watched the others in my group a little suspiciously as I ate. They seemed like perfectly normal protos. There was none of the blankness in their eyes I associated with blands, nor the sluggish indifference. I wondered when it would start to show. Some of them were talking with each other, telling which gestatories they came from, speculating on what we would be asked to do. I couldn't bring myself to say anything.

The drug must have been wearing off, because when we were herded into the shower room and I could throw my gray uniform into the laundry I felt a surge of hatred for it, and beat it against the wall a few times first. Showering, I fantasized that I could wash away all the neuterness. When we all filed into the roundroom, it came to me that I would never sleep in a bed as long as I lived. I would never eat in a cafe. I would never enter human space again, except as an intruder. My world—my place—would be one of dingy gray service corridors. Worst of all, I would soon cease to care. Soon, my brain would start to dull from the natural acuity of childhood into the vacancy of the adult bland. I looked down at my body, till today so normal and so right. Now I knew the truth. I was a mistake of nature.

Feeling the sharp bite of despair, I sat down with my back to the wall and drew my legs up with my arms around them. I laid my head down on my knees, to block out all sight of what was around me. I tried to remember the multiplication tables, thinking that if I kept my mind going, maybe it wouldn't get neuterish, even with all these neuters around me.

Someone touched my shoulder, and I looked up. A new group had come into the roundroom. They were only a little older than us, but unlike us, you could tell they were blands. I had never seen an adult bland naked before, and I stared. They looked just like old children.

One of them was kneeling in front of me. It said, "Come sleep with us. You'll feel better."

"No," I said.

It didn't press the point, merely shrugged and went off to the center of the room where they were all settling down in a tangled blandball on the cushiony floor. I turned my face to the wall and laid down with my back to them all. I slept that way all night.

The next morning, I began to learn how to be a bland.

We woke early when the automatic lights came on in the roundroom. The routine after that was much like being at the creche: we went through hygiene, crowded around to get new uniforms from the bin, then went into the refectory for breakfast. After that, the "newbies," as they called us, gathered in a room where a human supervisor came to talk to us.

"Here at Brice's, you won't get to say, 'I'm just a bland, I can't do that,' " she told us. "We've got a lot to teach you, and we've got to do it in the next nine months, before you start going dumb on us. So you're going to have to pay close attention every day, no excuses. There's nothing we teach that's so hard a bland can't do it. We know, because we've trained thousands of you. If any of you start lagging behind, we figure you've decided not to cooperate, and you'll be shipped out. Got it?" She looked around, but no one said they hadn't got it.

She divided us up into small groups then, and gave us our assignments. I was with four others assigned to the kitchen. When we came in, there were already five older blands working there with a supervisor. The supervisor told us our jobs. Mine was to help wash up the dishes from breakfast. When I saw the mountain they formed on the counters, I thought there was no chance I could get it done before lunch. An older bland was already at work on them, moving sluggishly. As soon as the supervisor went off, it winked at me and said, "I'm Hyper."

"You are?" I stared, thinking it had to move faster than that to convince me.

"That's my name, stupid," it said.

"Oh. I'm Tedla."

"You ever done this before?" it said. I shook my head. "Well, never mind, I'll teach you."

"What's to learn?" I said disdainfully.

It drew itself up, doing a perfect imitation of the pompous tone of the supervisors. "Maybe some places there's no technique to washing dishes. Here at Brice's we've got *standards*."

I glanced nervously over my shoulder at the supervisor. But Hyper had judged her distance perfectly; she couldn't hear.

"Here, you scrape and rinse," Hyper said, giving me a long-handled brush. "I'll bring the dishes to you."

With the supervisor out of sight, Hyper earned its name. It kept up a steady stream of advice to me—what leftover food to put in the garbage can, what could be washed down the drain; how to set a pot aside to soak; how to load the dishes in the machine; what soaps to use for what purpose. Its tone was alternately teasing and bossy. "Don't be so conscientious," it said, after having nagged me a thousand ways to do it right. "You've got to let the machine do *some* work. The essence of this job is knowing the capacities of your machine."

"Did they send you to dishwashing school or something?" I grumbled.

"This is it, kid," Hyper said. "You're learning from the expert."

The supervisor happened by then, and Hyper's attitude suddenly changed. It became silent, sullen, and slow. She watched us work for a few seconds, then said, "You learning your lesson, Hyper?"

It mumbled, "Yes, ma'am."

When she went off I glanced at my companion, wondering what that had been about. Hyper whispered, "I don't normally work down here. I'm here as punishment for sassing."

"You sassed a supervisor?" I asked, surprised.

"Are you crazy? If I'd sassed a human, I'd be digging ditches in the Lower Beyond. I sassed another bland."

"That I believe," I said ruefully.

"Are you being impertinent?" it said officiously.

"What are you going to do, make me wash dishes for it?"

The supervisor called out, "Cut the chatter, you two, and do your job."

We worked in silence for a while. I could overhear the supervisor teaching the blands who were cooking lunch for the humans. They were discussing how to make a sauce of the exact right consistency—smooth, translucent, neither runny nor sticky. It sounded very complicated. I wondered if they would ever expect me to learn that. Our own lunch was already cooking in big boiling pots—a root vegetable we call groundnut, if I could judge by the smell.

The humans had separate dishes that we had to load in a special machine. I had never seen fine china before, and I admired it as I was rinsing. The plates were light blue, painted with delicate designs of cherry blossoms. They were so pretty, they looked out of place down in this rough, industrial kitchen. I felt sorry for them.

"Never use the harsh soaps on the good china," Hyper instructed as we loaded the human dishes. "And make sure not to use any soap with sulphur compounds on the silver, or you'll be up reshining it all night."

"How do I know if the soap's got sulphur?" I said.

"Read the label. You can read, can't you?"

"Of course I can." It had just never occurred to me that blands would have to.

There had been over sixty of the plain stoneware bland-plates; there were only a dozen of the china. "Is that how many humans are here?" I said.

Hyper glanced over its shoulder to locate the supervisor. "Right."

"What do they do?"

"They train us."

"Is that it?"

"Well, they have to eat a lot and get massages and ped-icures so we'll know how to do it."

"Is that the only reason this place exists? To train blands?"

"That's right," Hyper said.

I managed to learn more as we unloaded the clean dishes and stacked them ready to use again. Brice's was set up like one of the elite private houses in a convergence. Until that moment I hadn't known there was such a thing—I had thought everyone lived in the community and order houses. "Only the most powerful mattergraves and elec-tors have private houses," Hyper explained, "and they're not really private, of course—they belong to the commu-nity. But they're where the community heads live, and do their entertaining and business."

"Is that the kind of place we're going to?" I said, im-pressed.

Hyper nodded. "The ones who graduate are."

No wonder they were training us specially. The matter-graves and electors needed better blands than the run-of-the-mill person. I began to think it wasn't just a cruel hypocrisy, the way everyone kept telling us how lucky we were.

The blands were beginning to come into the refectory for lunch, and we were pressed into service carrying huge pots of food out to serve them. It wasn't till the last one left that we got to sit down ourselves and eat. When we came back into the kitchen afterwards, I saw all the dishes stacked dirty on the counter again, and groaned.

"What did you think, that they were going to stay clean all day?" Hyper said.

It went faster this time, since I knew the techniques, though I still didn't do them to Hyper's satisfaction. The dishes from the humans' table upstairs were much more complicated this time—we had not only china, but silver, wood, crystal, and basketry to clean. Each material had to be handled in a special way. By the end of the day, I had learned more about dish care from Hyper than I had thought it was possible to know.

I stayed on the dishwashing detail for five days, until I could do it in my sleep. On the last day, Hyper's punishment was up, and I was left alone. By doubling my pace, I was able to accomplish the same amount of work it had taken two of us to do before. At the end I was exhausted, but the supervisor was impressed.

"You're a good worker, Tedla," she said.

I felt quite pleased with myself until the supervisor left and one of the older kitchen blands pulled me aside.

"Don't you ever pull a stunt like that again," it said.

Astonished, I said, "Why not?"

"They'll start to think it's a one-bland job, and expect the rest of us to do it all the time."

I realized the sense in that. I had been so intent on pleasing the humans, I had forgotten who my real common interests lay with. The humans had all the power over me, but none of them would ever be my friends. At first, it was a bitter thought.

When my five days of dishwashing were up, I was rotated to cook's assistant, and I learned all about washing, peeling, and chopping vegetables, trimming meat, stirring and mixing, and all the other tedious jobs the cooks didn't like to do. But what I was really learning was how to be a bland. I learned to slow my pace and cast down my eyes when humans were watching. I learned not to answer when humans spoke, unless it was a direct question, and then to answer in as few syllables as I could. But I also learned that the blands were an interlocked team, and if one of us sloughed off, all of us would suffer. We worked hard even when the humans weren't there—in fact, especially when they weren't there. We weren't doing it for them, we were doing it for each other.

There were some in my class of newbies who had a hard time adjusting. One, named Tick, was petulant and rebellious, and kept arguing with the supervisors. "Why should I do what they say?" it would tell us in the round-room, when all we wanted was to sleep. "Why should we have to haul the garbage while they laze around all day?" After a week, when it became clear that Tick was not growing reconciled, they began to take it away for medical treatments. The next time I saw Tick, I recognized in its face the docile indifference of the tranquilizer drug they had given me. But unlike me, they didn't stop medicating Tick after the first injection. They kept it drugged for weeks on end, and after a while it grew listless and stupid as well as content. Soon we all noticed that Tick was too easily confused to keep up with the training. Shortly after, it disappeared from our roundroom.

"We decided that Tick would be happier somewhere else," one of the supervisors explained.

We never talked about it in the roundroom, but we all got the message. Strangely, though, I never imagined that the change in Tick was anything more than the speeding up of a natural process. I firmly believed that the same thing would be happening to the rest of us before long, as the neuter neurochemicals faded our initiative and leached away our ability to learn. Tick's vacant stare had only been a harbinger of things to come. Of course the thought frightened me. I kept a close watch on myself and my age mates, trying to catch the first signs of the dumbing.

I can see what you want to ask; Capellans think so individualistically. The answer is no, it never occurred to me to attempt escape. What would I have done if I had gotten away? In a few months, I knew I would be incapable of living on my own; I would need humans to take care of me. They were my only security. I had to learn to please them.

In my mind, I was going through a process I can only describe as withdrawing from humanity. It was a relief, in a way. A bland's life was so much more predictable than a human's. I could count on being housed, fed, and clothed, and all I would have to give in return would be work and obedience. I would never again have to exert myself to do something beyond my abilities. I would never have to be worried or frightened. I would never have to justify my existence. I could simply turn my back on all the demands and rigors of humanity.

For the first month and more they rotated us newbies through the more menial jobs, so we would learn good work habits and grow accustomed to the routine. After the kitchen, they transferred me to Maintenance. There I worked on building repair—painting, revarnishing, caulking—and learned about the mechanical systems like plumbing, electricity, ventilation, recycling. Brice's naturally had a chapel on the top floor, and I spent one blissful five-day period as gardener's assistant—watering, repotting, and trimming growing things. I loved being in the chapel, and this was my only chance. As neuters, you see, we didn't go to chapel because there was no point. We had no gods inside us. That is, we were like animals and plants—part of the overall sacredness of life, but incapable of becoming aware of it. Humans who didn't search for their gods were often said to become like neuters—unaware, unconscious.

Too soon, I was transferred to Cleaning. It was then I got to know the human spaces in a way even the humans never knew them—down to every cranny where a dustball could hide. On night shift, we shined brass reliefs on the doors with tiny brushes and polished marble floors till we could see our reflections. By day, we changed the humans' linen and scrubbed their bathrooms. The hardest part of cleaning was staying out of the humans' sight. Human space was interwoven with a hidden web of service corridors for us, called bland-runs. In some places, we had peepholes to see whether a human was about; elsewhere, the rooms had infrared detectors. Every suite of human quarters had graydoors to give us access—and escape. To be caught in a human's space was horribly shaming for us. The whole skill lay in never letting them guess we were there.

By the end of my introduction to Brice's, I understood why it took sixty blands to keep a dozen humans comfortable.

The month of rotations had sorted us out in the supervisors' minds. They had identified our attitudes and abilities. Our numbers had decreased by five, including Tick. We were now ready for our permanent assignments.

On the day before the assignments were handed out, I was working in Laundry. One of the newbies in Cleaning came down with a rolling bin of towels and sheets, and whispered to me, "Quee says they're all meeting in the big vocatory, arguing about who gets which of us."

We blands had the means to know virtually everything that went on in human space. We rarely paid any attention, because so little that went on concerned us. This was different.

"Do you know where I'll be assigned?" I asked. I was desperately hoping to be trained for gardening.

My friend shook its head. "We'll try to find out."

By refectory, the whole list of assignments was circulating in whispers around the tables. Quee told me, "You're going to be a Personal."

"What's a Personal?" I asked.

"Canto and Laki are Personals," an older bland told me. I didn't know either of them well. No one did. They spent more time with the humans than any of us, and seemed to hold themselves a little aloof, with a proud, aristocratic air. I was disappointed, but stoical. Doubtless the humans knew what was best for me.

The next morning the supervisor read us the list of assignments, and we all pretended to be surprised. There were four of us to be trained as Personals. Only one lucky bland had gotten gardening. I went over to the corner of the room where the other Personals had gathered near Canto and Laki. They were looking us over critically.

"What's a Personal do?" one of the others, a red-headed bland named Mallow, said.

Laki answered. "When you leave Brice's you'll get assigned to a guardian—one of the important humans, like a mattergrave or elector. Your job will be to make that human's life comfortable."

"How?" I said, unable to imagine what a human might need a bland for.

"You'll see," Laki said.

When the supervisor dismissed us to go to our places, Canto and Laki led the rest of us upstairs to a wide place in the bland-run where some lockers stood. As we stood there, they stripped out of their gray jumpsuits and began to put on layer after intricate layer of clothing from the lockers—underwear, stockings, shirts, pants, coats, cravats, and gloves. We watched, dumbfounded. When they were done, the two of them looked transformed. They were in tailored black uniforms with gold buttons, wide cuffs, and white fabric gloves. The rest of us exchanged glances, unable to imagine how they would perform any work in those costumes. They combed their hair carefully, then led us straight through a graydoor into human space.

The room we entered was a lounge: beautifully veined lignis walls polished to a sheen by the industrious cleaners, a deep red carpet, two fireplaces with shining fenders and andirons, and upholstered furniture arranged informally for conversation. The room had a snug and woody atmosphere, with opulent glints of metal and glass, and a lingering smell of firesmoke. We newbies, feeling uncomfortably like intruders where we were not meant to be, fidgeted. But Canto and Laki stood by one wall with their hands clasped at their backs, their posture very erect in their elegant uniforms, their faces completely blank. Mallow mimicked them, but looked silly, and we broke out in a nervous giggle. Just then the door opened on silent hinges, and a human entered the room. We crowded together, afraid we would be scolded for getting caught in human space.

The man who crossed the room to take a look at us was named Supervisor Mondragone. Up to now, we had seen little of him. He was an older man with a strict and critical expression, who always dressed as precisely as a diagram. One by one, he asked our names, studying us as we stared at the floor and fidgeted. At last he sighed. "Dear me," he said. "What material. We have a long way to go."

He raised his voice to the tone humans used when giving us instructions. "You blands are going to have to learn some new rules. As Personals, you are going to be spending a good part of your lives among humans, and you will have to learn the rules of human space. Unlike other blands, you will need to know how to talk to us, and listen to us, and move among us without attracting attention by your neuterish behavior. By the time I'm through with you, I will expect you all to be completely invisible and completely indispensable to your guardians."

He turned to Canto and Laki. "Find them some uniforms before bringing them back tomorrow. You know where they're kept. Teach them how to dress. I'll need to see some progress in their manners soon."

"Yes, sir," Canto said expressionlessly.

"You may go to your duties now."

The two older blands bowed and left through the human door, as if it belonged to them. We all stared after them.

"Now," Supervisor Mondragone said, "let's start with your carriage."

He spent the morning teaching us how to move. "Imagine there is a string attached to the top of your skull, and it's pulling you toward the ceiling," he said. We learned to stand without slumping, and walk without shuffling. He made us practice graceful movement, and gave us exercises to do in our own time. We even learned to hold our heads up while humans were near, and cast down only our eyes.

Shortly before lunch, he took us to the dining room, where Canto and Laki were at work setting the table, and he left. The two blands then took over our instruction, explaining the purposes and placement of all the dishes I had once learned to wash. There were strict rules about where every piece of silver went, and which dishes were used for which course, and how the linen napkins were folded. Each of us practiced by setting a place; then Canto and Laki shooed us away into grayspace, but instructed us to watch the meal carefully through the peephole.

I had never seen humans eat like this before. Unlike us, they seemed almost as interested in *how* they ate as *what* they ate: They held their bodies stiff, handled the eating tools in a particular order, and seemed to be saying ritualized things to each other. Canto and Laki served them from the sideboard, moving silently around the table with the serving dishes and pitchers of drink, always removing used plates or silver, brushing the crumbs from the tablecloth, proffering silver basins to wash in. The point seemed to be to remove all evidence that food *had* been eaten, and leave only evidence that food remained to eat.

After the humans left, we came back in, and Canto and Laki discussed what had happened like critics after a performance, dissecting what had gone wrong and right. Things I had not even seen loomed large as mistakes in their eyes: carrying the linen towel on the wrong arm, forgetting to place the candied violets on the jelly mold. I had never dreamed that anyone worried about such things, least of all blands.

But the most astonishing thing was how they spoke of the humans' behavior.

"Supervisor Calder didn't eat much of the ragout," Canto said. "Is she still dieting?"

"I don't think she likes the fruit-meat combination," Laki answered. "She didn't go for the orange duck last week, either."

"Do they mind you watching them like that?" I asked nervously.

"It's our job to watch them," Laki said. "How else would we know what they want? If they have to ask for anything, we've already failed. That's the first rule of being a Personal."

We were to hear that instruction over and over in the next few months: know what they want before they even want it.

We ate what was left over in the serving dishes, sitting right there at the humans' table, though it made us newbies nervous. "We don't have time to go downstairs," Laki said. "There's too much to do."

When we finished, I expected to have to clear off the table, but Laki said, "That's the scullions' job." We left the table as it was.

I had already figured out that Laki was the stricter one, with higher standards. Laki was an attractive bland with curly black hair, pale skin, and dark eyes with long lashes; but it always had a tense and anxious look that kept us from really relaxing. When they decided to split us up, Mallow and I ended up assigned to Laki. I knew we would get a workout.

Laki led us through the bland-runs to the humans' private quarters. Now the focus turned from food to clothing. Laki took us into one man's closet, lined with dozens of different outfits, and explained to us what sort of clothing was appropriate for different occasions. Humans, it seemed, wore different colors and styles depending on the time of day, season of year, purpose of the occasion, and relative status of the others at a gathering. Some outfits were elaborate with sashes, ties, cuffs, collars, and medals; others had a studied simplicity. There were a dozen different types of shoe, hat, belt, and undergarment, all with a different purpose.

"Why are there so many rules?" I asked, overwhelmed.

"Because knowledge of the rules shows the quality of the person," Laki said. "There are plenty of people who don't pay any attention to what they wear. That just shows they're not the best class of human, and the others look down on them. Your job is to make sure no one ever looks down on your guardian."

Laki demonstrated by choosing a dinner outfit to hang out on a wooden clothes-form in the bedroom. The bland carefully inspected every piece of clothing, and taught us how each material needed a different kind of cleaning, and you couldn't trust the laundry to get it right without specific instructions. Shoes and metal ornaments needed to be polished before each use. The laundry had delivered a load of freshly cleaned clothes, and Laki taught us how to wrap them in scented tissue and fold them for storage in the drawers.

After we had taken care of one man's clothing needs, we moved on to a woman's quarters. The outer clothes were much the same, but the undergarments and "informals," as Laki called them, were different. When we had arranged her clothes, Laki announced we were done.

"What about the rest of the humans?" I asked.

"There's only four of them with high enough status for a Personal," Laki said.

It was the first inkling I had had that even our humans, who seemed so monolithic from downstairs, were divided into ranks.

We met the other Personals in the bland-run by the lockers, and Canto and Laki argued about how to get all their work done before dinner. In the end they decided Laki would do grooming, and Canto would get uniforms for us and teach us how to wear them. Laki didn't seem pleased. "You owe me now," it said to Canto.

As we headed down the bland-run, Canto told us, "When you're really a Personal, you'll have to do grooming three times a day, when your guardian has the time: first thing in the morning, just before dinner, and before bed. They all have different tastes about grooming. Some of them want baths, others want showers. Some use cosmetics. Some want to be shaved twice a day. You have to learn what each human wants."

We came to an equipment room where a dozen uniforms were stored, in all their many pieces. We rummaged around till we each found a complete set. Most of them had missing buttons, stains, and ripped seams from hard use. "You'll have to fix those tonight," Canto said. "You can't show up looking like ragamuffins."

Canto drilled us in putting on the uniforms, and we practiced walking in them. It felt strange and tight; yet somehow, in the uniforms it was easier to move with the haughty, human air Supervisor Mondragone had taught us that morning.

"Let me give you some advice," Canto said to us. "Keep the manners they teach you for human space in human space, and don't bring them into grayspace. Take them off with the uniform. Otherwise the rest of the blands will think you're holding yourselves above them, and trying to be human."

We exchanged silent looks, since Canto and Laki had that reputation in the roundroom anyway.

By that time we were very tired, but we had to go back to the dining room to prepare for dinner. This meal was even more formal and elaborate than lunch. Again we watched through the peepholes. Laki seemed jittery and made several mistakes even we noticed, but it covered for them skillfully. Afterwards, when we were all gathered in the bland-run, it broke down in tears. "I'm rotten at this," it said. "I'm never going to learn."

Since Laki seemed like a complete perfectionist to us, we couldn't believe a word it said. Canto said sympathetically, "I'm sorry," as if it were the one at fault, and tried to put an arm around Laki's shoulders. Laki twisted away from the touch. With a fierce effort at control, Laki wiped the tears from its face and turned to Mallow and me. "Come on," it said, "I'll show you how to prepare the bedrooms."

So it was back to the humans' quarters to lay out the nightclothes, replenish the contraceptives and sexual aids, turn down the covers, and sprinkle scented water on the sheets.

We got down to refectory late, but the kitchen staff still had some leftover bean soup for us to eat. We sat at a table together in the empty room. I missed the noisy camaraderie of the other blands. I had not yet realized that a Personal is caught in the crack between the two worlds—spending its life with humans but never being one of them, isolated from the other blands but never able to escape them.

By the time I had repaired my uniform and gotten to the roundroom, I was so exhausted that I fell asleep at once. And yet, I had scarcely closed my eyes (as it seemed) when Laki was shaking me awake, whispering, "We've got to get up for grooming."

And so my new routine started—up before the humans so we would be ready with their drawn baths, scented oils, and heated towels. Then on to serve the meals, care for the clothes, and run whatever errands they sent us on. Our days didn't end till the humans were asleep. In the moments between our duties, Supervisor Mondragone drilled us in poise and bearing, and taught us how to talk politely and address humans with their myriad of titles. We learned the intricacies of ordering the courses of a meal, and presenting the dishes with artistry and taste. As we grew more advanced, we were permitted to help the humans dress, shave them, and arrange their hair and cosmetics. We learned manicure, pedicure, and massage. We learned how to pack clothes for travel. We even learned how to care for our guardians when they were sick—remedies for diarrhea, gas, colds, headaches, and heartburn. "Your guardians will be indispensable people to their communities," the supervisors told us. "They are too busy to take care of themselves, so you must do it for them."

There were a lot of "nevers" to learn. Never talk about your guardian's habits or gossip to the other blands. Never take a message. Never listen to conversations that don't concern you—but do listen in case anyone expresses a need or desire. Never tell another human what your guardian wants, but do tell the other blands—often.

They taught us to watch our guardian (and our guardian's guests) carefully, to interpret their gestures, tone, and body language, always thinking: Is he cold? Is she thirsty? Do they want anything? Can I be helpful?

I had been at Brice's three months when we hosted a dinner for clients. From the excitement of the older blands I knew how important an event this was. "This is our opportunity to impress people," Laki explained. "The better we perform, the better guardian we'll get."

Supervisor Mondragone was also keyed up. "We're going to have a guest list of forty this year," he said, watching us severely. "You are all going to be on duty that night. Besides Canto and Laki, two of you are going to have to serve."

"Tedla and Mallow can do it, sir," Laki volunteered. My heart gave a frightened leap, but I kept my eyes cast down and my face blank, as I had been taught.

Supervisor Mondragone stopped in front of me and said, "Tedla?" That was my cue to look up. "Are you ready for this?"

"I don't know, sir," I said.

"Well, we'll test you. Tonight, you two will serve dinner."

It was a complete disaster. At the outset Mallow got rattled and poured the wine into the water glasses. Coming

after with the molded ice and water, I had no choice but
to put it in the wine glasses. Supervisor Mondragone
glared at us, but we pretended as if nothing were amiss.
Then I dropped the roll basket and half of them ended up
under the table, so that the humans were kicking them to
and fro, and I had to scramble around on the floor picking
up the rest. By then we were so flustered we served the
salad on the fruit plates and completely forgot to brew the
coffee; the humans had to sit drumming their fingers waiting for it.

When I got into the bland-run afterwards, the other newbies were whooping in laughter at our mistakes. I was
angry and frustrated. Canto said to me, "Look on the
bright side. At least no one ended up with food in their
lap."

Laki was not so philosophical. "Now I'll catch it. I was
supposed to have taught you two. You were supposed to
know how to do this."

I thought my chances of being allowed to serve at the
great dinner were over; but the next morning Supervisor
Mondragone said to us, "Well, you can only improve. At
least you kept your composure; that was the important
thing." Our only punishment was to be assigned to serve
every other dinner from then on, to get the practice.

The preparations for the great day were elaborate. All
the public areas were hung with garlands and strings of
lights like fireflies, and every pane of glass and crystal
bauble was polished. Aircars brought in huge crates of
exotic foods, ice sculptures, and songbirds in cages. The
kitchen was in a total panic, baking pastries, constructing
fruit sculptures in aspic, and organizing their forces as if
for a military campaign. We Personals got brand-new uniforms that fit so well I felt perfectly elegant. On the day
of the dinner, an aircar imported a chamber orchestra of
musicians. They were the only human servitors brought in;
the whole point was to demonstrate the capabilities of
Brice's blands.

Supervisor Mondragone gave us a serious lecture that afternoon. "You are the only blands the guests will actually see; remember you are representing everyone else. If the guests get a bad impression of you, they will have a bad impression of everyone, no matter how hard all the others have worked."

We also got a nervous lecture from Canto and Laki. "Do well for us," Canto said. "This is our big chance to impress a guardian and get a good home. Don't drop any rolls." It had become a joke among us.

It was a cold and misty evening outside, but inside, Brice's was dazzling bright. The aircars landed and took off in a steady stream, whirring like huge bugs. Whisper and Trice were posted by the entrance, taking wraps. As the crowd collected in the reception room, Canto and Laki circulated with trays of hors d'oeuvres and drinks; Mallow and I kept their trays stocked, and as the crowd grew we also circulated with bottles, replenishing glasses. The humans were brightly dressed; some wore community garb, but others were decked out in feathers and gold chains. They were so intent on each other, it was easy to feel invisible. I was careful not to look any of them in the face, or touch them. Once, a woman began to ask me for something, then gave a start. "Oh my god!" she exclaimed to her companion. "I thought it was human." She gave a high-pitched laugh. I waited to see if she had a request, but now she was too embarrassed, so I melted away into the crowd to spare her feelings.

When the music changed, announcing dinner, we hurried to open the doors for the crowd. The great dining hall looked opulent, the table so loaded with flower arrangements, crystal, silver, and porcelain that it was a wonder where the food would go. Under Supervisor Mondragone's instructions we had divided the table into quarters, with Canto and Laki getting the most important people. Whisper and Trice carried in the trays of food that came up from the kitchen on carts, so the humans wouldn't have to glimpse a kitchen bland.

It all had to go like clockwork, and our biggest fear was that the kitchen would hold us up, and make it necessary to stall. But the humans were so engrossed in their conversations they ate slower than we had planned, and we had to pass whispered instructions back to the kitchen to slow down. "This is a good sign," Canto whispered. "It means they're enjoying themselves."

I had one human who was getting slightly tipsy and talking too loud. "Hold back on his wine," Laki whispered to me, "or the others won't enjoy themselves. Give him his entree first." I marveled that Laki had the presence of mind to notice my humans, when it had ten of its own to worry about.

The most dangerous part of the meal, for us, lay at the dessert, when we had to dim the lights to show off a dramatic flaming brandy sauce by way of a climax. My hands felt slippery with nerves as we lined up along the sideboard, watching each other for perfect timing. Laki hit the lights; then, as the conversation stilled, we all simultaneously lit our dishes and lifted them above our heads, the blue flames lighting our way to the table amid a smattering of applause. Whisper brought the lights up again, we served, and I knew the worst was over. Afterwards, the humans adjourned to the lounge for liqueurs, and our supervisors got busy striking bargains and soliciting business.

It was past midnight when we got back downstairs, but all the blands were still working on cleanup, and the mood was excited. They gathered round us at the refectory tables to hear our account of what the guests looked like, what they wore, what had happened. We celebrated by eating leftovers.

That night as I fell asleep with half a dozen other blands pressed close to me, I felt a brimming warmth for them all. We were a good team. We had accomplished a performance even a human might take pride in. I knew I could trust every one of the others around me.

I was no longer sorry to be a bland.

Three days later, the senior class started to leave. Laki actually looked happy for the first time since I had seen it; it had snagged a place in the household of the Polygrave, one of the most powerful humans in the world. It would be living at Magnus Convergence, the very center of all power. I was happy for it, but sorry to see Laki and Canto go. "We'll miss you," I said.

Laki hugged me. "You'll be a good Personal, Tedla," it said. "Don't let things discourage you here." I smiled at Laki's pessimism. We saw them off with a big round-room celebration.

〰️ Val interrupted. "Were they sold?"

"No, of course not," Tedla said, looking slightly shocked. "That would be slavery."

Val was taken aback. "Well, isn't that what you're describing?"

Tedla looked very troubled. "We weren't slaves. Neuters are never traded for money. Brice's was compensated for having trained us, of course—otherwise it couldn't have stayed in business. But it was the training being purchased, not us."

"Seems like a pretty fine distinction to me. Are neuters ever paid for their work?"

"No," Tedla said slowly. "But neither are humans. They're compensated in housing, food, clothing, and community, just like we are. Oh, humans may get a little pocket money from time to time. But a clever bland who wants money can steal more than the average human can earn. There are a lot of thieving blands. Not at Brice's, of course."

"Of course not," Val said.

❖❘❖ There was more work for us after Canto and Laki were gone, since we had to take over their duties. The four of us were now assigned each to take care of a particular human. We would rotate monthly, they said, to give us wider experience. When I was assigned to Supervisor Mondragone, I knew I was going to have to be letter-perfect every day.

He was very particular about dressing for dinner, and always required my help. I was nervous at first, knowing he would be watching my performance. But I grew used to his habits, and found I could usually anticipate what he would want. One day, as I was fastening his collar with a golden stickpin, he put his hands on my shoulders, looked at me seriously, and said, "You are doing well, Tedla. I'm very pleased with you."

It had been a long time—since I was at the creche, really—since a human being had praised me, or even spoken to me as if I were an individual. I felt a rush of pleasure and gratitude quite out of proportion to what he had said, and I think I must have blushed. He patted my shoulder. "Think of me as your friend, all right?"

Of all the humans, Supervisor Mondragone was the last one I would have expected to show any friendship toward a bland. I realized that humans were more complex than I had imagined. I went to serve dinner that night with a warm feeling inside me.

When others were around, Mondragone's manner remained strict and aloof; but when we were alone, he paid a lot of attention to me. He told me things about himself, and asked me questions. One day he ran his fingers through my hair and told me not to let the others cut it, because it was so beautiful. I always left his quarters feeling a cut above the other blands. Of course, I didn't say anything to them because I thought they would be jealous.

ᴈⅅ Tedla paused, looking indecisive. "There is something about me I have to mention, because it explains a lot of what happened."

"What?" Val said.

It looked down uncomfortably. "When I was young, I was quite attractive. You scarcely have a non-gendered word to say that. I'm not trying to boast; it was just a fact."

"Stop apologizing, Tedla," Val said. "I think I would have figured it out anyway. Most people would be happy to have your looks."

The neuter glanced at her fearfully, then down. "I hate them. There are times when I've wished I were malformed."

"Why?" Val said.

The neuter twined its hands indecisively. "Oh, humans can make use of looks to charm or manipulate each other, to get good mates or other things they want from the promise of sex. But what use are looks to me? It's like a stupid joke, a promise I can never make good on. My looks can only infuriate and disappoint people, and bring harm to me."

"Harm?" Val said seriously.

➤|← Slowly, by almost imperceptible degrees, Supervisor Mondragone's manner toward me changed. One day when he came out of his bath he asked me to dry him with the heated towel I had prepared. After several seconds he caught my hands in his and said, "Tedla, do you want me to like you?"

"Yes, sir," I said. And I really did.

"Then do something for me," he said. "Touch me right here. It will give me great pleasure."

He showed me what to do. I had seen him get an erection before, but I was so innocent I had only the haziest notion what it meant. This time he led me through it till he achieved satisfaction; then he took me in his arms and kissed me on the lips. "I love you, Tedla," he said. "You must not tell anyone. Do you promise?"

To be perfectly honest, I was merely puzzled about it at first. It was just another thing I had learned to do for a human, not that different from backrubs or shaving or cosmetics. The only thing that made me uneasy was the way it changed my supervisor. He grew very affectionate, and went out of his way to touch me and kiss me whenever he could. It was not unpleasant, merely out of character. It was the first inkling I had of how sexual desire can change a human's personality.

After that, it became a daily thing, always just before dinner. He taught me many techniques—the use of oils, massage, and various tools; ways to prolong his orgasm; how to recognize when he was ready, and what he was ready for. "Learn this well, and your guardian will always love you," he said to me. "You'll never be treated like other blands."

At first, he taught me only hand techniques; but soon he started to ask me to do things with my mouth and tongue, and I had to hide my disgust a little. Then one day when he was lying on the marble slab in the bathroom that we used for massages and body shaves, he reached up to touch my cheek and said, "Can't you take off that uniform? I would love to see your body."

On Gammadis we don't have the nudity taboos you have here on Capella—especially not neuters, who have nothing to hide from one another. Even so, I hesitated because it seemed so counter to all the ways we were being taught to behave in public, and I was confused. Nudity was for the closeness of the roundroom. Among humans, we were supposed to keep aloof, our identity hidden behind layers and layers of clothes.

But he sat up and began removing my clothes himself, slowly, as if it were a ritual. When I was completely naked, he ran his hands over my skin, then pulled me close to him, between his spread legs as he sat on the counter, so that I could feel his sex organs pressed against me. "Ah, Tedla, you can't imagine how much this means to me," he said.

It was true, I couldn't imagine. I could tell from the beginning that he wanted me to feel some sort of reciprocal passion toward him, but it was impossible. We simply aren't capable of sexual arousal. At first I had enjoyed his caresses, because I thought they meant affection for me. I still wanted to believe that. But I had begun to feel horrible doubts that this was about me at all.

꿈 Tedla paused for a long time. "Sex has no meaning to us, but we don't live in a nonsexual world. We live among you, and by your rules. We have to think about your sexuality all the time."

Trying to keep her voice neutral, Val said, "That doesn't seem quite fair."

Looking at its hands, Tedla said, "It's inevitable. Some humans—maybe all—are actually attracted by asexuals. Even your standards of beauty tend to be androgynous. I don't know why it is—the ambiguity of identity, perhaps, or the novelty of a transgender experience. Then there are people who are attracted to anything dangerous."

"What is dangerous about it?" Val asked.

"On Gammadis, sexual encounters with neuters are absolutely forbidden," Tedla said. "The idea is horrible, shameful, disgusting. Anyone found molesting a neuter would be ostracized, and penalized by the harshest laws we have."

"But it's done?"

"All the time," Tedla said bitterly. "Everyone condemns it, then they do it anyway. It's the central hypocrisy of my planet. They all learn not to see it. The only thing more forbidden than doing it, is talking about it. If we were on Gammadis, I would be risking everything to tell you."

"Are you serious?"

"Absolutely," Tedla said. "They would say I was inventing evil stories, slanders from a sick mind. You can't imagine the strength of their shame."

"But it's focused on you, not on themselves?"

"Yes. The more they love us, the more they loathe us." Tedla fell silent, its jaw clenched down.

Val said cautiously, "Are all neuters used sexually?"

Tedla shook its head. "Only . . ."

"The attractive ones?"

Tedla nodded.

>|< I exaggerated when I said they all do it. Actually, very few do it. It just seemed like everyone to me.

The types of sex he taught me next were the hardest for me to learn. On the day he first penetrated me anally I broke down in tears. He scolded me sternly, saying I had to show enjoyment, then kissed me and caressed me. "If your guardian is attracted to you, you have to act eager for him," he said. "It's the best way to be sure you'll be treated well."

I'm sure the other Personals must have noticed that something was going on with me. I grew tense and silent with them. Outside of Supervisor Mondragone's quarters, I focused completely on my work, burying myself in learning things, perfecting everything I did. I began to count the days till I would be rotated away to someone else, but I felt guilty about it, since one of the others would then surely take my place. I wanted to warn them, but couldn't bring myself to admit how far I had allowed him to go.

It was strange, how I blamed myself. He had complete power over me; I couldn't have rejected him. And yet, because he had persuaded me instead of ordered me— because he had secured my complicity at every step—I felt that somehow I was the one responsible. He sometimes told me that I had made him fall in love with me, that he had no power over himself when I was around, and I believed him.

One morning as I was walking down the bland-run with a pair of shoes in my hand to fetch some polish, Motivator Jockety stuck his head out the graydoor into his office and gestured me to come in. I was quite startled. The motivator handled discipline among the blands; we rarely saw him except when we were to be punished, and I had never been punished for anything. I was very nervous stepping into his office, wondering what I had done wrong.

He closed the door behind me and looked me over. He was not one of the humans who rated a Personal, so I knew little about him. In that small room, he seemed massive and imposing. He said, "Supervisor Mondragone says you are doing very well at your duties."

I looked at the floor and said nothing.

He stepped closer. His voice took on a false jocularity. "Oh, look," he said. "I've got something in my pants. What do you suppose it is?"

I knew what it was. It was pressing stiffly against the fabric. My mouth was suddenly dry. I tried to swallow, but only felt like choking.

He said, "Go on, why don't you see what it is?"

I didn't know what else to do. I laid down the shoes I was carrying and reached out to unfasten his pants, then pulled down his underwear till he was exposed. His penis was huge and pink, and pointing straight up.

"Oh dear," he said. "What are you going to do about this?" He put his hands against the wall on either side of me, so I was trapped between that huge penis and the wall.

There was only one thing I could do, if I wanted to escape. I would have to turn my mind off and simply get through it, like an awful job. I bent down and opened my mouth.

After he let me go, I was shaking so hard I had to stop in an equipment room to calm down. They all knew what a slut I was, I thought. Despite all of Supervisor Mondragone's warnings, I had let on. Now, just the sight of me was enough to inflame them. It was as if I were giving off some sort of signal. I was nothing more than the Brice's prostitute.

I had never felt so disgusted with myself.

My only hope was that my next supervisor would save me. On the day I heard I was going to be transferred to Supervisor Calder, I went through my duties in a haze of relief. She was a sallow, gloomy woman who was always full of ineffectual complaints, but anything was an improvement.

That afternoon, when I went to my old supervisor's quarters for the last time, I walked in on Mondragone and Calder, both lying naked on the bed drinking liquor. I stammered an apology and began to back out, when Mondragone called out, "Come in, Tedla! We've been waiting for you."

As I closed the door behind me, my heart was laboring hard with dread.

Mondragone's speech was slightly slurred by drink. He came over and put his arms around me, whispering in my ear, "I thought you could use some tips on how to get along with a woman."

Calder strolled over, her glass in her hand, and said, "It's very pretty when it's scared, isn't it?" Then, to me, "Well, take off your clothes so I can see what I'm getting."

That afternoon Mondragone taught me the basics of giving sexual pleasure to a woman. He taught me what parts of her body were most sensitive, and how to use the dildoes and vibrators and other tools. From the amused smile on his face as he watched me in bed with Calder, I knew with chilling certainty that he had never cared one bit for me; this was all just part of the curriculum.

Calder had very different tastes than Mondragone. She had a hard time achieving orgasm; when I failed to excite her she would slap me and curse. I quickly learned she needed to be almost in pain to become aroused. The things she wanted me to do to her should have disgusted me; but I had already learned to absent myself and become an automaton, merely obeying, not really there. Unlike Mondragone, she didn't really mind when I didn't act eager; in fact, she almost preferred to think I was doing it against my will.

I knew that six months had passed when a new class of newbies came in. Now we, who had been the new ones, were the seniors teaching a confused and tearful bunch of children how to become what they really were. On their third day there, we decided to hold a collation for them, to cheer them up. We naturally had no access to liquor or drugs, so instead we smuggled pans and noisemakers into the roundroom. While some of the blands sat around the edges drumming, the rest of us joined hands in the middle and danced.

I don't know what happened to me that night. The deafening noise of the drumming, the wild dancing, the rhythm—it all took me out of myself. I felt lifted into a trancelike world where I could spin and spin forever. I was no longer attached to my body. The hateful things I did in the day fell away—they were no longer part of me. I danced till I became transformed.

The next day, as I led one of the newbies through the rules of setting table, it occurred to me that I had become Laki: strict, tense, and unhappy. I no longer smiled or joked with the other blands. I held aloof from them not because I was better but because I felt soiled by human contact. I was sure they would discover me if I got too close.

The clients' dinner was coming up again, and I looked forward to it eagerly, because it was my passport away from Brice's. By that time I had been rotated twice more, and was serving Supervisor Gladden. She liked to talk. She preferred to get her sexual gratification in the morning, just after getting up. The act itself was usually blessedly short, but she would sit and analyze it afterwards, asking me constant questions as I tried to get my duties done. I answered as little as possible. I wished she would just do as she pleased with my body, and leave my mind alone.

One day, she was quizzing me, asking, "Didn't you get any pleasure out of that? What did you like most? What's my greatest asset?" I was impatient because we had a busy day ahead. I was dressed and laying out her clothes, hoping she would get the hint and start moving, so I wouldn't be late at breakfast.

I have no idea why I finally broke. She said something like, "Tell the truth—what do you really feel?" and I simply exploded.

"I really feel that you're all a bunch of perverts," I said. "You disgust me. I hate your sex. I hate you. I wish you would just leave me alone."

That was all I said. I was trembling too hard with rage to get any more out. But it was enough.

She sat very still for several seconds, staring at me while the color first left her face entirely, then rushed back. Then she got up, very cold and deliberate, and put on a robe. I went into the bathroom, pretending to do something, but really because fear had replaced my anger and I was sick and quaking inside. I heard her place a call. Soon she answered a knock at the door. When I came out of the bathroom, Motivator Jockety was there. I was so frightened I froze. I couldn't move or speak.

Jockety took me by the skin at the back of my neck and shoved me toward the door. The pain made me cry out, and he growled, "Keep quiet, you." He shoved me down the hallway then. We came to a room I had never been in. It looked very much like this room—tile floor, no windows. There was a bed, a table, some chairs, and an adjoining bathroom. Jockety released me, and I turned to face him. He was a good foot taller than I, and a hundred pounds heavier. He had not yet shaved, and his face was bristly with beard. I saw he was in a terrible rage.

"I'm sorry," I said. "I didn't mean it. Please."

"Sorry's not enough," he said. "You think we allow insolence at Brice's? You think blands get to talk back?"

"No, sir," I said.

Two other humans came in the door—Gladden and another man. Jockety didn't turn to look; he was completely focused on me. I expected him to strike me. Instead, he took my white shirt in his huge fists and gave it a wrench. The fabric ripped in two from collar to waist. He stripped it off my back. Then he took my pants and wrenched them violently open from waist to crotch, pulling them down around my ankles. I stood before him, quaking and naked, trying to shield myself with my hands. He and the other man took me, each on one side, and dragged me to the table. They bent me over it, crushing my face into the surface. Gladden took my wrists and stretched my arms out over my head. The other man spread my legs and tied my ankles to the table legs with my stockings. I could see Motivator Jockety unfastening his belt and trousers. Then he moved behind me and set to work.

They raped me over and over again. In that first four hours, every human in the building came into that room to abuse me in some way in sight of the others. They raped me anally and orally, sometimes both at once—they laughed and made jokes about that. It went on till blood trickled down my legs and every thrust was agony.

For the first hour I thought that they would stop if I only wept and said I was sorry and promised never to talk as I had done again. By the second hour I realized that nothing I could say or do would keep them away from me, though I still begged for release. By the third hour I was in hysterics—sobbing as a pure bodily reaction, like hiccups. I simply couldn't stop.

In the fifth hour they turned more brutal and sadistic. By then my tormentors were down to three—Jockety, Calder, and a man named Pardee. They strapped me to the table and beat me with belts and switches—never quite enough to break a bone or leave a scar. Calder had a small needle and thread with which she took stitches in my skin. The thread was soaked in something that stung like fire, and left swollen, itching red welts behind. They all laughed as she stitched their names in my buttocks, thighs, and stomach. The letters stood out in burning red.

From time to time they rested, eating snacks to revive themselves, talking about what they ought to do to me next. They spoke of horrible things, crippling mutilations. At the time I didn't know that anything was stopping them; all the tortures they described seemed utterly real.

They did other things I won't make you hear. At the end of six hours they started pretending they were going to let me go. Once they actually gave me my clothes back, but before I could leave, Jockety came in the room with an apparatus for giving electrical shocks. They all laughed and stripped me naked again. Jockety taped wires to my body, then set out to see if he could induce a convulsion while he was sodomizing me.

It didn't work. He tried again and again, and at least got whatever satisfaction can be got from raping a child in excruciating pain.

◊◊◊ Val had been trying to show no reaction, but now she finally flinched. Tedla paused, as if becoming aware of her again. Its face was very white; the words were coming out one by one, hot drops on raw skin. It said, "I'm sorry to make you listen to this. I know this isn't what you wanted to hear. But someone needs to know the truth."

It drew a shaky breath. "I've often wondered why they chose me," it said. "I was no ringleader. I hadn't really rebelled, just broken under pressure. If they had wanted to ensure my obedience, the mere threat of rape would have served as well as the real thing. It simply wasn't necessary."

It was silent a few moments, then said, "I think perhaps

it had nothing to do with me. I didn't know it then, but what they were training me to do was terribly illegal. They could have been punished severely, if any of the humans had testified against the others. They needed some way of ensuring silence among themselves. That's why they all took part—they had to implicate themselves in front of the others, so all of them were equally guilty."

"But that doesn't explain the torture," Val said.

"No," Tedla said. Slowly, as if forcing the words out, it said, "I think that happened because they simply enjoyed it. They were evil people."

The last sentence was said almost in a whisper, but with such force that it could have been shouted.

>}{< I was completely shattered. In a single day they had reduced me to an object of utter revulsion. My legs were caked with blood, filth, and semen; my face and hands reeked of their bodies. My skin was covered with red, itching welts. Even my mouth had the taste of them, sticky inside. I couldn't move without pain, and I couldn't be still either.

When they finally gave me my ripped clothes back and told me to go, I wanted to find a place to hide. Not the roundroom; I couldn't bear that the other blands should find out what had happened. The roundroom was our inviolate refuge; I couldn't bring this new person back there, this disgusting thing they had made me into. I went to the shower, and stayed there as long as I could, washing. I washed out the inside of my mouth with soap to get rid of every trace of them. But it was still inside me.

I didn't take off my coveralls that night. I went off to the edge of the roundroom, against the wall, and wouldn't speak to anyone, or let them touch me. They all knew something horrible had happened; I could feel the fear spreading out all around me. It was doubtless what the humans intended. The blands all knew if it could happen to me, it could happen to them. The fact that they didn't know exactly *what* had happened made it all the more frightful.

The next day I was still in terrible pain, but I tried to go about my duties for fear they would send me in the aircar to a clinic, and the curator would want to examine me. The thought of someone touching me again made me freeze up, as if my muscles were all locked. But I couldn't do my work. I was too jumpy and fearful to concentrate on anything. I kept breaking down in tears for no reason. They finally sent me back down to the roundroom, and I spent the rest of the day in the shower. The cold water soothed the burning of my skin, and my shame.

That day, the supervisors all gave the other blands a little lecture about me. They said I had shown gross disobedience, and had been punished. Everyone else would be punished too, if there was more disobedience. After that, the blands started giving me silent, resentful looks for not having known my place, for not living up to the Brice's rules, and getting them all in trouble. Not a single one sided with me; their loyalty was all to the humans. I learned a valuable lesson: There is no solidarity among blands. We tolerate no independence or rebellion that might jeopardize the group. We police each other as effectively as ever the humans do.

After a week there was not a mark anywhere on my body to show what had happened—a complete void of evidence. But my mental state had gotten no better, and I think the supervisors began to be worried they had gone too far. It was not their consciences bothering them; it was money. The clients paid them to create docile, obedient, unquestioning blands; instead they had created an edgy, hysterical one. They might lose all their investment in my training if the damage couldn't be repaired in time.

They tried to make it up to me with kind words. But the only thing that helped was the cessation of their sexual demands. After that day, no human at Brice's ever touched me again, or asked me to touch them.

The client dinner was coming up fast. We had to train and prepare. On the big day I felt as brittle as an egg, ready to shatter and crack. But the other Personals pulled me through, and the night went well. The next day Supervisor Mondragone called me into his office to congratulate me. I had been chosen to go to the Polygrave's house in Magnus Convergence. I felt overjoyed at the thought of seeing Laki again. I would actually have a friend where I was going.

"You must do your best to represent Brice's well," Mondragone said.

"I will, sir," I said.

We blands said our good-byes to each other that night. The roundroom, as we say in our proverbs, was spongy with tears. But I felt ecstatic to be leaving. The next morning, as we waited in our gray coveralls for the aircar to take us away, I felt like I had been reborn, as surely as if I'd been through the birthpool. Whatever I was bound for in life, I knew it had to be better.

I was just fourteen.

Chapter Five

֍ It was late before they finally fell asleep, Val on the bed and Tedla curled up in the chair. It seemed like she had scarcely closed her eyes when the sound of the door opening woke her. She sat up blearily and saw it was just a robot delivering breakfast.

Tedla had not stirred. Val got up to check out the food. There was only enough for one and it looked unappetizing anyway, so she stretched, wondering if there was a cafeteria in the building. Tedla was still sleeping as if drugged—who knew, maybe it had been—so she quietly slipped out the door into the hallway.

There was a light showing under the door into the observation booth next to Tedla's room, so she knocked on it softly and looked in. Magister Gossup was there, his chin resting on his fist, staring at nothing. Most people, on seeing that austere and unreadable face, would have hesitated to disturb him; but Val went in.

He turned to look at her silently.

"You haven't been here all night, have you?" she asked.

"No, I just got here an hour ago. I have been viewing the recording you made last night."

She sat down facing him. The window into the next room was opaque. "What do you think?" she said.

"I wish to god I hadn't seen it," Gossup said.

152

"I know what you mean."

There was a short silence. At last Val said, "Well, it certainly shoots down Magister Surin's ideas."

"In what way?" Gossup said. He looked very tired.

"Tedla's problems obviously go back a lot farther than the last twelve years," Val said. "It was already in a shaky mental state when it arrived here. Tampering with more recent mentation patterns won't do any good. The original graph Surin's using as a pattern is the graph of a torture victim."

There was a long pause. "Yes, I suppose you could argue that," Gossup said at last. Watching him, Val had a sudden strong instinct that he was the key to this situation; winning him over was her only hope.

"They're going to go ahead anyway, aren't they?" she said. "It doesn't matter whether it will do Tedla any good."

His face gave away no hint of his inner thoughts. He said evenly, "WAC is pushing it very hard, yes. But that doesn't mean it will happen. There are others involved in the decision."

"You?" Val said. "Are you involved in the decision?"

He looked directly at her. "I am working for WAC, Valerie. So are you."

She felt a moment of claustrophobia. She was caught in a tiny space, and it was getting smaller, closing in around her. She forced herself not to sprint for the door. "Magister, I have an idea," she said. "Let me take Tedla home with me again, just for a while. Tedla was so at ease with us. Leaving it here, cooped up in a room that makes it think of that experience—it's inhumane. We're making it crazy ourselves."

"I know—" Gossup started to say.

"If security's a problem, WAC can put surveillance on my copartment," Val said. "That way, they can keep an eye on Tedla every second of the day, just as if it were here. We'll sign any form you like."

"You're too close to this, Valerie," Gossup said. "You need to go home and rest a while. Get some distance."

"Will you ask them? Will you try?"

He paused a moment, then said, "All right. I will try. Tedla would obviously prefer to be with you, and I agree that keeping it here is not kind. Now will you go home?"

"Thank you, Magister," Val said warmly.

She left the room feeling cautiously optimistic—not so much because she believed his promise as because she believed the feeling behind it. Gossup felt as trapped as she did, she was sure of it.

She stopped at the security desk to ask the guard for the nearest place to get a decent breakfast. He said, "You'll have to go back up to the main complex. There's a caf on ground floor."

"Fine," she said, glad to know a little bit more about where she was.

The caf proved to be run on a Chorister license, and so was heavy on flowers, ferns, and other harmonic foods. Val loaded her tray with enough to smuggle some back to Tedla. As she was heading for a table, a familiar figure hailed her. Magister Surin was sitting alone at a table, drinking a cup of very un-harmonious espresso. She hesitated, but he gestured her over to join him. Wary but curious, she went.

"Please sit down. I'm afraid we got off to a bad start yesterday," Surin said when she came up to his table. "I hope you didn't get the impression we're not pleased to have you on this project. Really, we are."

It was quite disarming. Val said, "Well, I hope you didn't get the impression I'm opposed to any treatment. I'm not. I just want to make sure we don't do something drastic before we know all the facts."

"Absolutely, I couldn't agree more," Surin said warmly. "That's the problem dealing with these marketeer types. They always want instant answers. The trick is to give them one so they'll go away and let you do your real work."

Val glanced at him. He looked completely at ease in this setting, too. It was mildly irritating. "You've dealt with marketeers a lot?" she asked.

"Oh, yes," he said in a tone that implied it was an everyday thing. "You learn the tricks of the trade. They really don't care how you solve the problem, as long as you do it."

"But who gets to define what the problem is?" Val said.

Surin laughed. "Good comeback," he said. "Worthy of Magister Gossup himself." He took a sip of coffee, watching her. "You know, I'd never met him before this. He's truly hard to figure out. I understand now why there was opposition to his nomination to the Magisterium."

Aha, Val thought. So that was what this was about. "Oh, really?" she said casually. "I wasn't following the debate." In reality, she had had no access to the debate.

"It was the usual arguments you hear whenever another Vind achieves a position of power: Their alliances and motives are unclear, they're up to something only they know about."

"Oh," Val said. "Xenophobia."

"Absolutely. So, have you known him long?"

She nodded. "He was my thesis advisor."

"He certainly thinks highly of you."

Val wasn't sure how to take this. "Really?" she said.

"Oh, yes. Are you going to follow him into politics?"

Val looked at him, startled. The thought had never entered her mind, but it told her a lot about how Surin's mind worked. He saw her reaction and immediately backtracked. "Sorry. Rude question. It's really been a treat for me, to watch Gossup handle these Gammadian reps. You can tell he's a master."

"Oh, is that what he's been doing?" Val said.

"Hasn't he told you?" Surin said. He had clearly pegged her as a minor player now. "He's the perfect salesman, so subtle you'd never know he was on our side if you didn't . . . well, if you didn't know. WAC was quite jumpy about sharing any information with the delegates free of charge, but Gossup persuaded the old tycoons that a relationship of trust based on an initial show of generosity would be most profitable in the long run. You see, the Gammadians are quite ingenuous about the value of their own information. They're like any isolate society: They assume the advantage is all on our side, because we have the spacetravel technology. They think their own information is of little value to us. If they only knew."

"How interesting," Val said, suppressing her irritation at being lectured on introductory xenology. Surin was obviously enjoying the sound of his own voice; if she kept quiet, she might find out something useful.

"Apparently, we always have this initial advantage when dealing with a new planet," he went on. "We have to take advantage of it while it lasts. So Gossup's been tantalizing them with our wares without teaching them our mercenary ways. No sense in disturbing their innocence, is there? It'll be gone soon enough."

A terrible suspicion struck Val. "It can't be easy to hide how an information economy works. They must be strictly controlling what the delegates see and hear."

"That's the name of the game," Surin said smoothly.

Which meant that the delegates couldn't be allowed to question anyone who knew Capellan society well enough to spill the beans. Even if that person was one of their own citizens.

No wonder it was the last twelve years of Tedla's memories that Surin had diagnosed as the problem. They *were* the problem. Just not Tedla's problem.

Val rose. "I've got to get back," she said. "I want to be there when Tedla wakes up."

"Here, I'll walk with you," Surin said, springing up.

She headed for the public elevator, but Surin stopped her with a friendly wink and said, "I'll show you a short-cut." He led her through an unmarked door into an empty service corridor that unexpectedly made her think: grayspace. There was a freight elevator next to a concrete stairwell. Surin pushed the Up button. As if continuing a casual conversation, he said, "The thing I can't get any sense of is Gossup's politics. Do you know where he stands?"

Val shook her head. "We never talked politics much."

"I mean, he's not one of those wacko radicals who want to de-commodify information or something, is he?"

He had intended only to be genially provocative; he had no idea that Val was married into a whole family of wacko radicals. She said, "Actually, I think the free information people have some good points."

He pretended to be intrigued. "You're joking, right? Those people want us to return to some sort of primitive state of nobility that probably never even existed."

"There are plenty of cultures that get along fine without buying and selling information," Val said, mostly to needle him.

"None of them has an interstellar trade economy. Come on, commodification of information is the only thing that's made space travel economically feasible. It's the only commodity whose value equals its transportation cost. We'd be exporting biologicals or photonics if it paid. But our trading partners can build the machines and grow the organics much cheaper than we can send them, if they just have the codes and specs. If information were free, the way the radicals want, then there would be nothing to trade, and there goes the only incentive for interstellar ties."

Val had heard all these arguments; in fact, she had used them all herself with Max. She also knew his answers. "They would argue that the artificial restriction of information, in order to make it a scarce commodity, hampers the exchange that creates new ideas, and hinders change."

"Poppycock," Surin said. The elevator arrived, and they stepped on, but he kept talking. "An information economy creates *incentive* for new research and new ideas. Our whole planet's economy is based on generation of innovations. That's the thing about information. You sell a person a widget, and he needs more widgets pretty soon. You teach him how to make widgets, and he never needs you again, unless you invent a better widget. We've always got to have some new product. That accelerates change.''

"They also say the information trade creates a culture of paranoia."

Jokingly, Surin said, "I'm not paranoid. Are you paranoid?"

"No, but someone paranoid may be listening to us," Val gave the old retort.

They had reached the seventh floor. Surin led the way through a door that let onto the corridor where the wayport was located, but from the opposite direction than the public elevators. Val thought she would get rid of him when she thumbed the wayport lockplate, but he followed her to the other side. The guard at the security desk had changed; Surin waved at him and he gave a respectful, "Morning, Magister Surin."

Walking down the hall toward Tedla's room, Surin said, "Listen, how long do you think this interviewing thing you're doing will take?"

"I thought we agreed on five days," Val said, a little tensely.

"I know, but if I could get going any sooner, it would give me some breathing space, make my life easier." He came to a halt by the observation room door. "What do you say?"

So this was payback time. Fair exchange for all the information he thought he'd given her. It struck her then: He didn't just want to impress the capitalists. He wanted to do the project. It was his chance to make a name for himself. She forced herself to smile and said, "I'll see what I can do."

"Thanks, Val." He patted her shoulder. "Listen, it's

been great getting to know you. We should have lunch some time."

"Sure, I'd like that," she said.

She went into the observation room and closed the door behind her. The room was empty. She allowed her face to contort into the grimace it had been wanting to make for half an hour. "Self-important prick!" she said to the empty chair. But putting up with him had been worth it. She understood a lot more now than she had.

When she entered Tedla's room, it was empty. Alarmed, she called out Tedla's name. There was no response. She looked behind the bed, then went into the bathroom. Tedla was sitting in the dry bathtub, wrapped in a blanket.

"What are you doing there?" she said.

"Val," Tedla said wanly. "I thought you weren't coming back."

She sat on the commode, studying Tedla's face. "Why would you think that?"

"I thought you were disgusted with me," it said softly.

Seriously, Val said, "You still think it was all your fault, don't you?"

"No," Tedla said, but the denial was unconvincing.

"Listen, Tedla. You haven't done anything wrong. Not in my eyes, or the eyes of anyone else on Capella Two."

There was a short pause. Tedla didn't respond. Val said, "You haven't told me what you're doing in here."

"I had to get out of that room," Tedla said. "I've been sitting here thinking how easy it would be to tear up this blanket into strips, and make a rope. I think that ventilation grate would support my weight. They're crazy to leave me alone like this. I was wondering if they wanted me to try."

She didn't think it would be reassuring to say, "Don't worry, you're under surveillance," so she just said, "No, they don't." After a moment's thought she said, "You didn't think anyone wanted you to kill yourself before, did you?"

"No. I didn't think anyone would care. I'm still not sure

why all of you do. I guess I don't know you Capellans as well as I thought I did."

Right then, Val would have been glad to know a little less about Capellan motives. She paused. "Tedla, do you still want to go home with me?"

She saw the first spark of life in Tedla's eyes since yesterday. "Could I?"

"Sure you could, if that's what you want. Yesterday you wanted to stay and have the treatments."

"Not if there's another way to get out."

"Is that the only reason you wanted the treatment? To get out?"

"I don't know. I was crazy yesterday. They'd been probing me and photographing me, giving me drugs. Please let me go home with you."

Val took a deep breath. "All right. We'll give it a shot. You have to stay quiet until we get out, all right?"

"All right," Tedla said.

Val led the way out into the hallway. Tedla walked close at her side, its eyes on the ground. When she came to the security desk, the guard rose nervously. In a calm, take-charge voice she said, "Surin asked me to take Tedla up to his lab for another scan. Do you have the checkout tablet?"

As the guard looked around his desk for the nonexistent tablet, Val drummed her fingers impatiently. Finally she said, "Oh, just give me something to sign."

The guard gave her a slate, and she scribbled a signature.

"I can't let this person through the wayport, Magister," the guard said, nodding nervously in Tedla's direction.

"Don't worry, I'll authorize it," Val said confidently. "Come on, Tedla." She turned to lead the way down the hall. The guard looked after them uncertainly, but apparently her invocation of Surin's name won out over his doubts. When the doors opened, she waved Tedla through. "Wait with the guard on the other side," she said loud enough for the man at the desk to hear. Then she stepped through herself.

Tedla was waiting for her alone in the corridor. She glanced toward the security desk; no alarm seemed to have gone off yet, so she turned away from it, leading Tedla down the hall toward the service door. They passed only one person on the way, a nurse wheeling a large machine. She didn't even glance at them. When they came to the unmarked door into the stairwell, Val pushed on it. It was locked from this side.

"Damn!" she said. There was a small, reinforced-glass window in the door; she peered through it. Two doctors were coming up the steps on the other side, talking. She rapped vigorously against the glass to attract their attention, then pointed to the door handle. One of them opened the door. "Thanks," she said. "I didn't want to go all the way around."

"Sure," the man said, then continued on. Val and Tedla started down the steps.

Uncertainly, Tedla said, "Aren't we going up to the lab?"

"No, you idiot, we're going home," Val said.

"Oh. I thought you'd changed your mind."

"I guess I was convincing, then," she said.

Tedla looked at her. "You're not authorized to do this, are you?"

"Well . . . not exactly."

"Are you going to get in trouble?"

"I guess I'll find out," Val said.

Once they came out into the crowded public lobby by the caf, it was easy to blend into the stream of pedestrians heading toward the waystation. Val bought two tickets for them and waved Tedla on through. She was mildly astonished that it had worked. It was amazing to find what you could get away with if you acted like you had the right to.

When they got home, Deedee was so delighted to see Tedla that she completely ignored Val's presence. Even

Max looked genuinely pleased. When Deedee had dragged Tedla off into her room, Max said in an undertone, "What happened? You looked pretty grim when you called."

She said, "Max, I don't normally believe in conspiracies. But there's really one going on here."

"Tell me," he said seriously.

"Later. First, I've got to make a call. I think you'd better lock the doors, and don't let anyone in. Tedla's not supposed to be here."

Max's eyebrows rose. Val headed for the studium terminal. At the door she stopped and looked back. "By the way," she said, "I don't think we'd better count on that contract with WAC."

Magister Gossup took her call right away. "Val, where are you?" he said.

She couldn't remember him ever using her nickname before. Making her voice even calmer than his, she said, "I'm at home. Don't worry, Tedla's with me."

He was speechless for several seconds. Then he said, "Valerie, what are you up to?"

"Nothing," she said. "Just what we all agreed. I get five days to interview Tedla before we reevaluate about the treatment. Tedla felt more comfortable at my house. You said yourself you agreed."

"I said—" he started, then thought better of it. "Never mind. It doesn't matter now." He paused indecisively.

"Magister, I need you to make sure WAC leaves us alone till the time is up. No goons on my doorstep frightening my daughter, okay?"

Evenly, he said, "Valerie, you're going to have to bring Tedla back to the curatory. I'm sure you realize that."

"Of course," she said, "after five days. If it still wants the treatment."

Magister Gossup closed his eyes for a moment. "Don't do this to yourself, Valerie. Your whole career will be ruined. Everything you have worked for, gone."

Her stomach muscles clenched. He was her friend, he

always had been. She had counted on him. Now she knew the boundaries of his support. "I'm right about this, Magister," she said. "It's better this way for everyone. For Tedla, for the delegates, even for WAC. Nothing bad is going to happen. I swear it."

"You cannot promise that. You don't have control of the situation."

Frustrated, she blurted out, "If all of you would just trust Tedla a little, instead of trying to be so underhanded and full of subterfuge, maybe you'd find a solution everyone could live with. Why don't you just tell Tedla what's going on, and ask for its cooperation?"

Gossup looked at her bleakly. "After the way it has been treated, Tedla has no reason to be loyal to Capella."

"After the way it's been treated, it has no reason to be loyal to Gammadis, either," Val said.

"Well," he said. "There is something in that." For a moment he seemed to debate with himself, then said, "Let me speak to Tedla."

Tedla was sitting cross-legged on Deedee's bed, looking at a book with her. Val said, "Tedla, Magister Gossup wants to speak to you."

Tedla looked up, awestruck. "Kpatksiro Gossup? The xenologist?"

"Do you know him?" Val said.

"We studied his work at C4D."

"Of course. I keep forgetting your training. Yes, that Gossup. He's on the studium screen."

When Tedla sat down nervously in front of the terminal, Gossup said, "Hello, Tedla. How are you feeling?"

"Very good, Magister. It's an honor to talk to you. My tutor, Magister Delgado, made us read nearly every word you've written."

"Doubtless to take issue with them," Gossup said drily. He and Delgado had been notorious rivals, once. All the same, it was clear that he was pleased by the information.

Score one for Tedla, Val thought. She left the room and closed the door behind her.

Max was in the dinery. Val sank down on a chair, weary with tension. He put a cup of coffee in front of her and sat down. "All right, what's going on?" he said.

She told him everything that had happened at the curatory. He listened quietly, shaking his head in disbelief from time to time. At the end he said, "That's diabolical. What made them think they could get away with wiping someone's memories for their own profit?"

"What's the value of memories?" Val said a little bitterly. "Only what the market will pay."

"I think I'm making you into a radical," Max said.

"Besides, what's to stop them, as long as no one finds out? A deranged alien with no family and no ties on Capella Two—who was going to complain?"

Max reached across the table and squeezed her hand. "I'm proud of you, Val. You did the right thing."

"I hope you're willing to live off righteousness for a long time," she said glumly. "I've probably blown my whole career."

"And I love you for it," he said.

The studium door opened, and Tedla came out, looking a little glazed. It sank into a chair. Max got up and fetched it some coffee without a word. Val finally said, "Well?"

"You *did* get in trouble, didn't you?" Tedla said.

"You might say that," Val said.

The neuter looked at her closely. "Why were you willing to risk it?"

"Oh, it's just one of my personality flaws," Val said. "Ask Max. I'm always biting off more than I can chew."

Tedla looked dissatisfied with this answer. It said, "Humans always feel like they have to belittle themselves when they do something out of goodness or compassion. You always act as if you have to deny you have good motives. We blands are ashamed to seem too smart; you are ashamed to seem too good. I don't know why you set

up these standards of behavior for yourselves, then deny
it whenever you get too close to them."

"Caught you," Max said, grinning at Val.

"Stop it, you two," Val said. She needed to change the
subject. "Did Gossup say you could stay here?"

"He didn't know," Tedla said. "He asked me if I
thought you would go to the nets. What did that mean?"

Val and Max looked at each other. Max said, "You do
have that option. WAC must be shaking in its boots, thinking you might do it."

"I don't have any proof, just suspicions," Val said.
"No one ever said an illegal word to me. It was all im-
plications."

"But you could tell the nets about the Gammadian delegation. That would still blow WAC's negotiations. Everyone would be clamoring for access to them."

"You knew about the delegation?" Tedla said.

"Since yesterday," Val nodded.

"Why didn't you tell me?"

"I'm sorry, Tedla. I should have. There was so much
else going on. . . . What did Gossup say about them?"

"He asked if I was willing to speak to them. I couldn't
believe he had to ask. People from my own planet! Why
wouldn't I want to speak to them?"

"That was all he said?" Val probed.

"Yes. Why?"

Val was done with secrets. "They're very worried that
you'll tell the delegates things about Capella that might
interfere with trade negotiations. They're trying to keep
your compatriots in the dark about the value of their information."

Tedla looked incredulous, then laughed. "And they
think the delegates would ask a *bland* about those things?
Or believe me if I told them?"

Val and Max exchanged another look. Val said, "You
know, that's probably true. They may be worried for nothing."

Max broke out laughing. "They need a xenologist on this project!"

Val began to laugh, too. "To do them justice, that's what they hired me for—background cultural research. I don't suppose—" A thought struck her. "You know, I've still got an access card for WAC's secret files on Gammadis. I bet they haven't thought to cancel it yet." She felt through her pockets and found it, a little bent from the fact that she had slept on it last night. She leaped up. "I'm going to go try it out. Don't interrupt me for a while."

Sitting down at the studium terminal, she fed in the card. Almost immediately, a WAC logo appeared on the screen, and a mechanical voice prompted her to give her thumbprint for identification. With a qualm of apprehension, she pressed her thumb against the optical reader. The screen was silent for a long time, and she was preparing herself for disappointment, when Access Approved flashed on the screen. She gave a little whoop of triumph. Then, suddenly, she was inside the database.

Scrolling through the contents, she felt overwhelmed. There was a mass of it—hundreds of thousands of files, almost completely unindexed, raw data just as it was received off the PPC over sixty years ago. WAC clearly must have considered the Gammadis episode closed, or it would have spent some money processing the data. She opened a few files at random, to get a sense of what was there; she found geological reports, soil chemistry, atmospheric measurements, botanical catalogues. All dry as dust. The paired-particle device had been too limited to transmit more than the occasional image or graph, so most of the files were simple text. Doubtless the maps and models were all among the confiscated data.

Scrolling through screen after screen, Val searched for anything that looked ethnographic. At last, realizing how much there was, she asked the sorter to search for the key word "Tedla." She received an avalanche of filenames. Giving a low whistle, she sat clicking her thumbnail against her teeth, debating how to approach this. Choosing a file that looked different from the others, she was rewarded with a detailed anatomical description. "Gammadian proto-humans possess the precursor organs of internal genitalia for both sexes," the doctor wrote; "the wolffian structures (male) and mullerian structures (female) are maintained in fetal form through puberty, when one set develops and the other is absorbed. In neuters, based on examination of this subject, both sets atrophy and are absorbed. While hormone treatments could presumably give it secondary sexual characteristics, it could never develop natural genitalia at this stage (age 15)."

This file did contain a picture: a much younger Tedla standing naked before the camera, its face blank, eyes avoiding the lens's gaze. Val quickly closed the file. This was more than she wanted to know about the anatomy of someone she had come to think of as a friend.

She asked the sorter to list the "Tedla" files by author; this revealed that nearly all of them were Alair Galele's weekly reports. She opened one at random, and immediately her attention was caught. While the other researchers had prepared formal reports full of statistics and technical analysis, Galele's were like hasty diary entries, full of subjective reactions, written in a breathless flurry of abbreviations and half-sentences. Val began to understand Gossup's reaction to Galele. Her tutor had no patience for sloppy methodology, and Galele was sloppiness incarnate. Still, there was something charming about his enthusiasm.

She glanced at the clock at the bottom of the screen. She had already been in the database for half an hour. It was only a matter of time before they detected her and shut her out. Quickly she commanded the machine to download all the "Galele" files to her own private cache, followed by the rest of the "Tedla" files. She sat watching filenames flash across the screen; then a blue message appeared: Access Denied.

"Damn!" she said, hitting the chair arm.

From the other side of the studium door, Max's voice came: "What happened?"

"They caught me."

"Too bad."

"Well, I got something. I'm not sure what yet."

She went to look. Through some quirk, the sorter had wasted time downloading not only the files by Galele, but also a mass of messages sent back to Capella *about* him, including a number marked Urgent and Confidential. When she weeded them out and arranged the files by date, it appeared that she had gotten most of Galele's early reports, but only a few additional useful files.

Val opened the first report in the chronological list and began to read from the beginning.

Down to the planet at last! No offense to august ancestors, but their spaceship is a damned crib, not meant for extended living, and three months was too much muscle-cramp and togetherness. At least we got a linguistic crash-course before braving the planet.

Cruised low coming in. Beautiful place—vegetation everywhere—very rural—fewer signs of habitation than expected—no wonder First Contact team was surprised to find advanced civilization—population doesn't seem sufficient.

At airfield were welcomed cordially by assorted muckety-mucks, very glad to have us here & learn about us, etc. etc. They are quite used to the idea of us, thanks to four years of advance work by F.C. team.

Gammadians here are tall, willowy, very beautiful—strong faces, light skin (presumably due to subterranean living, since sunlight has high UV content). Friendly, cordial, cultured, but with a reserve or slight wariness—one can scarcely blame them, not knowing our true motives.

They took us down to their "convergence." Entire city is underground. Large population center—250,000—in elegantly designed subterranean city. Not at all what you'd expect—very bright & airy—organized around light wells & air shafts—very clean. Their principal building mat'l., called lignis, is actually a viscous liquid which hardens in air, so they merely carve a cave out, shape the lignis into rooms with compressed air, & leave it to harden, when it becomes extremely strong & capable of polish, like wood or agate. The city, as a result, looks like a series of bubbles, all curves & grain, quite a pleasing effect. Learned all this from one of our hosts as we were descending into city center. My Gammadian seems sufficient—understand better than I talk—but waving of hands helps.

They took us to a giant reception in a large, elegant hall lit by "piped" sunlight (optical fiber?). Fermented beverages, unidentifiable plant products (quite good), fewer animal parts. Modified vegetarians? Many long speeches, a choir for music, important (I assume) people to greet us. Greeting is by touching palms of hands together & briefly intertwining middle fingers. Sexual symbolism? I talked much in broken Gammadian about our desire to learn from them.

Striking uniformity of age, both in city & at reception. No one under 15 or over say 75. Seems a city of the adult & middle aged. All healthy, not a sign of any illness, defect, or deformity. They are probably controlling what we are allowed to see. Even so, the obvious comfort & wealth is impressive.

Sat down to a long & bibulous banquet which had me yawning (ship time was over 20 hrs.). Servitors were young men & women in livery. At last I glimpsed one of the third sex—at least, I assumed so—clearing away dishes along the perimeter of the room. "It" was smaller than other Gammadians, dressed in a drab uniform. Gone before I could get a good look. There must not be many of them. I tried to ask my table-mates, but could not make myself understood.

They are debating where to send us. One school of thought is that we should all be kept here at the seat of learning & center of civilization (presumably so they can monitor us), another holds we should be scattered out among many communities with varying histories, industries, & customs (presumably to separate us so we can't conspire). I favor the latter, but was careful (as F.C.s warned us) not to voice my opinion, though they tried to sound me out.

They were very eager to know what I wanted to study. I told them life cycle, & they seemed a little taken aback—perhaps there is no discipline that addresses such topics here. They kept asking if I were a geneticist or physiologist (at least I think that's what they meant).

Clearly, our arrival has produced a crisis of sorts in their leadership. Since they have no centralized hierarchy, factions appear to be competing for control of us, & it appears likely we may be parceled out to equalize power. The function of the banquet was, I suspect, to size us up & decide who would be awarded to which group.

At last they let us go to our rooms—a private one for each of us, quite a luxury after the ship. Mine is a suite of connected bubbles—bedroom, bathroom, closet or dressing room, breakfast room, study, lounge. Lavish use of space. They supplied towels, toiletries, robe, lounge wear, night clothes, slippers, & food in case I get peckish at midnight. Also what I take for soporifics and sexual aids (!). The bedroom has translucent lignis walls lit from behind, quite lovely. The bed is monstrous and round. Can't figure which end is up. The arched ceiling over it is low & the walls are cozily close: like the primeval cave or womb. Comforting thought.

Galele's next report was dated a week later.

They have put us through an exhausting obligatory tour of the great monuments—libraries, historic sites, natural wonders, great rooms (architecture being entirely interior). We saw some ruins that greatly excited the archae-

*ologists; if they prove as old as the natives claim, we may
have to revise the diaspora chronologies. Much travel by
mechanical means. The usual self-congratulatory lectures.
A nice thing: they are great lovers of beauty, natural &
manmade. Landscape like an article of religion: they believe in "treading lightly" on nature. Will probably be
much market for Gammadian art.*

They took us to a famous opera, Cloverine—*a tragedy
about the evil olden days when there were families! Pro-
tagonist was a woman of talent & ambition who is weighed
down by social demands to have and care for babies. She
is debilitated by pregnancy, betrayed by a fickle husband,
exhausted by demands of motherhood, but stubbornly
clings to her children (the fatal flaw?), struggling to support them. In the end she dies & the children—the oldest
now a delinquent—are consigned to the state anyway.
Gammadians seemed to find this tale most pathetic and
satisfying. I was taken aback. They noted my reaction, &
asked whether we oppress our women by "making" them
rear children.*

*Most extraordinary: There is no kinship system. None.
They have entirely dispensed with the family as social unit.
Only one of my guides knew who her parents were, and
she had never met them. None knew siblings or children
of their own. By their account, this is deliberate. Once,
long ago (in Cloverine's time), there was "clannishness,"
as they put it, but it was engineered out of their social
system, along with other ills such as "factionalism," eth-
nicity, inherited social class, and nation-states. (All
sources of divisiveness.) Even gender no longer divides
them, since they grow up entirely without it. (Was their
sexual development also engineered?)*

*Children grow up in institutional "gestatories," raised
by professionals, never knowing their parents. On matur-
ing ("matriculation"), they join an order or community,
institutions that perform all economic, governmental, and
social roles. All major resources are communal, not indi-*

vidual. The order or community offers cradle-to-grave se-curity. Housing, food, spending money, medical care, social support, access to information—all through the or-der or community. No one needs *a family.*

Patternists form orders: they are focused on information creation & control, like our infocompanies, but not so commercial. Communities are *commercial, but materially oriented, like our governments—they specialize in build-ing, manufacturing, agriculture, ''sapping'' (harvesting tree sap), other basic economic activities. They are hier-archical, ruled by mattergraves. All are decentralized: hundreds, perhaps thousands, of orders and communities arranged in loose networks, scattered geographically in many convergences. No wonder they are at odds how to handle us. They have no apparatus for making global de-cisions, only local ones. No, not even that—communal ones.*

I know now why I see no poor. No one can be poor who belongs to an order or community, since they take care of their own. The only poor are the placeless ones, outside the system by their own choice. My guides say there are few; I can see why. How would they support themselves? Where turn in an emergency? No family, no property—independence is impossible. Or at least, undesirable.

Caught sight of another neuter, cleaning rooms in a hallway. It scurried away before I could get close, like a shy animal. I must find where they all live.

Finally, the decision about what to do with us. The ''scatter them widely'' faction won—probably less from fear of us (we are not very fearful) than from eagerness of all the competing orders and communities to have an alien visitor of their very own. Fancy being a status sym-bol.

I am to be assigned to a patternist order in Tapis Con-vergence, a midcontinent backwater. Apparently they pegged me as a patternist type. I will be the only Capellan at Tapis, which suits me fine—all the more opportunity to foster ties with the locals. I shall be "adopted" into an order—they simply cannot relate to us as long as we remain outside their social system. Mine is an order of "questionaries." No precise Capellan parallel, something between journalist and social scientist.

I will be sorry to leave this convergence. It is lively and lovely. There are three central lightwells ringed by stacked balconies. They grow trailing plants to drip over the balconies, and wind the leaves through with little sparkling lights, so that it looks like a green waterfall by day, a cascade of stars by night. Everyone goes to lean on the balconies and people-watch. There are strolling musicians, and the music echoes nicely up and down the shaft. I asked one minstrel if he belonged to an order. Yes, of course— he busks in his spare time, just for the joy of it.

Their dress is colorful and creative, but rather unisexual—I can tell no difference between that of men & women. Men may wear jewelry & feathers in their hair, women wear boots & overalls if they please. Reflects the egalitarian nature of gender roles. Exposure of sexual organs is frowned on (though, I gather, practiced in certain "wild" settings by young people). I have gotten a rather Puritanical sense from them, but not gloomy or repressive—more high-minded & stoic. The main variation in dress is between orders & communities, each of which have a characteristic color & cut of clothes, a kind of uniform, though interpreted very individualistically by members. When "off duty," they wear anything they please.

They tell me Tapis is a very "liberal" convergence, though what that means I don't know. It was said as if I should welcome the news.

The head of my new order came to fetch me. She is called Ovide Hornaday Questionary—a smallish dynamo with a droll, sarcastic sense of humor. I liked her instantly.

Soon we were joking like old buds. How well this is all turning out!

We traveled to Tapis by aircar, a conveyance that specializes in meal extraction—lurching, nauseous swoops both up & down. I barely managed to keep hold of my dignity & breakfast. I have no idea what keeps the damned vehicle aloft, which added to my discomfort. Interstellar lightbeam travel I can manage, but this suspension in air is terrifying.

Tapis proves to be just as lovely as Magnus Convergence. Though smaller, it was designed with a real eye to architecture. Their central "shaft," as they call the lightwell, is very irregular—each floor is a different geometric shape stacked on the one below. A triangle on a hexagon on a rhomboid, & so forth. At one point there is a six-story waterfall right down one side of the lightwell. Each order and community in the convergence has its own subsidiary shaft, with all its facilities opening off it, and radiating hallways that intersect confusingly with the hallways of other stacks, so that I know I will be lost most of the time. I praised the beauty of the place to Ovide, and she said it has always been a center of the arts. It was, she said, the place where the Sensualist Movement originated 40-plus years ago. This was not, I gather, what it sounds like, but rather a school of aesthetic & religious thought that later verged into social reform.

Ovide has assigned me a guide named Annika Hornaday Questionary. I asked thoughtlessly if the names meant they were related, & received a rather disapproving response from young Annika. Seems the second name is called the honorific; everyone chooses one to honor some mentor they admire. So they often indicate schools of thought or political alliances within the order. The first name is given at "birth" (i.e., matriculation), and people have no choice about it. The last name indicates the order or community one belongs to. I am now Alair Galele Questionary.

Annika is very bright, but young and rather naively doc-

trinaire. She spent our first tour feeding me the party line about her culture. She is quite aware of the evils of gender discrimination, apparently having studied it in history, and has formed the idea that I come from a gender-biased culture. "We have no subordination of women," she told me (her tone implied I ought to be apologizing). "Our socialization process is almost entirely without gender bias. We are raised in a strictly egalitarian environment. We never have to separate our identities from role models of one sex or the other. Protos see women and men in every role: nurturing, authoritarian, educational, physically demanding. They form no stereotypes or prejudices. As a result, very few feel uncomfortable with their sex, since it carries so few cultural or behavioral restrictions with it."

I think I was hearing her thesis.

She feels that the Gammadian social arrangement is responsible for the almost complete absence of war & strife. When she went so far as to say there was no conflict, I finally challenged her. She admitted bad things happen— "But who wants to dwell on them?" Don't know if this denial is political or personal. I pushed—what sort of bad things? People cheat, fail to meet their goals. I pushed more. Lying? (Yes.) Theft? (No, property mores too communal.) Murder? (Uncomfortably, yes. She claims it is occasional.) Rape? (I didn't know the word, so described it. She said there was no word for it, quite disgusted at the idea.) Very enlightening conversation. Made her very uncomfortable.

My quarters here are more modest than at Magnus, as befits a member of a not-very-large order—though I still have bedroom, workroom, lounge, kitchen, and bathroom to myself. There is a wall screen, but no entertainment on it—just information services. Every day the place is cleaned and linen replaced by invisible elves. I never see them. I asked Annika who my benefactors were and she said, "The blands do the cleaning." I asked if it were appropriate to leave them a tip, and she said, "Oh no, don't encourage them.'' (Odd. Why not?) I shall try it anyway. And some day I will lurk in my room to see them.

Meals are served in a communal hall, though there are also restaurants and cafes on the Questionaries' shaft (''Questishaft'') where one can eat privately for a fee. For the moment, I prefer the refectory. It is completely automated. The menu is listed on a screen, and you simply touch the items you want. Presently they appear on a roundtable server, and you take your tray to a table. Afterwards you bus your dishes to a similar roundtable, and they disappear. All quite neat & efficient. The first time we went, Annika introduced me to a tableful of questionaries who were quite friendly & curious, and rather surprised I wasn't being given a more VIP treatment. I tried to convince them that would be counterproductive.

''Don't worry,'' one man said ironically, ''it wouldn't suit Ovide's agenda. No doubt she wants you mingling with the riffraff.''

I was very curious what this meant, but the others seemed uncomfortable at the man's statement, so I couldn't pursue it. I will have to look him up privately. His name is Gambion.

I got all the other usual questions—what my planet is like, what I'm here to study, what's my impression of Taramond. I'm getting very good at answering without saying much. The F.C.s would be proud.

The second night there was a reception in my honor. They gave me questionary regalia to wear—black pants and high-necked, long-sleeved shirt, with a scarlet sleeveless robe (knee length) over the top. Surprisingly comfortable. The more distinguished members of the order wear sashes across the chest, and medals. Black boots, and for very formal occasions (or outdoor work) a hat. Women & men dress the same, of course. We looked like a flock of marsh blackbirds.

Ovide introduced me all round, and I answered the 10 questions again & again. They are quite excited to have me, and all want to show me their research. No way to tell them I'd rather see their living arrangements.

I saw Gambion there, and made a point to go over to him. Annika was trailing me, so I asked her to fetch me a drink. Gambion watched as she left, and said, "She's very pretty. Are you screwing her?"

I was taken aback. Was this the vaunted sexual equality? I stammered, "Is that . . . expected?"

"Only if she's offered," he said.

"She hasn't."

"Probably wise to keep your distance anyway. Ovide might get jealous."

From which I had the revelation that Ovide and Annika are lovers. Is this an added implication of the names?

I had a thousand questions then: homosexuality, monogamy, teacher-student relations, privacy strictures, sexual taboos. But I wasn't sure this was the proper setting for such intimate matters; then Annika came back. So we exchanged pleasantries for a while. All quite boring and socially acceptable.

The next day I asked Annika where people go to enjoy themselves when they're not at parties for visiting aliens. "I go to Heller's on the main stack," she said, "but you wouldn't want to go there."

"Why not?" I said.

"It's for young people."

"Oh, my poor ego!" I said.

She was immediately concerned that I was serious. "I'll take you, if you want."

"No, tell me where the decrepit old people go."

"There's a coffeehouse the senior faculty like."

"Are you sure I can hobble that far?"

"It's right on the Questishaft," she said seriously. The girl has not a trace of humor.

"Well, show me the way," I said.

It proved indeed to be a place offering specialty coffees (bless the Diasporans and their terraforming kits—they knew what was really important to bring along). In addition, there was a bar that served a very good fermented grain beverage they call hopscotch. Very few people were there, so we took a table alone.

"Tell me, Annika, what do people here do when they fall in love?" I said.

"Why, are you in love with someone?" she said, startled. I think she half suspected I was making a pass at her.

"No, this is what I study," I said.

"You study love?"

"Among other things. Mating habits, sexual mores, that sort of thing. It's often a key to understanding a culture. Tends to be an emotionally charged topic."

"Oh."

"So answer my question."

"Well, they often move in together..." Her voice trailed off. I waited, expecting more, but no more came. I couldn't tell if she were uncomfortable.

"Does this embarrass you?" I said. "Is it inappropriate for me to ask?"

"Oh, no," she said.

"Well, go on then. Is there such a thing as marriage any more?"

"There's partnership," she said, "when two people have a lasting relationship. But they don't have to be in love to become partners. It helps, of course."

"Does partnership have any legal standing?"

"No. There's not supposed to be any obligation on either side. No property or anything. But, you know..." She looked down. Something was bothering her.

"Do you have a partner?" I asked.

"Ovide," she said. There was no hesitancy to the admission, so apparently no stigma was involved here.

"Is that public knowledge?" I asked to make sure.

"I hope so," she said.

"Why?"

"Well, the whole point is, she's supposed to be helping

me, sponsoring me. Like she's done by letting me be your guide. Everyone envies me. But I'm not sure any more that that's a good thing. People are sniping at me, you know. They can be so petty. It doesn't matter as long as I've got Ovide's protection. But if she dumps me . . . She could, you know. Any time she decides she likes someone else better. There's no obligation. I could dump her, too, but why would I? It's my whole career at stake.''

''So you feel pretty insecure?''

''That's right. Insecure.''

''Do you love her?'' I asked gently.

''I don't know. I suppose I do. I need her, that's the thing. I was never going to be anything till I caught her eye.''

''Does this happen to many young people?'' I asked. ''Partnership with an older person, a sponsor in their order?''

''Only to the lucky ones,'' she said.

''But you don't feel very lucky right now.''

''No,'' she said.

''Well, I'll tell her what a good job you're doing,'' I said.

She looked up at me, and I saw the first flash of real warmth in her eyes. ''Thank you,'' she said.

I felt sorry for the girl, but couldn't tell why she thought her problem was so earth-shattering. Adolescent angst, no doubt.

Some of Annika's observations about gender roles appear to be true. Male & female roles are not at all distinct. Women will ask men to help them in a task requiring strength, but only as one might ask a person with good eyesight to read a sign, or a person with a good voice to lead a song. There is no sense of superiority or inferiority, just difference. To me, Gammadian men seem less aggressive than Capellans, certainly less than Oremen. They dominate conversations less, do not lead the way when walking. Women quite unconsciously assume more competitive roles than in gender-polarized societies, for instance in arguments or shared tasks. Both men and women seem less judgmental of the other sex, watch each other less, manipulate less. They still flirt quite overtly, but not while business is involved—only in social situations.

Q: Can it be they have, as Annika claims, a violence-free society (or close to it)? Can one eliminate crime and conflict by the simple expedient of eliminating gender tension?

The above observations may be quite superficial, coming as they do from an afternoon strolling around the Questishaft and sitting at a cafe table, noting down behaviors and eavesdropping on conversations. Annika thought me quite lazy, to spend my time lounging at a cafe while I could be doing research.

Ovide called me in to chat. She apologized for neglecting me, said she'd been busy. True to my word, I told her Annika had been taking care of me nicely.

"You have been shocking the pants off her," Ovide said, looking at me in that forthright, humorous way she has. "Every night she comes home rattled about something else you've done or said."

I realized then that Annika was spying on me for Ovide. It had been naive of me not to realize it before.

"I'm sorry if I violated any standards of behavior," I said. "But . . ."

"Yes?"

"Well, I think Annika needs a little shaking up."

Ovide broke out laughing. "So she does. You are good for her, I suppose." She grew thoughtful then. "I'm sure you've realized by now that there are a lot of things that need shaking up around here."

She seemed to be fishing for some reaction from me, and it made me quite uncomfortable. I am not foolish enough to criticize their social system to a member of the power structure, even if I wanted to, which I don't.

Seeing my difficulty, she adopted a more businesslike tone. "I want to put the resources of the order at your disposal so that your research will go smoothly. It would help if I knew what you hope to learn."

The unspoken question: What is your agenda here? Of course, I don't have an agenda, but try to convince them of that. I said, "I don't know what I'll learn until I learn it. Really."

I must have seemed evasive. She said, "I hope that your findings will prove useful to us as well as to you."

Ordinarily, I would have assumed that this meant, I hope you justify the current power structure. But her remark about things needing shaking up had thrown me badly off balance. I stammered some cardboard cliché about helping them understand themselves better. I'm sure she thought I was hiding what I was really up to. But I'm blessed if I know what she is up to.

Did I ever say these people are Puritanical? I was absolutely wrong! I have just come back from my first casual visit to a Gammadian at home, and my impression of them has taken a complete turn.

Gambion asked me over for "dinner and a swim." Annika did not altogether approve of the company I was going to keep, which reinforced my impression that Gambion is of a different clique than Ovide. When I asked if it were appropriate to bring a gift, she said absolutely, and offered to help me choose one from a little shop on the Questishaft. She picked a specialty cheese with a worm in the center; I suspected her of rather pointed symbolism, but she assured me it was a great delicacy, and the reaction I got when I presented it was quite appreciative.

As a senior patternist, Gambion lives in very nice quarters—quite a lot more spacious and, of course, more personalized than mine. There were three other guests: a thin, artistic-looking older woman named Auri and a young couple, Linna (the woman) and Bors (the young man). At first I could not sort out their relationships. From the conversation I gathered that Auri and Gambion were partners, and had been for years. She must have been his sponsor when he was an up-and-comer, since she is somewhat older. But then someone referred to Gambion and Bors as partners, despite the fact that Bors and Linna were sitting on a couch with their arms around one another. I finally had to call time out and ask directly.

It turned out there were three partnerships among the four people: Gambion and Auri, Gambion and Bors, and Bors and Linna. So the men were maintaining two relationships at once, one homosexual and one heterosexual. I asked the women if they also had other partners, but they laughed and said they didn't have the energy. They seemed quite amused that I found it odd.

"Don't people pair off where you come from?" Linna asked.

I replied, "If we want more than one partner, we do it serially, not all at once. Though it doesn't always work out that way."

I also learned that Auri, Gambion, and Bors—a three-generation triad—all had taken the same honorific, "Tappany." What they have created is, in fact, a pseudo-family based on a chain of teacher-student (or sponsor-protégé) relationships rather than blood. Linna, being outside the "family," had the slight formality of an in-law.

Since no one seemed at all secretive or self-conscious, I ventured to ask, "Are same-sex partnerships as common as cross-sex ones?"

They disagreed—Auri holding they were not, Gambion holding they were, Bors siding with Gambion, Linna tactfully abstaining. From the discussion, I gathered that sexuality is seen as a spectrum, with bisexuality the "normal" state, and strict homo- and heterosexuality the rare extremes at either end. However, value judgments are not attached; the attitude is very much chacun à son goût.

Either the conversation or the drinks were making me

a little overheated, and I was glad when Gambion suggested we repair to the pool. Everyone picked up their drinks and went to the back door, which opened on a large, domed common area. It was brightly lit with piped sunlight, and full of growing plants—even small trees— that formed secluded little glades where people could sit privately. Streams of water ran in stony beds to an irregularly shaped pool in the center.

We chose a place near the edge of the pool, where there were chairs and a table to set our drinks on. Then my companions proceeded, without the slightest self-consciousness, to strip naked for their swim. I could not escape it—I began to do likewise—but at the last I could not bring myself to take off my briefs. They all looked at me curiously—I expect they had been hoping to see if Capellans were made the same as Gammadians—but no one said a word. They dived in, all but Auri, who said she didn't want to get her hair wet, so merely dabbled her feet in the water. Since the rule seemed to be "no clothing in the pool," I sat down at the table.

Presently Linna came back and stretched out on a nearby stone ledge to dry in the "sunlight." I didn't want to appear standoffish, but couldn't think of a single topic of conversation to broach with a pair of stark naked women. Fortunately, Linna and Auri were looking at a fortyish woman across the pool from us, standing on the edge playing some game with a man in the water (she was naked, of course).

"She says she's not ever going to do her duty," Linna said resentfully.

"Doesn't surprise me," Auri said, her voice sharp with disapproval. "Why should she? Her fortune's made." She looked at Linna appraisingly. "Have you applied for a license?"

The subject seemed to fill Linna with gloom. "Yes. I'm waiting for the test results. It's not a good time, but then, when is? I might as well get it over with, and I need the money.''

I couldn't imagine what they were talking about.

"It's not so bad," Auri said. "You shouldn't believe all the stories people tell. Some women do it again and again, just for the money.''

Linna looked faintly disgusted.

"What are you talking about?" I finally said.

"Procreation," Auri said.

"You mean, pregnancy?" The two women nodded glumly. "You don't want it?''

"No, why should I?" Linna said a little defensively.

I thought about it. The reward of pregnancy is to have the baby; but children here are raised in creches, apart from their parents. "Do you ever get to see the child?" I asked.

"You can if you really want to, for the first two weeks," Auri said. "They counsel against it, because you get emotionally involved. I didn't choose to see mine.''

"Then what's the reward?" I said.

"Money," they both said simultaneously.

We got into quite a discussion then. Linna's attitude, it seems, is quite widespread. And why not? They have reduced motherhood to mere babymaking. As a result, to keep the population up, the orders and communities have to bribe women to reproduce. The financial rewards are substantial, enough to pay off the debts all young people incur to their communities for training. It is, they assured me, one reason women are often more well-to-do than men. There is no penalty for the woman who chooses not to reproduce, other than the censure and gossip of other women. But I think I detected in Auri's and Linna's condemnation a thread of private envy.

"Do you get to choose the father?" I asked.

"Of course," Linna said, "assuming your genetics are compatible.''

"And who decides that?''

"The Order of Matriculators."

"They are the ones who issue the licenses?"

Both women nodded. *"They guard the genetic pool,"* Auri said. It struck me then that something of the sort is needed. Since no one knows who they may be related to, involuntary incest is a real possibility.

At that point, the two men came back, and the women immediately changed the subject. I wondered whether pregnancy was an improper topic to discuss in front of men, and if so why the women had been so open with me. Perhaps they didn't quite consider me a man. I was an alien first, male second. My inability to disrobe in front of them might have been fortunate after all. Preserved at least some of my magnetic mystery. (Ha!)

No one moved to put their clothes back on till after we had eaten dinner, and I eventually grew accustomed to the sight of breasts bobbing in front of me. It is, perhaps, a good thing that the treatments on Capella seem to have killed my libido. I felt not the slightest stir of sexual interest the whole evening.

"Why don't I ever see the people who clean my room?" I asked Annika the next day.

"There aren't any people who clean your room," she said impatiently. She was already upset with me because I had tried to draw her out on the subject of pregnancy. *"Can't you ever talk about anything* important?" she had said. Perhaps the subject is a tender one with her.

"What do you mean?" I said. *"I thought you said the blands clean my room."*

"That's right," she said. Then, when I still looked perplexed, she explained as to a child, *"Blands aren't people."*

At first I thought it was a linguistic problem. *"I thought 'bland' was your name for a neuter worker,"* I said.

"That's right."

"Neuters aren't people?" I was dumbfounded.

She looked as if I were a hopeless imbecile.

"What are they, then?"

"They're . . . unfortunates. Children who never matured."

I was beginning to understand. "Are they mentally handicapped?"

"Yes," she said. "They're slow and childlike. They need looking after."

"I would like to see one."

She had barely been containing her frustration with me, and now it boiled over, hissing. "Why are you so interested in all the dirty, disgusting things? I thought you were going to want to know about our art and our thoughts and our culture. All you care about is what's gross and indecent."

I was perplexed and a little worried by this reaction. First, I had no notion how I had provoked it. The only subjects I had broached that morning were pregnancy and neuters. Neither one seemed particularly dirty or indecent to me; obviously, I was missing something. Second, I could sense another negative report on its way to Ovide. That in itself I could deal with, as long as it went no further. What I didn't want was for anything negative to get back to the First Contact team. My credibility isn't the best with them, and I don't want my chain jerked for no reason. So I opted for conciliation.

"I'm sorry, Annika. You've got to remember I'm still new here. I don't know a lot of things you take for granted. If I'm saying something offensive, you've got to tell me."

"Well, I did," she said, a little embarrassed now at her outburst.

"Thank you. And I do care about your art and thoughts and culture. At Magnus I went to an opera that taught me a lot. Maybe you can take me to some more."

"All right," she said, immediately brightening.

This led to an entire week of relentlessly high culture. It wasn't entirely useless. Art—representational art, at any rate—can be extremely informative, since it thrives on the clashes and inconsistencies that throw all custom into high relief.

Yet Annika was almost comically unable to relate the plays we saw to reality. To her, these were sources of cultural pride, not actual depictions of society. When I would question her about the actions of a character, she would say, "Those things didn't really happen."

"But they could have happened, couldn't they?"

"That's not the point. They're symbolic."

"What do they symbolize?"

"The greatness of our culture."

The girl is a dyed-in-the-wool chauvinist.

One day I managed to escape the clutches of Annika's cultural hegemony tour and made my way to the coffee house alone. The proprietor is a bustling, busy woman who is very friendly & curious about me. I managed to strike up a conversation with her. Seems she is not a patternist, but "factor" of a community that manages establishments of entertainment all over the convergence on a kind of franchise system. I.e. the restaurant actually belongs to her community, but she manages it and trains postulants (young people not yet firmly attached to an order or community) in the business. I asked her if the postulants did the washing up and cooking, and she laughed heartily. "No, the blands do the dirty work," she said.

"I've never seen one here," I said with interest.

"Good," she said, smiling a little nervously. "I don't want the customers losing their appetites."

Apparently the mere sight of a bland is enough to put one off one's feed. Now I was really curious. "But they do the cooking? Does everyone know that?"

"I expect so," she said a little reluctantly. "We're not a fancy place that can afford human chefs. People know, they just don't want their noses rubbed in it. But I keep my blands clean, let me tell you."

Since she had said "my *blands,"* I asked, *"Do they belong to you?"*

"Of course not." I could tell she was on the edge of being offended, and was making allowances for my outlandish ignorance. *"They belong to my community, same as I do."*

"Could I see them?"

Now she definitely turned frosty. *"I don't think so,"* she said. *"They're scared of you. If I let you in their space, I wouldn't get a lick of work out of them the rest of the day."*

"They know I'm here, and where I'm from?" I asked. She nodded. This might explain a great deal. *"Why are they scared?"*

"Don't ask me," she said, giving an exaggerated shrug. *"Who knows what notions get into their heads."*

I was going to ask something else, but she rose and said, *"I've got to get back to work."* Her manner had cooled considerably. Apparently I am fated to offend everyone here without knowing what I've done.

Since the damage was already done, though, I chanced one last question. *"Annika, my guide, says the blands clean my rooms, but I've never seen them, either in the room or in the hallways. Why is that?"*

She drew closer, apparently fearing the other customers would hear my question, and said in a low, hurried voice, *"I daresay you have a graydoor in your quarters."* When I shook my head, she added, *"Yes, you do,"* and left.

When I got home I searched carefully. I found it in the kitchen—a small, gray metal door I had taken for some kind of utility access panel. It had no knob or latch, and fit flush with the metal frame. I got a knife from one of the drawers and slid it into the crack to see if I could trip a latch or something. At that moment I heard a short exclamation behind me and turned to see Annika standing there, looking as horrified as if she'd discovered me butchering puppies.

"What are you doing?" she said.

It was perfectly obvious what I was doing, so I said, "Seeing if I can open this door."

"That's the graydoor!" she said, in a tone of utter disgust.

"I know," I said.

A variety of emotions crossed her face—horror, fear, repulsion. At last she burst out, "You are such a disgusting little man!" and stormed out of my quarters.

I was perplexed. I sat down in my lounge, still holding the knife, my self-image a little bruised by her description of me. I had clearly violated a behavioral code—one was apparently supposed to ignore the fact that neuters existed. But the intense emotion of her reaction seemed out of proportion.

I was almost relieved when Ovide sent a message calling me into her office. She offered me tea, then sat looking at me a little sadly, like a grandmother regarding an errant child. "I'm afraid I am going to have to replace Annika as your guide," she said.

"I swear I don't know what I did," I said. "Whatever it was, it wasn't deliberate. I'm sorry."

"It wasn't any one thing," Ovide said. "She just found the assignment too challenging to her notions of good behavior and good taste."

Meaning, of course, that I had behaved neither well nor tastefully. "Someone's got to explain these things to me," I said.

Ovide paused, then set her teacup down with care. "There are a lot of people here—Annika is one—who don't like to think about ugly or negative things. It's a quirk we have. Annika said that was all you ever wanted to talk about—the bad side."

I thought about it. In a way, she was right. "I like to look at conflicts and contradictions, because they illuminate so much about a culture," I said. "Where a culture is most *itself* is not in the areas where it is complacent, *but where it's under attack, either from outside or in. The boundaries where it has to defend itself, and so define itself.''*

"Our culture is not under attack,'' Ovide said, then added deliberately, *"unless it is from you.''*

"No!'' I said at once. *"Absolutely not. We have no desire to change you or meddle in any way. We only want to learn. What I'm saying, Ovide, is that every society has self-contradictions and seeds of instability in itself. I'm beginning to understand where a few of yours might lie.''*

She looked at me very seriously and said, *"We have a lot to learn from you, Magister. But remember, it's a dangerous thing you're doing, trying to probe beyond peoples' self-deceptions.''*

It was a remarkably perceptive thing for her to say, considering how little she'd known me. I said, *"I spent a long, hard time coming to understand my own self-deceptions.''*

"Are you the better for it?''

"Yes,'' I said. *"I was not a very good person, once.''*

"Well,'' she said, *"only we can decide what is good or bad for us, or what delusions we want to keep.''*

"Absolutely,'' I said. *"Only my ignorance has gotten me into trouble. As soon as I understand you, I swear I'll be a model citizen.''*

She smiled then, and I felt the screws loosening. She wasn't going to report me. We parted on good terms.

I think I have learned something important from Annika. Her reaction is more honest than anyone else's. I hit a nerve with her, one of those sensitive spots that reveal a tension point. But what is it?

I must be more on my guard.

Chapter Six

⚓ That evening after Deedee had gone to bed, Val joined Tedla in the studium. All day she had been half expecting WAC to show up, but there had not even been a call.

Tedla was sitting on the bed, legs drawn up. When Val sat down, the neuter gave her a fleeting smile. "What are you thinking about?" she said.

"The people from my planet," Tedla answered. "When do you think I can see them?"

"In a week, maybe," Val said. Less than four days were left for her. The passage of time made her anxious.

"Why so long?" Tedla said.

"You really want to see them, don't you?"

"Why does everyone doubt that? You've never been an exile. You don't know what it's like. I never thought I would hear my own language again, or talk to someone who knows . . . well, what to think of me."

Gently, Val said, "But Tedla, what they think is that you're not human."

"Yes, that's the point. I'm *not*. It's not that I dislike the way you are. You're just fine, for you. But I'm not like you."

"If you're not human, you sure do a damned good imitation of it."

"Yes, I know," Tedla said, leaning forward to look at

her seriously. "That's just it. It's an imitation. I've spent twelve years learning to pass as one of you. Learning how you talk, how you think. I can imitate you well by now. But that's all it is."

Val felt some misgivings. "Would you go back if you had the chance?"

It looked poised on a knife-edge. "You think I could?"

"It depends on the negotiations, I suppose. But if they reopen contact . . . it would be up to you and them, then."

Tedla let out a breath. It looked keyed up, expectant. "Of course I'd go back! For twelve years I haven't even dared to hope it could happen."

"I can't believe you'd want to, after what you told me last night," Val said.

"You don't understand."

"No. I don't. I'm not convinced this isn't just another self-destructive impulse."

Tedla looked taken aback. "I need to tell you more, then," it said.

"I'd like that," Val said. "I'd particularly like to know how you met Magister Galele."

"All right. But I have to tell you about another person first."

When Tedla looked down to collect its thoughts, Val hit the Record button on the terminal again. The red light flashed as Tedla began to speak.

❊ On the day I left Brice's, a random event changed the entire course of my life.

Mallow didn't feel well that morning. During the four-hour aircar trip to the Brice's agency at Magnus Convergence, it became sicker and sicker. By the time we arrived it was in such pain that the pilot dropped it off at a curatory. We later learned the verdict: appendicitis.

The illness would have been of no great consequence, except that Mallow had been scheduled to go to a patternist order at Tapis Convergence, and the elector herself, who was visiting Magnus on business, had been intending to take it back that day. The agents were in the embarrassing position of having to inconvenience the head of an order. They argued it over right in front of us as we waited in the loading dock for transport to our new assignments. At last they told the other three Personals—Whisper, Trice, and me—to wait till they had the problem sorted out.

We waited about two hours, watching the other Brice's blands disperse to the delivery vehicles, never to be seen by us again. I kept thinking of my reunion with Laki. At last a nervous, worried-looking young man came out and ordered us to follow him. We trooped through a door into human space. It made me uneasy, because we were still in our gray coveralls, our identity uncamouflaged.

The man led us into an office where two women were waiting. The one who rose to look us over was in questionary colors, with a sash of office. She was a small woman with a brisk and kindly manner. My eyes met hers for a second before I had a chance to drop my gaze decently to the floor.

"That one," she said decisively.

There was a whisper of papers, and the other woman said, "Tedla." The young man said something in an undertone, and she cleared her throat. "Oh. That's the one scheduled to go to the Polygrave's house."

"So?" the client said. There was a challenge in the word.

"It's . . . had special training, elector."

"All the better."

"You might not find it as satisfactory as the others."

"A Brice's bland? Not satisfactory?" the elector said.

The agent quickly changed tune. "All our blands are qualified. Take that one if it's what you want. We'll replace it if it doesn't work out."

"Good," the elector said, having gotten her way. The two agents conferred with each other in an undertone.

My world had just turned upside down. Everything I

had earned, everything I had started to count on, had been snatched away. I wasn't going to live at Magnus. I wasn't going to see Laki. I stared at the floor, feeling wronged.

They exchanged a few words about payment, then the elector took my papers and said, "Well, Tedla, follow me."

I did as I was told. I never saw Whisper or Trice again.

The elector led the way out to an aircar pad, where her private vehicle was waiting. I knew she wouldn't want to sit next to a neuter, so I found a spot on the floor of the luggage area in back, and strapped myself to the wall. We took off with a swoop that left my stomach on the ground. The elector glanced back at me, saw my bleached face, and said peremptorily to the pilot, "Go easy, Massower. You'll make the child sick."

I took heart a little from that. The elector seemed like a decent person, unlikely to mistreat her blands. But I still had mixed feelings about going to Tapis. I had grown up near there, and had actually been there once. But I dreaded the thought of meeting any of my creche-mates again. If any of them had stayed in the area after matriculation, and I was to be serving a prominent elector, then it was a horrible possibility.

We flew a long time straight into the westering sun. When I peered out the window, I saw grassland below us, mile upon mile stretching to the horizon, broken only by wrinkled, branching watercourses shaped like roots. I had never imagined so much grass in my life; it was like an ocean. The sun was on the horizon when we began to bank and descend in spirals, and I glimpsed below us a cleft in the prairie where a river rushed through a deep, shadowy gorge. On the plain at the edge of the canyon was a complex of aboveground buildings and a small airpad. There was nothing else: no lights, no vehicles, no sign of any habitation. Just grass.

When we were down and the pilot killed the engine, the silence was stunning. The elector began to unbuckle her straps, so I did the same. Timidly, I said, "Is this where I'm going to live?"

She turned around to look at me. "Yes. You are going to be serving a very great man who once did service to our order. He is one of the wisest and most learned men alive."

I was so bewildered by now that I couldn't think of another question. The pilot opened the door and the elector climbed out. I followed her.

The wind struck me right away, blustering against my ears and pushing me off balance. I was to learn it never stopped out here. I looked around; all seemed bleak and deserted—nothing but some round-topped sheds, a water tower, and grass.

An elderly bland was approaching us across the airpad, followed by another one in gray coveralls, pushing a luggage cart. The elector called out, "Pelch! I have a job for you." She took me by the shoulders and steered me firmly forward so the old bland could see me. It had a tight, curly mat of gray hair and mild, crinkled blue eyes. It took some gold-rimmed glasses from its pocket and put them on to survey me. It looked like a studious old elf.

"It's for the squire," the elector said, meaning me. "A personal valet. Do you think he'll be pleased?"

"I have no idea," Pelch said.

"Well, take it down and clean it up," she said. She handed Pelch her carrying bag. "These are the clothes I want it to wear. Call me when you're ready. I'll go see the squire now."

"He's in the river room," Pelch said.

A significant look passed between them, and she said with a note of concern, "Is he all right?"

Pelch merely shrugged. The elector walked off quickly.

"What's your name?" Pelch said, eyeing me skeptically.

"Tedla, sir," I said without thinking, then blushed. Its air of authority had made it seem human.

Pelch's eyebrows rose and it said drily, "We can do without the 'sir.'" I felt like a fool. "Well, come along, Tedla," it said with an air of taxed resignation. "I suppose we'll have to find room for you."

We descended a set of plain, poured-stone steps into the stark, utilitarian decor of grayspace. Pelch led me down a corridor with a plain tile floor, exposed ductwork, and harsh white lights. After a day of strange places, it seemed relaxing and homey, a space where I could be at ease. It even smelled of blands.

We came to a hygiene station where five or six shower-heads hung over open drains in the floor. "Wash yourself up," Pelch said, taking a rough, threadbare towel from a cupboard and hanging it on a hook for me. "Be sure to soap your hair." It left.

I did as I was told. As I was drying myself, another bland about my age peeked in curiously. It had a gnomish face with oversized ears and a huge mouth. When it grinned, I saw it had crooked teeth.

"Hello," I said.

"I'm Britz," it said. Its teeth whistled when it talked.

"I'm Tedla." I draped the towel around my neck and went to the bench where Pelch had left my new clothes in their sack. Britz looked on curiously as I took them out. There was a white silk shirt cut wide in the sleeves and ruffled at the neck; tight-fitting blue knee breeches with gold buckles; sheer stockings; and black polished shoes. The materials were very fine; they seemed too good for a bland.

"Am I really supposed to put these on?" I asked Britz, since there was no one else to ask.

"I suppose you could show up in a towel," it said.

It had a point. I had already put my coveralls down the laundry chute; this was my only choice. I sat down and started putting them on.

"What's your job, Britz?" I asked.

"I was the squire's Personal. Are you going to take over now?"

"I don't know. I don't know anything, even where I am."

"You're at Menoken Lodge."

That didn't enlighten me much. "How many blands work here?"

"In the household, just nine. But we're a working ranch. If you count the hands and herders, there are more than a hundred."

"How are you treated?"

Britz screwed up its face. "Not bad. Old Pelch is a worker bee. 'Are you getting *all* the dirt? In this household we *wax* the wood. How do you expect to meet the squire's standards if your work's no better than that?' " As it gave Pelch's words, Britz took on a pose of such perfect mimicry that I surprised myself by laughing.

"Who's your supervisor?" I said.

"Pelch."

"You mean you don't have a human supervisor?" This made me a little alarmed. I imagined a household of anarchy, disorganized blands running into each other.

"Just the squire, and he doesn't care what we do as long as he doesn't find out about it. Pelch pretty much runs things. Pelch has been with the squire all its life, and knows what he wants."

I had finished dressing, and stood up, feeling self-conscious in the finery.

"I'm supposed to bring you up to the demi-lounge when you're done," Britz said.

I followed it. We passed a bustling kitchen where five or six blands were at work. It seemed like a relaxed, busy place. We threaded up a metal stair to an unmarked door, where Britz knocked. Pelch quickly opened it. The old bland inspected me on the stair landing, and finding I met its standards, let me through into the small room on the other side.

I had clearly passed into human space. The room was decorated in teal and white. A huge couch was set against one wall; on the other was a massive mirror with a counter before it, and polished granite basins with shining spigots. The carpet felt bouncy as moss.

"Wait here," Pelch said severely, and left.

Alone, I sneaked over to the mirror to look at myself. The new clothes made me look tall and skinny. The effect would have been passably elegant, if it hadn't been for the frightened expression on my face.

The elector came in, filling the room with noise and presence, as humans do. She looked me up and down and said, "That's more like it. You've done wonders, Pelch!" She pursed her lips critically, fingering my hair. "Fetch a scissors. It looks too girlish. That may have been the Polygrave's taste, but it's not the squire's."

Pelch obediently produced the scissors, and I saw blond ringlets fall onto the blue carpet as she snipped. "There," she said with satisfaction when she was done. "It looks like a perfect young gentlebland." She smiled at her own witticism, since there was no one else in the room to appreciate it.

"What am I supposed to do?" I asked, quaking inside.

She said seriously, "Squire Tellegen is a noble but melancholy man. Your job will be to make his life pleasant and cheer him up in any way you can."

I had no coherent idea then why it seemed like such an impossible demand, or why I felt such a sense of despair at succeeding. Now, it seems simple: They wrench a child from the only home it has ever known, dehumanize it with abuse, whisk it bewildered to a place it's never seen—then ask it to cheer someone up. It defies common sense.

She led me out into the house. I had never seen such a beautiful place. We crossed a darkened, grottolike room. Its domed ceiling had a circular skylight that let in a bluish light from the fading sky outside. The walls were constructed as if from ruins overgrown with greenery. Rivulets of water ran down pebbled stream beds inset in the floor to the center of the room, where a sunken pool glowed with azure light, and lazy fish turned to and fro. The room was filled by the trickle of water and the smell of greenery.

The next room we entered was as dramatic as the first was subdued. Exposed wood beams jutted high into a cathedral ceiling. One whole wall was glass, rising twenty feet to the massive beams. That end of the room jutted out like the prow of a ship over the chasm where the river raced far below. Outside the glass, where a precarious balcony overhung the gorge, I could see mist rising against the fluted black cliffs opposite. We descended a staircase to a sunken area where furniture was arranged around a central fire pit. There was no one in the chairs. The only person in the room stood looking out the glass wall into the frightful black chasm beyond.

We came to a halt near the fireplace. "Prosper," the elector said, "I have brought you something."

The man at the window turned to us. He was elderly, but stood absolutely erect, with a poise and command that made me think he must have once been in charge. He was tall and lean, and his clothes were subdued but elegant. His eyes, when they fell on us, looked tired and passionless, like a hot fire that has burned down to coals.

The elector pushed me gently forward. "An addition to your staff. A personal valet. A trained one, this time."

The man's eyes narrowed as he focused on me. I saw the quick flash of intelligence in them. He glanced at the patternist behind me. He had figured something out about this situation that I didn't understand.

"What is it, a bland?" he said.

"Matriculated nine months ago, and straight from training at Brice's. You will be its first guardian."

His brows drew together angrily. "Ovide, what possessed you to bring this poor child here as if it were some sort of gift? Take it back where it belongs. I don't need another bland. This whole thing is abhorrent to me."

With all I had been through that day, this last rejection struck me like a blow. Hopelessness whirled up in my brain. What did they do with blands rejected by their guardians? Was I never going to have a home?

The elector's hand had been resting lightly on my shoulder; now her grip tightened. "Stop jumping to conclusions, Prosper. You've completely misunderstood. I was at Magnus today, at the Brice's agency, when I learned that this bland was slated to go to the Polygrave's house as a Personal. I know the Polygrave. Believe me, you will be saving it from a very unpleasant life if you will just be my accomplice and take it in."

I knew it was a lie—she had picked me before ever hearing of the Polygrave, and never would have seen me if it hadn't been for Mallow's illness. But the tale was close enough to the truth that I would have no trouble remembering it.

I couldn't tell whether he believed her. He hesitated, as if debating whether to resist, then gestured me to come over to where a lamp cast a pool of light on the floor. I went, emotions battling in my tired mind. He studied my face in the light. I snatched a look at his own face. He had once been a handsome man, but now looked wan and neglected.

"Brice's, eh?" he said to me. "I visited there once, years ago, when old Brice was still alive. He had some very advanced ideas about training blands. He always demanded the best from them. It was a good place, then." He paused as if waiting for me to say something.

"It's still a good place, sir," I said.

"They trained you to be at ease with humans, did they?"

"Yes, sir."

With a gentle touch on my chin, he tilted my face toward the light. "Such beauty," he said softly. "What a waste for the world. And a burden for you."

Despite all my training, our eyes met. I stood there

transfixed, feeling that he saw into my soul, and understood every particle of my being. There was compassion in his face, but it wasn't just for me. It was for all blands, all humans, caught in this terrible trap together. His eyes wandered away toward the black precipice outside the window. His sadness seemed to fill the air, like silence.

At last he turned back to me. I had recovered my manners, and my eyes were decently downcast. He said, "What's your name, child?"

"Tedla, sir."

"Would you like to stay here?"

"Yes, sir. Very much."

"All right, then. I could use a Personal with some training. Britz is not adequate, despite all Pelch can do." His voice sounded resigned, but when I stole an anxious look at him, he smiled kindly. "Go down and have them feed you. Pelch will explain your duties in the morning."

I turned away in time to catch the look of satisfaction on the elector's face.

That night I was so tired that I fell asleep as soon as I hit the roundroom floor, and never even stopped to think that I was sleeping in a pile of perfect strangers.

It was different the next morning, when I was wakened by the stirring of the others around me. I looked around and didn't recognize a single face. The roundroom itself was drab and threadbare, and the neuters around me all seemed old, slow, and work-worn.

I spied Britz then, still asleep. One of the old neuters was poking it with a foot, and Britz was pretending not to notice. I crawled over to it. "Britz," I whispered, "you've got to show me what to do."

One eye came open. "Oh, Tedla," Britz mumbled. "Am I glad you're here." Then it suddenly sat up in a panic. "Oh my god, I've got to get the squire's coffee! Why does he have to get up so early?" It scrambled out of the roundroom into the hygiene station, but by then all the showers were taken by the older blands, who gave Britz an "it serves you right" look and took their time. We stood and waited, Britz fidgeting impatiently.

"Can't you just skip the shower?" I whispered.

"No, Pelch inspects us."

I noticed then that Pelch had not been among us in the roundroom. "Where is Pelch?" I asked.

"It has a private room, with a bed," Britz said significantly. "Says the roundroom is bad for its back."

I had never heard of a bland sleeping in a private room before.

One of the showers finally opened up, and we crowded in together, soaping each other down quickly. Britz then snatched a suit of threadbare livery from a locker and began to put it on hurriedly. I had left the fine clothes from yesterday lying on a bench, but now I found them hanging neatly in a locker. I put them on, but simplified the jacket by ripping off some gold trim. It looked too gaudy for my taste. I was hurrying down the hallway after Britz when Pelch came out of a door and stopped me.

"Where do you think you're going, dressed like that?" it demanded.

"I was going to help Britz," I said uncertainly.

"Oh, no you don't," Pelch said. "I don't want you learning bad habits from that scamp. You stay down here till I've had a chance to teach you how the job ought to be done." Pelch headed for the kitchen then, and so I followed. It didn't seem like the time to say that I already knew how the job ought to be done.

I stood watching, feeling useless, as the kitchen blands prepared breakfast. They worked smoothly together, as if they had practiced this routine a thousand times. Scarcely a word was exchanged. Meanwhile, Pelch was making up the day's menus and checking the inventories of food, using an electronic scroll. Watching it, I had a hunch no one ever got away with stealing food from these cupboards.

Britz came flying down the stairs in a panic, saying there

was no cream upstairs. One of the kitchen blands silently handed it an earthenware jar of cream, and it started upstairs again. "Britz!" Pelch called out severely. "Use the silver."

"Oh, right," Britz said, backtracking to get a silver creamer. No one said anything, but they were all shaking their heads.

After the humans had eaten breakfast—there were apparently only the two of them in the house—we sat down around the large wood-block table to eat. The food was good, and plentiful, but the company was silent. Pelch eyed Britz and me critically as we ate, and finally said, "I can tell we're going to have to increase the food budget, with two voracious children in the house." Britz nudged me and rolled its eyes in a "don't pay any attention" signal.

After breakfast the blands dispersed to their duties. Pelch said, "I suppose I'd better get you doing something useful."

The old bland led the way upstairs through the blandruns. The house was laid out in three levels—public rooms on the top, private human quarters in the middle, and grayspace on the bottom. Because it was built into the cliff, the rooms on the east side had windows. Pelch paused at a graydoor and peered through the hole; finding the coast clear, it led me into a large bedroom that looked out over the gorge. Now that it was day, I could see that the house was placed at a curve of the river, looking upstream toward a vista of waterfalls and rapids framed by black cliffs. The view was dramatic and gloomy to my eyes.

The bedroom itself was as beautiful as every other human room in the house, decorated sparely with black enamel furniture. The ceiling was an abstract in stained glass, backlit with piped light. At the moment the room was rather disheveled—the bed unmade, clothes and towels strewn about. "You can straighten this up when we've finished," Pelch said.

Our first stop was a guided tour of the closets. The squire's taste in clothes was elegant but a little out of date. Every garment was of the highest quality, but some of it was in a shocking state of disrepair and neglect. Pelch explained how the squire liked to match his colors and fabrics. In the midst of the lecture it broke off and said, "You won't be able to live up to his standards, you know. He is very particular. No bland has ever satisfied him since I was his Personal."

Timidly, I said, "When was that?"

"I've been serving him for forty years," Pelch said proudly. "I was only a little older than you when I became his Personal, and he was in his twenties."

"Why did he have a Personal then?" I asked.

Pelch seemed quite pleased at the chance to tell the story. "He was a prodigy. Do you know what that means? A genius. Geniuses have a way of burning themselves out, so his order gave me to him, to make sure he ate and slept and didn't have to worry about things." Pelch's eyes took on a gleam of reminiscence. "I lived through some wild years at the beginning. He was involved with a group of artists then—they called themselves the Sensualists. They were an unruly bunch, full of passions, but they changed the face of art.

"But the movement fell apart, or the artists did, and Squire Tellegen moved on to write about ethics and legal reforms. We lived in Magnus for ten years, in the very heart of power. I served meals to all the great mattergraves and electors with these hands, when he was working for reform. They all looked up to him. But then the politics changed, and he was no longer so welcome, so we moved out here."

"Why does he run a ranch?" I said. It seemed very peculiar for a great social reformer.

"Oh, the order had somehow inherited the place, and he wanted the peace and quiet, so they let him live here. The ranching is only a hobby. He's waiting here, and working. Some day the electors will change their minds about him, and he'll go back to the world in glory."

I could see that this last was a cherished notion of Pelch's. I had now formed a picture of this oddly unblandlike bland—resourceful, passionately loyal, resentful of a world that didn't appreciate its guardian properly. And jealous of youthful upstarts usurping its place. For all its good qualities, Pelch was going to be an obstacle to me.

We went on into the luxurious bathroom, and Pelch described the squire's schedule. "He rises very early, but don't you disturb him then—he likes to meditate and write. At seven he takes coffee. He then dresses for breakfast, and dines with his guests, if any. He spends the rest of the morning in the studium. Lunch is served in the morning room. In the afternoon he takes care of ranch business, and may need you to dress him and bring his gear if he goes out riding. He bathes and shaves just before dinner. Dinner is always formal, even on days when there are no guests. But usually there are. People come from all over the world to visit him. You will treat them all as if they were mattergraves. No giggling or horseplay."

The thought was so inconceivable that I said, "They did teach me how to serve humans."

"Oh, yes," Pelch said with disdain. "Brice's, or some fancy place like that. Well, we have our own standards here."

Pelch gave me a long lecture on the squire's habits and tastes then. I later discovered that nearly all of it was wrong. Perhaps once it had been right, but people change with time, and blands don't. Pelch still thought of the squire as the young man it had once served.

"Does the squire ever travel?" I asked.

Instead of answering, Pelch said indignantly, "Who told you to call him that?"

"What?" I said, confused. "Everyone calls him squire."

"That's just a nickname, something his friends use. To

you, he's Prosper Tellegen Lexigist. You can call him Lexigist Tellegen.''

I knew it was ridiculous, but I said, ''All right.''

''He goes to Tapis maybe twice a year, but it's me he takes with him. He went to Magnus before the current regime came in.''

I was beginning to think my training would be wasted here, but that was the humans' business. All I could do was what they told me.

There was an alcove off the bedroom, hidden by a standing screen. Pelch said, ''Don't you go in there. That's the squire's devotional. He is a very spiritual man.''

Although it spoke with the same pride as always, there was an anxious note in the old bland's voice. It struck me then that there was a risk for a human who took his religion too seriously. Justification had to be an anxious time not just for the humans but for those who loved them as well. And there was not a doubt in my mind that Pelch loved Squire Tellegen with all its heart.

Pelch left soon after, and I spent the morning straightening up the bedroom and going through the closets, sorting out the clothes that needed attention. At the end, the group of clothes I considered fit to wear was pitifully small. There was a whole collection of shirts with ink stains on the cuffs and sleeves. I took an armload and headed down to the laundry.

There was a lone bland working in the laundry, tall and lean and moving as slowly as if its veins ran with syrup. We had slept together the night before, but I introduced myself anyway. It looked at me dully, paused a long time, then said its name was Scamper. Obviously, the name was someone's idea of a joke.

I showed it the shirts. It looked at them like a sleepwalker, then said, ''Those are clean.''

''They've got ink stains,'' I said.

It shrugged. ''Machines don't get ink out.''

"No, you have to pretreat the stains. Don't you have any alcohol-based solvents?"

It looked at me as if I were speaking some alien language.

"Where's your supply cabinet?" I asked. It acted like it didn't understand. I spotted the supply cabinet and asked, "Can I look?" Scamper shrugged and turned away as if the problem were no longer its concern. I finally found the proper solvent in a bottle crusty with age. I sprayed it on a shirt, watched the ink stain dissolve, blotted it away, then took the result to Scamper. "See?" I said. "It works really well."

Scamper didn't react. I left the pile of shirts and the bottle sitting next to them, and went upstairs again. When I came back down to prepare for serving lunch, Pelch cornered me in the hallway and said angrily, "What do you mean by coming down here and passing out orders to the other blands?"

I was astonished. "I didn't pass out any orders. I just asked Scamper to clean some shirts. I thought that was its job."

"You don't decide what other blands' jobs are," Pelch said severely. "I'm the only one that passes out assignments here."

"I'm sorry," I said.

At Brice's they had spent months teaching us how to get along with humans, but not a word about getting along with other blands. I was beginning to realize that the latter task could be far more complicated. At least our relationship to the humans was well defined.

Pelch wouldn't let me serve lunch. Instead, we stood together in the serving-pantry, watching while Britz served. Pelch gave a running commentary on all the things Britz was doing wrong. The surveillance made Britz very nervous, and it got muddled and clumsy. I couldn't imagine what the humans were thinking. The climax came when

Britz was clearing away plates and let a dirty fork drop so it stuck in the elector's hair.

There were four guests coming for dinner. After the debacle at lunch, Pelch decided that I would assist Britz. I was still not considered trustworthy enough to appear before the humans, but Pelch was grudgingly ready to concede I might know how to organize the dishes and brew the coffee.

"That Pelch makes me crazy," Britz said to me when we were alone. "It's always trying to interfere. It'll never leave me alone."

With good reason, I thought silently.

"Did you get the lecture about the good old days?" Britz said, grinning. Then it launched on a mimicry of Pelch. "Why, forty years ago I served his food and washed his clothes and cleaned his quarters all by myself, with just these two hands. Blands *worked* in those days."

I was still laughing when I said, "Listen, Britz. If Pelch doesn't horn in at dinner tonight, would you let me serve?"

Britz's eyes grew big. "*Let* you? I'd *pay* you to do it. I hate serving. They're always glaring at me."

"All right, then."

While Britz was dressing the squire for dinner (Pelch didn't trust me to do that, either), I went into the dining room to check everything out. The table was set all wrong, so I quickly rearranged it. No one had thought to chill the wine or slice lemons for the water, so I hunted up an ice bucket and ran down to the kitchen for the lemons myself. Then I rearranged the serving dishes in the pantry so we could get at them easier.

Dinner didn't go as smoothly as I wanted, but compared to lunch, it was elegant. When the humans were seated and I appeared with the wine, Squire Tellegen's eyebrows rose a hair, but he said nothing. I poured in the proper order, by rank—which I deduced from their clothing, as I had been taught. I then followed with the water and fruit, ghosting around the table so they scarcely noticed my presence. The fact that their conversation never paused showed me that my timing was right. As I poured his coffee after the meal, Squire Tellegen said to me in an undertone, "I see Pelch already has you hard at work."

"Yes, sir," I said, my eyes downcast.

The next morning Pelch had its weekly conference with the squire, and came down bristling. Britz had had the presence of mind to disappear, so Pelch turned on me. "Who gave you permission to serve dinner?"

"Was there a complaint?" I asked innocently. If Pelch had been a human supervisor, I never would have dared a retort like that; but it wasn't.

"I expect you to do what I tell you from now on," Pelch said.

"I will," I said.

With an ill grace, it said, "The squire wants you to dress him for dinner tonight. And you will serve again."

"Yes, Pelch," I said.

I had won the first round.

That afternoon when the squire came to his bedroom for grooming, he seemed very sad and pensive. I had his bath drawn and waiting—hot, the way Britz said he liked it, but lavender-scented the way *I* liked it. When I offered to undress him he waved me away absently, so I stood by in silence and took his clothes as he dropped them, checking them as I put them into the closet or laundry chute. He went into his bath and I laid out his dinner clothes, the shoes freshly shined and the buttons polished. When I went into the bathroom he looked startled, so I said, "Would you prefer me to wait outside, sir?"

"No, no, go about your duties," he said. So I busied myself heating his towels and preparing the shaving tools. When he stepped out of the bath, I was waiting with the heated towel. He said hesitantly, "I took this all for granted once. Now it seems quite decadent."

"Hasn't Britz been serving you properly?" I asked, turning away to mix the shaving lather.

"Britz is a normal bland," he said. "It did the minimum it could get away with."

I smiled to myself at the implication that I was different.

I turned around with the razor to indicate I was ready to shave him. He had wrapped the towel self-consciously around his waist, and was looking at me apprehensively. "You're trained to shave, are you?" he said.

"Yes," I said, startled that he would think otherwise. With a visible effort, he sat down on the edge of the shaving ledge. "All right," he said. "Be careful."

"Have you been shaving yourself?" I asked, astonished.

"For ten years or more," he said, glancing at me with a shadow of amusement.

"You must be very good at it," I said, checking his face critically.

"One does get that way."

I motioned him to lie down. "It's easier for me," I explained. He did as I told him. At first he was very tense, but as he realized I wasn't going to slit his throat, he relaxed. When I had finished his face, I draped a hot, scented washcloth over it so his pores would absorb the moisture, and stood looking down at him. He hadn't had a body shave in a very long time. I knew it was my duty to do it, but what had happened at Brice's made me reluctant to offer a service so sensual. Making my voice very cool and professional, I said, "Would you like a body shave?"

He dragged the cloth off his face to look at me. I couldn't meet his eyes. Gently, he said, "Another day, perhaps."

I smiled at him, feeling light as air at the reprieve. "Tomorrow I'll give you a manicure," I said decisively.

I helped dress him—fastening cuffs, pinning on his medals, slipping on his shoes with the tortoiseshell shoehorn. When we were done, I stood back to inspect him. He was terribly elegant, and very handsome in my eyes—

thick gray hair, a high, intellectual forehead, a long, straight nose, and decisive chin. He smiled at me and said, "Do I meet your approval? May I go down now?"

I had forgotten one thing. I whirled around and snatched up the bluebird feather I had found to decorate his lapel. It was the only modern, stylish touch in his conservative appearance. I tucked it in, then stood back to admire the effect. Very gravely, he laid his hand on his chest and bowed to me, and I broke out laughing. He touseled my hair with a smile, then we parted—he to his guests, me to the dining room to prepare.

During dinner, one of his female guests commented on the feather he still wore in his lapel.

"Ah, yes," he said. "Nasatir tells me it's very stylish. I can't take credit for it—it was my new bland's idea. I can tell this one's going to spoil me rotten."

"Well, it's about time *someone* spoiled you," the woman said warmly.

As we were cleaning up from dinner, I asked Pelch, "Has he ever had a partner?"

"Dozens," Pelch said, glad as always to share its superior knowledge. "When he was young, he had so many admirers he could have his choice. Later, he settled down. For ten years, at Magnus, he lived with a young man who was his protégé. It nearly broke his heart when that one left for a more powerful patron. He's been alone ever since."

I wondered if that accounted for his sadness.

It also gave me a twinge of anxiety. It occurred to me that perhaps celibacy was one gap in his life that the elector had arranged for a Brice's bland to fill. I simply couldn't know—nothing would ever be stated out loud, even if that was the expectation of me. That evening, I had to steel myself to go up to his room to prepare his bed and warm his robe.

When he came in, he seemed tired and preoccupied. He sat on the edge of the bed and let me take his shoes off, then slowly began to shed the rest of his formal wear. After several minutes of silence he said, "Are you sad, Tedla?"

"No, sir," I said.

He sat there looking at me with his cravat half untied. "This afternoon you seemed so gay, it was like hearing a snatch of music I'd almost forgotten. But now you're very quiet. They've made you welcome, haven't they? Pelch has been good to you?"

"Yes, sir," I said.

"Then what is it?" He reached out and took my hand, and sat looking at it against the aged skin of his own hand. "How long have you been a bland?" he asked, looking up into my face.

"Nine months, sir."

"Are you used to it?"

It was the most astonishing question he could have asked me. Coming at me like that, it woke a wave of confusion inside me. I had thought I was quite reconciled to my state—happy, even. But when he asked me, my body answered for me, and tears started to my eyes. "No, sir," I said.

He sat there looking at me as if his heart were hurting. He reached up to wipe a tear from my cheek with his thumb. "Poor child," he said softly. "I wish there were something I could do for you."

I fought to get control of myself again. My supervisors at Brice's would have scolded me for being so blandlike as to break down in tears in front of my guardian. I pressed my mouth together and took his jacket to the closet. He undressed silently and put on his robe, then turned to his bed. I finished putting away his clothes, then stood there, still not knowing if he would want me sexually, but sensing that if it came at all, it would come now. He looked at me from his bed, hesitated, then said, "That's all, Tedla. I'll see you in the morning."

"Thank you, sir," I said. Once I was on the other side of the graydoor I leaned against it, weak with relief and gratitude. He didn't want me that way. It wasn't going to be part of my duties.

I think that was the moment I started falling in love with him.

I soon began to stake out my territory among the other blands. There were jobs and areas of the house where I, as the squire's Personal, was unquestionably in charge, subject only to Pelch—the bedroom, the dining rooms, the serving pantries. I soon began to rearrange things the way I wanted them. Britz was quite willing to accommodate me, but some of the other blands were very set in their ways, and resisted any change to their routine. I learned to wheedle them, and joke, and reason, and if all else failed I went to Pelch. Pelch usually received my suggestions with an ill-humored scowl and a lecture about how I ought to know my place. Then, if I was right, I usually got my way.

Pelch and I ought to have been allies. We shared a lot of things—intelligence, high standards, and a desire to make our guardian happy. My arrival had even eased Pelch's life by taking a large burden off its mind. Once it figured out that I knew what I was doing, the old bland pretty much left me to manage the squire's comfort and turned its attention to other aspects of running the house. But even though we reached a guarded truce, Pelch's jealousy constantly got in the way of our really liking one another.

Here on Capella Two I've learned that all human societies contain competing camps. In other cultures, the lines of division usually fall along gender or kinship or rank. Among us blands, the divisions were all by age. Britz and I, the youngsters, were much more energetic and flexible and curious than the older blands. We were constantly getting warnings about our boldness and impertinence. I attributed it all to neuter timidity till one day Mimbo, a wizened old bland in the kitchen, rolled up its sleeve and

showed me the scars on its arm—hard, ropy skin, dead
and white. "You know what that is?" it said. "That's
where a supervisor held my arm in a pot of hot oil because
he thought I was being sassy. When I was your age, they
could do that to blands, and nobody cared."

It shocked me into silence. Pelch, who was nearby, said
to me, "You've got Squire Tellegen to thank that people
can't do that to you. He was the one who got them to pass
laws against abuse of blands. You'd have no legal protection today if it wasn't for him."

It was the first inkling I'd had that there were laws protecting me. Up to then, I had assumed that nothing held
humans back but their natural goodness.

The blands seldom liked to talk about the old days, but
now and then they would get started among themselves,
and Britz and I would listen, frozen to our seats in horror.
I learned that there had once been a sport called skeering,
where humans set a bad neuter loose in the woods and
hunted it down with throwing-knives. The climax was always the butchering, which was done not by the humans
but by blands they'd brought along, to teach them a lesson.
No bland was allowed to come back from a skeering until
its hands were soaked in blood.

After hearing this, I understood their caution better, but
I still couldn't help being irritated by it. After all, things
like that didn't happen any more. They didn't need to live
their lives slinking around in fear.

By Brice's standards, none of the blands at Menoken
Lodge worked very hard. The older ones had learned to
draw out their duties to take up the maximum amount of
time. But Britz and I were often able to finish our jobs
early and have some freedom. No one cared what we did
then, as long as we stayed away from the humans. We
explored all the bland-runs in the house, and risked life
and limb scrambling on the cliffs outside. But our favorite
thing was to go to the barns, where they kept the machinery and horses for working the ranch.

Squire Tellegen was only symbolically in charge of the ranch—there were three other humans who supervised the ranch blands. The ranchers rarely ate with the squire or mixed with his guests, not being the same rank of human. And we household blands almost never mixed with the ranch blands. They had a roundroom in one of the outbuildings, but most of their time was spent on the range, tending the herds. They seemed like strange, weathered, laconic creatures to Britz and me. I'm sure we seemed quite pampered and soft to them. We often wheedled the stable hands to let us pet and feed the horses, and we naively envied their jobs.

I found that my own job called for some ingenuity at manipulating humans. As soon as I completed my inventory of the squire's closet, I brought the dire situation there to his attention.

"You need new clothes," I said to him.

He dismissed the suggestion with a wave of the hand. "No, I don't. I've got too many as it is."

"They're all worn and stained and ten years old," I said. "I don't know how I'm going to keep you dressed the way you ought to be."

"Learn to reject vanity," he said philosophically.

Since he was in a good mood, I said, "It's not vanity. It's decency."

"Give it up, Tedla," he said. "I am not asking the order to spend any money on clothes for me; they have too many other demands to satisfy. Use your ingenuity. I'm sure you have some."

I thought it over, and decided he'd given me permission to solve the problem. The next time Elector Hornaday came to visit—as she did almost weekly—I maneuvered to catch her alone in the hall before dinner. I couldn't initiate a conversation, but I gave her a significant look which prompted her to say kindly, "How are things going, Tedla?"

"He needs new clothes," I blurted out. "And he won't ask you."

"Really?" she said, a little skeptical. "I'm surprised Pelch hasn't been nagging my ear off."

"Pelch is busy supervising blands," I said.

"Well, make a list of what he needs. Be specific. Put down colors and sizes. Can you do that?"

"Yes, ma'am," I said. I hesitated, and she looked at me curiously. "Please don't tell him," I said.

She smiled. "All right. It'll be our secret."

The next time she came, I slipped her the list, and she winked at me conspiratorially. Within a week, a huge shipment of boxes arrived with most of what I had asked for. Pelch was puzzled by the delivery, and asked me what I knew about it. I played dumb, but reported that Elector Hornaday had been criticizing his clothes at dinner. Pelch shrugged at the unaccountable acts of humans, and said, "Well, take it all up to his closet."

"Can I get rid of some of the tattered old things he's wearing?" I asked.

"Yes, of course," Pelch said. "You ought to keep an eye on his clothes. He never knows when he needs new ones."

"Yes, Pelch," I said obediently.

The squire never even noticed.

Or perhaps he did, and just kept it to himself. He watched my gradual settling-in with a great deal more interest than I had expected from a guardian. My disdain for blandlike sloppiness seemed to give him a sort of tolerant amusement. "You are a philosophical curiosity, Tedla," he said to me one day. I hadn't the faintest notion what he meant, and looked at him askance. He said, "Fifty years ago, a bland like you could not have existed. It gives me pleasure to think I have helped create a world in which you could come to be."

It was a little disconcerting to be treated as an individual again. He watched my moods and sometimes even asked what I was thinking, as if blands thought. It threw me off my balance.

I watched him, too, of course. Much of what I saw concerned me. To me, Menoken Lodge was a glorious haven. To him, it was a prison. He was being eaten away inside by a parasite of loneliness.

He spent a great portion of his day reading, thinking, and writing. When he came up for grooming and dressing, he was sometimes preoccupied and pensive, scarcely noticing my presence; at other times, he would talk to me about something he was thinking—learned subjects far over my head, to which I could only respond with an occasional polite "Yes, sir," or "I see." I could tell he was pining for human companionship. There came days on end when there would be no visitors, and he grew restless and bored. When someone would finally show up for dinner, he would be vivacious and lively for an evening; when they left, he would subside into an irritated melancholy.

I asked him once why he didn't go visit the convergence—he seemed to long for it so. He said, "I have chosen seclusion. I need to be away from the distractions of urban life and social prominence. I've done all that; now is my time for quiet."

And yet, he fretted. He had a coterie of core admirers who came over and over, and whom I got to know well. At least three of them were ardently in love with him. He knew it, too—he would lead them on with warmth and charm all evening, and then just as some real intimacy seemed imminent, he would withdraw, and retreat to his lonely room. It drove them to distraction, but they always came back. I think he needed them. He needed to feel admired and loved; he drew sustenance from it. But always he had to be their impossible dream—floating just beyond their reach, remote and unattainable.

They often begged him to come back to Tapis, and end his exile. He needed to hear that, too. In fact, when they hadn't said it recently, he would angle for it, leading the conversation in such a way that they would have to say it again. Then he would smile and decline graciously, saying he needed the peace to work on his book.

One night after he had entertained a group of visiting younger scholars from Paltrow Convergence who had come to meet the great man, he sat on the edge of his bed with his head in his hands, lost in dejection. I stood by waiting for him to undress, but he seemed unaware of my presence. "I have become so irrelevant," he said, ostensibly to me, but really to himself. "Everything has moved on without me. It doesn't matter that I exist any more."

His words struck fear into me. It was still a month before his justification was due, but they were the words of a man who has no intention of living for another year. I saw the precarious security I had attained evaporating under my feet. I sat down beside him on the bed, feeling hollow inside. He looked up, as if startled to find me there.

"It matters to *me* that you exist," I said.

It was a terribly presumptuous thing to say. But he did not get angry. Instead, he looked at me with a kindness that made me ache inside. "The loyalty of a bland is a terrible test of our humanity," he said softly.

The next month, shortly before justification, he decided to go out and oversee the roundup and branding of the new calves. He called me into the library and said, "Tedla, do you know how to ride?"

"No, sir," I said.

"Well then, I'm going to ask Jimmicky to give you some lessons. I will need you with me to help around camp."

"Yes, sir," I said.

I was terribly excited at the prospect of learning to ride a horse and camp out. Even Pelch had to smile at my eagerness. Pelch had been out to the roundup many times.

"You don't mind my going, do you, Pelch?" I asked.

"No," it said. "I'm too old for it. He is, too, only he won't admit it. I'm going to give you a medicine kit for when he finds out. He'll be pretty crabby on the second day.''

I got reams of other advice from Pelch—how to set up the tent, prepare his bed, handle his washing and grooming. I wouldn't have to cook, for which I was grateful, but I would be in charge of the squire's coffee, tea, and liquor. I knew how trusted I had become that they let me have the liquor. Usually, it is kept strictly locked away from blands. In fact, it's a tradition that if any bland can get ahold of alcohol, the whole roundroom is entitled to go on a binge. A roundroom full of drunken neuters is not a sight most humans find amusing.

Jimmicky was one of the stablehands Britz and I had pestered—a soft-spoken bland who knew all the horses as if they were a roundroom, and felt as shy and uncomfortable with other blands as most blands feel with humans. Since we had only three days before leaving, my lessons amounted to no more than how to stay on top and keep the horse from taking advantage of me. Jimmicky itself was coming along to saddle and feed and groom. Mine was to be a good-natured bland-horse (as we call a gelding), prettily striped, yellow and chocolate. When it first came out to meet me, the creature looked enormous—the stirrups were nearly at eye level, and I couldn't imagine how I was going to get up. When the animal nuzzled me with its nose, smelling my pockets for treats, it nearly knocked me over. In monosyllables, Jimmicky taught me how to greet my horse. Our horses are very intelligent; there are sounds that are like a language to them. Skilled riders don't even need reins—they just guide their horses with whistles and clicks.

We set out very early in the morning, when the grass was still dewy, so that we left a broad trampled track behind us, a dark swathe in the silver. The squire rode ahead on his tall red mare, and Jimmicky and I rode behind, our horses loaded down with equipment. The animals all seemed frisky and excited to be getting out, and it was hard not to catch the feeling. The sky was a pale blue with high, windblown clouds. Our path lay westward through low, rolling hills sprinkled with a dusting of flowers. The wind was at our backs.

When we paused at midmorning to rest, the sun was beating down, and the scent of hot sage was all around us. Stretching my legs as the squire drank his coffee, I found a patch of prairie flowers, where hundreds of tiny white butterflies were feeding. When I walked through, they all rose around me like an upside-down snowfall, and I was bathed in white wings. I laughed, imagining how they must tickle the flowers.

When I returned to the camp, I found that Squire Tellegen had been watching me. His smile was shadowed by a look of loss. "If only that joy of first discovery were still in me," he said when I sat down beside him. "You are so much more alive than I, just from having lived less. It's as if my substance has become stretched, thinned out with each passing year, leaving no room for wonder."

When we resumed our travel, he called me up to ride beside him. He had become bored with solitude, and wanted to talk. "Tell me what you see," he said. "I want to see this land through your eyes."

At first I was reluctant. He was such a deep thinker, I knew that bland-talk wouldn't hold his interest. I couldn't begin to speak with all the allusions and nuances of his learned friends.

When he figured out what I was thinking, he laughed. "Believe me, Tedla, I get very bored with learned discourse. It becomes predictable after a while, moving by its own tenets and forms. It will be refreshing to hear something simple."

"Blands are simple all right," I said.

"I meant uncomplicated," he said, looking at me closely. "But perhaps I misspoke. I don't think you're uncomplicated, Tedla. In fact, you are more of a mystery to me than most humans."

He had made me feel self-conscious, so I tried to distract him by doing as he had asked, and turning his attention to the landscape.

Looking out from the hayloft at Menoken Lodge, I had thought the prairie was a bleak land, unvarying, without landmark or interest. Now that I was out in it, I saw I had been wrong. The grass was all shifting currents of color. In most places it was a bleached, grayish green—but then the wind would come along and press it into silver. There were streaks of umber and pale yellow flowing around the hills, and deep green in the hollows.

"All the colors have meanings," Tellegen said to me when I had pointed it out. "A true plainsman knows what they all signify, and can read the landscape. He can know what lies underneath the ground the way a cook knows whether the dish is done from the color of the surface. To him, the vegetation reveals water, and type of soil, and even buried things abandoned by the ancients thousands of years ago."

"Can *you* see those things?" I asked.

"No," he said. "The only landscape I can read below the surface is the terrain of words."

From far away, the hills all looked lush and velvety, and I imagined lying down on them, cushioned on a luxurious carpet of grass. But whenever we came up to them, they were covered with the same sharp, dry grass as grew everywhere else, and the ground was infested with tiny cactus and sand burrs. There was something frustrating about it: We kept riding toward soft hills in the distance, but up close our daily journey was nothing but prickles.

Tellegen laughed when he heard this. "Are you suggesting it's a metaphor for life, Tedla?" he asked.

"I don't even know what a metaphor is," I said, though in fact I did.

"Well, think about this, then: You *can* lie down on man-made grass. We've bred it and changed it so it makes our lives soft and pleasant for us, but the price is, it needs us to survive. Tame grass would die out here. You can tell this grass is natural because it's unyielding. All life is the same way. Even people.''

We talked about a thousand crazy things like that. I gradually lost my self-consciousness and my fear that he would laugh at me. It became a kind of game: I would make an observation, he would turn it into a parable or conundrum before my eyes. He seemed heartily amused, and the long, hot afternoon passed swiftly.

The shadows were beginning to make the contours of the land dramatic when we came to a shallow, pebbly river. There was a grassy ledge nearby, and there Squire Tellegen instructed us to pitch the camp. Jimmicky and I worked at setting up the tent, caring for the horses, fetching water, and starting the fire while he strolled down to the river, writing in a notebook. Jimmicky said to me in a low voice, "Does he always pester you this way?"

"No," I said. "He's bored, with no one to talk to."

Jimmicky shook its head. "I'm glad I don't have your job."

I hadn't considered it an onerous duty to talk to him, but now it struck me that most blands would. For a moment I felt uncertain that I had acted right. Then I thought to myself, Pelch would have talked to him. That made me feel more confident.

Jimmicky fixed the squire's dinner first, and we waited till he had eaten it, then fixed our own. Afterwards, when I brought him some coffee, he was shuffling a game of cards he had brought along. He said, "Sit down, Tedla. I need a partner."

"I can't do that, sir," I said. "It's too hard."

"Don't worry, I'll teach you."

"I'm too old," I said.

He broke out laughing. "You, old?"

I was a little annoyed at his deliberate misunderstanding. "I mean, too old to learn new things. I've been a bland more than a year now." He knew as well as I did that blands' brains began to atrophy at nine months, and we got progressively more stupid with age.

In a serious voice he said, "I will be very displeased if you don't play with me."

Of course, I sat down then. Without another word, he dealt.

We had played card games at the creche, but the deck he used was an adult one, much more complicated than I had seen. There were five different communities of cards, arranged into generations, with "cousin" cards crossing the boundaries. We actually used the antique kinship term, though it meant nothing to me.

He explained the rules of the game, but I didn't recognize the cards very well, and kept making stupid mistakes. He won hand after hand.

"You know, it's not very much fun for me if I win all the time," he said.

I gave him a sullen glance, thinking it served him right for trying to play with a bland.

We played some more, but I was getting very sleepy, and he finally gathered the deck into its case. I had not noticed how dark it had gotten till I looked up at the sky, and gave a little gasp of amazement.

I had never seen so many stars. I got up to get away from the fire's light. From one horizon to the other, the sky was simply spattered with them, thick as flour spilled on a black floor. The big streak of the galaxy arched overhead. Away off in the darkness, I could hear the river rushing over its bed.

I felt Tellegen at my side, also looking up. "Which one is the aliens' star?" I asked. A docent had pointed it out to me, once, but I didn't remember.

"You can't see it now," he said. "Only in winter."

He pointed some other things out to me, though. He showed me the ecliptic and the zenith, and one of our neighboring planets, and the patterns of the constellations.

The air had gotten very chilly, and when I shivered he said, "Are you cold?"

I shook my head. I hadn't realized what it would mean to be out here, exposed to the transparent sky at night, with no shelter anywhere. It was like being suspended over a chasm, not sure of what kept you from falling. I wanted to clutch the ground, but there was nothing to hold onto but grass.

"Does it frighten you?" he asked gently. I nodded.

He put an arm around me, and I was grateful to have an anchor, somehow imagining that he was more firmly rooted to earth than I, and could catch me if I fell into the sky. In a hesitant voice I said, "Do I have to sleep out here all night?"

"Would you like to sleep in the tent?" he said.

I nodded. I knew we had staked it firmly down, and at least inside I wouldn't be able to see the emptiness above.

"Well, it's a big tent," he said. "I expect there's room for you. You'll have to be very quiet, and not disturb me."

"I won't," I said.

Pelch was wrong; he was very cheerful the second day. I was the crabby one. My body ached in a thousand places, and it was sheer torture to climb on the horse again. Tellegen noticed how stiffly I moved but didn't say anything, for which I was grateful.

Beyond the river, the land began to rise and got more rugged. Away off in the distance we could see blue hills against the sky. Here, the land seemed exaggerated, oversized. The day before, the hills had merely been undulations; here, they were presences, towering over us.

We reached the roundup site shortly after noon. We topped the crest of a ridge, and suddenly saw below us a wide river valley that narrowed like a funnel to the south. At the narrow end, where the hills hemmed the river close, were herded thousands upon thousands of head of cattle, grazing on the abundant valley grass. There were temporary pens and chutes set up, and we could see the ranch blands moving through the herd on their tough, wiry horses. Blue smoke rose from their camp.

As we came down the steep hill path, one of the men in charge saw us and came riding across the river and up the path to greet the squire. I had been riding next to him while no humans were about, but now I fell back with Jimmicky. As we came down into the valley I listened to the two men talking about business—the health of the herd, the number of calves, what percentage to cull for market. Squire Tellegen listened to all the details, and asked probing questions that made me realize he was genuinely interested.

Jimmicky and I split off to set up the squire's camp at a spot he showed us, well upstream from the blands' camp, so we would have clean water. When we were done, Jimmicky settled down to sleep in the warm sun. I knew I ought to wait at the camp where my duties were, but all the activity was going on by the pens, and I was curious. I decided to go locate Squire Tellegen, so I could keep an eye on him. When he headed back to the camp I would run ahead so I could be there, waiting for him.

I walked past the blands' camp. There was only a single large tent set up—their roundroom, I assumed. A cook with a crippled leg was preparing a huge pot of stew and baking bread in a portable metal oven. It gave me a suspicious look, so I didn't stop.

The blands had set up the cattle pens in a chain. The first pen was a corral large enough to contain almost a hundred of the beasts, sorted out from the larger herd farther down the valley. The buffs were huge black animals, very shaggy, with manes that nearly covered their short horns, and sharp cloven hoofs. Two ranch blands on horses were in among the crowd of cattle, sorting out the calves and driving them one by one down the chute to the second pen for branding. I watched them, entranced by the unconscious grace and skill of their movements. They were using only soft pad-saddles, like pillows, and guiding the horses with their knees and whistled commands. The horse and rider seemed like a single entity, their motions were so coordinated. Rushing into the crowd of cattle, wheeling round, dancing sideways, then charging forward—the horses seemed to know exactly what they were doing, as if they could think with their riders' brains.

I spied Squire Tellegen standing at the fence, watching. There was a human with him, so I hung back; but presently the man left, so I ventured closer. When Tellegen noticed me, he said with some surprise, "Hello, Tedla. Have you come to watch?"

"Yes, sir," I said, checking his face closely to make sure it was all right.

We stood there together for a while, both absorbed in the show. As we watched, one buff grew angry at the herders, and charged with her horns down. The horse slipped agilely away, but banged up against the fence, smashing the rider's leg. The bland didn't cry out, but the others had seen the accident, and rushed up to help it off the horse. Within a few seconds, another bland was on the horse and back at work, while the first limped away, leaning on a companion. Tellegen followed it with his eyes, frowning.

"Will it be all right?" I asked.

"I expect so," he said. "They're very hardy. They won't accept human medicine; we've tried again and again. They have their own remedies that they trust more."

The horse seemed scarcely to notice that its rider had changed; the new bland had the same rapport with it.

"The buffs are a hybrid," Tellegen explained to me. "They are part domestic cow, part native buffalo. We'd hoped to get the docility of the tame cattle and the hardiness of the wild. But they're still dangerous beasts. I suppose there's no way to get a creature that can survive the winter on the range without a savage disposition."

"Do the blands stay with them all year?" I asked.

"Yes," he said. "These blands aren't like you, Tedla.

For them, being penned up at Menoken Lodge would be torture. They're wild creatures, too."

We walked on to view the activity in the second pen, where the branding was going on. Here, the blands were working on foot. As the calves came in, the blands skillfully roped them, tripped them, and tied their legs; then a human recorded the calf's sex and weight, took a blood sample, and gave it a serial number, which the blands branded onto its ear with an inkgun.

"We keep track of the lineages, to ensure genetic diversity," Tellegen explained.

"Are there bland cattle?" I asked.

"No," he said. "Humans are the only mammals with a sex that can't reproduce." He looked down at me. There was a hesitant, sad note in his voice. "Nature had to make us this way, because we threatened to overrun the planet. Now that we have learned better, we still must endure the punishment."

He said "us," but I knew he meant "you."

That evening, after he had eaten dinner, he lit the lantern and went into his tent to write in his notebook. I finished washing up the dishes, then sat by the riverbank, listening to the stream gurgle by. Jimmicky had disappeared somewhere. There was a sweet scent of vegetation cooling after release from the hot sun—letting out its breath, perhaps, freed as I was by the approach of night. The sun had just set, and the sky was salmon and blue in the west. The hills were outlined in overlapping shadows against the sky.

A wind blew past, and the grass around me rustled. It brought the faint sound of voices from the blands' camp just downstream. I rose, hesitating, and glanced at the squire's tent; but I knew he wouldn't need me or miss me for an hour at least. As silently as I could, I sneaked away down the riverbank.

When I got within earshot, they were singing. One had a stringed instrument, and another was drumming. It sounded strange and wild. The phrases blew my way on the wind; I could barely understand them, because the herders' accent was so strong. But the tune spoke to me, lonely and searching. It made all our roundroom songs sound like jingles and nursery tunes. This was music that came from the grass hills and the hoofbeats, from wind and harness and hard ground, sweet as the scent of grass and ruleless as the weather. There was no trace of anything human in it.

I was still in the shadows outside the circle of their campfire, but I could see their weathered faces, like eroded stone or knotty wood, lit by the fire. Their bodies were lean and wiry. Everything about them seemed alien and free.

I heard a soft step behind me, and turned to look. Squire Tellegen had followed me. He said nothing, just smiled at me then stood there at my side, listening to the music. At last, in a voice that was barely a breath, he said, "What drew you down here, Tedla?"

Carried away by the moment, I said, "Squire, could I go with them some day? Could I go herding?"

My question took him completely by surprise. He blurted out, "Do you want to leave me, then?"

The pain in his voice was so unexpected by me, that I hung there, torn between my affection for him and the first real glimpse of freedom I had seen since the day when I wasn't born. I glanced back to the campfire, then to his face again.

He quickly regained control of himself. Gravely, he said, "Tedla, if you want to go with them, I won't stop you. I want what's best for you. Spend the night with them. See if that is what you really want. I won't need you until the morning." He turned and left then, walking away stiffly, like a man trying to prevent himself from looking back.

The ranch blands had stopped singing, and were roasting something over the fire now. They were talking low among themselves, and I heard their laughter. I stood there, longing to step forward into their circle, but feeling as if an

invisible barrier stood between me and these free neuters.
The squire had been right; I was not like them. I was tied
too firmly to humanity.

I turned and walked back toward the squire's camp.
When I got there I sat down quietly outside his tent, twisting a strand of grass in my hand. Presently, he looked out.

"You came back," he said, and there was a terrible
happiness in his voice.

"I haven't fixed your night-drink yet," I said.

I thought he would say more, but he just looked at me
for a long time, then let the flap drop between us. I relaxed
and went off to put the kettle on the fire.

His justification came only three days after we got back,
and the whole house was on edge. Though I had come
back from the roundup feeling confident, I quickly caught
the prevailing anxiety. All of us were completely dependent on his making the right decision.

His friends and admirers sent him many messages in
those three days, but he refused to read any of them, and
they just collected on his desk. Pelch fretted that he wasn't
taking anyone else into account. On the eve of his justification day, he told Pelch to have us all leave him alone
so he could spend the next day in prayer and reflection,
speaking to no one from sunrise on. The morning after, I
prepared to go up to his room feeling hollow inside with
dread. But I found him standing there, looking out his
window pensively. I said nothing and he said nothing, but
I'm sure he saw how radiant I felt. When I went downstairs
Pelch was waiting, its face haggard with worry. When it
saw my face I thought it was going to hug me.

After justification, it was as if he had a new lease on
life. He allowed me to coax him into some changes—getting his hair professionally cut again, stocking a better vin-
tage of wine than penny-pincher Pelch wanted to buy. His
friends showed up in droves, and as winter set in and we
began baking and preparing for Leastday, Menoken Lodge

seemed almost cheerful. Outside, the plains were desolate and wind-whipped under a glowering sky, and the river gorge became choked with ice, but inside we were a cozy family.

The roundup trip had changed my relationship to the squire. After coming back, I had half expected us to fall back into more formal roles, but Tellegen would have none of it. He often dawdled at dressing in order to talk to me, and on evenings when he had no guests he now insisted that I play cards with him.

At first I resisted, telling him I was too stupid. He didn't argue or try to encourage me. He simply said, "I am your guardian, Tedla. I have a right to ask you to do this." Almost against my will, I became interested. It was like any other exercise—hard and painful at first, but soon becoming pleasurable. The feeling of intense concentration, the sense of order coming out of disorder, my growing control—it was all unexpectedly satisfying. It got so that, when he was occupied and I had nothing else to do, I would secretly take the cards out of his desk and play games with myself so I could get good enough to amuse him.

But he was very good at cards, and it was hard to satisfy him. One night when I had kept the game going longer than usual, and felt quite pleased with myself, he burst my confidence by saying, "That's not good enough, Tedla. I need you to challenge me, or I won't be amused."

"You should get a human to play with you, then," I said.

"It intrigues me to have you," he said. I thought he meant as it would intrigue him to see a dog sit at a table. I was a novelty, a diversion, something he could show at parties—a card-playing neuter.

But I now think it was an experiment. He wanted to see if I was capable of learning, and if so, how fast. How disappointed he must have been. Every time he tried to teach me something different I would resist, wanting to keep doing the old things I already knew. I wanted to settle back and coast, not to exert myself or compete, not to have to try—or fail—again. I had been given a license in life to cease struggling, and he was revoking it. Of course I resented it.

I was angry at him the first night I beat him. He had been irritable all day, criticizing me for little things, complaining about the other blands' work, and the whole household was grumbling. By the time we sat down to cards, I was secretly vindictive. I became so caught up in the run of the tricks that I didn't even notice he was losing till he laid down his cards and said, "Your game."

I didn't believe it. I looked at my remaining cards, then at his, and saw I could not help but take him. He was watching me carefully, as if to note down my reaction. I felt a rush of anger. "You let me win," I accused. He had tried that a few times, early on, thinking it would encourage me, and found it had the opposite effect.

Now he shook his head. "I played as well as I knew how. You just played better."

"That's not true!" I said. My frustration boiled over. This all seemed part and parcel with the day. "I don't want to play any more," I said.

He looked mystified. "Tedla, you just won. You said you couldn't do it, and you did. Doesn't that give you any pleasure?"

"No," I said.

"Well, it gives *me* great pleasure," he said.

He could not know how much it threatened me to think I could win. If I were better than him at anything, then I would have to question the natural order that placed him above and me below. I did not want to question that. To question that was to start questioning everything. Nothing would be safe once I took that step.

I don't think either of us fully understood how dangerous was the territory he was leading me into. His indulgence tempted my thoughts into unrealistic paths. Not that I was in danger of forgetting I was a bland—the other blands saw to that. It is impossible to sleep in a roundroom and maintain any sense of separation. But I was getting far too interested in humans and their doings.

It was shortly after Leastday that we learned that one of the aliens was coming to Menoken Lodge.

Down in the roundroom, we had been only vaguely aware that another, larger, delegation of aliens had arrived on our planet. Looking back on it, I realize WAC must have sent the second contingent before the first had even arrived. They must have been very confident of their diplomats' ability to win us over. I wonder what they would have done if we had proved to be hostile barbarians who had killed or enslaved their First Contact team. Fortunately for them, we were ready to give their researchers a courteous welcome.

Well, almost all of us. Even in such an enlightened roundroom as ours, a great deal of ignorance lingered, and ignorance breeds prejudice. When Pelch came down, looking slightly flustered and worried, and told us the news, some of the blands declared they wouldn't have anything to do with an alien.

"Who knows what we might catch, touching its towels or washing its dishes?" said Dribs, one of the cleaning blands. "Do you know what kind of diseases they carry?"

"The aliens are humans, just like our humans," Pelch said, scowling.

"That's not what I heard," Mimbo said. "I heard they're deviants, born with sexual organs. They can copulate in their cradles."

"You're a fine one to be criticizing anyone's sex," Pelch said tartly. "Remember your place. The alien is our guardian's guest, and that's how you'll treat him."

But a core of the neuters stayed fearful and rebellious, and nothing Pelch could say would sway them. Pelch finally looked at me. "*You're* not going to give me any back talk, are you?" it said.

"No, Pelch," I answered. In fact, I was almost equally torn between curiosity and revulsion. Everything Dribs and Mimbo said was true. But if Squire Tellegen was going to let an alien in the house, then I wanted to see it.

"You see?" Pelch said to the others. "Tedla's not scared, and it's going to have to serve the alien. You others should be ashamed of yourselves."

From their looks, I could tell that if I did end up serving the alien, no one was going to let me in the roundroom without a thorough washing.

The only way for Pelch to have won would have been to tell the squire and have him talk to the rebellious blands. But Pelch never wanted our guardian to know that it had less than total control of the situation downstairs, so the trump card was out of the question. In the end, Pelch had to compromise. It agreed that no one would have to wash a contaminated dish or towel or sheet against their will. We would make separate arrangements to clean everything the alien touched, in a kind of quarantine. Pelch itself would do the dirty work, assisted by Britz and me.

The night the alien was scheduled to arrive, it was cold, so I went to the river room to light the fire and prepare hot drinks, just as if we were expecting normal guests. Squire Tellegen was waiting there, reading as if aliens came to his house every day. When I heard their voices approaching down the hallway I busied myself at the sideboard, my back turned to them.

There were three of them: Elector Hornaday, a vestigator named Nasatir, and the alien. When the elector introduced "Magister Galele," the alien spoke up in enthusiastic but wildly accented Argot, saying that "Magister" was his title, rather like "Questionary." It sounded like something he had had to explain quite a number of times.

Squire Tellegen offered them all drinks. When I turned

around with the tray, I got my first good look at the alien. My first impression was of a little brown troll-like man. He had a mop of thick, uncombed brown hair and a mustache. He looked rumpled and studious. When I held out his drink on the tray, he looked straight at me with a sharp, humorous twinkle in his eye. Startled, I quickly lowered my gaze.

I went into the next room and ducked through the graydoor. The other blands were all clustered by the peephole into the river room, taking turns staring at the alien with exclamations of thrilling horror. "Get back to work, you bums," I hissed. "Do you want me to tell Pelch?"

"Oh come on, Tedla," Britz said. "You get to see him all evening."

"No, I don't," I said. "I can't just stand there staring at him, you know." I joined them at the peephole. "Let me look," I said. When Dribs moved away, I pressed my eye to the hole. The alien was sitting there, listening alertly to a conversation between the elector and the squire, his eyes shifting from one to the other as if looking at them would help him understand. When he spoke, he waved his hands in a jerky, uncoordinated way, and I feared for the drink on the table beside him.

I backed away from the peephole. "Get the hors d'oeuvres," I said to Britz. Then, to Mimbo, "How's dinner coming?"

"Not ready yet," Mimbo said.

"It won't ever be, if you don't get downstairs," I said.

"All right, all right." They broke up and trooped away, exchanging whispered comments.

When I went back in to serve the hors d'oeuvres, their toddies already needed replenishing, so I went to the sideboard to heat some more. The alien was giving an enthusiastic account of his researches. Whenever he came to a word he didn't know he just blundered ahead, making up something. Listening to him, it was sometimes hard to keep a straight face; but all the humans were being polite, and not letting on.

He broke off in the middle of an explanation of alien theories of individualistic and communitarian cultures, and which ours was, to say, "I have wanted to ask most ardently, do you have concept of natural equalism here?"

They were all staring at him blankly, unable to decipher what he meant, so he tried again. "The notion that humans are made equal."

"No," Tellegen said. "That is absurd. All humans are unique. Each has his or her own blend of abilities, deficits, and moral strengths. To say we are equal is degrading, as if we were mass-produced machines, interchangeable parts."

"Eh?" the alien said. It seemed to mean, "Please go on."

"A notion like that would be pernicious to society, as well. It would mean that those blessed with superior ability would have no obligation to develop or exercise it for the common good. Talent comes weighted with obligation—a higher standard of behavior and achievement. We cannot encourage people to shirk that duty."

"And what of those without abilities?" the alien said.

"Everyone has some sort of ability," Nasatir said. I had come to his side to offer him hors d'oeuvres. He glanced up at me and said, "Even blands have abilities."

I offered the tray to the alien. He was looking at me expectantly, as if for a reaction, but I kept my expression perfectly blank. I found it a little offensive to be noticed, but told myself he didn't know any better.

"This is an interest," the alien said. "I wanted to meet you, Lexigist Tellegen, because of your champion of asexual rights."

When they had figured out what this meant, Nasatir said, "*Rights* may be a strong word."

Tellegen suddenly spoke up, very forcefully. "It

shouldn't be. We shouldn't have to backtrack and temporize at the thought that they have rights."

"Well, in some abstract philosophical sense, perhaps," Nasatir conceded.

"I'm not talking philosophically now," Tellegen said. "I'm talking about the basic morality of our social system. It is simply unconscionable that two-thirds of us should live off the labor of the other third. The exploitation of blands is corrosive to our humanity."

There was a startled silence. The alien looked very alert. "Then you do have concept of natural rights?" he asked. Since no one seemed to understand, he said, "Human rights?"

"Yes, of course," Nasatir said. "It's a subject much discussed."

"But neuters aren't human," Tellegen said bitterly.

"You think this is wrong?" the alien pressed him.

Elector Hornaday interrupted. "That's what we call the Troubled Question, Magister Galele. Their nature is something we haven't resolved."

I had never before heard her speak not as the squire's friend but as the head of his order. Her tone was a clear warning to Tellegen. He looked disgruntled, but obeyed her by falling silent. The drinks were hot, so I served them in the quiet that followed. I noticed that the fire had gotten low, so I fetched more wood from the bin and knelt on the hearth to get it burning again.

The alien had completely missed the interplay between Hornaday and Tellegen. He said, "Your opinion, lexigist?"

Tellegen stirred uncomfortably in his seat, then gave his elector a stubborn, defiant look. "I can only give you the personal opinion of an old man. I have no evidence to advance, only experience."

"Eh?" the alien said attentively.

"I have seen more genuinely noble behavior from certain blands than from three-quarters of humanity," Tellegen said. "There are ways in which we could aspire to be more like them. Their innocence, their patience, their gentleness with children and animals, their fortitude in suffering. The fact that, despite all we have done to them, they can still love us."

My back was to him, but I heard his voice change, and I somehow knew he was aware of me. He said, "The love of a neuter is more pure and selfless than any human love. They throw their very souls into your hands. It can cut you to the heart."

The fire was going again, but I knelt there very still, not daring to turn around or face him.

The alien said, "So you think they are equal to humans?"

"Some of them are. There's not a doubt in my mind," Tellegen said.

"You are the first person I have heard to say that."

"I am very nearly the first to think it," Tellegen said. "It would make me very unpopular in certain circles."

I rose quietly to escape the room. I caught a glimpse of Elector Hornaday's face; she looked deeply troubled.

I crossed the empty dining room to the serving-pantry to see how dinner was coming. Britz was just bringing up the fruit plates. "What's going on in there?" it asked eagerly.

"That alien is completely crazy," I said.

"What do you mean?"

"He thinks blands are equal to humans."

In my mind, it really was the alien who had said it. The thought that my own guardian could hold such a belief was simply inconceivable.

I made my last-minute preparations, then returned to the river room to give Squire Tellegen the signal that dinner was ready. I stood in the doorway, but he was deeply involved in conversation, and didn't see me at first.

"Give yourself some credit, Prosper," Nasatir was saying. "You woke up the whole world to the abuse and inhumane conditions of their lives. Because of you, their lot has improved immensely.''

''There are still abuses,'' Tellegen said. ''It is an abuse in itself to have total power over them.''

''Speak for yourself,'' Nasatir said, a little exasperated. ''Most of us don't have power over even one bland. Here you live, with half a dozen of them, whose only purpose in life is to keep you comfortable. If you're so concerned about power relationships, why don't you turn them all loose?''

It was a rhetorical question, of course; but Squire Tellegen looked troubled by it. He was about to answer, then decided against it, frowning at some inward debate. The alien's head was turning from one to the other of them like a cat watching a ball. He obviously didn't understand the nuances here. He finally ventured, ''Is to turn them loose not possible?''

''No, of course not,'' Tellegen said, dismissing the idea with a gesture. ''They are incapable of fending for themselves. Their welfare is our responsibility.'' He looked away toward the window, where the river gorge yawned. His voice was heavy with emotion. ''We have an ancient myth, Magister Galele, about two brothers, one wise and one foolish. The foolish one was tricked by a jealous woman into putting on a shirt that then burst into flames, but did not consume him. He was in such agony he could not move or speak. There was no way to get the shirt off. For the rest of their lives, the wise brother was forced to carry the foolish one around on his back. He was horribly burned by the flames himself, but unable to abandon his brother. It's usually taught to us as a fable on the evils of kinship, but what it really foreshadows is our relationship to the unsexed. Their agony is ours, because we cannot abandon them.''

There was a complete silence in the room. I stood there, transfixed by the conflict I saw in my guardian's face, and horribly uncertain what it meant. At last he looked up and saw me standing there. For a moment our eyes met, and he truly looked like a man in flames. Then he said neutrally, "I believe our dinner is ready. Shall we go in?"

Magister Galele would have been glad to go on talking about neuters over dinner, but the others firmly turned the conversation to more polite topics. I had intended to keep a sharp eye on what the alien touched, but I found myself preoccupied and anxious for the squire. He kept up the conversation graciously—I think he could have done that in his sleep. But I knew him well enough to see his turmoil.

He urged Elector Hornaday and Vestigator Nasatir to stay the night, but they both had appointments the next morning in the convergence. I had expected the squire to stay up late talking to the alien, but when the other guests were gone he turned moody and pensive, and soon pleaded exhaustion. They touched hands and wished each other good night.

I was standing by to show the alien to his room. As soon as we were alone in the hall, he asked my name and what my position was. Of course I answered, but it made me nervous. He kept on asking things—how long I had been here, how old I was, whether I was happy here. It was so offensive to be grilled by a human who had no rights over me that I pretended to be dumb, and not understand him. He must have gotten the message, because he gave up by the time we reached the guest room. When I asked if there was anything else he needed, he said, "No, thank you, Tedla. You've been very kind."

I quickly cut across to the squire's room through human space. There was no one around, and it would have taken longer by the bland-run. I found him standing at the window, still fully dressed, staring out into the dark, ice-draped canyon. A cold wind was blowing snow against the glass with a hissing sound. There was something about the squire's posture that filled the room with loneliness. It was killing him, I thought.

Softly, not sure he would want me there, I went to his side. He turned to look at me, his face a perfect mirror of the desolation outside. He put a hand on the back of my neck to draw me closer. For a while he was quiet, just looking at me. Then he whispered, "Tedla, do you have any idea how much I love you?"

For a moment I hung poised on the edge of the solid ground I knew, where I was a bland and he was my guardian and our relationship to one another was prescribed down to the last detail. Then, without ever deciding, I stepped off the edge and was falling. He had beckoned to me for help, and I threw everything I had after him.

I put my arms around him and clung tight, my face pressed against his neck, my breath coming hard. He returned my embrace strongly, protectively.

"I never intended to tell you," he said. I could feel his lips moving close to my ear. "I thought it was better not to let you find out. But I realized tonight that if I don't tell you, the whole world is going to know. I'm not going to be able to live with this inside me."

I didn't say anything. My self was rushing back into me with a painful force. I had fully expected never to be loved again. I had accepted a life without any individuality or worth. Now, I was cherished by a man I had come to trust and admire more than all the world. I knew I was really there, because I was the thing his arms encircled, the thing his love defined. I felt weightless, buoyed up by the intoxicating moment. We stood there for a while in each other's arms, rocking a little to and fro.

"Tedla," he said uncertainly. I felt tension return to his body. I pulled away and looked at him. The conflict was back in his face.

"I don't want this to change you. I need you to stay just the way you are." He took my face in his hands, gazing at me with a troubled smile. "I love the way you think, and the way you're frightened to find yourself thinking. I love your patience with me, and the way you get annoyed when I am crotchety. I love your vulnerability, and your innocence, and your sadness. I love the fact that you are so much more than you think you are. You would not be precious to me if you were human. What I love is the fact that you are a bland."

He drew a shaky breath, like a man who felt himself falling and couldn't stop himself. "You trust me, don't you."

I said, "Yes."

"I want to earn that. I want to protect you, and keep you safe. I never want anything to harm you. But—"

He ran his thumb over my cheek, very lightly. "God help me, I also love your beauty. Tedla, would you be willing to spend the night with me?"

It would be disingenuous to say I hadn't seen it coming. But I felt completely different than I had at Brice's. Here, I knew I was perfectly free to say no, and nothing would ever happen to me. But I didn't want to say no. I loved the squire deeply. I wanted him to love me. He was so gentle, so generous, I yearned to be close to him, and if there were any pleasure or comfort I could give him, I wanted to do it.

All the same, a little quake of nervousness went through me. To give him my body as well as my heart would change everything between us. It would change our lives in a hundred ways I couldn't imagine. It truly was a precipice.

I thought to myself, "I can say no," and said, "Yes."

He kissed me very gently, then hesitated, with a trace of anxiety. "You're sure?"

I thought of leaving him in the loneliness I had found him in, and said, "I'm sure."

I undressed him the way I did each night, hanging his clothes away in the closet and bringing him his robe. Then, as he sat on the edge of his bed watching with fearful anticipation, I took my uniform off and laid it carefully over a chair. When I was completely naked, he looked at me from every angle, as if I were an art work newly revealed to him, and what he saw delighted him.

"You are so beautiful," he said. "It makes me ashamed of what I have become. Once, I was like you. Look at me now."

"You look beautiful to me," I said shyly, and meant it. He was not flabby or sagging, as old men get; he was still lean from abstinence and exercise. His body had the marks of a long life on it, but there is nothing ugly about that.

"If I thought you were capable of flattery, I would suspect you," he said, smiling.

I had expected him to take the lead, to show me what he wanted; but when it came time he turned oddly shy and awkward. It was clear he had never been to bed with a bland. He had no notion what to do or how I might give him pleasure. I realized that I was going to have to guide him—yet I couldn't let him know that I had been trained. The idea would revolt him, and I was afraid that if he knew my past I would revolt him, too.

Slowly, I began to show him things I thought he would enjoy—simple, natural things, the sort of things that seem obvious once you know them. Gradually, he relaxed; the tension and complexity left him, and he was able to submerge his mind in sensation. For a while he became quite passionate, and I think I was able to give him a kind of pleasure, and a kind of release, he had not had in many years.

But for me the best part came after all his sexual energies were spent and we lay pressed close against each other in bed, drowsy. The wind was blustering against the window, but we were warm together. My cheek rested against his chest, and his arm was around me, and he stroked my hair, from time to time bending over to kiss it. All down my body my bare skin pressed against his, and I felt in that intimacy a perfect safety, as if his love formed a protective sphere around us, and nothing could ever penetrate that barrier.

When I woke the next morning, the chill light of an overcast dawn was coming in the room, and the bed beside me was cold. I raised my head and saw him standing at the window again in his dressing gown. There was a terrible tension in his body.

He heard me stir, and turned around. "Tedla, can you forgive me?" he said. His face was distorted with remorse.

I rose on one elbow, still a little confused with sleep, but alarmed by this new turn. "For what?" I said.

"For using you this way." He sat down on the edge of the bed. "I was not myself last night. I was carried away by base urges; I couldn't control what I did. It was shameful of me to coerce you this way, to make you satisfy my needs. It's not your fault. I swear to you it will never happen again. But if you don't trust me, if you feel you can't be comfortable around me any more, I will arrange for you to go elsewhere, to serve another—"

"No!" I cried out. I was fully awake now. His mood was frightening me. I reached out to touch his hand where it rested on the coverlet, but he snatched it away, as if afraid of my touch.

"No, please," he said, "I can't trust myself. I thought I was a better man than this. I thought I was stronger, but I'm not."

It was horrible, like a nightmare, to find out I had made him ashamed. The room seemed cold, and I was naked; I pulled the covers up around me, shivering. I suddenly saw myself without the illusions of last night. Of course he was shamed to have loved me. I was a bland. My touch was pollution.

He saw my misery, and it made him desperate. "I didn't mean to harm you, Tedla. Anything but that."

"I understand," I said numbly. The inviolate bubble that had seemed so strong last night was gone. I wasn't the person I had thought. I was still a bland. This was all my fault.

I threw the covers aside and got out of bed. I went into

his bathroom and turned on the shower, scalding hot, then made myself step into it and wash. When I got out I returned to the bedroom and started putting on my uniform. The squire was still sitting on the edge of the bed, exactly where I had left him, frozen in thought. When I was ready, I said, "Do you want to dress, or shall I bring your coffee first?"

He turned to look at me bleakly. "Tedla, I am the one at fault here. Last night I betrayed everything I have spent my life working for. What I did to you was a crime. I could be put in prison for it. I know, because I was the one who wrote that law, and persuaded all the orders and communities to accept it. I have worked all my life to protect people like you from people like me." He closed his eyes, distracted by inner contradictions.

"Do you want your coffee?" I asked again.

At last he squared his shoulders and rose. "No. I want to wash and dress." He came to the bathroom door, where I was standing, and paused, looking at me. "Please don't come in," he said. "For your own safety, you must keep your distance from now on."

His words were saying one thing, his eyes were saying another. I saw it clearly: He wanted to take me in his arms right then and there. I hesitated, not knowing which one of his minds to obey.

"Go get my coffee while I wash," he said. "We'll begin the day just like all the others. Thank god no one is in the house but the Capellan magister. He'll never suspect."

"Yes, sir," I said.

I was about to go, but he stopped me. "Tedla, we must forget last night, and make sure it never happens again," he said.

He didn't mean that, either. His face, his whole body told me he was more in love than ever. Last night hadn't been the end. It was just the beginning.

I left by the graydoor then, as if nothing had changed. But in fact, everything had changed.

Chapter Seven

❧ **The next morning there was still no message** from WAC or UIC. Val found the silence unnerving, so as soon as she could get into the studium she punched Magister Gossup's number.

When Kendra answered, she said, "Hi, Val," without any trace of coldness. "He's not in."

"Who's he been meeting with?" Val probed.

"Oh, WAC, Epco, you name it. Should I tell him you called?"

Val hesitated a moment. "Yes. Tell him everything's just fine."

After cutting off, she sat a few moments, thinking, *Epco*? Had Shankar stepped into the ring?

It would explain the silence. If the two infocompanies were battling over control of Tedla, then they might be leaving the Gammadian with her only because any other arrangement would require one or the other of them winning.

Shrugging, Val called up Galele's reports again. She skimmed rapidly through reams of bloodless information he had collected in carefully orchestrated visits to a matriculatory, gestatory, and midway house. One passage caught her eye:

Finally got my first close-up look at some asexuals, who were employed in caring for the infants at the gestatory.

Terribly disappointing. They do, in fact, appear to be mentally disadvantaged. My guide assured me they can talk, but I could not induce them to utter a word to me. When my group entered the nursery, the three blands on duty retreated to a corner where they huddled, staring at the floor, with all the signs of intense fear. When my efforts at rapprochement produced no result, their supervisor spoke sharply to them, ordering them to answer my questions. Even that had no effect. They were quite unable to do it.

They look much like humans—no obvious deformities or physical characteristics of retardation. I was surprised that they were allowed to care for the infants, since the job requires (it seems to me) a considerable amount of judgment and responsibility. The gestagogues laughed and said they never had any problems, that the neuters were quite capable where children were concerned. It made me suspicious that the behavior I was witnessing was a social performance, the conventionally "correct" response for a bland. There is no way to find out, short of getting a neuter to talk to me alone—not a likely thing. The humans quickly hustled me away. They seemed both protective and embarrassed, as if I had discovered the mad relative in the attic.

Apparently, there is no way to diagnose neuterism prior to puberty. All Gammadians, it seems, are born with X chromosomes, so that sexual differentiation is a matter of selective gene activation. Everyone has the potential to be any sex. I asked whether neuterism was inherited, but they answered that there is no way to find out, since lineage records are sealed for confidentiality. It struck me then: If neuterism is random, people free to look up their own relatives would necessarily find that they were related to neuters. The whole system of sacred secrecy, though justified by lofty social ideals of "non-tribalism," seems perfectly constructed to keep anyone from realizing they are the parent or sibling of a neuter. Is this a byproduct, or an underlying purpose?

Felt the need to check my observations with someone else, so called up Magister Mackey, our geneticist, who is working with the Matriculators, the most secretive and insular of all the orders. Asked if she knew what causes neuterism. She laughed ironically and said, "As if they'd let me study that."

I was quite interested by this response. "Don't they want our help finding a cure?" I asked.

"They don't need our help," she said. "These people know as much about genetics as I do. They're pretending ignorance. The more I reveal I know, the more they shut down."

I asked if they had given her access to the lineage records, and she laughed again. "Not a chance," she said. "No one touches those. Absolutely all they want from us is artificial gestation."

"You think they could cure neuterism if they wanted to?"

"If it's curable. If it's even genetic, and not environmental or viral or something. They claim they don't know, but I don't believe a word of it."

This left me very thoughtful. Up to now, I have assumed that my difficulties at probing certain subjects were the result of social convention, misunderstanding, embarrassment. I had not considered deliberate concealment.

Mackey's attitude, though paranoid on the surface, makes sense. Why would Gammadians want to cure neuterism, and thus eliminate the most useful part of their work force?

Ought I to be thinking of neuters as a social class, rather than a gender?

Much food for thought here.

Galele recorded two more encounters with neuters after this, each more frustrating than the last.

I can't even get them to look at me, much less respond. They meticulously avoid eye contact with humans. I think the message is multiple: first, submission ("I am not dangerous, do not harm me"); second, tuneout ("I am not listening, so don't try to communicate with me"). Humans accept their avoidance as respectful in some circumstances, sullen and dull in others. I suspect there is yet a third, more hidden message—"You are irrelevant to me, so don't try to impinge on my life or I won't respond." I find this very passive-aggressive, almost rebellious, but other humans don't find it so. Perhaps I am overanalyzing, and there is in fact no coherent thought in their minds at all.

I can't help noticing that neuters perform many of the tasks assigned to females in gender-differentiated cultures: child care, cooking, cleaning, etc. They appear to occupy the economic role of women, but not their social or sexual role. Is this significant?

At last, paging through, Val found the passage she was looking for.

Very promising development: Ovide invited me to a dinner party at the home of a mentor of hers, Prosper Tellegen Lexigist. In his youth he was part of a movement called the Sensualists—lofty, high-minded young artists and thinkers who advocated connection to nature and discovery of the god within through sensory experience. I gather they became rather notorious for free love, but also produced some great art and poetry. Tellegen was their theoretician. He later underwent a well-publicized religious conversion and became a crusader for humanitarian reform. Ovide spoke of him with great affection and respect; I rather suspect her of being sweet on him. I was to be something of a diversion for him, I think.

We went in the dreaded aircar. The great man has retired to the most remote place imaginable—a ranch far out on the central plains of the continent. But when we arrived, the place was jam-packed with aircars: pilgrims and protégés come to see him. We descended into a large, elegant mansion where a lively soiree was in progress: a dozen or more of the acutest, most unconventional people I have yet met.

Tellegen himself is a tall man, refined and elegant, a true elder statesman and philosopher. After meeting him, I've changed my mind again: there is a Puritanical streak in this culture. Though the most gracious of hosts, he seemed emotionally elusive, remote and priestlike among this crowd of loving devotees. He asked Ovide curiously about events in the convergence: obviously he follows the politics closely. I got a better sense of the factionalism there.

Convention seemed to exercise no limits on the conversation here, as in Tapis: people talked openly about topics I've had to dance around delicately for months. I actually got a conversation going about neuters. In lofty theoretical terms we debated whether they are human (Tellegen believes so, others disagreed), whether the concept of natural rights applies to them (again, Tellegen took the radical view). Curious: while everyone else (so far) denigrates neuters as brutish and dull, Tellegen appears to idealize them as innocents—beings untouched by human corruption, children of nature. A sharp, ironic man named Nasatir challenged him with hypocrisy, since he lives a pampered life supported by a large staff of blands. Why, Nasatir demanded, didn't he grant his own blands rights? The reply: the entire social system is unjust, and an individual cannot act justly within such a context. Despite the ready answer, Tellegen seemed quite troubled and vexed by the challenge.

We were served by a strikingly beautiful adolescent of perhaps 16, with the poise and reserve of a young aristocrat cast unexpectedly into servitude. Despite its clearly servile role, several minutes passed before I realized it was

*a neuter, and not some young relative met with hard luck.
The others in the room completely ignored its presence,
pontificating away on the subject of blands as if it were
deaf or incapable of understanding. It showed no reaction,
though I watched closely. I thought it looked out of place,
as if wrenched from everything it understood, sleepwalking
through a life of degradation. The irony and poignancy
both were lost on my companions.*

*After a sumptuous banquet, Tellegen asked us to stay
the night. I was ready to comply, but Ovide had to get
back, so we unfortunately took our leave. I am extremely
eager to return. Partly because Tellegen's acumen and
unconventional views may give me some insight. But
mostly because I think he would be able to answer my
simple, factual questions about neuters. What is their intelligence? Their abilities? Do they have any emotions, any
point of view? I am longing to get past that invisible barrier that hedges round the closed society of the blands.*

*Managed to wangle myself another invitation to Men-
oken Lodge, Prosper Tellegen's ranch house-cum-salon.
This time, went alone and stayed the night. Gathered much
valuable information which I will write up some time.*

*Tellegen's neuter servant was again in evidence. Its
name is Tedla, and it clearly enjoys a privileged position,
since Tellegen is a fond and indulgent master. Tedla is
less skilled at maintaining the dumb brute pose than any
other neuter I have observed. I am now convinced that it
is a pose—at least in this case.*

*When alone with me, Tedla was impassive and mono-
syllabic, but surreptitiously curious—sizing me up as if to
determine if I posed a threat. Given the restrictions on eye
contact, this was a complicated maneuver, which I at-
tempted not to reveal I noticed. When Tellegen is present,
however, Tedla is openly relaxed, almost to the point of
showing real character. This seems to both amuse and
confuse Tellegen. Case in point:*

We were talking about the legal rights of blands, one of Tellegen's favorite topics. As happens often, Tedla was in the room, silently serving us some completely redundant drink or other (I half suspect it of hanging around to eavesdrop). I asked Tellegen whether he thought blands even knew they had legal rights. He said confidently, "I expect so. The grapevine among blands is awesomely effective." For some reason we both became aware of Tedla then, though it was doing nothing but standing there pretending not to listen. Perhaps the pretense had become a little obvious. Tellegen turned to it kindly and said, "Tedla? Do the blands know their rights?"

"Your blands do," it said. "Outside, where they need to, it's a different story."

Tellegen looked startled and a little peeved that a teen-aged underling had dared to contradict him in front of company. But he smiled with an indulgent condescension. "You have barely been anywhere else in your life, Tedla," he said.

"No, sir," it said, looking down submissively.

"So you could scarcely be expected to know."

"No, sir."

Tellegen settled back in his chair, having confirmed his opinion and established dominance again through the gentlest of means. He continued our conversation. When I looked at Tedla several seconds later, it was watching him surreptitiously with a slight, wry smile, as if it understood perfectly the irony of what had just transpired.

Anyone who understands irony is no mental defective.

Later that day, something even more remarkable happened. It was after dinner, and we were speaking (I think) about blands' intelligence. As usual, the person most likely to be able to enlighten me was employed clearing away the dishes, and not allowed to speak. For some reason Tellegen began gently teasing Tedla. For a while it put up with him stoically, but when he didn't stop, it rather abruptly left the room. Presently another bland came in to take over, giving the feeble excuse that Tedla had been taken ill. I was very curious to see how Tellegen would handle this open insubordination. At first he ignored the situation, as if to deflect my attention. But presently he left the room. When he came back, he seemed pensive and moody. "I am afraid I must confess to being a fraud, Magister," he finally said. "Here I have been passing myself off as an expert on blands, and I don't even understand what is going through the head of the one I thought I knew best."

This was an extraordinary speech from a Gammadian. Up to now I have met no one who would have admitted that anything at all could be going through the head of a bland.

The next morning Tedla was back, perfectly obedient again, and looking quite unintimidated by whatever discipline its master meted out.

I am extraordinarily keen to get Tedla to open up to me. It will be a touchy business, I can tell. Despite its behavior with Tellegen, the bland is shy and suspicious with strangers, as if apprehensive of maltreatment. I will have to seduce it as carefully as a nervous virgin.

When I got back to Tapis, I found a troubling message from the First Contact group. They warned me to stay away from Tellegen—he's under some sort of cloud. Very confusing—I've seen no evidence whatsoever—here he is revered. So I went and asked Ovide point blank. She scoffed, said my friends were talking to reactionaries, & I should pay no attention.

I don't know what to do. The F.C.s' word is supposed to be our law—but have they got the wrong end of the stick? I would hate to give up visits to Tellegen's. I have learned more from him than any three others combined, and like him enormously. More to the point, there is Tedla. I can't bear to be cut off from the only asexual who will even look at me, much less speak. This is really frustrating.

*   *   *

There was no further mention of Tedla or Tellegen for over twelve weeks. Then, a short note:

Made what I pledge will be my last visit to Menoken, to put a proposal to Tellegen that he lend me one of his blands for testing & research. I meant no harm by it, and thought he might be glad to further my studies. Am unable to fathom his hostile reaction. If any negative reports come of it, I can easily explain.

Val sat back, wondering what lay between the lines of that entry. She heard movement out in the dinery and called, "Tedla?"

The studium door cracked open, and Tedla looked in. "Come in," Val said. When the neuter obeyed, she saw it had a rag over one shoulder and a scrubber in one hand. "What are you doing?" she said.

"Cleaning your cupboards," Tedla said. "The last person who lived here didn't do a very good job of it."

Not the slightest bit pleased at the symbolism, Val said, "Well, stop it. You're a guest, not a house servant."

"I want to. Please, it's the least I can do. I can't stand not being useful."

"If you want to be useful, sit down and answer some more questions. Did you ever wonder why Magister Galele stopped visiting the squire?"

Tedla looked blank. "Stopped? When?"

"After his first two visits."

"He never stopped," Tedla said. "He came like clockwork, every week. Sometimes twice."

Val felt a smile grow slowly on her face as she understood. Tedla said, "What is it?"

"He 'forgot' to report it to his superiors," she said. "They'd told him to stay away."

"Really?" Tedla looked astonished. "How do you know?"

"He said so in his reports."

Leaning forward in fascination, Tedla said, "You have his reports here? Can I see them?"

Immediately regretting her openness, Val said, "Actually, I'd prefer you didn't, at least not yet. They might contaminate your memories. It's very revealing when you disagree."

Tedla sat down on the bed, obviously disappointed, but resigned.

Val said, "For example, he didn't report his first visit to Menoken Lodge quite the way you did. He says there were over a dozen people there, and he didn't stay the night."

Tedla was silent for a moment, then said, "That's impossible. I couldn't forget something like that."

After a moment of hesitation, Val said, "Oh hell, you've already told me your version in this case, so you might as well read what he has to say."

She copied out the passage and rose to give Tedla the chair. The neuter settled down eagerly. On seeing the first sentence, it smiled. "He writes just like he talked. I can hear him saying this."

Tedla became absorbed in the account then. After finishing, it leaned back in the chair, looking troubled. "I can't explain this. I must be wrong." It turned to look at Val. "I *can't* be wrong! That memory's the most vivid thing in the world, in my mind. I would have staked my life on it. Am I crazy?"

"Maybe Galele is wrong," Val suggested. "He did have a reputation for sloppiness."

All she knew for sure was that she needed to be skeptical of one of her sources. She just wished she knew which one.

Reading Galele's report put Tedla in a reflective mood. Val said, "Do you want to tell me some more?"

Tedla fidgeted with the dishrag, twisting it between its hands.

"What's the matter?" she said.

"I shouldn't," Tedla said. "I've been thinking about it. I shouldn't have told you all that last night."

"Why not?"

Tedla shifted as if the chair were upholstered with needles. "It could do such harm—terrible harm."

"To you?"

"No, to Squire Tellegen. His memory. On Gammadis, he is respected, even revered. His whole life work was based on that. Even now, if people found out about us, all his reforms would become a ribald joke. His writings would have no moral authority any more. It would destroy everything he did."

Watching the neuter's face, Val came to a realization. "You still love him, don't you?" she said softly.

Tedla looked away, lips pressed tight together. "That doesn't mean for me what it does for you. For you humans, the sexual part is so powerful it drowns out everything else. You can't imagine love could take over your whole being, even without it."

"Tedla, why does it make you so guilty?" Val said.

"He was my guardian!" Tedla said angrily. "I was supposed to be protecting him. Even if it was from himself."

For a moment Val was silent, counting the contradictions in that statement. At last she said, "No one on Gammadis is ever going to hear about it from me."

Tedla gave her a worried glance. "I know. I trust you. It's just that . . . this part is very personal."

After a long silence, Val said, "I'd really like to hear it."

Steeling itself, Tedla said, "I owe you so much. I don't want to be ungrateful."

She cleared the screen and hit the Record button.

❊❊ I can only tell you this the way I remember it. Maybe my memories aren't as good as I think they are. But if I start doubting myself now, I'll lose track of everything.

Squire Tellegen had thought our secret was safe because there were no guests on that night but Magister Galele. What he had forgotten was that there were nine blands in the house who all knew I hadn't been in the roundroom, and who scarcely needed a map to know where I *had* been. But they were not the squire's problem. They were mine.

When I entered the kitchen that morning, the blands were gathered in a knot, but their conversation broke off quickly when they saw me. Everyone went about their business, trying not to look at me. The breakfast preparations were way behind schedule; the blands must have been so caught up in gossip that nothing else got done.

"Where's the coffee?" I asked, dismayed. "The squire's asking for his cup, and you haven't even started brewing it."

"Oh, hold your hat on," Dribs grumbled.

"You'd better get moving," I said to Mimbo, who was getting out the fruit for breakfast. "They'll be sitting down in a few minutes."

"Oh, we're taking orders from *you* now, are we?" it said.

"Well, where's Pelch?" I asked, looking around.

"Sick," Mimbo said, as if it were none of my business.

At that moment Pelch came in, looking not so much sick as ill-tempered. Our eyes met, and from clear across the room I could see that the tension between us was now full-fledged hostility. On Pelch's part, at any rate. I had nothing against Pelch; it was a hardworking bland and a good supervisor. But now its emotions were involved.

I turned to check on the coffee situation. Dribs was moving with agonizing slowness, so I snatched the cannister away and started making it myself, working fast. I held the silver urn under the drip spout till I had a cup's worth. "Bring up the rest as soon as it's ready," I said to Britz.

I delivered the squire's cup, then hurried down to the morning room to make ready for breakfast. I found the alien wandering around the vestibule studying things, so I steered him firmly into the breakfast room and told him the squire would be down shortly. He wanted to talk to me, but I quickly evaded him by ducking back into gray-space.

Neither fruit nor coffee had come up from the kitchen, so I was obliged to go down again. I found everything in a state of chaos; something had burned on the stove, and a cloud of smoke was hanging around the ceiling. Mimbo had backed into a serving-tray, and I glimpsed blands on their knees picking food off the floor and putting it back on the plates. I snatched up the coffee and left. The less I knew about all this, the better.

"Ah, at last," Squire Tellegen said a little accusatorily when I came in with the coffee. There was a short silence as I poured, first for the guest, then for the squire. There was barely enough. Then the two men resumed their learned conversation.

"Legally, it's fraught with undesirable consequences," the squire said. "If they were defined as human, they would lose all the special protections we have designed. Without guardians, they would be subject to the depradations and exploitation of the evil side of humanity. Their special status is necessary for their own protection."

"Do they ever run away?" the alien asked.

For a moment the squire was dumbfounded by such a strange question. "Where would they run to?" he said. "To live like animals in the woods? It seems unlikely."

When I got back into the pantry, Britz was just showing up with a plate of half-burned, half-raw toast. "That's not what I need!" I said. "Where's the fruit? I need more coffee. Run down and get some, quick."

"Sorry, Tedla," Britz said. "It's crazy down there."

"I noticed."

I thought of dumping the pathetic toast in the waste bin, but didn't know when I might get something else to serve, so I took it in.

"Do they commit crimes?" the alien was saying. Every question he had was more outlandish than the last.

"Petty crimes, occasionally—thievery, sabotage, witchcraft."

"Witchcraft?"

"Silly superstitions, yes. Major crime is rare. Occasionally there will be a renegade who goes berserk and has to be put down. . . . What is this?" The squire picked up one of the pieces of stone-cold, charred toast.

"I'm sorry, sir," I said. "Pelch is sick. The rest are doing the best they can."

"That is no excuse." His voice was uncharacteristically severe. He handed me the plate of toast. "Take this back. Tell them they all know their jobs, and should do them."

"Yes, sir."

Ordinarily, I would have shrugged off his tone; this morning it stung. As I carried the plate away, the visitor's eyes followed me curiously. I suddenly wanted him gone. He watched too closely; he made us think in ways we would never dream of, otherwise.

Britz came in with the main dishes as I was dumping the toast. I inspected the plates carefully, picking out some hairs and bits of food that looked stepped on, then took them in.

"You will find it a sensitive topic," the squire was saying. "All our fears center around them, as our guilt does. We fear them changing, becoming more like us—or us becoming more like them. We fear them outnumbering us, turning on us, ceasing to love us."

He wasn't looking at me, but there was a change in his voice on the last words that made me know they were addressed to me. I kept my stony composure till I escaped back into the pantry, then leaned back against the wall, my hands over my face. Britz came in with the fruit plates then.

"Tedla, what's wrong?" Britz whispered.

"I don't know what I'm supposed to do any more," I said.

"What do you mean? Just carry the plates in."

Britz was right. Just carry the plates in. That was all I had to do. It was no more complicated than that.

The alien left before noon, and all of us were glad to have him gone. Britz and I set to work stripping his room and washing the laundry in strong bleach. I was glad to be safe in grayspace, where I knew the rules, and everything was clear-cut.

But by evening, even that security deserted me. When I went up to dress him for dinner, and later for bed, Squire Tellegen was preoccupied and barely looked at me. I rushed through my duties in order to get away from his silence. I was glad to escape back to the roundroom. But when I lay down in my own familiar place, the other neuters, instead of settling down around me, drew away and left me lying there alone. They didn't say anything; they didn't need to. Everything I needed to know was in the way they recoiled, as if my body were a tainted thing. They no longer wanted to touch me.

I hadn't expected the isolation. By day I kept up a civil facade, speaking only about work. By night, I retreated to the edge of the roundroom, as if it were my own choice, as if I didn't want their companionship. But the loneliness began to weigh me down. Only Britz was still friendly to me; but the reason, as I occasionally glimpsed in its eyes, was pity.

Now, it seems strange to me that, except for Britz, they all blamed me, and not Squire Tellegen. I suppose it was because they had known him for years, and thought of him so kindly. I was the new element in the equation; therefore, I was responsible for this unsettling disruption. Then again, it's in our nature as blands to despise each other.

For a week, Squire Tellegen spent a great deal of time in his devotional, praying and meditating. With me he was remote and silent; with the others, short and snappish. The whole house grew tense and unhappy. I was completely miserable.

At last one afternoon, when he was writing in the library, I came in to serve him a hot drink, and he looked up at me thoughtfully. "Tedla," he said. I stood before him like a perfect automaton, my hands clasped behind me, my eyes cast down. In a puzzled voice he said, "Have you ever thought of running away?"

I knew what was going on then: The alien's strange questions were making him doubt everything he knew. I said, "No, sir."

"Well, perhaps not you. Do you think other blands might do it?"

"None I've known, sir."

"Good. I thought not."

I hesitated, wondering if that were the end of it. He was silent, and I was just about to turn and go when he said, "I haven't seen you smile in days."

I looked up at him. "I haven't seen you smile, either," I said.

It was a terribly impertinent answer, but it seemed to thaw him a little. "Do you watch me?" he asked.

"Of course I do," I said.

"Do you think we can ever be friends again?"

I was so desperately lonely, all my caution fled the room at the slightest sign of kindness. "I hope so," I said.

As he watched me, a sad smile grew on his face. "Don't look at me like that, Tedla. I can't stand it. Sit down and we'll play a game of pijico."

After that we slowly resumed our old routine of cards and conversation. But it wasn't like before. There was a tension of restraint between us, like the spring on a mousetrap pulling back and back. If our hands came close, we both flinched away. From time to time I would catch him watching me, like Britz—but in his eyes it was both pity and maddening longing.

Soon we learned that Magister Galele was coming to

visit again. This time, I was not worried about catching an alien disease. It was another sort of germ I was worried about: a virus of the mind.

He came alone. When I met him at the door to take his coat, he greeted me by name, as if we were old friends. I was polite and aloof.

I remember the second visit chiefly for what happened at dinner. They had both drunk more than was good for them, and were feeling quite jolly. I began to regret not having diluted their drinks more, because the squire was talking quite unwarily. I passed word down to the kitchen via Britz to hurry up the main course.

When I entered with their plates, Magister Galele was saying, "I would eagerly like to test one, but Ovide won't hear it. I want to know if they're bona fide of subhuman intelligence, and if so, why, eh? Are their senses less acute? Are their memories unable? Do they really have blunted affect?"

"The standard answer to all would be yes," the squire said ironically.

"But what is the evidence?"

"Why, it's common knowledge," the squire said, then laughed. "There is no real evidence, Magister. I suspect, if we looked, we would find that there is a range of abilities in their population, as in ours." I was replenishing the water in his glass when he said, "Tedla here is an interesting case. It's pretending to be a model neuter right now, because you're here. But when no one is looking, it's quite bright."

This made me feel very defensive. I was not *pretending* to be a model neuter—I *was* one. No bland could have been better. If he was dissatisfied, it wasn't fair for him to say so to company.

He sensed something in my manner, and said, "Tedla?"

I set the water pitcher down on the sideboard and turned to face him, my eyes on the floor, as if waiting for an order. "Yes, sir?"

"What's the matter?"

I sneaked a look at him. There was a fearful fondness in his eyes. I said, "I'm not pretending."

"Oh, so this is the real you we are seeing?"

I nodded.

"Silent, obedient, and impassive?"

He was teasing me. It made me angry and a little frightened that he would do it in front of the visitor.

Smiling, he said, "I'm sorry, have I embarrassed you?" Since I did not answer, he turned to the alien and said, "I don't know whether this answers your question about intelligence, but Tedla can beat me at pijico, and I was once considered an expert."

I felt frozen. First of all, it wasn't true—I had never beat him; he just let me win from time to time. But more than that, why would he claim such a thing, implying I thought so much of myself that I would try to compete with a learned man? He was making me a laughingstock in front of his visitor, the butt of a condescending joke— the neuter who didn't know its own limitations and aspired to strut in front of the world, a monkey magister. I was so angry with him I snatched up a tray and turned to the graydoor.

When I was safe in the serving pantry, I slammed the tray down loudly. Britz was just coming in with a plate of puff pastries. It said, "Wow! What's with you?"

"Britz!" I said, quickly unbuttoning my livery coat and stripping it off. "You've got to go in there and serve them."

Britz's clownish, big-eared face took on a comical look of bewilderment. "Why?"

"They're talking about me, and I can't stand it," I said. I made Britz put on my coat, which made it look even more comical, since I was taller and the skirt came down below Britz's knees. Britz would completely break the dignity of the occasion, and serve Squire Tellegen right.

"I'll be you, Tedla," Britz said, and took on a pose of

dignified, aristocratic reserve. At that moment it was maddening to know that was how the other blands saw me. I whacked Britz on the butt with a tray. "You brainless bland," I said.

It saw I was genuinely upset and dropped the act. "What am I supposed to say? The squire will ask for you."

"Tell him I got sick," I said. Sick of him and his jokes. "I'll go do your job."

"Here, take my apron," Britz said, pulling it off from under my coat. I tied it on over my white silk shirt and seized up a tray of dirty dishes.

When I got down to the kitchen, they all looked at me curiously and asked what was going on. I tried to give a civil answer, but they could tell I was smarting. Britz had been assigned to scrubbing pots, so I rolled up my sleeves and set to work. The others snuck curious looks at me as I worked, since they'd never seen me do menial labor. I was grimly glad to prove I could do it.

Half an hour later we were wiping the counters and putting away the pots, when Britz came flying down the stairs shouting, "He's coming! The squire's coming down here!"

The consternation was as great as if aliens were invading. It was the same thing, in a way—an event so untoward and out of all ken that the only rational response was terror. In thirty seconds every bland had melted away, leaving me alone in the kitchen. I wanted to run as well, but I knew it would only make things worse. If the squire was angry enough to break all natural law by coming into grayspace, there was no place on earth where I could hide.

He entered hesitantly, as if uncertain where he was, which may have been true. I had been wiping off the stove, so I kept on as if he weren't there. He came over to me.

"Tedla, what are you doing down here?" He sounded more bewildered than angry.

"I'm working," I said, continuing to do so.

"Are you really sick?" he said. He laid a hand on my forehead to feel for fever.

"I'm not sick," I said.

"Then what's all this about?"

He truly didn't know. Without looking at him, I said, "I don't like being laughed at."

Astonished, he said, "I wasn't laughing at you. I was bragging about you. Don't you recognize praise when you hear it?"

"For a human, that might be praise," I said. "For a bland, it's mockery. And it's cruel."

Tears were stinging my eyes, but I didn't want to cry, so I angrily wiped them away. He was looking at me as if nothing in his life had ever been so mysterious.

"Tedla, I would never do anything cruel to you," he said.

"I know that," I said. Suddenly I felt terribly ashamed of myself, for being so self-centered, for making him come down here. It all became so unbearable that I began to cry. With only the slightest hesitation he took me in his arms. I clung to him, my face pressed against his shoulder. "Please forgive me," I said in a choked voice.

He stroked my back comfortingly with one hand, the other cradling my head. "Poor child," he whispered. "You weren't made for this life. I wish there were something I could do to save you."

He kissed my forehead and pressed his cheek against it. Then, as if there were nothing he could do to stop himself, he slowly kissed my lips. I knew there were probably nine pairs of eyes riveted on us, but I didn't care. In his arms I felt completely invulnerable.

"My dear, dear partner," he whispered. He used the word that meant "love-partner," the word older humans use for the youths of their infatuation. It made me giddy to hear it.

I pulled away and wiped my face with the apron. "I'll go set out your night things," I said.

"Yes, do that," he said. His voice was charged with the knowledge of what I meant.

When he came up to his room, I was waiting for him. This time he was ardent from the beginning, as if the abstinence had stored up feelings that had to explode out or destroy him. It was as if he couldn't get enough of my body. I gave myself over to him completely that night. His passion burned hot into the night, fed on infatuation, guilt, and shame.

The next morning I woke with my head on his chest, his arm still around me. He was staring at the ceiling. When he saw I had roused, he kissed me, then resumed his thoughts.

"You know, Tedla," he said thoughtfully, "there was a time in my life when I believed that the quickest way to my god was through the senses. I believed in experiencing things to the full, taxing myself to the very limit. Then I grew older, and began to doubt that I could achieve transcendence that way. Until now. Now, it's all coming back to me, what being really alive feels like. It's close to something—insanity, enlightenment, I don't know which."

He looked down at me, so I smiled at him. It made me feel blessed to see him so happy.

I don't know what love feels like for humans. For me, that first time, it was like having an endless spring of water inside me. It was full, and buoyant, with a tingle of lightning always in the air. I loved the squire with the perfect trust and intensity of youth. I had no notion that the weightlessness could ever turn to vertigo, or that, floating, I might ever look down and see a chasm.

After that night, there was no longer any question of my going back to the roundroom. I became his permanent bedpartner, except when guests stayed overnight and the risk of discovery was too great.

In the months that followed, everyone noticed the change in the squire. He was more vivacious and charming at dinner, and the parties started growing more frequent. He took up old interests and projects neglected for years. He even flirted with his admirers, though it never led to anything. "Are you coming out of exile?" one woman asked him. "Tell me it's true."

Elector Hornaday was the one who came closest to guessing the truth. One night she looked at him and said, "I could swear you were in love." The fear that she would guess nearly froze me to the floor. But I shouldn't have worried. His friends' faith in his morality was too blind. I could have stood on the dinner table and shouted out the truth, and none of them would have believed me.

The other blands scarcely knew what to make of such a scandalous situation. They might have tried all the old bland methods for keeping me in line—sabotaging my work, playing tricks with my clothes or food—if it had been anyone but their own guardian involved. As it was, they imagined me to have power over them, whether I did or not.

The situation was particularly hard on Pelch. Before I came along, Pelch had believed it knew Squire Tellegen through and through, and loved him without the slightest reservation. Now it felt betrayed; it grew waspish and critical of everyone, its temper stretched tight as a drumhead. As time passed, it became less and less able to cope with its duties, in constant emotional turmoil as it was. The result, ironically, was that I became the conduit of information about the squire's wishes. Not that he ignored Pelch or stopped giving it authority—Pelch just didn't listen to him, as full of resentment and disapproval as it was.

One day when Pelch was handing out incorrect orders I dared to say, "Pelch, I don't think that's what he wanted."

It turned on me in a rage. "Have you served him for forty years? Did you watch him grow up and become what he is? How do you know what he wants?"

Dribs immediately took Pelch's side. "If he wanted you to be our supervisor, he'd say so."

"All right," I said, shrugging and letting it drop.

Or so I thought. Later, Pelch cornered me alone. "You are destroying him," it said, its voice shaking. "Before you came, he was the most moral man alive. You've corrupted him, made him into something he's always hated, just to get power for yourself. I've seen how you act with him, how you flaunt yourself and tempt him, till he can't help but give in. If any harm comes to him, it will be your doing."

I was terribly shaken by Pelch's words. I brooded on them as I went about my tasks that day, wondering if it was true. Had I brought corruption into a healthy house, like some disease contracted at Brice's?

At last, when I couldn't stand it any longer, I went upstairs. The squire was alone in the library, reading. I came in quietly and sat down on the floor at his feet, laying my head on his knee. He said quietly, "What is it, Tedla?"

"I just want to be close to you," I said.

He stroked my hair, and smiled at me tenderly. "You are a great comfort to me," he said.

I sat there for perhaps ten minutes, just soaking in the reassurance of his presence. It was the only reassurance left to me.

The isolation from my own kind drove me more and more toward the human world. It wasn't just Squire Tellegen, either. There was Magister Galele.

He came often to Menoken Lodge, and I grew quite accustomed to having him around. There was absolutely nothing imposing about him: enthusiastic, disheveled, quite unable to keep himself in order. He treated me with an informality I found disturbing at first, then disarming. He was constantly trying to draw me out in a way no other human—not even the squire—did. I thought it was a game with him; later I learned it was what he was trained to do.

He acted as if it gave him great delight when I was impertinent, and when we were alone he often teased me to get a saucy answer. Sometimes I would indulge him; at others, I would tease him back by being solemn and proper. I was a little apprehensive how Squire Tellegen would feel about my growing friendship with the alien, so in company I concealed it under a layer of formality. To his credit, Magister Galele seemed to understand.

One evening he was there with a party of half a dozen questionaries, and managed to spill wine all over himself before dinner. He could be amazingly clumsy. As the humans were all exclaiming and dabbing him with napkins, I said, "I'll take care of it if you'll come with me, Magister." He followed me downstairs, still joking at his own expense. When we got to his bedroom I made him take off his shirt so I could take it away to be washed. When I got a good look at it, I found it was all caked and spotted with the remains of other meals, besides ink and coffee.

"When did your blands last wash this?" I asked.

"I haven't the faintest idea," he said.

"Give me your burnous," I said. It was just as I thought. The overgarment was filthy, too—though because of the color it showed it less. Now I itched to turn him out of all his clothes and give them—and him—a good scrubbing. "I'll clean these for you, and give you something of the squire's to wear," I said. "I don't know what your blands were thinking, to let you out like this."

"They don't actually have much to say about it," he said, mightily amused at my tone.

"Well, they're neglecting you," I said. "You shouldn't let them get away with it."

He laughed. "Give them a break, you tyrant. They're not assigned to me personally. There aren't many people as favored as your mas—guardian is."

"I bet you could get a Personal, if you asked," I said. Of course, I had no idea; but an alien magister seemed like a very important person to me.

"I wish I could," he said. "I live in the order house.

We all share the blands' services. I barely even get to see them."

"Oh," I said haughtily, "institutional blands."

"Definitely not up to your standards," he said, smiling. "*They're* certainly not interested in talking to me."

I said tartly, "I daresay they're interested in what they find in your pockets. They're probably laughing themselves sick, behind your back."

"Really?" He looked as if I had just revealed something wondrous. "Are you serious, Tedla? That's how they act when humans aren't around?"

I gave him a look as if to say, "Are you a complete innocent?"

He got terribly excited then. "Tell me more. What else do they do when they're alone?"

I couldn't imagine why he wanted to know, but I was instantly suspicious that it was likely to get someone in trouble—probably me. Looking down, I said, "I didn't mean it. It's not really true."

There was a short silence. Then he said gently, "Tedla, what are you afraid of? Will someone punish you for talking to me?"

"No," I said.

"Well, then?"

I couldn't explain to him how our private world was ours alone, and no human ever came prying into it for a good reason. I couldn't tell him how invasive his question seemed, or how I feared what he might do with the knowledge. None of this was possible to explain to a person who had no notion how the world worked.

"I've got to get this soaking," I said of the wine-stained shirt in my hands. "I'll get you some clothes." I left hastily, and when I came back he was silent and thoughtful.

He was as lively as ever later in the evening, though. After dinner, as they were all still at the table drinking liqueurs, someone asked him how his researches were going. He said enthusiastically, "Excellent! I'm actually making some progress at last. I turned up some evidence of an asexual subculture. Up to now, everyone's denied there is one. But did you know that blands act completely different when we're not around? They laugh at us, and joke! They're also socially differentiated—some of them feel superior to others. A kind of occupational stratification.''

There was a chilly silence around the table. Finally a woman said, ''They laugh at us behind our backs?''

I was standing against the wall with my eyes firmly fixed on the carpet. I was praying he would have the sense not to say where he had found out, and that none of them would remember whom he had left the room with earlier.

As if he hadn't noticed their reaction, Magister Galele said brightly, ''Yes. I would love to hear a 'human joke,' wouldn't you?''

Someone gave a nervous titter. ''I don't think I would, actually.''

''New horizons in humor,'' a man said drily.

''Now I've heard everything,'' another chimed in.

That night when I was lying in Squire Tellegen's arms, he looked at me and said, ''Do you really ridicule us behind our backs?''

''No,'' I said.

He studied my face with a troubled frown. ''Tell me the truth, Tedla,'' he said.

''We talk about things that happen to us during the day, and laugh at them. Sometimes people do funny things. We'd go crazy if we couldn't laugh.''

He relaxed. ''Somehow, I couldn't bear to think of you mocking me in front of the other blands.''

I was mortified that he would think such a thing. ''I would never do that,'' I said earnestly.

He smiled and kissed me. ''Bless you. I thought I knew you better than that.''

But I lay awake thinking his suspicion was well founded. I lied to him and deceived him all the time, in little ways. All blands did that, to make their lives easier. There were things I would never reveal to him. I even pretended a false eagerness for lovemaking, because he got such intense pleasure from it.

He had an alien in his arms, and didn't even know it.

It was not long before Magister Galele was back, this time in the afternoon, and alone. When he saw me he grinned and said, "Damn! I forgot my laundry." But I knew Dribs was just behind the wall in the bland-run, listening to us, so I didn't answer.

The moment I showed him into the library, Galele burst out, "Did you notice my little experiment the other night, Tellegen? Damn, but I hit a nerve, eh? Right on the face. What a reaction! I'll tell you, it's those sensitive spots that really show up the soft belly of a culture. You people have had armor plating up to now."

I stood at the door trying to catch Squire Tellegen's eye so he could tell me if they required refreshments. I desperately wanted to leave. This man was beginning to frighten me. He had no sense of danger.

The squire seemed to be thinking the same thing. He said carefully, "You need to realize, Magister, those were some of the most liberal, open-minded people in all the orders the other night. If you had said the same thing in another setting, your researches might have been short-lived."

"Oh, I think I know how to choose my moments," Galele said confidently. "I haven't been studying you people all these months for nothing. Though up to now you've been hard eggs to crack—so urbane and humane. Even Tedla is a master of the polite brush-off."

I could feel tension charge the room like an electric current. I was standing with my back to the door, clutching the knob so hard behind me that my fingers ached. In a tight voice the squire said, "Have you been trying to interview Tedla?"

" 'Trying,' yes. That's a good word. Actually, Squire, that's what I've come to ask you about." He looked at me. "Don't leave, Tedla, this concerns you. Tellegen, I need your help. Tedla has potential to be an excellently valuable informant. It's got access to information no human can give me, and the intelligence to put it language-wise. I don't think I'll ever find another asexual with those qualities. If you would let me spend some time with it . . ." He broke off at the look on Squire Tellegen's face.

In a voice more ominous than I'd ever heard him use, the squire said, "I must ask you, Magister, not to speak to Tedla. Not another word."

If I had worked for any other guardian, I would have been on the way to retraining before the day was up. The things I knew could have destroyed the squire and all he stood for. No one keeps around blands with dangerous secrets when someone is poking around for information.

Galele, of course, had no notion of any of this. He looked from one to the other of us, bewildered. "But what harm could come of it?"

"You don't yet know our world well enough, Magister," the squire said. "I am responsible for Tedla's safety. You could put it in terrible danger."

"I wouldn't do that," Galele said earnestly. "I could preserve Tedla's anonymity, if you like. No one would know."

He kept on for a while, arguing about how valuable the information would be, how it would lead to greater understanding between our worlds. I could see the tension building in the squire, and at last it exploded out.

"I told you no!" he said in a voice he barely controlled. "Leave my house now! If I ever see you nosing around my blands again, I'll run you off myself."

Galele was perfectly stunned, and backed away, speechless. I quickly swept the door open for him to leave. He looked at my face, then at Tellegen's. He was a little flushed with embarrassment or anger, but he said nothing.

He ducked out the door, and I quickly followed, closing it behind me. I hurried ahead down the hall to fetch his coat.

As he took his wrap from me, he said, "Tedla, what got into him? What did I say?"

"Don't you ever learn?" I whispered, glancing over my shoulder. "Just stop asking questions."

"I'm sorry," he said. "I hope I didn't get you in trouble. I thought he would be happy to help." He saw the fear on my face, and said in concern, "Will you be all right?"

"Just get out," I pleaded. With a slight hesitation, he turned to go.

When I got back to the library, Squire Tellegen was pacing, still perturbed. "Is he gone?" he demanded. I nodded. He came up to me and took me by the shoulders. "We have to stop, Tedla. It's too dangerous. Someone is going to find out. We can't go on."

But I saw in his face that it was far too late to stop.

That evening, he told me to build a fire in the river room. It was not a good sign. Whenever a black depression was coming on him, the river room was the place he chose to go. It had been months since he had last spent an evening there alone. Pelch was terribly worried when it heard, and kept casting accusatory looks in my direction.

I looked in on him halfway through the evening. The fire had burned low, and he was simply sitting on the couch before it, staring at the coals. I tiptoed in to put more logs on. When the fire was going again, I turned around to look at him. He was watching me with an expression very close to grief.

"Tedla, what is going to become of you?" he said.

I was already on my knees, so I settled back on my heels to look at him. "I'm going to serve you forever," I said.

"I am old," he said. "My life is drawing to a close. You are young. You will have many years after I die."

He was thinking of death again. I felt like something

cold was growing inside my chest. I put a hand on his knee. "No. You can't die. I want you to live."

"I have done you terrible harm," he said.

"No. I love you."

"I need to know you'll be safe. That's the least I owe you."

"I'll never be happy anywhere but with you," I said.

He reached out and touched my cheek. "Do you know the worst thing I have done to you? The thing most likely to bring you harm?" He paused, then said, "I have nearly made you human."

He leaned forward and kissed me then, very tenderly. I closed my eyes and savored the sensation of his lips against mine, the press of heat from the fire at my back, the absolute completeness of the moment. I desired nothing, expected nothing.

After that I joined him on the couch, nestled up against him with my head on his shoulder and his arm around me. We watched the fire die together, as the river roared down the black canyon outside.

In the next weeks the house seemed more quiet and lonely than usual, without Magister Galele's visits. I realized how much I had come to enjoy his chatter, his curiosity, his outrageous questions. I think Squire Tellegen noticed it, too. Once, while we were playing cards, he asked, "Did you like him, Tedla?"

"It's not for me to like or dislike your guests," I said.

But I realized that I *had* liked him, in a way. Menoken was a grave and melancholy place without him.

And so I was both startled and pleased when the squire told me one morning that he had invited Magister Galele back. "Will he stay the night?" I asked.

"I don't think so."

I met Galele at the door. He looked at me warily. "How are you, Tedla?"

"Fine, sir," I said in my best distant servant manner,

because I knew it would madden him. It did, too, till I glanced at him to gauge his reaction, and he realized I was teasing.

I showed him into the library, just like before. But this time Squire Tellegen said to me, "Please leave us alone, Tedla. I want to talk to Magister Galele privately."

This surprised me a great deal, since no one ever thought that having a bland in the room made their conversations any less private. I could have listened at the graydoor, but that would have been disobeying, so I went down to the kitchen to bide my time, brewing some coffee for them since I had nothing else to do.

Presently, Britz came in and said that the squire was looking for me. I dashed up the stairs two at a time, paused outside the graydoor to regain my composure, then slipped in.

Magister Galele was not in the room. The squire was standing alone behind his desk looking grim and severe. A tremor of apprehension passed through me as I approached and stood waiting for his orders.

"Tedla," he said formally, "you know I have never ordered you to do something against your will."

"No, sir," I said.

"Well, now the time has come when I must give you such an order. I want you to promise that you will obey me."

I stood there, filled with misgivings, searching his face to see what this meant.

Sternly he said, "Tedla. I asked you a question."

My eyes fell to the floor. "Yes, sir," I said softly. "I'll obey you unless it will bring harm to you."

He came around the desk then, and took me in his arms, crushing me to his chest. When at last he let me go and looked at me, there were tears in his eyes, but he was smiling. "What I have to ask you will very nearly break my heart, but nothing worse than that," he said.

Horribly alarmed now, I said, "What?"

"I want you to go back to Tapis Convergence with Magister Galele. I want you to assist him however he asks, and to think of him in every way as your guardian."

Stricken, I cried out, "Forever?"

"Of course not," the squire said. "Nothing lasts forever."

"When can I come back to you?"

He paused. "When I decide."

"Who will be your Personal?"

"Don't worry about me," he said, smiling. "You can be more use to him now than to me. Do what he tells you. Learn what you can from him."

He was sending me away to remove temptation from his life. He knew that as long as I was living in his house, he would not be able to keep away from me.

That part was bad enough. But—Magister Galele? A few weeks ago, he had thrown the alien out of the house for asking to talk to me. Now, he was giving me whole to the person most likely to pry. "What if he asks me questions?" I said.

"Tell him what it's proper for him to know," Squire Tellegen said. "I rely on your discretion."

He was crazy, trusting his secret to a bland and an alien. It was almost as if he wanted to be found out. I clutched at his coat. "I don't want to go," I said.

Gently, he said, "It's not your decision. You have to trust that I know what's best for you."

"No!" I said.

His voice grew stern again. "Tedla, you promised to obey. Now go say good-bye to the other blands. Magister Galele is waiting."

"Now?" I cried out.

"Yes, now. Go on." He pushed me to the graydoor.

I was completely stunned. I stumbled through the graydoor and down the bland-run, too shattered even to cry. When I reached the kitchen, Pelch was getting the blands started on dinner. I fell into a chair at the table. Irritably,

Pelch said, "What's wrong with you now?"

"I'm not going to be here tonight," I said. My voice sounded strange. "He's sending me away. I have to go with the alien."

I saw a look of triumph grow on Pelch's face. "Ha!" it said. "I knew it! I knew he would come to his senses."

The other blands were all gathered around now. They looked less pleased than Pelch, since this was another disruption to their routine. Whatever they thought of me, at least I did my share of work.

"What will you do for the alien?" Mimbo said.

"I don't know."

"I'm sure you'll think of something," Pelch said nastily.

My feelings were already battered, and this was too much. I rose and turned to leave. Britz stopped me. "I'll miss you, Tedla," it said. "I wish you didn't have to go."

I gave it a desperate hug. "I'll miss you, too, Britz," I said, my voice breaking. I turned to look at the rest of them. "I'll miss you all." My eyes came last to Pelch. "Even you, Pelch," I said.

I had nothing to take with me but the clothes on my back. I climbed the steps slowly, dreading what lay ahead. Magister Galele was waiting in the hallway. There was no sign of the squire.

"Tedla, I can't tell you how pleased I am," Galele said, as elated as a little child. "Believe me, you have nothing to fear."

He didn't know what he was talking about.

We boarded the aircar together. He sat up by the pilot, I sat in back. As we took off I stared blankly ahead, feeling as if there were nothing left inside me.

When we landed at the convergence, Magister Galele led me straight down into human space, as if it were proper for me to be there. I had never been in the human parts of a convergence, and my first impressions were confused:

huge spaces, wild colors, waterfalls, and jostling crowds. There was not another bland to be seen. I trailed my new guardian, feeling horribly conspicuous, aware of every glance that came our way. At last I whispered to him, "Magister? Isn't there another way for me to go?"

He looked a little puzzled, then said, "Well, if there is, I don't know it. I can barely find my way around this place on good days."

So I was obliged to follow him. There was no supervisor who knew where to direct me, no bland to show me the way through grayspace. I wondered how I was going to find the roundroom. I hadn't felt so lost since I was a child, with Joby in the curatory.

At last we came to his quarters, a small apartment off a secluded spoke. The place was a complete shambles: papers, clothes, and food strewn all over, burned-out lights, and a musty smell. As I stood looking around me in horror, he started apologizing for being so unprepared to have me there. "This is the last thing I was expecting; we're just going to have to improvise," he said. He poked his nose into the studium and said, "This can be your room. I'm afraid there's only a couch; will you mind?"

"I'm not going to sleep in the roundroom?" I asked fearfully.

"You mean, with the other blands?" he said. "Certainly not. I don't want you getting lost among the order's blands. You don't work for the order. You work for me."

This was incomprehensible. Everyone worked for an order, even Squire Tellegen. "Who's going to be my supervisor?" I asked.

"Me, of course," Magister Galele said.

He didn't understand. The supervisor was the one who meshed all the blands' work together, so they functioned smoothly as a team. I couldn't be a team of one. I had to work with other blands. I couldn't do my duties otherwise. But he knew none of this. I felt horribly out of place.

He disappeared into the studium, and began excavating

the couch from under heaps of books and dirty clothes. It made me terribly anxious to see a human doing work to make room for me in human space. "Don't do that, sir," I said. "I'd rather sleep in the roundroom. Please."

He frowned at me. "I want you close by, not somewhere off six floors away. What if I need you at odd hours?"

A horrible thought struck me: He meant that he needed me sexually. I felt sick. So Pelch had been right about what my duties were going to be. I stared at the floor, trying to distance myself from the person this was happening to. Somehow, I had to make myself accept it.

"You know," he said, "I don't have extra towels or anything. We'll have to dig some up tomorrow."

So I wasn't going to be allowed to use the blands' hygiene station, either. He wanted to bathe in the same room with me.

He opened the closet door and exclaimed in satisfaction, "Ah, at least this is empty." He turned to look at me and said, "Where are your clothes?"

He was perfectly insane. "I'm wearing them," I said, as if he couldn't see.

"You mean that's all you own? Where are you going to get a change?"

"Doesn't the order have uniforms?" I said hopelessly.

"I don't want you wearing those disgusting gray things," he said.

I was completely miserable. I sat down on the couch and stared at the floor. He kept on talking, but I tuned him out. There was nothing but grayness in my head.

"Tedla?" He was standing in front of me. I looked up blankly. "Don't go neuterish on me," he said.

I looked away indifferently, saying nothing. What did he expect? I *was* a neuter.

He stood there looking at me for a little while, then finally left. I barely noticed. My mind was off.

I sat there the rest of the evening. From time to time I could hear him talking to the viewscreen, but I paid no attention. As night came on, I expected him to come in and demand my services to satisfy his sexual needs. Every time I thought about it, I froze up in terror. I didn't even know if aliens had organs like humans did, or what they did to stimulate themselves. Whenever I began to drift off to sleep, I would remember what I had to do, and start awake, my heart racing.

Of course, he never came. I never told him what I thought that first night. When I got to know him better, I didn't dare—he had a very prudish streak. But of course, I didn't know that then.

The next morning I woke up curled on the couch underneath a blanket I had never seen before. For a moment I puzzled at how it had gotten there; then I saw the clock and leaped up in dismay. With no other blands to nudge me awake, I had overslept. It was horribly late, and I could hear Magister Galele already moving around in the kitchen. My first day with a new guardian, and I had acted like some lazy slug of a bland.

When I came into the kitchen he was pouring coffee for himself. "Ah, you *are* alive," he said on seeing me. I thought it was a rebuke, and looked down, mortified.

"I'm sorry, sir. I don't normally sleep late."

"Well, you were pretty worn out last night. Coffee?" He held out the pot as if offering me some. I shrunk back, sure I was misunderstanding.

"Have you already bathed and groomed, sir?" I asked.

"Yes. Go ahead," he said.

I was silent. If he had already done it, what was I supposed to go ahead with?

"The bathroom," he said. "It's all yours."

So we were to take turns using it. I blushed, feeling stupid and self-conscious. "Is there anything you need first?" I asked.

"No, I'm fine."

As I showered, I planned out my day. There was a lot

of work ahead to get this place spruced up and back in order. Somehow, I was going to have to find out which blands I was to be working with.

When I came out he was sitting in the lounge drinking coffee. He had left some food lying out in the kitchen. Our apartments are not like yours, with food dispensers. We have little areas for preparing foods from scratch. Since I didn't know where the refectory was, I decided to risk eating some of his food while he wasn't looking. I didn't intend to take enough for it to really count as stealing.

He came in as I was wolfing down a slice of bread. I put it down, embarrassed and unsure what he would think. He said kindly, "Why don't you bring it out to the table?"

I obeyed, but it was horribly uncomfortable, eating next to a human. I hurried to finish.

"Is there something you would like me to work on first?" I asked, rising.

"I didn't have much in mind," he said. "I'd just like to talk."

My face must have shown my consternation, because he said, "Is there something wrong with that?"

I couldn't think of a polite way to say it. "I . . . I can't talk. I've got too much work to do."

"You do?" he said, surprised.

"Yes." I looked around. "This place. I can't let you live like this. I've got to find the cleaning blands and get them in here. I've got to go through your clothes, your grooming supplies—"

He looked like he was going to protest, but then restrained himself. "All right," he said. "Do whatever you think is best."

"You're going to have to leave for a while," I said, not trusting him to know.

"Why?" he said.

"So the blands can come in and do their work."

"Why can't they do it while I'm here?"

"They just . . . can't. They'd be ashamed."

He looked mystified. "You're not ashamed."

Little did he know. I said, "I'm your Personal. I *have* to be here with you. Please, just let me handle the blands."

"All right," he gave in, "as long as you will tell me what they say and do."

He was out of his mind, but I'd known that. "All right, I will," I said.

When I got him shooed out of his rooms, I could relax at last. I quickly turned to the graydoor. There was no difficulty finding the cleaning blands; they had parked their equipment cart just down the bland-run, and were sitting around it, taking a break. "Hi," I said, coming up. They eyed me incuriously. "Are you assigned to clean the alien's quarters?"

One of them, a middle-aged bland with a disgruntled expression, gave a short laugh. "For all the good it does. He won't let us do it."

"What do you mean?" I said.

"He's always there when we come through. We can't get in."

"Well, he's not there now," I said.

The bland shrugged as if there were nothing it could do. "We've already been past that door."

I looked back down the bland-run. They had passed it by maybe thirty feet. "Oh, come on," I said. "Can't you go back? It's filthy in there."

"Sorry," the bland said, sounding not the least bit sorry. "We come down the run from that direction. We don't go the other way. If people hang around so we can't get in, that's their problem."

I was astonished at this attitude. The bland eyed me as if I were a simpleton. "You new around here?" it asked.

"Yes. I'm Tedla, the alien's Personal."

They exchanged looks among themselves. Their spokes-bland said skeptically, "The alien's got a Personal?"

"Yes," I said, a little touchily.

"What does Cholly say about that?"

"Cholly" didn't sound much like a human name, but I said anyway, "Is that your supervisor?"

One of the other blands gave a dry laugh.

"Well, who *is* your supervisor?"

They all stiffened visibly. The talkative bland exchanged a look with one of its silent cohorts. "Supervisor Moriston."

"Where's his office?"

"*Her* office is on level four." The bland paused. "I wouldn't go to her if I were you. She's in a really crabby mood today."

I hesitated. My situation was so odd, I needed a supervisor with some understanding, not one with a temper. "Maybe I'll have my human talk to her," I said at last.

There was a squeak of wheels down the bland-run, and a laundry cart rounded the corner, approaching. The bland I'd been talking to said, "Hey, Cholly."

The bland pushing the cart said, "Hey, Gibb." It came to a stop, leaning on the cart and looking at me with open suspicion. Everything about Cholly was narrow: thin body, sunken cheeks, sharp nose. Its eyes were sharp and intelligent, but made me uneasy. I couldn't tell its age.

Gibb said, "This bland says it's the alien's Personal."

"Is that so?" Cholly said. Its face was unreadable.

"It wants us to go back and clean his place."

"He's not there now," I said, hoping Cholly could break the impasse.

Cholly abruptly straightened up. "I'll do it."

"Thanks, Cholly!" I said. "It's really nice of you."

I set off down the bland-run then to explore my new space. I quickly found that the network of grayspace in the convergence was immense, tangled, and completely unmarked. The only way to navigate was by asking directions of the small groups of blands I met frequently, desultorily going about their tasks. They did not seem at all surprised to see a new face; I realized there must be new blands all the time, here.

Whenever I came to a set of stairs I headed down, and soon I arrived at level three, which was grayspace. The facilities here were immense. I peeked into a huge, echoing refectory where several hundred could have eaten at once. On the next level down, there was a whole cluster of roundrooms, color-coded. Across each door was a gate governed by a badge reader. It struck me that all the blands I'd seen were wearing color-coded badges on their uniforms, doubtless to keep them sorted into their proper teams. It was all so impersonal and regulated that I began to realize how odd my experience had been up to now.

Soon I found the laundry, which seemed to go on for acres. I managed to wheedle some extra towels and linens from one of the blands working there, whose name was Bink. I asked, "Does this laundry just serve the Questishaft?"

"East Questishaft," it said. "The westblands have their own facilities."

"You mean there's another whole refectory and roundrooms and everything on the other side?"

Bink nodded. "We don't see much of the westblands. They think they're real hotshots because the elector's house is over there."

"How many blands do you think there are in the convergence?" I said, quite amazed by the scale of everything.

Bink shrugged. "How would I know?"

"There must be thousands just on this shaft."

"Maybe," Bink said. "I just handle these ten machines, that's all I know."

They all seemed like that, as if they'd staked out their little piece of territory where they could control things, and ignore all the rest. I suppose they had to be that way. If they had paused to reflect on what tiny cogs they were, it would have been too demoralizing.

When I got back to Magister Galele's quarters (after wandering around lost for a while because I'd forgotten what level they were on), I found that Cholly had done the

quickest once-over imaginable, not even bothering to replace the burnt-out lights or scrub the mold in the shower
stall. I realized that I was going to have to stay and su-
pervise the cleaning blands after this.

Magister Galele got back when I was just halfway
through his closet, having created a mound of dirty clothes
on his bed. He came right into the bedroom with an armful
of sacks. "What are you doing?" he asked in astonishment.

"Sorting your clothes for cleaning," I said, uncomfortable to have him watching. "Do you want me to leave?"

"Is this one of your normal jobs?" he asked.

I wondered what Personals did on his planet. "Yes,
sir," I said.

"Then carry on," he said. "But first, I brought something for you." He held out the bags.

I couldn't imagine what he was up to now, but I took
the bags suspiciously, and looked in them. There were
clothes inside—brand-new clothes purchased for money in
one of the human shops. Since I had just been noticing the
deficiencies of his wardrobe, I said with satisfaction,
"Good. You need these."

"They're for you, Tedla," he said, watching for my
reaction.

Astonished, I said, "What would I do with them?"

"Well, one normally wears clothes."

I took them out of the bag to look more closely. "I can't
wear these," I said.

"Why not?"

"The colors." I showed him a red and black vest. "You
see? Those are questionary colors. They're only for people
who belong to the order."

Sitting on the edge of the bed, he said, "So the blands
don't think of themselves as working for the order?"

I saw then that it was all some sort of test, and I was
supposed to give the right answer, but I didn't know what
that was. I froze up in fear of getting it wrong.

Encouragingly, he said, "Is it that your first loyalty is to the blands, and only then to the order?"

"It's not like I have to choose," I said.

"What if you did have to choose?"

"I'd do what my guardian told me," I said.

I had thought he would be pleased with that answer, but he looked dissatisfied. I had no idea what he wanted. Wanting to mollify him, and not sure how, I picked a pair of black slacks and a white shirt from the pile of clothes, and said, "Maybe I could wear these." Quickly, I stripped off Squire Tellegen's livery and slipped into the new clothes, then went to look at myself in his mirror. They were decently subdued, but still looked quite elegant on me. I looked at myself from half a dozen angles, terribly pleased with the effect. In fact, I had to force myself to stop looking, lest I seem vain.

Magister Galele was smiling broadly. "You know, Tedla, if you just got a decent haircut, no one would be able to tell you from a human."

My pleasure froze inside me. "*I* would," I said coldly. Now he was the one who looked mystified.

Later that day he got me to tell him what I had found on my trip into grayspace. I didn't feel as if I were informing on the blands, as I would have at Menoken, because I owed these convergence blands nothing. I was a stranger here; it wasn't my home. I knew Magister Galele better than I knew any of the blands. So I let him ply me with questions about how they acted and talked in grayspace.

In the next days, I made slow headway on improving his quarters, his wardrobe, and his person. There were some awkward moments when we had to negotiate grooming. His Capellan nudity taboos made him very sensitive. We finally reached an agreement: I would shave his face but not his body, cut his hair and nails but no massages. I had to stay away when he was bathing and dressing. But he had to give in on some things, too. I wouldn't wear human colors for him, or go out into the convergence. Each of us thought the other was making much of nothing.

I told him Supervisor Moriston's name, and that he had to talk to her. He said, "Yes, yes, I will," and then didn't. As a result, I stayed in limbo. I learned to avoid the supervisors, which was easier than you might think—they spent as little time as possible in grayspace, and every bland knew their schedules and movements. I hoped I wouldn't run afoul of them before I went home again.

My status among the blands was even more equivocal. I learned that when Magister Galele had first arrived, rumors had flown through grayspace about the aliens—they fed on blood, and had strange hypnotic powers. At first, Cholly had been the only bland willing to set foot in Magister Galele's quarters. Cholly had always had a reputation for strangeness, and its willingness to serve the alien had only enhanced that.

"He really likes Cholly," a young bland named Pots confided to me. "Cholly says—" It stopped guiltily.

"What?" I asked.

In a furtive whisper, Pots said, "Cholly says he's promised to make it human some day."

"That's ridiculous," I said.

"I don't know," Pots said. "He gives it weird things."

"What sort of things?"

"Alien power objects."

I was completely astonished by this, and when I next had a chance, I said to Magister Galele, "Do you know a bland named Cholly?"

"I don't know any blands but you," he said.

When I told him what Pots had said, he was intrigued. "Where could they be getting this?"

My arrival, of course, had upset Cholly's little scam. The blands would often gather around me, asking questions they didn't dare ask Cholly.

"What's he look like naked?" was a favorite one. But I had to tell them I didn't know.

"Cholly says he sleeps in his clothes," a bland said.

"That's true," I admitted.

"Does he bathe in them?"

"I don't know. He won't let me see."

"What do you think he's hiding?"

I couldn't tell them. They all knew I slept in his quarters. Strangely, it made them regard me with a kind of awe as well as suspicion. My reputation made it easy to wangle favors out of them. I soon superceded Cholly as the main conduit of information about the alien. It did not make Cholly like me.

By the time I had been there three weeks, I was very lonely. To the blands, I was an object of scandalous rumor, only a little less unnatural than Magister Galele. To the humans, I didn't exist. On the couch at night, my isolation gnawed at me, and I would dream of Squire Tellegen's warm arms around me. I longed for the day when I could go back home and be myself again.

When I went down into grayspace one day, I found the kitchen in an uproar, and the cleaning blands racing around getting out banquet tables and chairs. I saw Gibb, and asked what was going on. "The humans decided to have a big collation tonight," it grumbled.

"Why?" I asked, since there wasn't any holiday near.

"Some human made room."

"Oh," I said indifferently.

Just then, a heavyset woman with black brows like plumes of toxic smoke spotted us. The supervisors weren't normally in grayspace at this hour; today was obviously different. She came striding over. From the way Gibb melted into the hubbub, I gathered that this must be the infamous Supervisor Moriston.

"You there," she said to me, "where's your uniform and badge?"

I looked down obsequiously. "I don't have one, ma'am."

"Who are you? Who gave you those clothes?"

"I'm Tedla, ma'am. Magister Galele's Personal."

"Oh, I've heard about you," she said ominously. "You've been filching supplies."

"Only for my guardian," I said defensively.

She advanced a step, and I retreated till my back came up against the wall. "You tell him I'm not going to tolerate any unsupervised blands in my area. If he wants to have a Personal, he has to come to me. He can't just sneak in a bland like this. You have to be processed and assigned a team, like everyone else. Got that?"

"Yes, ma'am," I said.

"Now, either get ready to do some work, or get out of here."

"Yes, ma'am," I said, and fled. When I got upstairs, Magister Galele was not in, so I waited nervously for him to come back. The confrontation had left me feeling more insecure and out of place than ever. I decided to beg him to let me go home.

Soon I heard him at the door and went out to meet him. But when I saw his face I thought she must already have tracked him down. He looked very perturbed.

"Bad news, Tedla," he said. I was opening my mouth to apologize for having made trouble when he said, "Squire Tellegen is dead."

In between two breaths, my entire world collapsed. I stood staring at him, too stunned to react. "No," I whispered.

"I'm afraid so," he said grimly. "He 'made room,' as you people say. There's to be a memorial collation tonight, and I'll have to show my face. I can't say it puts me in the mood for celebrating."

I sank into a chair; my legs wouldn't hold me up any longer. I couldn't grasp it. I couldn't imagine the world without the squire. I looked at Magister Galele, dazed.

"Did you have any inkling of this?" he asked.

Wordlessly, I nodded. The squire had given me ample warning. In fact, now I saw his sending me away in a different light. It hadn't been to remove temptation. It had been to remove me, so I wouldn't have to be the one to find him. The thought stabbed me through. I pressed a hand to my mouth and squeezed my eyes tight to keep in the tears.

Magister Galele put a hand on my shoulder. "You were really fond of him, weren't you?"

I nodded. He squeezed my shoulder. "I'm sorry, Tedla."

He left me alone for a while then. I still sat there in the chair. The world was circling around me like a whirlpool, spinning, ready to drag me down. I struggled to keep my head up, above the terrible dark water below me.

I would never go back to Menoken Lodge. The household there would be broken up, the blands all sent off to other places. I would never see any of them again. After forty years, Pelch would have to learn to be a bland again, and serve another guardian. I could only imagine its grief. At the thought, my breath caught again, and I sank a little further into the inner blackness.

Pelch would blame me, of course. It would think the squire's guilt had finally forced him to do the moral thing, to justify himself for having fallen so far below his ideals. Perhaps Pelch would be right.

With that thought, I could barely hold my nose above the surface of my grief.

The conscientious part of my mind reminded me that Magister Galele had to go out, and I ought to choose the proper combination of clothes for him, since he wouldn't know what was appropriate to wear at a memorial. I needed to make sure no one would laugh at my guardian.

Then: Magister Galele was my guardian now, forever. I would never see Squire Tellegen smile at me again. We would never play cards, or ride out onto the prairie. He was gone.

With that, the blackness pulled me down.

I managed to get through the rest of the day, though my

mind was all emotion, no thought. As I set out Magister Galele's clothes, the tears ran down my face at the thought of how I had done the same for Squire Tellegen. When I went in to shave him, my hands kept jerking and I had to give up and let him do it, or risk hurting him. He looked at me and said, "I won't be gone long tonight, Tedla. Just long enough to be decent."

He checked his messages before leaving. I was in his bedroom when I heard him exclaim, "My god, there's a message from him!" I came out into the lounge just as he began to play it on screen.

Squire Tellegen's face looked drawn and full of strain. His cheeks were dark with stubble, as if no one had shaved him in days. He looked out from the screen, paused a moment, then I heard his voice say, "Magister Galele. I barely know you, my friend. It is strange that you are the one to whom I have bequeathed the thing most precious to me in all the world. Use it well. I have only one request, one obligation, to ask of you in return: When the time comes for you to return to your own home, take it with you. There is no other solution. This planet holds no future for it. Please, take it with you."

The message ended. The screen hissed gray, empty. Magister Galele stood staring at it for several seconds, then turned around to look at me, his face a mask of dismay. "Tedla, I don't know what to say. This is horrible. I can't do it. I feel awful to deny a man's deathbed wish, but it just can't be done. He has no idea what he's asking. I don't have the power to take someone to Capella. I'm sorry. You understand, don't you?"

I couldn't imagine why he was asking me.

He paced around the room for a while, very agitated. "How could he put me in this position?" he said. "How could he do this to me?"

"You're going to be late for his collation," I said. My voice sounded mechanical.

He looked at me, terribly troubled. I recognized what

was in his face: He had never expected, or wanted, to be responsible for me. The thought of it terrified him. "We'll think of something," he said, sounding far from sure. "We'll solve this."

He left then. I went over to the screen to replay the message. I didn't listen to the words. I watched his face, seeing in it the knowledge of what he intended to do. For a moment, I felt a terrible anger toward him for abandoning me.

But when the message was over and the room was still again, what came to me in the silence was simply this: There was no one left to love me.

It was like floating in dead space, still able to breathe and think and live, but with nothing to do for the rest of my life but exist, never touching another living thing. The silence around me seemed absolute, the emptiness impenetrable.

Barely thinking, I walked into Magister Galele's bathroom. He had some medications, so I swallowed a whole bottle, washing them down with water. Then I found his razor. While I could still think, before the drugs took effect, I sharpened it methodically, then ran a tub of warm water. I knelt beside the tub and laid my arm on the edge, wrist up. It was hard to bring myself to do it, and the first cut was not deep enough. After I had cut my right wrist and saw how fast the blood came out, I went back and cut the left again, then plunged my hands into the water, thinking it would keep the blood from clotting. The sight of the bathwater turning pink disgusted me, and I turned away, trying not to watch.

It seemed like I waited there a long time. Presently my stomach began to cramp and I felt dizzy, so I laid my head down on the edge of the tub, feeling cool porcelain against my forehead. My breath was short and I could feel my heart laboring. My last thought was to wonder how Squire Tellegen had done it.

*   *   *

From somewhere far away I became aware of a voice, an anguished voice, calling my name. For a moment, in my confused state, I thought it was Joby. Then the present seeped back into my mind, still indistinct and dreamlike.

I was lying on the bathroom floor where I had collapsed, and there was blood all over me. Magister Galele was kneeling beside me, a look of intense distress on his face. He was saying my name. When he saw me look at him, he jumped up, saying, "Oh my god, oh my god." Soon he was wrapping my wrists tightly in bandages. He picked me up and carried me into the bedroom, laying me on the bed.

I heard him talking to someone on the viewscreen in a strange language. His voice was high and panicky. I was feeling horribly nauseous—sickening waves that made my throat contract and my mouth water. I knew I was going to vomit, but I didn't have the strength to move. At last I groaned. He turned and saw me. Putting a strong arm around me, he helped me over to the basin and held me while I threw up all the poison I had taken. It felt good to be rid of it. I leaned weakly against him, and he hugged me tight, then made me drink some water. It tasted terrible, but he wouldn't let me turn it down.

He took me back to the bed then. I was shivering now, so he fetched a blanket and wrapped me up in it. Then he sat down, taking me into his arms. My head was cradled in the crook of his elbow, and the warmth of his body made the cold of mine more bearable. He was talking constantly in a jumble of two languages, but I understood none of it. I thought he was being very kind, making me comfortable so I could die without suffering. I fell asleep in his arms.

It was a couple hours later that the curator arrived—an alien curator, only the second alien I had ever seen in the flesh. He examined me and tried to ask me questions, but I felt too sluggish to respond. Magister Galele hovered nearby, talking anxiously. He looked all nerves.

At last the other alien turned to him and said, "You ought to send it to a curatory."

"I can't do that," Magister Galele said pleadingly. "Don't you see? They'll blame me. I was supposed to be responsible for Tedla's welfare, and then I let this happen. They'll kick me out for sure. Oh god, how could I be so stupid?"

"Calm down, Alair," the curator said impatiently. "They won't blame you." He paused. "Unless there's a reason to."

Magister Galele looked stricken then, as he realized even his own countryman doubted him. The curator turned back to me. "I don't have any Gammadian blood, and it would be too risky to give it Capellan. All I can give it is saline."

"Well, do that, then!" Galele said.

As I watched the curator insert a needle in my vein, it slowly came to me that they weren't trying to help me to a painless death, as decent humans would. They were trying to make me live.

"No," I protested weakly. "I've got to die." I had to make these crazy aliens understand. They didn't know what they were doing to me.

Magister Galele sat down at my side and rubbed my shoulder. "Tedla, forgive me," he said. "I didn't know you would take it like this. I had no idea how you felt. I promise I'll be a good guardian to you, and do as Squire Tellegen would have wished."

It all came rushing back to me then, why I was in this humiliating position. I didn't want another guardian; I wanted Squire Tellegen back. Barring that, I wanted to die, but they weren't going to let me. I began to cry in grief and frustration.

"Stop, Tedla, stop," he pleaded, but I couldn't stop. He took me in his arms again and rocked me gently, talking soothing nonsense. I buried my face in his shirt and cried till I fell asleep again.

Over the next few days, as I slowly recovered against my will, he was always there. He fed me and talked to me, and when I became distraught he comforted me. He held me in his arms to soothe me to sleep. By the time I was strong enough to realize it, there was a bond of love between us that neither of us had expected, and neither of us could escape.

Chapter Eight

⟳ As Tedla's voice faded away, the only sound in the studium was the scarcely audible hum of the terminal. Val finally leaned back in her chair, letting out a breath. "Why didn't you tell us this wasn't your first suicide attempt?"

Tedla stared at its hands lying in its lap, wrists upturned. Val couldn't see any scars. "I didn't think you needed to know," it said faintly.

"Are you out of your mind, Tedla? We could have given you some completely wrongheaded treatment, thinking all your problems came from leaving Gammadis." She realized her voice had a scolding tone, and corrected herself more gently, "I'm sorry, it just upsets me to think we could have done you more harm, through our ignorance. It was crucial for us to know this."

Tedla's voice was so low she could barely hear the answer. "You people go around admitting things all the time, as if it made no difference."

Val realized that it was shame preventing Tedla from looking up. "I'm confused," she said. "I thought that on your planet, to kill one's self is honorable."

"For humans," Tedla said.

"Not for neuters?"

Tedla shook its head. "It's only humans who get to decide when to end their lives. Neuters are innocents, and

296

ought to trust humans to know when their lives are drawing to a close. They're supposed to let us die without suffering.'' Finally, Tedla looked up at her. ''I was so confused by the way I'd been treated, I started to act as if I were human. But I wasn't, so I didn't succeed. It taught me my place. I wish I'd learned it better.''

Gently, Val said, ''Well, I'm glad you didn't succeed.''

''Failure is not permitted on Gammadis,'' Tedla said. ''If someone tries and fails, like I did, it's so shameful the other humans just leave him alone till he does succeed. No one talks about it. It's disgraceful. It would pollute his memory.''

''So that's why you couldn't believe Magister Galele was trying to save you?''

''No Gammadian would have done the same, except out of contempt.''

''That sounds terribly heartless.''

''Being human is hard.''

Max and Deedee returned from the playground before lunch, and Max suggested that Tedla might like to accompany them on a visit to his parents' house. Val shot him a wary glance; but when Tedla was out of earshot he said, ''We can't keep it prisoner, you know.''

''Well, be careful,'' she said.

When they were gone, she sat down at her terminal to look up Galele's reports again. As she had expected, there was not a hint in them of any suicide attempt. There was, however, a suspicious two-week gap, which had earned him a reprimand, to which he had replied with a defensive memo and a mass of cobbled-together information, much of it repeating earlier reports. It should have been obvious that something was going on. Clearly, no one had been paying attention.

She had gotten no further when the chiming of a priority message interrupted her. The preview button revealed that it was Magister Gossup.

He looked somber. "I am uncertain whether this will be news to you or not," he said.

"I haven't heard anything," Val told him.

"The Gammadian delegates have learned about Tedla's presence here, and the . . . circumstances we were attempting to deal with."

Val gave a low whistle. So even WAC's information-control had limits. "What does this mean?"

"They have requested to see Tedla immediately. We have no grounds to refuse."

"All right," Val said, letting out a breath. "Tedla will be pleased."

"I am glad someone will."

"Why did you think I might know?"

"Well, we have no idea who leaked the information."

Val looked at him in astonishment. He should have known her better. "You think I did it? How could I? I don't even know where the delegates are, much less how to contact them."

"I didn't say you had done it, Valerie. You simply might have been informed by . . . other parties."

"Oh, I see—I'm a conspirator." His lack of trust was galling, and unexpected. "What is my motive supposed to be?"

Gossup paused, as if considering the most diplomatic way to answer. "Someone less sophisticated than yourself might have thought that ingratiating themselves with the delegates would ensure a place on the next Gammadian expedition."

"Well, I'm not that dumb," Val said.

"I didn't think so. I am glad to know I was right."

There was an awkward pause. At last Gossup said, "Someone will be at your home soon to escort Tedla to WAC headquarters."

"All right," Val said, not daring to let on that she had allowed Tedla to leave the house. As Gossup was reaching out to cut off the transmission, she said, "I've gotten some more interviews. I think you ought to look at them."

For the barest instant she could have sworn she saw apprehension on his face. "Very well," he said. "Send them to my cache."

When she had finished transmitting, she quickly placed a call to her in-laws. "They haven't gotten here yet," Joan told her. "Should I have them call you?"

"Yes," Val said. "Instantly. Before they do anything."

Out in the other room she heard the door open, and Deedee's voice calling, "Momma! Momma!"

"Never mind, Joan, I think they're here," Val said, and quickly got up to see.

"Momma! Some men followed us," Deedee informed her excitedly.

Val looked up at the adults. Max was trying not to show how disturbed he was. "We decided it was better not to lead them to E.G.'s house."

"God, yes," Val said.

"Is this because of me?" Tedla asked Val.

"Partly you, partly me," she said. "It's good you came back, anyway. I got a call from Magister Gossup."

When she told the news, Tedla's reaction was as much nervousness as pleasure. "I wish I'd had some warning. What am I going to say?"

It was the perfect opening for her to do some coaching. Instead, she deliberately smiled and said, "Just be yourself."

The physical location of WAC headquarters was a company secret. Though thousands visited on business or to work there every day, its carefully camouflaged location on the moon's surface was unknown to all but authorized employees—and, no doubt, to any rivals with the resources to find out. Since everyone arrived by wayport already inside the complex, there was no casual way to tell.

The buildings were constructed in one of the company's proprietary styles of architecture—Ultrabyzantine, one of the old Earth styles WAC had purchased and vigorously prosecuted anyone else for using. From the central way-port, visitors poured out into a massive cathedral dome studded with glittering mosaics. As Val stepped onto the transparent floor she saw that it was, in fact, a reflexive dome—below them, another dome yawned, brightly lit, a perfect mirror image of the one above: an ostentatiously wasteful use of space. Walking across the glassy expanse, as if suspended in midair, was disconcertingly acrophobic. She saw Tedla staring down and drew close to reassure it, but what the neuter murmured to her was, "I wonder who polishes the floor to keep it so clear."

A flock of doves flew artistically above their heads to-ward concealed nesting-niches in the dome. The WAC es-cort was heading across the transept toward the place where the altar should have been; there, gilded steps led up to a private wayport to the executive levels, under a canopy supported by writhing spiral columns and backed by a filigree reredo. Val wondered what it did to Pym and his ilk, to undergo a daily apotheosis just to get to work.

The guard disputed Val's authorization to pass through the wayport. To her surprise, Tedla quietly informed their escort that it had no intention of going any farther without her. They stood waiting as the guard placed a call, then waved them both through. Her transubstantiation author-ized, Val mounted the steps.

They found themselves in a sumptuous hotel lobby, de-serted except for staff. Still following their escort, they ascended a brass and glass elevator to the third floor, where they found not a hallway full of doors but a turquoise-paved antechamber into a connected set of suites that clearly took up the entire floor. Their guide knocked on one of the doors, then held it open for them.

Magister Gossup was sitting on a couch with a tall man who rose as soon as they entered. He had a fine-boned face and fair skin that gave him a refined, slightly effeminate look to Val's eyes—an impression reinforced by his luxuriant hair, which he wore swept back from his face and falling to his shoulders. But there was nothing effeminate about his icy blue eyes, or the frown line between them that gave him a critical expression even when he smiled.

The first thing out of his mouth, when he saw Tedla, was, "Yes, that's the one."

Tedla stopped dead just inside the door, and exclaimed, "Vestigator Nasatir! Do you remember me? We met at Menoken Lodge."

The Gammadian said something in a strange language. His tone was imperious and peremptory. Tedla's eyes fell to the floor, and the eager, hopeful look was bleached from its face. It muttered a two-syllable reply. Nasatir said something else, apparently a question. Tedla hesitated, then with a visible show of will raised its eyes to meet the delegate's. "Are you able to speak Capellan?" it said.

"Of course," the delegate said sharply, displeased.

"I would prefer their language, if you don't mind," Tedla said softly.

Nasatir seemed about to give an indignant retort, so Val said, "Thank you, Tedla. That is very considerate."

Nasatir's eyes turned to her, so she said, "Hello. I'm Magister Valerie Endrada," and held out her hand as Galele had described the Gammadian greeting-gesture. They touched palms and twined fingers, and Val decided it did have a sexual connotation, or at least a sensual one.

"I am pleased to meet you," Nasatir said in a completely different tone—not warm, but respectful.

Val turned to Gossup. "Magister Gossup, I don't think you have met Tedla in person."

Gossup came forward to shake Tedla's hand. "I am quite pleased to meet you, Tedla," he said. "I wish it could have happened sooner."

With a furtive glance at Nasatir, Tedla said warmly, "I

feel honored, Magister Gossup. I have always admired your work.''

"That gives me pleasure. Please have a seat," Gossup said. He returned to the couch himself.

Was he on Tedla's side after all? Val glanced at Nasatir and saw the expression of bafflement that he quickly concealed. The Gammadian took a chair to Val's left, across from Tedla. His back was rigid, and he sat tensely forward; his eyes flicked from Gossup to Val and back again, obviously uncertain of his footing. Tedla looked equally uncomfortable, but its eyes were on the floor.

"What is your role, Magister Endrada?" Nasatir asked. "Please forgive me if I get your language wrong. I've had very little practice." He seemed to be trying not to look at Tedla.

"I am a colleague of Magister Gossup's," Val said. "I'm here as a friend of Tedla's."

Nasatir looked puzzled and slightly suspicious. "What do you mean, 'friend'?"

She wondered what there was about the word that didn't translate. "Tedla's been staying at my house for the past several days," she explained.

Much more warmly, Nasatir said, "Ah, you are the one who has been caring for it since . . . thank you. We are indebted to you. I hope you weren't inconvenienced."

"Not at all," Val said. "It's been a valuable opportunity."

Nasatir said, "We were quite chagrined to hear the story of its shameful behavior. Please accept my apologies. I'm afraid it's badly disturbed—you can scarcely blame it, after all it's been through."

Val should have been prepared, but still she was taken aback to hear him speak of Tedla as if it weren't in the room. She said, "Believe me, I don't blame Tedla."

There was an uncomfortable pause. Nasatir had clearly heard something in her voice that wasn't in her words. He said delicately, "I understand that it has been full of stories."

Val glanced sharply at Gossup. He looked noncommittal. Tedla's face looked gray. "I have conducted some interviews," she said. "Is that what you mean?"

"Has Magister Gossup spoken to you about them?" Nasatir said.

"No."

"I have to warn you, then, not to give this bland's tales much credence. I have no idea what has inspired it to utter such falsehoods and filth. It's beyond my understanding, except that the poor creature is quite unbalanced." He finally looked at Tedla. His outward benignity clearly hid a steely anger.

"I'm sorry if we have gotten the wrong impression," Val said. "Can you give me an example?"

"Quite easily," Nasatir said confidently. "There is a place called Brice's on my planet. It's an experimental training center, serving the academic and scientific community. Not the kind of place that would train blands for a mattergrave's house, or for any domestic position at all. This bland got all that wrong, because it was never at Brice's. Doubtless it heard of the place, and thought that having been trained there would sound more prestigious than the truth. The whole story was fabricated. Believe me, we made it a point to look up this neuter's past."

Val looked to Tedla. Its face was chalky white. It sat with its shoulders hunched forward, staring at its knees.

Nasatir went on, "That part is relatively trivial and easy to disprove. The allegations concerning Lexigist Tellegen . . ." Here his voice changed. It was clear he took a personal affront. "I knew Prosper Tellegen. Many people did. He was a deep thinker and a highly moral man. One of the few truly great men I have known. Why this bland should turn on him, with these revolting slanders, I have no idea. Certainly, Tellegen never showed it anything but the greatest kindness. Too much kindness, perhaps. And this is the way it repays him.''

Val was staring at Gossup. She had sent him the interviews about Tellegen only this morning—she glanced at the time display on the room screen—a little over an hour ago. How had he watched them and conveyed their essence to Nasatir in that time? And why had she not told him they were confidential?

She looked at Tedla, expecting reproach, but its face looked completely blank. ''Tedla?'' she said. ''Do you want to answer?''

Tedla shook its head.

''He's saying you lied. That you made it all up. What are we supposed to believe?''

In a dull voice, Tedla said, ''He's right. I did make it up. It's all lies.''

Nasatir settled back in his chair, at ease.

There was a long silence. At last Val said, ''You're saying I'm a complete dupe?''

Tedla wouldn't look at her. ''I'm sorry.''

''Don't blame yourself, Magister,'' Nasatir said sympathetically. ''I'm sure it was very convincing. Perhaps the bland even convinced itself, in its confusion. Living among you has obviously sexualized it. You would have had to know our culture very well to see how preposterous it all was. Believe me, for any true Gammadian, the thought of physical contact with a neuter is completely revolting.''

He sounded sincere. If Val had not been watching Tedla closely, she would have missed the expression that glanced across its face—a look of deep outrage, swiftly hidden. Until then, she had been uncertain what to think. After that, she knew.

Nasatir went on, ''The whole controversy over this bland has been one unfortunate misunderstanding after another. From our point of view, the sooner we get it all behind us, the better. We don't wish to make an issue of it from now on."

"That is very generous of you, Delegate," Gossup murmured.

Nasatir smiled at them both genially. "Well, no harm done." He rose. "Come along, Tedla."

Tedla sat unmoving, looking dazed. "Excuse me?" it said uncertainly.

Patiently, Nasatir said, "We're sending you home, Tedla."

Tedla looked at Val. "Do I have to go?"

Val managed to keep her voice even. "It's up to you."

Turning back to Nasatir, Tedla said carefully, "Under what circumstances will I return?"

"Circumstances?" Nasatir said, almost on the edge of laughter.

"What will my status be?"

As if to a silly child, Nasatir said, "What do you think it will be?" He turned to Val and Gossup. "You see how you people have confused it. I think it would be better if you left us alone."

Suddenly, Tedla rose from its chair, facing Nasatir tensely across the coffee table. "No. Please stay."

Neither Val nor Gossup moved. In a kind but stern voice, Nasatir said, "Tedla. You should know that the elector of the Tapis questionaries has empowered me to act as your guardian. You need to remember what that means, before I become displeased."

With an enormous force of will, Tedla looked him in the eye and said, "I am sorry, Delegate Nasatir, but I can't acknowledge your jurisdiction over me. I'm willing to discuss returning to Gammadis, but not under those conditions."

Nasatir burst out, "Oh, this is ridiculous." He turned to Val angrily. "What do you think you'll gain by teaching it to talk like that to me? Who are you working for?"

Val said, "Delegate Nasatir, your dispute is with Tedla, not with me."

With bitter sarcasm, Nasatir said, "Oh, yes. You are going to get me to negotiate with a bland." He turned to Gossup. "Perhaps I have not made myself clear. The return of this neuter is an absolute prerequisite to diplomatic relations. This is not a negotiable point."

Gossup rose to calm the waters. "I think it would be better if we adjourned to think things over," he said. "Delegate Nasatir, let us speak to Tedla. I'm sure we all want the same thing; we just need to find how to get there."

The delegate looked thoroughly displeased at the prospect of letting Tedla out of his sight. Gossup said, "Tedla, would you and Valerie wait in the blue room for a moment?"

As Val rose to leave, Nasatir surveyed her with a cold eye. She didn't bother with parting pleasantries.

As soon as they were alone, Val said, "Tedla, I'm so sorry. I had no idea Gossup would tell the delegate what you told me. I've violated your privacy. It was totally unethical. I feel horrible."

"It was my own fault," Tedla said.

"No, it wasn't. It was ours. Those interviews were confidential. I wouldn't blame you for telling me to get out of your life forever."

Tedla gave her an apprehensive look. "Is that what you want?"

"Of course not!" Val reached out and squeezed its hand. "I was so proud of you when you stood up to him," she said.

"You sound like Magister Galele," Tedla said.

"We Capellans like people with courage."

"I'd forgotten what it was like to be a bland," Tedla said, preoccupied. "I've gotten so used to the way you people treat me. I didn't know I was going to argue with him, till I did. It was horrible behavior. I acted human. But the strange thing was, I even *felt* human. What felt wrong was acting like a bland. He was right, you people have done something to me. You've corrupted me." It turned to her with a troubled look. "Val, I don't think I can do it. I'm not a bland any more."

She wanted to hug it. "Bless you, Tedla," she said warmly. "It's about time you noticed."

The door clicked, and Magister Gossup came silently through. He said in an undertone, "Valerie, I was not the one who told him about your interviews. He brought them up to me himself, shortly before you came. I haven't even seen the latest ones. I don't believe he's seen them either; he's only heard a summary. From whom, I don't know."

Val felt the clutch of paranoia. "Someone must be listening on my home terminal."

"Well, it isn't WAC," Gossup said. "It's someone trying to sabotage the negotiations."

"Epco?"

"It's a possibility. You need to be cautious; they are sabotaging you in the process."

He was right; the forces at work here would crush her career without a thought. There was nothing personal about it. She was just in the way.

Gossup turned to Tedla. "Delegate Nasatir just reiterated to me how essential it is for you to return. He is quite adamant about it. I am not sure why. Do you know?"

Tedla shook its head gravely.

Gossup sighed. "At present, he is making it a condition for further negotiation. That means it will be WAC's desire, and my duty, to persuade you." His voice sounded perfectly neutral. Watching, Val felt her confidence in his support ebbing. He went on, "Is there any demand you might have, any condition that WAC can meet, that would make it possible for you to return? I can assure you, the company's full resources can be brought to bear."

Tedla looked overwhelmed. "What could WAC do?

Change a thousand years of history? Make me human?''

Very delicately, Gossup said, ''You realize, don't you, that the latter option might be technically feasible?''

Tedla drew back, and its voice turned frosty. ''I know you could change my body. It wouldn't make me human. Not for me, not for Delegate Nasatir.''

Gossup quickly retreated. ''I'm only trying to raise a variety of options.''

''What options can there be?'' Val said.

''There are always options,'' Gossup said sternly. She got his message: He was expecting her to be his ally. She could redeem herself by somehow twisting Tedla's arm into consenting. The thing that left a foul taste in her mouth was the knowledge that she could probably do it if she tried—and Gossup knew it.

''I need to think about it,'' Tedla said. ''I need to go home and think.''

''Could I persuade you to take a room here?'' Gossup asked carefully.

''No.'' There was a resolution in Tedla's face that Val had never seen there before. ''I will go home with Val.''

''A number of people would feel more comfortable if . . .''

''I will go home,'' Tedla said firmly.

''Very well,'' Gossup said, with a significant look at Val. She had her assignment. At that instant, she felt a bitter anger at him, for putting her in this position.

The Magister walked them out through the lobby, pausing for a low-toned conversation with the guard posted at the wayport. As they crossed the echoing dome, he said to Tedla, ''What did the delegate say to you when you first came in?''

''He asked me why I thought I could justify myself,'' Tedla said expressionlessly. ''But it wasn't what he said. It was the language that mattered. All this time I've been wanting to hear my own language spoken, and forgetting that humans and blands speak it differently. It's a dialect

we use. It sounds simplified, almost childish. That's why
I had to speak your language. I realized I couldn't answer
him in a human dialect without sounding arrogant and presumptuous, and I couldn't make myself talk like a bland.
Not any more.''

Val looked at Gossup. She wondered if he still thought
there were options. To her, there only seemed like two:
self-destruction or betrayal.

The sun was setting when they reached their home wayport, giving way to a pink Gomb-light that made the egg-
domes of the copartment complex look like fluffs of cotton
candy against the jagged landscape. The port would normally have been crowded with commuters at this time, but
it was Allday, and only a few stragglers were about, loitering around the shop displays where the autoclerks were
ever ready to take their orders. UIC enclaves were secular,
so commerce went on around the clock and around the
calendar.

Val and Tedla headed up the hill, side by side. Val was
so preoccupied by her dark thoughts that she didn't notice
the steps following them till Tedla cast a quick glance over
its shoulder.

"It's not the same two that followed us earlier today,"
Tedla whispered to her. She also glanced back. It was a
man and a woman, wearing green coveralls instead of the
WAC security uniform of suit and tie. Each of them was
carrying a shoulder bag. The woman was grasping something in her hand. They were walking fast; their purpose
was clearly not to follow, but to overtake.

Grasping Tedla's arm, Val steered it into the walkway
of the housing complex adjoining her own. They were
soon surrounded by the copartment domes, which met the
ground in jagged shapes like broken shells. Breaking into
a fast walk, Val ducked under the eaves formed by one of
the overhanging dome-shells, dodging the clutter where
residents had staked out patio space with lawn furniture,

bicycles, and toys. Darting from dome to dome, she headed toward the fence separating this complex from her own. Behind, she heard a crash, then heavy footsteps, running. She broke into a dash, Tedla close beside her.

Tedla was first to reach the gate, and jerked it open. Val glanced back. Their pursuers were rounding the last dome at a run. She could see now what was in the woman's hand—a transdermal, doubtless a knockout drug. She dived through the gate after Tedla and slammed the latch down, but there was no way to bolt it. "Head for the main dome," she said. It was the closest structure, and with luck there might be people there.

They raced down the walkway. As they rounded the dome, they saw the entryway was lighted, and people were gathered on the steps. Tedla slowed hesitantly, but Val pushed it on through the door.

Only when she saw the decorations in the brightly lit common room did she realize that they had barged in on a wedding reception.

"Oh my god!" she said, horrified.

"What?" Tedla stepped nearer, alarmed.

"It's Elise and Radko's wedding," she said. "I was invited. I completely forgot."

There was a sound of scuffling from the door, and an angry voice. Val dragged Tedla with her into the reception line. There were too many people here for a covert kidnapping. "Quick, Tedla, what do Gammadians say at weddings?" she said.

"We don't have weddings," Tedla said, eyes on the door.

"Oh, of course. Well, how do you wish each other good luck?"

"We say, 'May you die in the bed of earth.' "

"Good Lord, that won't do."

They had come to the front of the line, and the bride said warmly, "Val! Max said you wouldn't be able to make it. I'm so glad you did. Thanks for your present."

Thinking she had the best husband in the world, Val said, "I'm so happy for you, Elise. May you sleep together on the bed of earth. That's an old Gammadian wedding saying." She dragged Tedla forward. "This is my friend Tedla, from Gammadis."

"Welcome to Capella Two," Elise said.

"I hope you'll be very happy," Tedla said, only a little flustered.

There was no sign of their pursuers. They collected pieces of honeyed ricebread—Val noted that it was a Chorister recipe; Elise must have paid a fortune for the rights. The music was being provided by a lutska ensemble using live goats—not top-of-the-line, but still more expensive than she would have sprung for. She spied Max at one of the long community tables, Deedee beside him, wearing her prized rainbow skirt, the only nongeneric article of clothing she owned. As Val slipped into the seat beside Max, she said in a low voice, "Am I glad you're here."

"I thought you'd forgotten," Max said.

"I had. Two thugs chased us in here. I'm sure they had more in mind than picking our pockets."

Deedee climbed out of her seat to show Tedla how her skirt flared out when she twirled around, a demonstration that always made her dizzy and giggly. Several older couples at nearby tables were looking on fondly. Val leaned close to Max to tell him what had happened.

"What are we going to do?" Max said seriously.

Val said, "I don't know."

"We can't let Tedla go back to that planet."

"I don't know if we can stop it."

"No. What you mean is, you don't know if we can stop them from taking it." Max had a challenging look. It made Val feel defensive.

"What do you expect from me, Max? I'm up to my neck in trouble already."

"I've got an idea," Max said in a very low voice.

Val glanced around to see who was listening. A young

woman had settled down next to Tedla, and was talking to it earnestly. Her body language was openly flirtatious. Val thought of coming to the rescue, but Tedla didn't seem in bad trouble yet, so she turned back to Max. "What?"

"I think we should post Tedla's story on the public nets," Max said.

"You're crazy," Val said.

"I'm serious. It would rouse public interest, and public sympathy."

"Max, I can name at least thirty-seven reasons why that's a terrible idea. For starters, WAC would hit the stratosphere."

"Let them," Max said.

"Easy for you to say. For seconds, that story is valuable. Tedla could probably get a good income from the royalties, if it were marketed right."

"And I suppose the xenologist who did the interviews would get a cut?" Max said.

"Well, yes, but . . ." She realized she was groping for excuses and flared angrily, "Since when is it a crime to try to provide for my family?"

Several people looked around at them, and Val tried to pretend it wasn't her with the poor taste to have a marital spat at a wedding. Tedla and the young woman had gone off to the edge of the dance floor and were taking turns whirling Deedee around in imitation of the older couples. Deedee was in heaven. The young woman was in for a rude surprise, Val thought.

"Val, can't you see? You're playing into their hands," Max said softly. "You're acting suspicious and proprietary, just like the marketeers want. The companies need us all to be alienated from each other, because it cuts off routes of communication they can't control. If everyone shared information openly, it wouldn't be a controllable commodity, and no one could profit from it. They need our behavioral collaboration to make their windfalls. Trusting each other enough to communicate honestly is the most subversive thing we can do."

"It's very noble of you, Max," Val said. "But I'm no subversive. I don't know why you've never noticed before."

"Maybe because you've never controlled any really valuable information up to now."

Val watched Tedla playing with her daughter and thought Max was right on one thing—Tedla was valuable information. Valuable enough to make its life perilous. Valuable enough that companies and whole planets were plunging into conflict over it. But the worth of any information lay in its scarcity. If nothing about Tedla were a secret, if every nook of its life were exposed on the massive scale Max was proposing, would it be safe?

She shook her head. "There's another reason we couldn't do it," she said. "Tedla's privacy. It would never consent. It denied everything today, just to protect people who have been dead for half a century."

"But if the choice is between exposure and slavery . . ." Max fell silent, watching Tedla across the room. "Do you think we ought to do something before that girl falls in love and ruins her life?"

"Yes," Val said decisively. "Besides, people are beginning to leave. This is the safest time to get to our house."

It was a short walk, but the path between the domes was narrow and dark. As they left the laughter and light behind, Val drew close to the others. Max and Tedla were walking ahead, she and Deedee behind. Max was teasing Tedla— unwisely, Val thought—about its romantic conquest.

"Don't pay any attention," she told Tedla. "He's just jealous."

"There was nothing sexual going on," Tedla said uncomfortably.

"Want to bet?" Max said. "What did she say?"

"She was telling me about her boyfriend."

"Do perfect strangers usually come up and tell you about their love lives?"

"More often than you'd think," Tedla said. "It used to puzzle me. Then I learned that many gendered cultures actually create an asexual class to act as confessors and counselors. It's as if people sense I'm a noncombatant. A neutral third party."

"What did she give you when we came up?" Max asked.

Embarrassed, Tedla said, "Her connection number."

"Aha!" Max said, as if that proved his point.

Ahead, a shadow materialized from the shrubbery, holding an object in its hand. Instinctively, Val grabbed for Deedee with one hand, Tedla with the other. Max said aggressively, "Who's that?"

The figure came closer, and Val recognized the WAC man who had escorted them earlier that day. He was holding a radio. "Go in the back door, please," he said. "Your house is secure."

Val gripped Deedee and Tedla harder. "Were you the ones who chased us coming here?" she demanded.

The man shook his head. "Why do you think we wanted you to stay where we could protect you?"

"Who were they, then?"

"We don't know. We didn't catch them."

As they walked to the door, Val heard him reporting their location to someone over the radio.

Val took care of putting Deedee to bed that night. As she bent over to kiss her daughter good night, Deedee said in a small voice, "Mama? Are the men going to come in here?"

"No, chick," Val said. "They can't come in here. You're perfectly safe. I'll always keep you safe."

After that, Val sat on the edge of the bed and read from one of the books Deedee loved and Max loathed till sleep began to take over, then sat looking at her daughter's face. Deedee looked so secure, so trusting, as if Val's promise were a protective spell. In the silence, broken only by the low, barely audible voices of Max and Tedla talking in the gathering room, Val realized she didn't have the courage to face what she had started. If it had been only herself, it might have been different. But now it was beginning to touch Deedee, and that she could not cope with. She was going to have to give in.

She turned off the light, then went into her bedroom. Lying on her bed, she stared at the ceiling for a while, then turned on the screen and flicked through her files till she got to Alair Galele's reports. She was beginning to feel a furtive empathy with the man. She wondered if he had had this ominous feeling of being swept forward toward an inevitable choice where no alternative was good.

She read:

At last—at long last—I feel I may have found a genuinely useful native informant. How astonished they would all be. They would assure me I was wrong, that I needed someone educated and aware, someone with an analytical intelligence. But Tedla is useful to me precisely because of its naiveté, its lack of education (i.e. indoctrination), its complete unawareness of the "right" answer. It has no agenda in speaking to me, other than to please me. I also flatter myself that, unique among Gammadians, it has begun to trust me.

We had some rocky patches at first. Of course, I was perfectly delighted from the outset, and thanked Tellegen profusely. On the ride home I kept checking the backseat like Orpheus, to make sure Tedla really was there, and I hadn't imagined it all. Tedla was considerably less thrilled than I. For the first week it wandered about with a stunned, disconsolate expression, as if marooned on a planet it had never seen. I had to restrain myself from calling Tellegen every ten minutes to ask for instructions and advice. I broke down often enough that he got a little testy with me, and told me I was being obsessive. He kept urging me not

*to interfere, just to let Tedla settle in and find its own way
of relating to me. At the time the advice was hard to follow,
since I was impatient to strike up a friendship; but now I
realize how good the advice was. Tedla is not at all like
the humans here, outwardly warm and inwardly cold and
secretive. With Tedla the cold (or is it fear? formality?) is
all on the outside. Once past that barrier, you're in a hurricane world of passionate loyalty, touching warmth, and
blackest self-blame. A breathtaking trip, if you have the
stomach for it. And they told me neuters were dull, phleg-
matic creatures. But I'm off the subject.*

*I am uncertain yet of Tedla's abilities, though that was
my first question. It claims not to be able to do a great
many things. I am uncertain whether to chalk this up to
cultural indoctrination, low self-confidence, or mere pro-
letarian work avoidance. Nevertheless, I believe my questioning is beginning to waken its interest in the world. It
is naturally observant, and is now learning (with my subversive encouragement) to put its observations into words.
It has even begun to volunteer information. This has
opened a whole new world to my study—a world I can
never enter, but merely record secondhand. Grayspace, as
Tedla calls it, is a thriving alternate culture not even native
Gammadians are fully aware of.*

As she paged forward, Val saw that Galele's reports
became more copious, and were increasingly filled with
Tedla's name. Skimming, she wondered at its repetition:
Tedla, Tedla, Tedla. Had no one noticed or cared how
much time the man was spending studying his informant?
Her eye lit on isolated passages:

*I am quite unable to characterize Tedla's thought pro-
cesses. Abstract language produces no reaction, but if I
can explain in concrete, narrative form it grasps a concept
readily. At one moment it will be quite lucid and logical
(though never theoretical), and the next it will retreat be-*

hind hidebound precepts, refusing to consider an idea because "That's not what the docents said." One moment it is a thorough martinet, the next a bundle of vulnerability. It is very aware of its own physical attractiveness—in fact, quite vain—but dashes any compliment as soon as it's uttered. I am quite perplexed how to please it—I'm constantly being made aware that my foot is in my mouth. Who would have thought I would have to learn to live with a teenager?

Gave Tedla a standardized intelligence test. My informant resisted and complained, telling me that such things were only for children, and it had lost the ability to perform them. I insisted, and was disappointed at the lower-than-average results. I will readminister it in several months, and in the meantime work on Tedla's self-fulfilling prophecies.

I am a little troubled by one aspect of Tedla's behavior. On occasion it acts almost seductive toward me. It has no sense of privacy, and would walk in on me in every conceivable state of undress, if I didn't speak sharply to prevent it (there are no locks on our doors). Yesterday it came into my bedroom looking quite melancholy. When I asked the reason, it complained bitterly about having to sleep alone. As it told me this, it sat on the edge of my bed, fingering the covers, and glancing at me in the most fetching way. The implication seemed to be that I was supposed to invite it to sleep with me. Needless to say, I did not.

I cannot decide whether this behavior is even conscious on Tedla's part. Is the youngster so profoundly innocent it does not understand the nuances of its actions? Or is it in fact trying to provoke me, or inflame me, perhaps to buy more security for itself, and a tighter bond to its protector? Or is it all in my mind?

My policy is to meet its flirtations, if that is what they are, with indifference. If the behavior is conscious, it will

*soon stop. Tedla is very perceptive, and extremely attuned
to my moods. To pursue any other course would be sure
disaster.*

*Interesting responses from my friends: On hearing that
I had acquired a bland, my friendly coffee-house owner
sat me down and gave me a long lecture on how to protect
myself from being taken advantage of. "Don't trust it out
of your sight," she said. "If you're not looking, it will be
thieving, or lazing, or playing you tricks, imposing on your
good nature." She appeared to think I was a mark ripe
for predation. The thought of my needing protection from
Tedla was so ludicrous I had to laugh. "My bland's only
about sixteen," I said.*

*"It doesn't matter. They learn their tricks young.
They're nasty, dirty brutes."*

*Since my bland is a good sight cleaner and more cir-
cumspect than I am, I found this hard to take seriously.*

*Gambion's reaction was totally different. I had invited
him and Auri over for drinks—my quarters now being so
presentable I have no qualms letting others see them.
Tedla has a perfect mastery of all the niceties of proper
entertainment, and served us with great style and relish. I
saw my two guests exchanging looks, and after the canapes
Gambion drew me aside and warned me quite seriously
about the dangers of "exploiting" my bland. I assured him
it was the farthest thing from my mind, but he persisted,
and it gradually dawned on me that he was talking about
physical intimacy (though he never said the words). In a
whisper he assured me that such practices will debase a
human, reduce intellectual capacity, sap physical strength,
and lead to disease.*

*I was quite alarmed by his gravity. "Will people assume
there is something going on . . . ?" I said.*

*"No, no, of course not," he said immediately. "I just
don't know the mores of your world, and wanted to warn
you of ours."*

"On our world it would be unthinkable," I lied, but convincingly.

"I am glad to hear it," he said.

It was quite a revelation to me that they had any mores at all on the subject, since nothing is forbidden unless it happens. The apparent strength of the taboo points to something deep in the Gammadian psyche.

Made some discreet inquiries to confirm Gambion's information. If anything, he gave me the soft version. Sexual relations with a neuter are viewed as something lower than bestiality. An exposed *"dirt digger"* (their euphemism, not mine) can be sure of never finding another sexual partner, and might even be expelled from the order. I must be terribly circumspect. I cannot afford even the whiff of such a scandal to touch me. Thank goodness for the treatments.

Blands clearly have a class culture, in the sense of expressive practices. But do they have a class consciousness? Obviously, they recognize themselves as a group, and some even recognize their treatment as oppression. But does this create solidarity? Would it ever result in collective action?

Tedla thinks not. *"We're too dumb,"* it says. But when I argued, Tedla came up with another explanation: that the blands are actually getting something out of the arrangement. *"We never have to worry where our next meal is going to come from, or make plans,"* it says. In other words, they are living the lives of domestic pets. I pressed Tedla on the concepts of freedom and self-determination, but they seemed quite foreign to it. Or they have been discarded as a fair tradeoff for security.

As the situation becomes increasingly clear to me, it is harder to conceal from Tedla my contempt for the exploitative system this planet hides under a veil of self-deceiving hypocrisy. Tedla has been thoroughly drilled in the psychology of dependence. WAC's profit forbids me from denouncing this system for what it is. But at times I think that if I could just start a tiny question, even in one young *person's mind, it would be worth the hundred years I've given up to come here.*

It may be my imagination, but Tedla appears to be getting quite attached to me. I find it touching, but also a little worrisome. I don't want it to get expectations I cannot fulfill. I have seen how deep its emotional attachments can become, and I am loathe to think of our inevitable separation. If this is merely adolescent infatuation with an older mentor, or even conditioned loyalty to a master, it still gives me a certain responsibility. I have such complete power over its life.

Got a message from the First Contact group, warning me to stop making myself so conspicuous, being such a character. *We must strive to bore our hosts. In banality is strength. I will attempt to comply.*

There was a soft knock on the bedroom door. Val blanked the screen, then called out, "Come in."

It was Tedla. Val sat up cross-legged on the bed and said, "What's on your mind, Tedla?"

The neuter sat down on the bed, looking pensive. It said hesitantly, "I've been thinking maybe I ought to go stay at WAC, as Magister Gossup suggested."

Val was silent. It was what she had been thinking herself an hour ago. But despite her resolve, now that Tedla was sitting in front of her she found it hard to say. Instead, she said, "You realize that WAC is on the delegates' side?"

"I know that," Tedla said. It looked down at the coverlet, tracing the quilting with one finger. "But you've risked a lot for me. I can never repay all you've done, and if any harm comes to your family . . ."

Val pictured herself saying, "You're right, as long as I thought I could get something out of you I was willing to take the risk, but now the odds have turned against you."

Would it be the truth? Instead, she said, "What does Max say?"

"I don't know. I didn't ask him."

"Did he tell you his brilliant idea?"

"No."

"What were you talking about all this time, then?"

Tedla glanced at her, embarrassed. "Um . . . you."

"Me?" Val said, astonished.

Tedla nodded, but said nothing more. Val said, "You can't leave it there. What were you saying?"

Choosing its words very carefully, Tedla said, "He's very worried about you. Did you know that?"

"No," Val said. "Why?"

Hesitantly, Tedla said, "It's the pressure of getting your career going. He's watched you constructing a professional persona to market—the bright, ambitious career woman. It's not your real character, he says. It's a marketable identity you've manufactured, a performance. But now he's worried that you're beginning to buy it yourself. He doesn't want you to turn into your own persona."

Val could tell that Tedla was reporting accurately; it all had the ring of Max's thinking. She could even imagine how she would have bristled hearing it in Max's voice, how angry she would have gotten. But somehow, the translation into Tedla's soft tones made it different. The information came to her straight, removed from the context of old arguments and annoyances.

"It must be hard to be a Capellan," Tedla went on. "You're all brought up to deceive one another, because openness might damage your saleability. How do you ever know if you're falling in love with a real person, and not a product?"

"I guess we don't," Val said.

Tedla glanced up at her. "Max does love you, you know. This wouldn't drive him crazy if he didn't."

It had been a long time since she had asked herself about that. She leaned forward and put her hand over Tedla's where it rested on the coverlet. "Thank you, Tedla," she said.

There was a thunderous noise from the gathering room. "Oh damn, what now?" Val said tensely. She scrambled off the bed. As she reached the gathering room, Max was emerging from the dinery. The noise was someone knocking on their door.

"Let me handle this," Max said.

Val heard a shriek of fear from Deedee's room. When she turned on the light, Deedee was cowering in her bed. Val took the child in her arms. "Don't worry, Deedee," she said, "no one's going to hurt you."

Out in the gathering room, Max was talking to the front-door viewer. They had never used it before. When Val emerged from the bedroom, carrying Deedee, she saw on the screen that the intruder was a stocky woman in a peace officer uniform. "Process server," said the speaker.

"At this hour?" Val said.

"Hold your credentials up to the viewer," Max ordered. The woman complied. Warily, Max opened the door.

"Tedla Galele?" the woman said.

"What's your business?" Max demanded.

"I've got a summons. Are you Tedla Galele?"

Val felt Tedla behind her, its light touch on her shoulder. "I'm Tedla Galele," it said.

The woman held out a slate. "I need your thumbprint and signature."

Tedla came forward, signed, and received a sealed envelope. The woman turned to go.

Max and Val both looked on as Tedla opened the envelope and read the document inside. When it looked up, its expression had a touch of irony. "The delegates have filed an extradition request before the Court of a Thousand Peoples."

Val let out the breath she hadn't realized she was holding. "I guess they didn't want to wait for you to decide," she said.

"They didn't want to acknowledge I had a right to decide," Tedla said. "Bad precedent."

Its face had the firm look she had seen before, briefly, at WAC. She asked, "Are you going to fight them?"

Tedla paused a long time. "Yes," it said at last. "I thought I wanted to go back. But I'm remembering a lot of things now." It looked to Val. "You don't know how I came to leave my planet. Even if you've read the official version, you still don't know."

"There isn't an official version," Val said. "The whole story's been suppressed."

"Then I need to tell you," Tedla said.

"Good. I'd like that."

"Can we go in the studium?"

Val hesitated. "As long as we don't turn on the terminal. It's not secure."

"You don't understand. I *want* you to turn on the terminal. I want whoever is listening to hear this part."

"Can I sit in?" Max asked.

"Yes," Tedla said. It looked at Deedee, who seemed far from any sleep. "You all can. I'm tired of this concealment. I want you to know the truth."

Chapter Nine

✳ A great many lies have been spoken about Magister Galele. It is time I told the truth.

The months following Squire Tellegen's death were very hard for me. Each morning I would wake up alone, and all the weight of my life would press me back. I had no interest in my duties any more, and had to drag myself through the day as if time had grown thick and slow, resisting my passage. Through all of this Magister Galele was there, feeding me pills and coffee, talking to distract me, giving me jobs to occupy my mind. But the most powerful tonic he gave me was affection. He was patient when I would stop responding to him, and held me in his arms when nothing else would cheer me. Say what you will about him, to me he was the kindest-hearted man alive, and I grew to love him dearly.

It was a very different feeling than the one I had had for Squire Tellegen, so different I didn't recognize it at first. I wasn't blind to Magister Galele's faults. He didn't inspire awe and admiration. In fact, I loved him because he needed me as badly as I needed him. We were both muddled and groping in a world of people who seemed to know exactly what they were doing.

He was his own worst enemy. Time and again I watched him sabotage himself. He was always ready to jump up and race off to do something without thinking it through. He was easily distracted, always sidelined by a good conversation or a novel experience. He could head off in sixteen different directions in a single hour. I had been trained to be systematic and methodical, and he nearly drove me to distraction at times. But I must say, he never bored me.

Even then, in those early months, I wondered whether his constant activity was a race to escape his own thoughts. I had many thoughts of my own to avoid, and I saw his perpetual motion through the lens of my mood.

"What a rich feast your planet is!" he would exclaim to me after relating some discovery he'd made. "You have such a thick, chunky gumbo of a culture. My own culture has become a watery bouillon, a mere broth of what it once was. But Gammadis—you never know what you'll find yourself chewing on."

And yet every now and then I would catch him brooding, as if thinking of his home, left so far behind him. My own homesickness ached like an ulcer, and I imagined his must be worse—fifty-one light-years worse. But if he thought I had noticed him, he would leap up, all good humor again.

There were odd lapses in his knowledge of our world. He had made great strides with the language since I first saw him, but was strangely ignorant of manners, style, and taste. Perhaps he was just naturally impatient with such matters. But I had been drilled in them, and so I drilled him. He called me his Master of Protocol. I wouldn't let him out in public until I'd checked that his shoes matched and his mustache was free of food.

"You act like my mother," he said once.

"I just want people to respect you," I said.

"You're such a prig, Tedla. If you weren't fifteen, I'd swear you were fifty."

"Grump, grump, grump," I said. I knew exactly what I could get away with. And if I could make him laugh, I could get away with nearly anything.

In the course of cleaning his apartment, I had come up against the irreducible mass of material he had collected, most of it notes and raw data he intended someday to process. I had shoved much of it into the closets, but it was constantly overflowing. One day I asked what he wanted it all for, and he stood staring at a stack of bursting boxes sadly, as if reflecting on his own inadequacy. "I ought to be indexing, translating, and digitizing it. I have to get it all in shape to ship back."

"You need an assistant," I said.

Something dawned on him, and he said, "Tedla, do you want to be really helpful to me?"

"I meant a human assistant," I said. "I'm not smart enough to do this."

"Oh, it doesn't take any brains at all," he said. "It's the most tedious, mindless work imaginable. It regularly bores humans into a coma."

I couldn't tell if he was serious or joking. He said, "Please? I'll teach you some things so simple a well-behaved ashtray could do them."

That was how he manipulated me into helping with his work. It wasn't nearly as simple as he made out. The records were in a jumble of formats and two languages, so he had me start out by scanning all the written matter and putting the recordings through the transcriber. Of course, I then had to correct the transcriptions. We devised a filing system, and that led to an index so he could look things up by date, name, or subject. Soon I was spending hours each day at the terminal in the studium. It cut into my other work, but he kept saying, "This is much more useful to me, really."

The truth was, I couldn't have kept busy just managing that one small apartment, and I was glad for the methodical thinking the clerical work took. Even if the world around me was shattering and shimmering with impermanence, I could create a tiny pocket of order in the clutter of Magister Galele's research.

He was still quite avid to get information about gray-space, and as soon as I felt able to go back among the blands, he began coaching me on what to look for. It was a long list: songs, stories, proverbs, pastimes, crafts, beliefs. Then he had more complex questions. Were there hierarchies among the blands, leaders and subordinates? What did blands think about humans? Did they have a sense of their own history? How did they keep antisocial elements in line? He would never just accept my opinion: Always I had to bring him concrete evidence, and explain what I thought the evidence proved, and why.

I was not even aware how profoundly he was changing the channels of my thought. He was teaching me not just self-awareness but social awareness. No one on my planet distinguishes blands and humans the way he did. To us, the differences are a matter of mental capacity; to him they were sociological. Always before, I had thought of blands as mere parasites on human society, completely dependent, incapable of creative action. Bland thoughts were just childish versions of human thoughts. Magister Galele taught me to see us as a group with our own original customs and modes of thinking. I didn't know it then, but I could never turn back once I had learned this. To *see* something you must cease to *be* it.

I am not sure it was entirely a gift. It is a peculiarly Capellan affliction, this need to articulate and analyze your own behaviors, thoughts, and creations. The more you analyze them, the more alienated from them you get, until you lose all the richness of unconscious act, and your glib articulation becomes the dominant test of who you are. It's certainly your test of intelligence, and very nearly your test of sanity. I ought to know.

I'm sorry, that was a digression.

An air of passive resentment permeated the grayspace of the East Questishaft. As I got to know the blands better, it seemed that most of their creative thought went into new ways of malingering and avoiding work. It's not that they were all lazy, though some were. It was a way of resisting and manipulating their supervisors, asserting control.

Their attitude toward humans was hostile enough to shock me. To them, the stereotyped human was a loud-talking bully, always in a hurry, always pushing. The blands had so little contact with humans, and the ones they did see were so dissatisfied with their own low status, that there was seldom any evidence to contradict their notions. After spending a while listening to their complaints and bitterness, I would feel like showering to wash off the bile.

"They ought to be grateful," I would say to Magister Galele.

"Why?"

"Well, where would they be without humans? It's the humans who take care of us."

"Seems to me you're the ones taking care of them," Magister Galele said. "Think about it, Tedla: You blands do all the work that's not purely intellectual."

"But the humans give us food, and shelter—"

"Who grows the food? Who builds the shelters?"

"But we wouldn't know how without them!" I protested. "We just follow directions. If you had a thousand thousand blands, they still couldn't build a convergence. They'd just mill around wondering what they were there for."

He said, "Tedla, you're a bigot. Do you know what that is? It's someone who lumps a group of people together and says they're all one thing or another."

I retorted, "I thought that's what xenologists did." I was getting very impertinent by this time.

He pretended to be outraged. "Oh, you ingrate! Is this what I get for teaching you irony?" He turned the serious teacher then, and said, "All right. But a xenologist reaches conclusions based on evidence and a chain of reasoning. A bigot's opinions are based on irrational grounds or no grounds at all. If you want to argue that blands are dumb, you have to bring me evidence. And it has to outweigh the fact that you were smart enough to do it.''

He was like that, a natural-born teacher. He was always challenging me, making me defend myself in words. If he had stopped to think what he was doing, he might have seen the danger in it. But he was enjoying himself too much. Once, after he had explained bell curves to me, and what you couldn't learn from them, he leaned back and exclaimed, ''I'd forgotten how much fun this was.''

''Were you a teacher on your planet?'' I asked.

''Yes,'' he said. ''I loved it.''

''Then why did you stop?''

His face took on an odd, closed expression. He said, ''Well, Tedla, life doesn't always go the way you expect it to.''

He didn't need to teach me that. I said, ''Maybe you can do it again whcn you go back.''

He gave me an odd look. ''What makes you think I'm going back?''

It had never occurred to me that he would be here forever. ''What about your home, your friends, your planet?'' I said.

''What about them?'' There was a trace of bitterness in his voice. ''It took fifty-one years to get here. The people I knew on Capella Two are all old now. If I went back, they would be dead. If I cared about going back, I never would have come.''

I tried to imagine leaving my home and all I knew forever. ''I couldn't do it,'' I said.

''Oh, you might,'' he answered. ''It would depend on how desperate you were.''

I wondered what had made him desperate. But his face had such an uncharacteristically grim look, I knew that topic was locked away.

It soon became obvious to me that I couldn't get the information he really wanted without going to the round-room. The roundroom was the only place where we felt truly at ease and private amongst ourselves, and as long as I wasn't part of that, the blands didn't wholly trust me. But I couldn't even get into the roundrooms without a badge and a team assignment.

"You've got to talk to Supervisor Moriston," I said to Magister Galele again after a couple of months had passed. I hadn't seen her since that one confrontation, and she had made no effort to track me down. I suppose she had enough blands to worry about without me. Not even humans go out of their way to create work for themselves.

Magister Galele was very reluctant. "What if she assigns you somewhere else?"

"Can't you talk to someone powerful?"

Embarrassed, he admitted, "Ovide doesn't even know you're here. I've been hoping I can just get away with it."

"Forever?" I said.

"Well, no. Of course not. I never thought . . . I suppose I'll have to do it, eh?"

"Eh," I said.

It took him several days to get up the courage, but he finally went to talk to Moriston. He came back looking flustered and angry. "What a dragon lady," he said. "She treated me like some under-evolved primate."

By liberal use of Elector Hornaday's name he had gotten a grudging promise not to alter my assignment, and had agreed to send me down for processing later that day. But when it came time for me to leave, he looked so worried and forlorn that I realized the thought of getting separated from me preyed on him. It was more than professional need for my information. The loneliness was eating him alive.

"You liven this place up so much," he said. "It's damnably quiet without you."

For a moment I felt guilty to be going back to the company of my own kind, abandoning him to his isolation. So I hugged him and said, "Don't worry, I'll never leave you. I'll always come back."

He was deeply moved. "You are the best thing that's happened to me on this planet, Tedla," he said.

Now I look back on my promise and think it was the thing he needed more than anything in the world. I kept the promise, too—for twelve years. When I finally broke it, I think it broke his heart. When he knew I wasn't coming back, it killed him.

But that was still a long way off.

When I entered Supervisor Moriston's office through the graydoor, a postulant with an electronic clipboard directed me into a tile-floored processing room. She took my thumbprint, the history of my assignments, and what I'd been trained for. Then she said, "Take off your clothes and give them to me." Silently, I did as directed. She put the clothes in a paper bag, wrote something on it, and left. I stood there waiting naked in the chilly room, rubbing my goosebumps. At length another woman came in, dressed in a curator's tabard. She started by taking a blood sample and sending it away for analysis. Then she made me stand under a bright light and inspected my body. I was worried that she would find the scars on my wrists; but the Capellan curator had used some medical adhesive that had made the cuts heal very cleanly, and they were not easy to see unless you were looking. At any rate, she didn't notice. She then asked me about a whole series of symptoms— warts, rashes, difficulty urinating, on and on. I kept shaking my head. At last she began pulling on a pair of latex gloves. She said, "Bend over. I've got to do a rectal exam."

My whole body began shaking at once. I backed away from her, unable to control myself. I knew what was going on now. They thought Magister Galele had been molesting me, and were looking for evidence.

"He hasn't touched me," I said.

"What do you mean?" she asked. I realized how incriminating my blurted protest sounded. Another word would only make it worse. I kept silent.

"Turn around," she said.

I had to, though I was shaking like someone with palsy. She was mercifully skillful and quick. When she was done, she told me to go into the next room, find a uniform in one of the bins, and wait.

I was soon sitting on a bench dressed in drab gray coveralls. Through a window into an adjoining room I could see the curator talking to Supervisor Moriston, who was nodding. At last the supervisor came in, with the postulant trailing her. Moriston's face was broken out in pimples, and she looked cross. She said to her assistant, "Did you check it for head lice?"

"No, do you want me to?" the postulant said.

"Better just shave it." The postulant went to a cupboard and got out some clippers. I watched apprehensively. I knew Magister Galele would be upset, but this didn't seem like the time to play the humans off against one another. So I sat without moving as the postulant ran the clippers over my skull, shearing away the curls. One ringlet fell in my lap and I stared at it, wishing I could save it; but a bland has no place for keepsakes.

When it was over I ran my hand over my smooth, bald skull. It felt cold and drafty. But Supervisor Moriston looked satisfied. "Stand up," she said to me. When I was facing her, she said in a too-loud voice, "Now I want some things clear. From now on you sleep in the roundroom. No more nights in his quarters. I don't ever want to see you out of a uniform again, not even in his rooms. If he asks you to do anything you wouldn't want me to see, you come straight to me. Do you understand?"

"Yes, ma'am," I said. It came to me then: She thought she was protecting me by making me look ugly and bland-like.

She handed me a blue badge. "You're on blue team. Your refectory time is posted downstairs. You know how to find your roundroom?"

"Yes, ma'am."

She dismissed me then.

That night it felt strange to be in a roundroom again, smelling the old familiar musk of close-packed bodies. I felt like a spy from human space, disguised in my neuter form. Cholly, Gibb, and Pots were all on blue team. When Cholly saw me in the shower, all shaved as I was, it said, "Did Moriston finally get to you?"

I nodded. Cholly's tone held no sympathy—more like triumph. I saw some others whispering and glancing my direction, and realized they must have been gossiping about me all this time, and now believed I had been taken down a peg. Nothing gives blands such satisfaction as to see one of their own kind put in its place. I wasn't sure how they would feel about touching me, so I didn't try to join them in the center of the roundroom. It was odd: I had expected to feel at home here, after my long exile in human space, and human beds. But I didn't. I was turning into a halfway thing, neither human nor wholly bland.

It was early the next day when I entered Magister Galele's quarters, but he was already up and drinking coffee. He greeted me with a charged mix of joy and horror. "Tedla, thank god! They sent me your clothes, without a word of explanation. It was like receiving the ashes of someone who died. Lord in heaven, what have they done to you?"

He wanted me to get out of the uniform and put my clothes back on. "I can't stand to see you like that," he said, really perturbed. I hesitated, but decided the odds of Supervisor Moriston coming to his quarters to see what I was wearing were pretty remote, and I might as well please him. But even after I had hung the uniform by the gray-door, he couldn't get over my shaved head. Outrage alternated with heartbreak all morning as I fixed his breakfast, shaved his face, and laid out his clothes.

"That woman's a tinpot tyrant," he said. "She's jealous of someone with better looks than hers, that's what it is."

I didn't dare tell him what I thought her real motive was. I said stoically, "It will grow back."

"That's not the point," he said. "It's not the hair I mind. It's seeing you debased and humiliated. That makes my blood boil."

I hadn't felt either debased or humiliated until he suggested it. To feel debased, you must have a feeling that you deserve better, which no bland has. But knowing he felt that way made me self-conscious and ashamed whenever he looked at me, and slowly I began to resent what had been done to me. It wasn't a familiar feeling, and I kept rolling it around in my mind, like a hard candy you suck on till it gets sharp against your tongue. Still, it wasn't really resentment for my own sake. I resented Moriston for going against Magister Galele's wishes, and causing him pain.

When the time came for me to leave that evening, he said, "I wish you didn't have to go. I keep thinking I'll never see you again."

"Think of all the good material I'll collect," I said.

That consoled him a little. "Be sure to watch for historical consciousness," he said.

It took a few weeks for blue team to stop noticing I was there and talk freely in front of me. When they did, I was astonished at what I found. You have done fieldwork, so you won't be surprised to hear that it had nothing to do with what Magister Galele expected to find.

Blue team was heavily involved in witchcraft.

In a way, it was an outgrowth of the petty sabotages all blands perform against people or other blands they don't like. They will polish the floor so the target of their malice will slip, or put extra bleach in the clothes to make the wearer break out in a rash. A really rebellious bland might spit in the soup. They whisper about poison, but never do it. They have an almost superstitious belief in the humans' ability to trace real sabotage back to the responsible party.

That was the joy of witchcraft. It caused harm that seemed unrelated to the actual perpetrators.

Blue team didn't stop with polishing the floor and passively waiting for an accident. They cast hexes to make the floor malevolent. They bewitched machines to make them pinch and burn their human operators, or give electric shocks. They sprinkled potions on the linens to make the humans sleepless with nightmares, or impotent. Magic lightbulbs made everything they illuminated look ugly.

Their main target was Supervisor Moriston. They spent hours inventing sorceries to make the woman's life a misery. She suffered from a constant succession of cramps, rashes, and infections for which blue team took credit and the other blands took warning.

Cholly was the ringleader. It was regarded with a kind of admiring terror by the other blands, and used its reputation to tyrannize even the reluctant ones into collaborating. There was a clique around Cholly, a bitter group of malcontents. The younger blands were completely cowed by fear of becoming their target. When Cholly's coven convened in the center of the roundroom, the rest of us huddled on the edges, whispering.

"You've got to be more careful," Pots whispered to me. I had taken its place as the lowest-status bland in the blue team roundroom. There was a much more rigid hierarchy here than at Menoken, based on age and closeness to Cholly. "You talk to Cholly too much like a human, and make it mad," Pots said. "You know, it already witched you."

"Really?" I said.

"Why do you think you ended up down here, in Cholly's power? Why do you think Moriston shaved your hair? That was Cholly's spell."

"How did Cholly do it?" I whispered.

"I don't know," Pots said in a fearful tone that made me think it did know, and didn't dare tell me. When I thought of the nearly unlimited access Cholly had to Magister Galele's quarters, the possibilities were endless.

"Is Cholly hexing the alien?" I asked.

"Are you kidding?" Pots said. "Where do you think Cholly got its powers? I told you the alien liked it. He must like Cholly more than he likes you, because he gave it stronger magic."

I soon learned that I had been just about the only bland in the East Questishaft not to know the story of my own bewitching. It had been one of Cholly's more spectacular successes. When I had first arrived, unwittingly challenging Cholly's monopoly on Magister Galele, everyone had expected a magical battle to erupt between us. Now I found out it had happened, and I had lost.

Of course, each day I would report everything to Magister Galele. I kept expecting him to scoff and ridicule us, but instead he was thrilled. "Such drama! Such tension!" he would exclaim. "The humans have no notion what a cauldron they are sitting on."

He explained to me the role of magical thinking, especially among oppressed and powerless populations. Every day he had some parallel example from another culture. It brought me back to reality to think I was witnessing an objective phenomenon, a mode of thought. If I had been trapped in East Questishaft with no one but blands to talk to, I'm sure I would have begun to believe in magic myself.

As time passed, he grew dissatisfied with hearsay. He said to me, "Do you think you could get them to let you participate?"

I was terribly reluctant. He didn't understand what a risk I was taking even telling him. Even if the witchcraft itself was absurd, the malice behind it was very real, and had a kind of power which I found disturbing. If it hadn't been for Magister Galele, I would have stayed as far away from it all as possible.

When he saw my face, he said, "Tedla, you don't believe in this hocus-pocus, do you?"

"No," I said defensively. "But if any humans found out, I'd be in big trouble."

He gave a quizzical smile and I realized I'd just implied he wasn't human. I started to apologize, but he laughed and patted my shoulder. "I know what you meant," he said. "I'm flattered, in a way."

But he still wanted me to try and penetrate Cholly's coven. Over the next few days he wheedled and cajoled me, and at last, against my judgment, I agreed to try.

I approached Cholly during the day, when it was cleaning Magister Galele's quarters. Oddly enough, now that Cholly had conquered me, it seemed to regard me as a kind of trophy rather than an enemy. Moriston's treatment of me was part of the reason. In Cholly's eyes, my shaving made me a natural ally against her. It was part of the illogic of it all that they held her accountable for her acts, while simultaneously taking credit for witching her into doing them.

I pulled Cholly aside into the bathroom and said in a low voice, "Listen, I want to get back at Moriston. Will you teach me to witch her?"

It gave me a long, appraising look. Its eyes were a strange, pale color, and you could see the whites all around the iris. I got quite uneasy at its silence. At last it said, "You'll have to obey me."

"Okay," I said, forcing back my misgivings.

"If I help you, I own you," it said.

I nodded.

"I'll tell you your task later," it said, and turned back to the cleaning.

That evening in the hygiene station, when I stepped out of the shower, I found myself surrounded by Cholly's crew. They hustled me over into a corner where Cholly was waiting, still dressed in its uniform. It looked me over, then drew something out of its pocket. "Do you know what this is?" it said.

It was a contraceptive diaphragm. "Is it Moriston's?" I asked.

"Yes."

"How did you get it?" I whispered.

"Never mind. Here, piss on it."

"What?"

"Go on."

They were all watching me, and I realized it was a kind of initiation. So I took the diaphragm and wet it with my urine. Cholly said, "Now tell your piss what you want it to do to her."

"Make her burn and itch," I said.

"Good." Cholly took it back and put it, still wet, in a plastic bag. "Next time you see her, you'll know your piss is inside her body," it said.

There was something primal about this revenge that made me quake with disgust and fear. Cholly saw my reaction, and smiled triumphantly. "All of us saw you do it," it said.

Now they had a hold over me. After that, since my obedience was ensured, they let me hang around their circle in the roundroom, listening.

They did a lot less actual magic than everyone believed. Most of their conversation was just vicious gossip and revenge fantasies. But Cholly also had a number of stories it liked to tell, usually late at night when the conscientious blands had all gone to sleep and only Cholly's crew and some younger hangers-on like me were there to listen. Cholly was a good storyteller. The slightly manic quality that made it seem so odd in daily life made it fascinating to watch in performance.

Cholly's favorite tale was about Brazen Potlicker Bland. (That was a joke; it had a name like a human.) Brazen had a cruel supervisor who pulled on his blands' ears if they misbehaved. Brazen had misbehaved so many times its earlobes dangled down below its shoulders, and it had to tie them back out of the way when it was working. (Cholly always acted out some funny business here, showing us how Brazen's earlobes got in the way.) The supervisor was so mean that whenever he went into grayspace to beat some blands, he left his soul behind on his dresser because he didn't want it interfering by making him kind. One day the supervisor went looking for Brazen with a big whip, to beat the stuffing out of it. (Here Cholly acted the part of the supervisor, glaring around at us as if we might be Brazen, which we all denied.) Brazen was so scared it nearly peed in its pants. (Here, Cholly shook and grabbed its crotch. We all roared with laughter.) It ran and ran, and finally came to the graydoor into the supervisor's room. It went through to hide, thinking that was the last place the supervisor would look. What should it spy but the man's soul sitting on the dresser. Being a thieving bland, Brazen couldn't resist taking the soul. Just then the supervisor came in, saw Brazen, and started chasing it. Brazen knew it was going to get caught, and had no place to hide the soul it had taken, so it swallowed it. But instead of going down right, the soul got stuck in Brazen's throat. (Here, Cholly showed us how Brazen's eyes got big and bugged out as it tried to cough up the soul.) When the supervisor caught Brazen, he tried whacking it on the back, and hanging it upside down, but nothing would bring the soul back up.

After that, Brazen had a soul like any human. It was smart as a person, but lazy and devious like a bland. It had many subsequent adventures in which it had internal conversations with the soul, which always spoke in a condescending, superior tone, just like a human, and always wanted Brazen to act human when it wanted to act like a bland. Cholly played both parts, Brazen and the soul. We thought the whole thing was hilarious, in a scandalous way.

I thought the stories were all just entertainment—though the kind of entertainment only bad blands would enjoy. Cholly used them to draw us into its subversion, and make us feel culpable. But Magister Galele was sure they had a deeper meaning. "Cholly is creating a collective culture by giving you a common mythic vocabulary," he said. "It's a technique of charismatic leaders. I wish I knew how deliberate it is."

What he most wanted to know was whether the blands were beginning to see their oppression as a collective problem, not an individual one. Up to this point, I—and every other bland I knew—had thought of mistreatment as the moral failing of individual humans. Once Magister Galele taught me that the system was independent of the individuals—the people could all be replaced and everything would stay the same—I could form the idea that it was the system that needed changing. Personal resentment changed into a sense of social injustice.

"Do you think they would understand, if you told them?" he would press me.

I shook my head. "No way."

But I understood.

One day a large box arrived at Magister Galele's doorstep. From the markings I could tell it had come all the way down from the Capellan questship. When he saw it, he gave an exclamation of satisfaction and said, "Come here, Tedla. These are for you."

They were all books and disks in Capellan. I thought he was joking, so I laughed. He said seriously, "I've decided you can't be really useful to me as an assistant unless you learn my language."

I was incredulous. "I can't learn another language. I can barely speak one right."

He absolutely refused to listen. We argued on and off for three days, and he finally wore me down. So every morning before lunch we sat down at the table for an hour, and he taught me Capellan. As I said, he was a wonderful teacher: funny, interesting, and involved. I so much enjoyed having his undivided attention that I tried to learn just so he wouldn't lose interest in me. Before too long, we were talking simple Capellan phrases to each other in the apartment. It was like having a private language only we knew.

Magister Galele did not entertain much; in fact, I was surprised at what a life of isolation he lived. But there were a few humans who came to his quarters from time to time. One was a man named Gambion, who enjoyed evenings of intellectual sparring. I did not like him. From the beginning he looked at me in a knowing way, as if with a sophisticated wink at what he assumed to be the relationship between me and Magister Galele. From time to time he would even touch me suggestively, as if thinking I was somehow available. It made my skin crawl.

I would work in the kitchen as they sat at the table drinking, and was astounded to hear how similar was the tone of Gambion's political gossip to what I heard in the roundroom. The difference was that the humans' gossip involved real power.

One day I had served them some food and was cleaning up when I heard Gambion's voice drop low, which always made me listen more closely. He said, "Ovide's in real trouble, you know."

"Really?" the Magister said. He sounded distressed.

"Yes, there's an election petition going around. She's too open to innovation. Her politics are the product of another time when there weren't so many threats. She doesn't understand what an age of anxiety this is."

"What are people anxious about?"

"You need to ask that? You, my friend. They're anxious about you."

"Us?" Magister Galele sounded astonished. "But we've done nothing. There are so few of us. We're completely under your control."

"It seems that way to you, I'm sure. But we have far less insight into your intentions and your powers than you have into ours. People are beginning to question the unrestricted access we've given you, without demanding the same in return. And then, there is your effect on our blands.''

"We have an effect on the blands?" The Magister sounded astonished.

"Oh, please, Alair, don't be so ingenuous. Of course, you must. But that's not important. What's important is that people *think* you do.'' His voice dropped even lower. I held my breath to hear. "You must understand by now, our system is extremely unstable. There's a vast population of them, more than anyone admits, and it's constantly growing. How are we to keep them under control? They're unpredictable. In the last twenty years we have eased up restrictions and improved their lot, but it's only made them more discontent. What chance do you think the humans in this convergence would have if the blands turned on us?''

"Oh, surely that's not likely," Galele said.

"You think not? How can we tell what's in their minds?''

It was a complete revelation to me that the humans feared us as much as we feared them. More, perhaps— because we understood the humans, or thought we did.

"People wonder whose side you would take, if the worst happened," Gambion said.

"Why, no one's side," Galele said. "We are strictly observers. Whatever our personal opinions may be, our employer obliges us to remain neutral.''

I winced. Gambion's question had been purely rhetorical; Magister Galele had assumed it was a serious option not to support the humans.

Gambion was silent for a moment, absorbing the indiscretion without reaction. At last he said coolly, "You have said very little about what the rest of the galaxy will make of us. We can't help wondering, you know. We think of ourselves as enlightened people. If we thought other planets were going to scorn us as barbarians, that would have a strong effect.''

"I know that, Gambion. That's precisely why I can't be open with you. I'm here to study you as you are now. Believe me, you will change all too fast when the conduits of information are turned on."

I took a damp cloth and went out to wipe the table. I wanted to see Gambion's face. He was watching Magister Galele with a controlled, appraising air. "People think I know you. Yet when they ask me the simplest question—what are you doing here?—I can't answer. What viewpoint do you support? I can only guess, from the company you keep." He glanced at me, but I knew it was Squire Tellegen he was thinking of. I was just the tangible evidence of that connection.

When Gambion took his leave, I came out and stood looking at the Magister till he turned to me.

"He doesn't like you," I said.

"What?" the Magister said, startled.

"I could tell from the way he watched you. You weren't paying attention. I don't think you ought to trust him."

He looked very unsettled. "That can't be right," he said.

But from that day he began avoiding Gambion.

It was not long after that he came into the studium when I was at work and said, "Tedla, you're really good with machines, aren't you?"

Actually, I wasn't particularly good with them; but he was unbelievably bad. I had never seen anyone who could get so mixed up when confronted by anything mechanical. He had recently gotten some equipment for recording visual-audio data, but after a few attempts had abandoned it and reverted to his old notebooks, written in crabbed Capellan hieroglyphs that broke into Gammadian whenever he quoted someone verbatim, so that no one but a perfect bilinguist could make head or tail of them.

All I said was, "I'm okay."

"No, you're really good. You know, when I'm on an interview, I don't have time to be worrying about equipment. I think it would work a lot better if you came along to set up the recorders and change disks and so on, so I can concentrate on what I'm doing.''

I thought it over. I was growing restless by now, never getting out of his apartment except to go into grayspace. If I could tag after him as a menial, I might be able to satisfy my curiosity about human space. My boredom made me bold, so I said, "Okay."

He looked pleased that I hadn't put up more of a fight. "Good. I can use your insights, too. I'm not sure I always catch the nuances you Gammadians see."

That was true, too, but I didn't say anything.

I was a little uncertain how his interviewees would react to my presence, but it turned out not to be a problem. When we went out, I trudged along loaded with bags of equipment and supplies, so obviously a packhorse that it didn't attract attention. As I would string cords and set up, he would engage the humans in some social banter that relaxed everyone. All he had to do was glance at me to see when I was ready, and then he could launch into his questions. Once the machines were running I would settle down cross-legged on the floor. No one ever minded me listening.

I learned a lot about humans this way. The first interview I went on was with a pregnant woman. I had never seen one before, and had to force myself not to stare. She was very self-conscious, and I realized that the public honor given to women who procreate hides a private shame. Magister Galele was extremely skillful at getting her to relax. I watched him play the clown for her, pretending to be more stupid and ignorant than he was, so she would laugh and want to teach him things. At first I felt annoyed at him—how could people respect him if he acted with so little dignity? But I slowly realized how he was managing her by deprecating himself. He got her to talk about some astonishingly intimate things.

"Will you be sad to give up your child?" he asked.

"In a way," she answered. "I had a dream the other night, about holding it in my arms. It was so small, and so alive. . . . But what can I do? No one would assign me a bland just so I could keep it."

"Wouldn't you consider raising it yourself?"

"Are you joking? I already have a full-time assignment. Besides, child-rearing is just mindless drudgery all day. I'd be no better than a bland."

It was something I heard over and over, their fear of becoming like a bland. It was why they feared sickness, and age, and all vulnerability, because it would make them like a bland. We were like their weak part, that they had walled off from themselves, and now no longer understood.

Observing the humans, I also learned a great deal about sexual culture. I was still very innocent. I know why you are looking at me that skeptical way: but you have to understand that sexual experience is not the same as sexual sophistication. What I didn't know were the verbal innuendoes, double entendres, gestures, hints, winks, all the ways you weave sexual meaning into your communication. All that is quite independent of sexual activity. In fact, I think it is often a substitute.

Magister Galele and I often talked about the interviews afterward—mostly in Capellan, which is a much more analytical language than ours. As my grasp of the language improved, he gave me Gossup's *Elements of Culture* to read. I labored a long time over that book, and not just because of the language. There were a thousand subversive ideas in it that shocked and disturbed me. From it, I learned that humans have always oppressed and exploited portions of their population, under a thousand different names and justifications. I learned strange new arguments about the rights of individuals. Worst of all, I realized there was nothing natural about our society—it was merely one way among many, and not even, perhaps, the best.

As the months passed, and the Magister increasingly

took me wherever he went, people began to notice. First they teased him and joked; then the ribbing became a little harsher. He always shrugged it off, or bantered back, but it made me touchy. Of course, they were all completely wrong about him. Everyone in Tapis Convergence assumed he was sodomizing me, a vice they understood. That he was educating me was beyond their comprehension.

My first inkling of real danger came during a visit to one of the midway houses run by the Order of Matriculators. I was very interested in this part of his research, since it gave me a chance to see the kind of place—perhaps the very place—I would have gone after matriculation, if only I had been human. The midway houses are where newborn humans live for nine months as their bodies mature and they make up their minds what profession to pursue. The orders and communities recruit promising candidates. In fact, the young people are generally made much of, as if they have achieved something extraordinary just by becoming human. Since they are freed from the discipline of the creche and not yet bound by the regulations of a community, the atmosphere is wild—and tolerated indulgently by the adults in charge.

In the end I did not enjoy the visit much. There was a strident arrogance in these young humans that did not become them. They seemed so pleased with themselves. Rulers of the universe, I called them mentally. They could not resist commenting on my presence, making me feel conspicuous. Perhaps it was because I represented the fate they had so lately escaped.

On the other hand, they were awed and intrigued at Magister Galele, and eager to display their cleverness to him. Magister Galele was in his element, joking and teasing his way from one interview to the next. I followed him around silently with a recorder.

Toward the end of the day he got into an intimate conversation with a young girl who so clearly wanted to have a sexual encounter that I sat nearby, itching with indecision whether to withdraw tactfully, or wait for him to ask me. He seemed to be encouraging her, and I could imagine why; I had often been puzzled by his completely celibate life. But at the last moment he broke off and told me we were leaving. As we walked away, I said to him in Capellan, "You led her on."

He looked at me, amused, and said, "Tedla, are you jealous?"

I was astonished at the suggestion, and quickly denied it. "I'd like you to have a partner worthy of you," I said.

But it wasn't strictly true. The fact was, we had become so close I had begun to think of him as mine.

All that day I had been aware that one of the postulant matriculators was watching us closely. He had wispy brown hair and a broad forehead, with close-set eyes that gave him an almost cross-eyed appearance. Something about him made me uncomfortable, but I couldn't quite place it.

As we were about to leave, I saw him again, loitering by the exit. This time the shock of recognition hit me. It was Zelly.

That was not his name any more, of course. He had a real name now, though I never heard it. I stared at him, thunderstruck, feeling a hot wave of shame, till his eyes flicked in my direction and I saw that he recognized me—had, in fact, recognized me from the beginning. My gaze fell to the floor, but not before I had seen his expression, as if I were a maddening blot on his past.

He addressed Magister Galele in a voice tight with forced aggression. "Do you think we don't know what you are really doing here?"

Magister Galele sized him up and responded calmly, "Here at this midway house, you mean?"

"No. Here on this planet. Interfering with our politics. Defiling our customs."

Carefully, Magister Galele said, "What has given you that impression?"

The young man gave an exclamation of disgust and discomfort. "You know what I mean. We all know what you're up to. You and that weeping baby, Ovide Hornaday." He said the elector's name with intense contempt.

By now, I could tell, the Magister was mystified, and quite curious. But he gave his standard response: "We are completely neutral in regard to your politics. We are only observers."

"If that's true," Zelly said in a venomous voice, "Why have you spent all your time hanging out with atomists and neuter-lovers?"

My eyes were on the floor, so I had no idea how to interpret the silence that followed. My own ears were buzzing with mortification.

Magister Galele said slowly, "I would be happy to hang out with someone else. Would you care to join me for a hopscotch?"

"No, not me," Zelly said. "It's Rustim that ought to talk to you. He'll set you straight."

"Fine. How can I get in touch with him?"

"I'll ask him. He'll talk to you, all right." He paused, then added with a particularly personal malice, "He'll talk to your bland, too. We'll be happy to set it straight for you."

I felt that he had finally gotten to the crux of his message.

When we had left and were walking down the corridor toward the central hub of the convergence, Magister Galele said in Capellan, "Well, that was enlightening. Not pleasant, but enlightening."

I was silent. My face still burned to think that Zelly had seen me like this.

Magister Galele began to talk about returning for some more interviews the next day. I said abruptly, "I don't want to go back."

"Why, because that punk was rude to you? He was out of line, Tedla. Don't worry about it."

I sometimes despaired of him. He felt so invulnerable, so immune to everything. "You don't get it," I whispered.

He stopped right there in the public corridor and turned to me. "What don't I get?"

I could feel people's eyes on us. Sooner or later they were going to stop making allowances for him. He was going to stop being the eccentric alien who didn't know the rules. "Not here!" I hissed. "I'll tell you at home."

By the time we reached home, he was embarked on another tangent and forgot all about it.

That evening I was silent and moody, and he finally asked me what was the matter. I wanted to tell him, but I felt too ashamed.

The next day we went back to the midway house, despite my misgivings. All day I hung back and kept my eyes down for fear of seeing Zelly again. The only time he came near us was near noon, when he handed Magister Galele a slip of paper and left without a word. The Magister glanced at it and put it in his pocket.

He wrapped up his interviews early that day, and had me pack up the equipment. I shouldered my load with relief and followed him to the door.

No sooner had we stepped into the corridor than we were surrounded: Two men took up positions on either side of Magister Galele, and I felt my arm seized roughly from behind. Something pressed against my buttock, and I heard a pop, then gasped at the bite of pain. It was a stinger, an instrument that administers a sharp little electric shock. It hurt like fire, but I didn't make a sound. "Like that, whore?" Zelly sneered in my ear. "You'll get more if you misbehave."

The men led us quickly away from the frequented corridors, and downward, by such a circuitous route that I was soon disoriented. Loaded down as I was, it was hard to keep up, and I got three more shocks in the buttocks to

keep me moving. At the last one, I finally gave a little
sound of pain, and Magister Galele turned around suspiciously. There was nothing for him to see.

At last they ushered us through a nondescript door into
a private dwelling. It was the type of dingy place the lowest-status humans occupy—just a single room with a bed
and sink, no private kitchen or bath, a well-worn carpet
and flimsy chairs. A man and a woman were waiting there,
sitting at a table. The lights were turned very low.

They gave Magister Galele a chair to sit in, and all gathered round. I crouched down silently on the floor next to
the door, still smarting from the shocks, and trying to look
invisible.

They had brought the Magister there to listen to a dia-
tribe. Their spokesman, Rustim, was a man with a huge
belly and very small eyes. He spoke in torrents, drowning
all response in the rush of his verbiage. I had never seen
Magister Galele so speechless for so long.

"We were a noble world before you came here. Now
we're in decay. Everywhere people are rebelling and questioning our great traditions. We had strong morals once.
Now, nobody wants controls on their behavior. You aliens
think you can weaken us by undermining our high standards. Well, there are some people who will still resist you,
who will resist you to the end."

In Rustim's mind, civilization was dangling by a thread,
menaced by a host of threats. He summoned fact after fact
to prove it, jabbing his thick forefinger at the tabletop as
if the surface held an invisible diagram. "I have evidence—evidence you can't deny—that Tapis is on the
verge of an uprising. No one's controlling the blands. We
used to know how to keep them in line. We used to have
things like skeerings to deal with the bad blands. You only
had to kill one, you see, but you cut open the body and
made it like a little basin, then brought the other restless
blands to wash their hands in the blood. That cured them.
They didn't just hear aimless talk of what might happen

to them; they smelt it and felt it. That got through to their brains.

"You're all so blind, you weepers, so sorry for them, you don't know what vicious vermin they are. I could show you evidence. People have found hex tokens in their rooms. They communicate with each other that way, like an underground network. They're all into sorcery, every last one of them. Don't you believe it when you hear an accident has happened to someone. That's no accident. It's witchcraft. It's all around us, everywhere. The blands don't work any more. All they do is cast spells. Some day you'll wake up in your bed, bleeding from every opening. Then you'll know your bland has gotten back at you.

"You aliens think we're so blind. You come here and try to stir up the blands, try to gather evidence that they're human. I suppose some day you'll want to raise them up over us and make us obey them."

He went on and on in the same vein, veering from blustering to threats to paranoia, then back again, till I lost track of any argument, and only understood the underlying rage. Magister Galele had enough sense not to try to argue. At first he sat listening, stunned and flushed. Then his eyes began wandering, as if he were thinking of how to escape. From time to time Rustim would pause for a breather, and silence would fall; then I could hear Magister Galele shifting uncomfortably, as if tensing to make a dash for it. I decided that I would leave the equipment behind if I got a chance to run.

"We're watching you, alien," Rustim said. "You and your bland." He rose then, for the first time since we had come in, and I saw he was a massive figure. He came slowly over to where I was, his footsteps heavy on the thin carpet. I stood up, my back pressed to the wall.

He came so close I could smell his breath and see the sheen of sweat on his face. With his eyes on me he said, "These atomists don't even have pride in being human. They think nothing of debasing themselves with their pubers. They even drag their catamites with them out in the open for a quickie during the day, and no one objects. And the pubers are so full of cum they think they're turning human."

Suddenly he raised his hand threateningly, watching to see what I would do. I braced myself for a blow, but didn't cower or beg.

Magister Galele leaped to his feet. Fiercely, he said, "Don't you touch it, Rustim. Whether you approve or not, there are still laws here, and I'll bring them down on you if you harm a hair on Tedla's head."

He looked very small beside Rustim, but very feisty. I held still, my eyes switching from one to the other of them, waiting. At last Rustim lowered his hand. "Get out," he said.

We gathered the equipment and walked away swiftly, neither of us very sure where we were. When we had put some distance between us and that little room, Magister Galele said, "I'm sorry, Tedla. I'm sorry to have exposed you to that. I had no idea what nut cases I was dealing with."

"*Now* do you get it?" I whispered.

He was silent a little while; then when no one was nearby he took my hand and squeezed it. "The world isn't made up of people like that, Tedla. Don't judge everyone by a few crazed extremists."

He still thought I was the one misinterpreting. Even with the evidence in plain sight, he couldn't see any danger. It gave me a feeling of helplessness, as if I were riding in an aircar headed straight for a mountainside. There was nothing I could do. He was my guardian; I was strapped to my seat.

That evening when I took off my uniform, the other blands noticed the burns on my behind, but I got little sympathy. "What do you expect, acting the way you do?" Gibb said.

All I wanted to do that night was sleep, but there was a tense air in the roundroom, and I quickly realized something was afoot. Cholly's crew was gathered at one side, talking, and the rest were trying not to watch them. I lay down among the outsiders, not caring if Magister Galele missed some data because of my laziness. But several of the witches looked over their shoulders at me, and finally one came over. "Cholly wants to talk to you," it said.

Reluctantly, I went. Cholly had a strange, animated expression, halfway between torment and elation. It looked almost human.

"It's time for you to do something for us," it said to me.

Sulkily, I said, "What?"

"The alien has liquor in one of his cabinets. Don't deny it, I've seen it. We need you to steal some."

It was a very serious offense, harshly punished. I knew I could probably get away with it, but my instincts still rebelled. I was not a bad bland. "Why don't you steal it yourself?" I said.

"Because you'd tattle," Cholly said nastily.

"No, I wouldn't," I said defensively.

"Besides, he keeps it locked now."

That was my doing, actually. I'd told Magister Galele where I kept the key, but I doubted that he remembered. I always fixed the drinks when he asked for it. "What do you want liquor for?" I said.

"Will you do it?"

I didn't answer. Cholly said with soft malice, "Remember what you did to Moriston? You want her to know?"

"Okay, I'll try," I said.

I stood there for a while, listening to see what they were up to. In my tired mind the memory of Rustim's ravings already had a surreal quality; but this brought them back with a jolt. If Rustim could have heard this, all his phobias would have taken on life. The blands were plotting some

truly major sorcery. Cholly was becoming Rustim's evil
shadow.

Moriston had been sick that day. "Did you see her?"
one of the blands whispered. "Her face was yellow. It's
our urine in her blood." Everyone had seen that she was
vulnerable, so Cholly had decided that the time had come
to make its move. Tomorrow night, we were going to steal
her soul.

The scheme was quite mad, like something out of
Cholly's tales. They thought that, without a soul, Moriston
would become like a bland; and whoever got her soul
would have the power to outwit everyone. "You'll see a
real Tumbleturn Day then," Cholly said.

The next morning I told Magister Galele everything, and
asked him what I ought to do. He thought it over a while,
but at last his interest in documenting a soul-stealing ceremony won out. In the midst of telling me about Xic soul-
stealing, he saw how uneasy I was and said, "There's no
danger of the humans finding out, is there?"

"Only if it works," I said.

He laughed. "Trust me, Tedla, it won't work. This is
just a harmless way of blowing off steam."

When I found the liquor was low, he actually went out
and bought another bottle, just so I could take it down to
the roundroom. I poured half of it into another bottle and
diluted the rest with water. The Magister thought I was
being terribly prudish. "Why not let them have their fun?"
he said.

"They're not used to it. They'll get just as drunk this
way," I told him.

I hung around Magister Galele's quarters late that evening, working on some translations, dreading to find out
what was going on in grayspace. The Magister finally
started to worry that I would miss something, so I braced
myself and went out to the kitchen to take off my clothes.
I had chosen a baggy uniform that morning; now I strapped
the liquor bottle to my body with some sturdy tape, then

put on the uniform over it. I couldn't bend over, but I hoped I wouldn't have to.

No one but blands saw me on my way to the roundroom. I could tell from the looks they gave me, and the way the ones from other teams avoided me, that news of Cholly's scheme was all over the Questishaft, and my complicity was well known. No one wanted to be caught in company with a conspirator.

When I got to the hygiene station, Cholly's coven surrounded me. When they saw the bottle they whooped with excitement and eagerly stripped the tape off my body, seizing the liquor.

"I'll take it," Cholly said. I was chilled to see how much authority was already in Cholly's manner. The others meekly handed the bottle over.

That night, every bland in the roundroom was forced to take a role in the weird ceremony Cholly and its crew enacted.

They started by making us form a circle, sitting on the roundroom floor. Inside, the six or seven main members of Cholly's cabal formed another ring. As we watched, they helped themselves liberally to the bottle, some of them coughing and grimacing as the fiery liquid burned their throats. When about half the bottle was gone, Cholly got up and went around the outer ring to give everyone a sip. I barely got enough to wet my mouth.

The inner circle began to sway in unison from side to side, chanting a strange incantation. Cholly would say the words, then everyone else would repeat them. They were in no language I had ever heard, but somehow seemed familiar for all that.

The speed of the chanting increased, and soon the inner ring were on their feet, dancing wildly in their circle, still chanting. Cholly gestured the rest of us to our feet, and we began to dance as well—at first hesitantly, then as the rhythm of the chant entered us, more loosely, till we were flying around the circle with wild abandon. I found myself shouting out the nonsense phrases with all the others. The liquor I had swallowed was making me elated and dizzy. The dim roundroom lights seemed to be pulsing, growing lighter and darker in time with our dance. As I joined the pounding rhythm, the distance between the outer and inner rings seemed to be changing—first they were very close, then very far, as if space itself had grown elastic. Reality was liquefying all around us.

A call went up—"Link arms, link arms! Don't break the circle!" We fell to the floor panting and grabbed hold of our neighbors. As the inner circle did the same, we saw Cholly standing alone in the center, holding something aloft, calling out strange, garbled words. It began to pass the instrument over its body, and I saw that it was a toothbrush—Moriston's, I had no doubt. As we watched, Cholly put the toothbrush in its mouth, just as Moriston must have done many times, and sucked on it till her saliva mingled with Cholly's. We watched Cholly swallow, and for a moment everything was perfectly still, poised between event and event in a stasis of expectancy.

Then Cholly's body went rigid. It fell to the floor, thrashing. The inner circle scrambled to get out of the way. Every muscle in Cholly's body was jerking and quivering. We watched, horrified. Then Cholly's mouth opened and a deep, booming man's voice came out of it. "Where are you?" it said.

It was not Cholly speaking, we were sure of that. Something else had entered the roundroom, something none of us could see, but all of us could sense. I clutched my neighbors on either side more tightly. My bare back, turned to the wall, felt cold and exposed.

Cholly's mouth opened again, and though its lips moved, the voice did not come from Cholly, but from far away, beyond the roundroom walls. It was a woman's voice this time, and it said, "I'm coming."

Then, out of the breathless silence, we heard the sound of a great wind approaching. I felt cold air stirring against my back. Beyond our circle, all light had retreated, leaving impenetrable dark. Past the heads of the blands across from me, I saw tree branches against the sky, and when I looked up there were tiny stars above us. I felt immense open space overhead. Then there was motion in the dark above me, as if something were swooping low out of the night, and I ducked my head down. Inside the circle, Cholly's body convulsed. Its spine arched painfully backwards, its mouth straining open. A loud, unnatural voice came from its motionless lips: "I am here!"

Suddenly, there was silence. Cholly's body collapsed and lay limp. No one dared to move.

We sat there a long time, our sweat turning chill, the dim roundroom walls once again around us. At last someone moved, and, as if a trance were broken, we all let go of one another's arms and drew away into a huddle on one side of the roundroom, leaving Cholly's body lying motionless by itself. It did not seem to be breathing.

Some of us got a little sleep that night, though I kept starting awake at the imagined sound of wings.

The next morning Cholly's friends managed to rouse it, though it acted very strangely—eyes staring and dazed, as if it barely recognized where it was. The rest of us avoided it. We showered and dressed fast. When we got to the refectory for breakfast, the blands from other teams asked what had gone on. All over the dining hall I saw clusters of blands gathered around the scattered members of blue team, mesmerized by the story. Agitation spread like infection across the room.

I was too troubled to join in the rumor-spreading—disbelieving what I had experienced, unable to either explain or discredit it. I knew exactly what Magister Galele would say, and I also knew with a certainty very alien to my nature that he would be wrong.

The time came for us to disperse to our assignments. Normally, the refectory was orderly as the blands began to leave; but this day, the gossip was too engrossing, and no one seemed to be moving toward the exit. The noise of talking filled the room. At last one of the doors to human space opened. In an instant, the blands all fell completely silent as they saw Supervisor Moriston enter.

She still looked yellow and sick, but very much herself. I felt a pang of disappointment, then shame at myself for feeling such a thing. I glanced around, and saw blank disbelief on the faces of other members of blue team.

"What are you dawdling for?" she said in her usual harsh, impatient tone. "Get going."

The entire roomful of blands stood staring at her in morbid fascination. I heard a whisper pass like a wind through the blands around me—"She's not human any more."

Used to absolute obedience, Moriston was at first unable to believe that her orders had had no effect. Then her face turned a ghastly shade of orange, and her fists clenched. She strode to the nearest table and said in a grating voice, "Get to your assignments, morons."

Who knows what possessed her to pick that table. It was the one where Cholly's coven was sitting. Of all blands in the room, the ones she chose to confront were the ones most positive in their belief that her soul was gone. They stared at her as if watching an animate corpse cavort in daylight. I'm sure they barely heard what she was saying.

In a rage, she seized one of them by its collar and dragged it to its feet. She gave it a rough shake. "Disobey me, will you?" she raged. She was raising her hand to strike it when she winced and put the hand on her side instead, bending over with a grunt of pain. Her postulant, who had been standing by the door watching, now rushed to her aid, alarmed. As the girl reached her, Moriston's legs buckled, and the postulant eased her to the floor.

"Now look what you've done!" the postulant said to Cholly's crew. She meant only to scare them; she had no idea that her choice of words confirmed the superstition that had the room in its clutch. When the postulant said,

"Carry her into her office," not a bland at Cholly's table moved.

We all saw terror come across the postulant's face then. Her eyes swept around her, seeing some three hundred blands assembled in silent disobedience, and herself alone. She rose slowly to her feet. Then she turned and fled toward the door.

For a moment after she was gone, the room was silent, except for Moriston's labored breathing. Then an inhuman shriek rose from the front table. Cholly was on its feet, quivering with manic energy. It danced forward to where the supervisor lay. The blands at the back surged forward to see, and I was pressed to the front. Cholly knelt over Moriston, pure insanity in its eyes. It was saying, "The soul, the soul," very fast under its breath. Suddenly it bent over her and pressed its mouth over hers, sucking the breath out of her body. She struggled desperately, her eyes very large. She finally managed to push Cholly away, then turned her head and vomited blood in a huge pool onto the floor.

As quickly as they had surged forward, the blands now surged back. Cholly was pacing wildly up and down, holding up its hands and shaking them. It was talking incoherently, as if giving orders, but the words made no sense. All around me the whispers rose: "It's got a soul, Cholly's got a soul!" And then: "It's human now."

Cholly stopped still, then turned to us. Its puny frame had somehow swelled; it looked imposing. "I'm your supervisor," it said in a commanding voice like Moriston's. "Kiss my ass, you pubers." Then, as quickly as it had become Moriston, it changed again. Fear came over its face. "They're coming!" it shrieked. "I hear the footsteps! Lock the doors! Don't let them in." It raced to the door where the postulant had disappeared, and began shoving a table in front of it.

Turmoil erupted. Some of the blands leaped forward to help Cholly barricade the door; others started back in terror; most milled around, surging this way and that, uncertain and frightened.

I fought my way through the tide of blands till I reached the door into grayspace. Behind me I heard a shout, and turned to see three of Cholly's crew racing after me. Thinking they intended to drag me back, I slipped out, slammed the door behind me, and shot the floor bolt. Moments later I heard the thunderous noise of tables being piled against the door. I turned and fled through the deserted corridors of grayspace.

"Magister!" I cried out as I burst into his quarters. "Where are you? You've got to help. Something terrible is happening."

He came out of his bedroom looking bleary and half-dressed. "What's the matter?" he said.

"Cholly stole her soul and she's dying, and the blands are all locked in the refectory—"

"Tedla, calm down," he said. He made me sit at the table and start from the beginning. Now, months of practice at observing and reporting paid off, and my brain clicked into focus. I described the events of the last night and morning in sequence. As he listened, his face grew very grave. "What's the situation now?" he asked.

"When I left, they were barricading all the doors. They're not bad blands, Magister. It's just that Cholly's gone crazy, and they don't know what to do."

He looked at me a little skeptically. Like every other human, he gave the blands too much credit for intelligence when it came to evil, and not enough when they were good. "Well," he said, "regardless, we've got to help them out. Let me get dressed, and we'll go down and talk to the supervisors."

"Not me," I said.

"Yes, you," he answered. "You're the only one who knows what's going on."

I waited in an agony of dread while he threw on some clothes, then I followed him out into the corridor. We had no sooner reached the main stair on the Questishaft than a siren went off. It was a horrible sound, starting low and climbing the scale like some primeval animal howl. It's strange that after so many centuries of civilization such a predatory sound can still strike terror in our hearts. All around the shaft people came to the doors of the shops, looking around to see what was going on. We passed one woman who had a hand-held public address radio pressed to her ear. She called out loudly, "We're supposed to evacuate the Questishaft! There's a bland uprising. They've taken hostages."

There were cries of fear then. Some people raced back into their shops to grab valuables and lock the doors; others headed down the spokes toward their residences; still more raced off to find partners and friends. I glimpsed a few shop owners trying to barricade the graydoors. It was useless; human space was so permeated by grayspace that for every access point closed there were three more alternatives. The entire convergence was just a warren of bland-runs.

Magister Galele grabbed my arm and began to walk at redoubled speed. Soon we were moving against the current of traffic as people began to flee. Some called out to Magister Galele to turn around, thinking he didn't know what was going on.

As we reached level four, the lowest human level, we saw a troop of civil-order martialists in helmets and heavy boots, deploying to cordon off the area where the supervisors' offices lay. We slipped in just ahead of them.

Inside the Facilities and Service office was a large lobby where, on normal days, people came to register complaints and requests relating to their blands. It was now crowded with martialists, supervisors, and postulants, all in a state of agitation. I saw Moriston's postulant talking tearfully to a tall woman martialist with sharp cheekbones and a close-shaved haircut, who seemed to be in charge. I pointed her out to Magister Galele. Boldly, he pushed right up to her.

"Excuse me," he said, "I think we can shed some light on this situation."

The martialist looked at him as if he were a buzzing insect. Undeterred, he pushed me forward. "Tedla was in the refectory when it all started. Tell them, Tedla."

The martialist didn't even let me draw breath. She turned away to say something to one of her lieutenants, who was holding a bullhorn. He raised it and announced, "All postulants and supervisors without direct instructions should report to the west shaft to assist supervisors there in maintaining order. Please move out now."

There was a general movement of people in the room, and we were pushed away from the martialist's side. Still hanging onto me, Magister Galele fought his way back toward her. Another martialist stopped us.

"Your bland should go to the westshaft refectory, sir," she said. "You need to evacuate. This is an emergency situation."

Just then another officer arrived and reported to the woman in charge, "Pacification force is here."

"Good," the martialist replied. "We need to get the murderous vermin contained quickly, or we're going to have to hunt them down all through their warrens."

"Are they armed?"

"They have access to knives, bludgeons, that sort of thing. There's also a lot of sabotage possible. We can't shut off the gas pipes because the controls are down there."

"Damn. How far have they spread?"

"That's what you have to find out."

A troop of about twenty martialists armed with batons, shockers, and projectile weapons came in. Appalled at the severity of force implied, I whispered to Magister Galele, "You've got to stop them! The blands aren't dangerous."

There was a stir at the door, and we heard a raised voice: "By god, you *will* let me in. I am elector of this order. Who called these martialists?"

"Ovide!" Magister Galele called out joyfully. As she came storming in the door, he pushed to her side. "I've been trying to tell these pea-brained police what's going on. They won't listen; all they want to do is push people around."

Despite the confusion around us, he had her attention. "What do *you* have to do with this?" she demanded.

"It's not me, it's Tedla," he said, pushing me forward.

"Tedla!" she said, startled to see me. We had last met in Squire Tellegen's dining room.

Worried that she, too, would stop listening, I blurted out, "Elector, the blands aren't rebelling. There's a few of them that think—well, never mind. What you need to do is calm them down and tell them you're in charge. They'll obey you, especially if you're kind."

She heard me out, then turned toward the head martialist and said, "Who called you in?"

"I did," said a large, imposing supervisor with a black beard. I knew from the blands that his name was Collum; he was in charge of red and yellow teams. "The vicious devils have got Ellia Moriston in there. We've got to get her out."

In a razor-sharp tone, Elector Hornaday said, "Supervisor Collum, you had no authority to call in the Order of Martialists, and they had no authority to declare an evacuation. We solve our problems within the order. You should have contacted me."

Collum was obviously under stress; now he burst out angrily, "It's your softness with these brutes that has made them rebellious in the first place."

"That's enough," Elector Hornaday snapped.

"No, it's not," Collum said. "We can't keep them under control, the way you hamper us with your 'humane' restrictions."

"I didn't ask for a critique of my policies," Hornaday said. She turned to the martialist. "Kindly get these troops out of here."

The martialist didn't budge. "Elector, this is a convergence-wide security issue. If the mutineers spread through the bland-runs, they could infect the other shafts as well. This is not just your problem."

"When they spread to other shafts, you may step in. Until then, this is a questionary matter."

Collum cried out in frustration, "While we stand here arguing about jurisdiction, they may be murdering Ellia!"

Elector Hornaday said, "I'm going down there and talk to them now."

Complete consternation showed on the other humans' faces. The martialist was first to recover. "I can't allow that, Elector. It's too dangerous."

"Are you in charge of my order house?" Hornaday said.

"They could ambush you."

"Elector?" I said. She turned to me. "When I left, they were all in the refectory, barricading the doors into the bland-runs. I don't think they will have left the room."

Hornaday turned back to the martialist. "Send a security team with me to the door, if you like. But we will try negotiation first."

Collum gave an exclamation of disgust. "As if they had brains to reason with."

The elector said to me, "Tedla, come with me. Magister, please stay here." She headed back into the supervisors' office complex then, plucking a postulant from the crowd to show her the way. Behind us, the officer gave some orders, and there was a rumbling hustle of martial boots at our heels.

We went down the stairway to level three. Here, the usual arrangement of space was reversed; human space consisted of narrow access corridors, and grayspace was the large area surrounding. I had come through the human halls to report to Supervisor Moriston's office, so I knew the way. I whispered to the elector how to get to the refectory.

The halls were perfectly deserted and quiet. As we passed doors into grayspace, some of the martialists stayed behind to guard them so we wouldn't get cut off. I was astonished how much tactical sophistication they imagined the blands to have.

When we reached the double doors into the refectory, we could hear noise from beyond—a rhythmic pounding, like drumming, and raised voices. Elector Hornaday turned to me. "What are they doing?"

"Magic, most likely," I said.

The martialists behind us tensed. One said, "Elector, should we fetch a welder to cut the door open?"

"It's not locked," I said.

Elector Hornaday tried it and found she could move one of the doors enough to open a crack. She cupped her hands around her mouth and said loudly through the crack, "You blands in the refectory—East Questishaft blands—please unbar the door."

The drumming abruptly stopped. She went on, "This is Elector Hornaday. There is no reason for you to be afraid. No one is going to harm you. But you have to let us in."

We heard tense voices on the other side, apparently arguing. Then there was a blood-chilling shriek and something crashed against the door. We all jumped back.

"My god, they're murdering her!" the postulant said.

I saw panic passing through the humans, and said quickly, "No. That's not what's happening. Elector, tell them you know all about Cholly. Say that Cholly needs help. Tell the good blands in the room to do the right thing, and let us in."

She looked at me a moment, then turned back to the door and gave my message. I knew the effect it would have: It would confirm all their superstitions about the omniscience of humans. They would know they didn't stand a chance.

We waited, hearing indistinct voices again. I was praying for them to listen and obey, because I knew what the humans' next step would be. "Come on, Pots. Come on, Bink," I whispered.

Suddenly, there was a loud concussion from beyond the door, then terrified screams and running feet. The fire detector sirens in the refectory began to wail.

"They've set a fire!" someone shouted.

Nothing strikes fear into residents of an underground city like fire. We are drilled from infancy to react swiftly if it breaks out. The martialists surged forward, pushing the elector back out of the way, and tried to force the door open. I was pinned flat against the wall of the hallway. As the troopers put their shoulders to the door we heard the sound of blands dismantling the barricade on the other side, dragging the tables out of the way. At last the door burst open. A crowd of terrified neuters surged toward it to escape the smoky room. I saw the lead martialist, with a baton in one hand and a shocker in the other, charge forward into the crowd, bringing the club down viciously into the face of the first bland in his way. The bland dropped to its knees, its nose broken, covered with blood.

One of the martialists was hustling the elector away down the hall, but not so fast she didn't hear the screams behind her. The shockers were going off like popcorn, and I could hear grunts of exertion from the humans as they brought their clubs down on flesh and bone. Too sickened to watch, I dashed down the hall after the elector. But when I reached the first door into grayspace, the martialist guarding it caught me by the arm and shoved me back toward the melee, saying, "Get back in there, puber."

"Elector!" I shrieked. She was too far away. I saw the martialist's shocker coming out, and tried to twist free and dodge it. He caught me in the shoulder. The shock flattened me. I fell to the floor, every muscle convulsing, struggling to draw breath. He nudged me with a boot, but I couldn't move. Someone called to him. I blinked through a field of crackling sparks, and saw he'd stepped away from the graydoor. With my last scrap of will, I forced my limbs to drag me through into grayspace.

It was like the kind of dream where you are pursued by some terrible danger, but your limbs will not move. Agonizingly slow, I first crawled, then stumbled, down the corridors of grayspace, propelled only by fear. When I came to the place where the cleaning carts were lined up, ready for the morning's chores, I fell to the floor in between two of them, hidden.

The fire siren had gone silent, but down the hall there were still shouts and screams of pain. It sounded methodical and deliberate now. I knew it was only a matter of time before the humans started scouring nearby areas for hidden rebels, so as soon as I could move I crept away into the maze of bland-runs. It was all deserted and silent. I climbed the southeast stairway, then doubled back to Magister Galele's quarters.

He wasn't there, of course. I fell onto the couch, my hands over my eyes, my skin still prickling and blobs of light floating through my vision. Then the blobs formed pictures: the baton breaking a bland's nose in a spurt of blood. A bland screaming, twitching from the pain of the shocker. Cholly, cut open like a basin, and all the other blands lined up to wash their hands in the blood.

I started up, trembling, wondering if it had really happened.

It was hours before Magister Galele came back. I hid until I was sure it was him. When he saw me he exclaimed, "Tedla!" in such a joyful voice that I rushed to his arms and buried my face in his burnous. He hugged me tight.

"Thank god you got away!" he said. "It's been driving me crazy. I've been down there, waiting for you. I thought you were trapped with those poor souls in the basement." He tensed; his voice was haunted. "It was a bloodbath. They were beaten. Disfigured, some of them."

"I know," I said.

He hugged me close again, as if to reassure himself I

was real. Softly, he said, "When I thought you were down there, dead or injured—" A tremor went through his whole body. I pulled back to look at his face and saw what a helpless tangle of conflict he was in. He went on, "I realized how much I . . . how much I . . ."

He couldn't say "love you." Instead, he blushed scarlet and looked away, as if expecting me to blame him. I couldn't imagine what was going through his mind.

"It's all right," I said.

He shook his head, then said in a slurred voice, "I want to deserve your trust. For once in my life, I want to deserve something good."

I hugged him tight and said, "You do. I'll love you no matter what."

He clutched me hard, as if holding back some strong emotion.

I slept on the couch that night—if a tense doze full of violent dreams can be called sleep. In the morning I felt exhausted, and Magister Galele didn't look much better. We looked at each other over the breakfast table, thinking of the part we had played in the previous day's events.

"What are they going to do?" I asked.

"There's going to be hell to pay," he said gravely. "I heard there was sheer panic in the other shafts when the news went around that our blands were in revolt. People will be screaming for more safeguards. The other electors and mattergraves are going to come down on Ovide like a ton of bricks."

"Are they going to investigate? Will they interview any blands?" I felt sick with dread. If they did investigate, there was not much hope for me. I had been one of Cholly's accomplices; I had even provided the liquor. At any point we could have stopped the whole conspiracy just by reporting it. We had chosen not to.

He saw what I was thinking and said, "I'll get you out of this, Tedla. I got you into it, after all."

It was brave and generous of him, but I knew he didn't have the power.

"I'll talk to Ovide," he said. "Don't worry, we'll think of something."

Right after breakfast he called the elector's office for an appointment. To both of our surprise, she agreed to see him at once. Quietly, her assistant warned him not to say a word to anyone until he had seen the elector.

He decided that I needed to come, and wouldn't hear a word of argument. My uniform from the day before was dirty and soaked with sweat, so I had to wear my human clothes. I decided they would make me less conspicuous anyway.

As soon as we set foot in human space, I could feel the change of atmosphere. All routines had been disrupted; people were gathering in clusters to talk. As we passed I heard their voices—grave, angry, frightened. For a moment I felt a rush of anger: What did *they* have to be frightened about? No human had had so much as a fingernail broken, unless you counted Supervisor Moriston. Resentment was so strange to my nature that I glanced at Magister Galele, thinking he was the one who had made me think this way. For a moment I wished I had never seen him. Then, repentant of my thought, I took his hand and squeezed it. Roused from his own preoccupation, he smiled tensely.

The elector's office was on an upper floor, in a suite of rooms that looked out over the Questishaft. When we came to the reception room, a vestigator waiting there called out, "Magister Galele!" I had never seen him before, and didn't think the Magister had either; but everyone knew who the alien at Tapis was.

"What was the Capellan role in the uprising?" the vestigator said.

"None, none at all," Magister Galele stammered, taken aback.

"You were seen down there, talking to the elector at

the height of the crisis. What were you saying?''

"Really, I can't tell you."

The vestigator's eyes fell on me. "Was this the bland involved?" he asked. I shrank back behind Magister Galele.

We were rescued by the opening of the elector's door. Two mattergraves and another elector issued out, looking grim. The vestigator's attention was distracted, and Elector Hornaday's assistant signalled to us from the door. We dodged behind a desk and into the elector's private antechamber.

"The snoops have been ambushing everyone in and out all morning," the assistant said apologetically. "I wish the elector would let us throw them out."

"Wouldn't that just make them more suspicious?" Galele said.

"That's what she says."

When we entered her office, Elector Hornaday was standing at the large window looking pensively out on the Questishaft below. When she turned to us, her face was strained and weary. Flatly, she said, "Magister, I need to know what your role was in yesterday's events."

I could see him snap into defensive mode. He stood there fidgeting a moment, then said, "Why does everyone think I had a role?"

She said impatiently, "You showed up on the scene with a great deal of inside information. We're not stupid, Magister."

He looked at me. I whispered, "Tell her the truth."

He nodded, but looked miserable. "This is so horrible. I never intended . . . You've got to believe me, Ovide. I was just trying to observe."

"I'm waiting," she said.

He told her the whole story then, standing there shifting from one foot to another. As she listened, her expression softened from accusation to a kind of hopeless resignation. When he was done, she sank into one of the office chairs, her chin resting on her fist. He sat gratefully in the sofa facing her. Since no one had invited me to sit, I remained standing.

"You have been a trial to me, Magister Galele," she said.

"I'm sorry," he said, utterly contrite.

"You know what the rumors are saying. That you somehow incited the revolt. That you have suborned our blands."

"Oh, no," he said.

"Those inclined to think of conspiracies don't have to go far on this one. Pretty soon we'll be hearing that it's the Capellan plan to undermine our social system by encouraging the blands to revolt. Once our planet is in chaos, you can then take it over."

"It's false!" Magister Galele said, really alarmed. "Absolutely false."

"I know," she said. "People who don't know you can't possibly give you enough credit for stupidity."

He winced and looked at the floor, just like a bland.

There was a long silence. At last the elector sighed and said, "I think you had better leave Tapis. Things might not be very safe for you here."

He didn't try to contradict her or ask why. He just said anxiously, "What about Tedla?"

Her eyes turned to me. I could tell from her expression that if Magister Galele was a trial, I was a problem impossible to solve justly. "You surprised me yesterday, Tedla," she said.

"Yes, ma'am," I murmured. I knew it wasn't a compliment.

"You were very levelheaded, and knew exactly what to do."

What she meant was, "You didn't act like a bland." I was silent. In the heat of the crisis yesterday, I had revealed too much.

She turned back to Magister Galele. "It would be better

if no board of inquiry ever had a chance to examine Tedla.''

She knew that it would be too hard for me to hide how Magister Galele had tampered with my training. He *had* suborned me. He hadn't intended to, but he had done it, and there was no undoing it. I was a piece of evidence better left undiscovered.

Magister Galele said, "Tellegen asked me to look after Tedla. He charged me very solemnly to keep it safe. I feel the responsibility keenly. I can't let anything happen that he wouldn't have wanted.''

"So this is all Prosper's doing?" Ovide said faintly. "That bastard.''

She came to a decision then. "I think you ought to take Tedla with you. Get it out of Tapis. Don't draw any attention to it. Just stay inconspicuous. It's the safest way.'' She studied his perplexed face for a moment, then looked to me. "Do you understand?''

"Yes, ma'am," I said.

"Good.'' She called in her assistant and said, "Have my aircar waiting in an hour. There will be two passengers for Magnus.'' She turned to Magister Galele. "Can you be ready?''

He was speechless at the abruptness of it. "But—'' He waved his hands incoherently.

"His research records,'' I explained. "Can someone send them?''

"What do they contain?'' she asked sharply.

"Nothing of interest to anyone but me,'' he said. "But to me, they're very important.''

I caught her eye and shook my head to signal that it wasn't that simple. All my reports on blue team's witcheries were there: our role, spelled out in the clearest detail.

She turned back to her assistant. "Make that two hours.'' To Magister Galele, she said, "Take the crucial parts with you. We'll send the rest. You know what I mean, don't you?''

"Yes," he said, but I knew he didn't. He was thinking academically, not politically.

"Show them out the back way, so the snoops don't get a crack at them," the elector said to her assistant. Then she turned to Magister Galele. "Good-bye, Magister. Knowing you has been . . . interesting."

His gaze dropped to the floor.

We raced back to his rooms, knowing how little time we had. When we got inside, I hesitated a second, then said, "Pack your clothes, Magister. I'll get the records."

"To hell with the clothes," he said.

Stubbornly, I said, "You'll need something to wear, and I know the records backwards and forward. Trust me."

It was the absolute reverse of the way it ought to have been, but he was too worn down to put up much of a fight. He meekly trooped into the bedroom, and I made for the studium.

All the recent, incriminating information was electronic, so I set the terminal to wipe every entry since I'd arrived, and began shoveling backup disks into a valise. I knew I ought to destroy them, but there wasn't enough time to sort them out, and Magister Galele would be heartbroken to lose the whole last year of work. I spied a stack of printouts that never should have been made, and stuffed them in on top of the disks. Then I began to systematically search the room for anything damaging. I had barely done the sweep when the Magister showed up.

"I'm done," he said.

"Did you pack your toothbrush and razor?" I asked.

"Oh. Right."

"Here, I'll do it. You go through the closet here for anything recent." I didn't think there was anything in there, but it was best to be safe. I jerked open his suitcase to see how well he had done. Better than I had expected, but he'd still forgotten socks and shoes. I raced to his bedroom to fetch them.

We left our rooms with him dragging the suitcase and

me toting the valise. When we got to the aircar pad, the pilot already had the motor running. We threw the luggage in the back, climbed in, and belted ourselves. As the aircar began to rise, Magister Galele looked back at me anxiously. I said, "Don't worry, Magister. If we just stick together, it'll be all right."

I was reminded that I had once said the same to Joby.

Chapter Ten

✴ It was drizzling rain when we came to Magnus Convergence, and I saw nothing of the landscape but gray pavement and fog. But inside, the aircar port was bright and busy. At the luggage desk, we found that the blands would deliver our bags to our residence so we wouldn't have to carry them. I looked to Magister Galele to see where we were going. "Capellan Emissarium," he said.

The supervisor handling the luggage put Magister Galele's suitcase on a moving belt. I didn't want to let go of the valise with all the data, so I looked at the supervisor to see what I ought to do. He nodded at a graydoor. I started off toward it.

"Tedla!" Magister Galele called out. "Where are you going?"

"With the luggage," I said. "I'll meet you there."

"I want you with me," he said.

I stood hesitantly, not wanting to argue with him in front of the supervisor, but not wanting to obey him either. I knew I ought to let the blands show me the way through grayspace.

"Come on," he said testily.

The supervisor was shaking his head at the eccentricities of aliens. I realized that residents of Magnus were much more used to Capellans, and might make allowances. So I shifted the valise to the other hand and followed Magister Galele.

Magnus was a much bigger convergence than Tapis. It had over a hundred shafts, each serving a separate order or community. At the very center were three massive supershafts arranged in a triangle and connected by broad, high-ceilinged hallways, so that you could almost always see sunlight. Everywhere were fountains and air sculptures and corridor cafes. I thought that the staff of blands maintaining it all must be immense.

The emissarium was located on one of the central shafts. It was set far back from the edge to make room for a broad plaza full of cafe tables, plants, and pigeons. As we crossed toward the bronze double doors, scarcely anyone spared us a look.

Inside was a quiet, lushly carpeted lobby. Behind a curved information desk a Gammadian receptionist sat. Magister Galele said to her nervously, "I need to talk to one of the First Contact team."

"Emissary Ptanka-Ni is in," she said.

"All right. Tell him it's Alair Galele."

Less than a minute later an alien emerged from one of the doors. With a quirk of surprise I realized that he was one of the original aliens we had seen so much of when I was in the creche, though his hair was now gray and he looked more world-worn than he had on screen. I also realized, from what Magister Galele had taught me, that the caste-stone on his forehead meant he was Vind.

"Alair!" he said, coming up to clasp the Magister's hand solicitously. "I have been trying to contact you since yesterday, when we heard the news about Tapis. I was getting worried. Are you all right?"

"Oh, yes, perfectly," Galele said. "I'm just going to have to impose on your hospitality a little."

The Vind's face didn't lose its look of cordial concern, but his voice became sharp. "Why, what's the matter?"

"A little political hot water, I'm afraid."

The emissary abruptly switched into Capellan. "This uprising. Can we be linked to it?"

"Well . . . I think . . . mistakenly . . . but there's some potential for that."

"We'd better talk in my office," the emissary said, and turned back to the door he had come through.

"Can someone take care of Tedla?" Magister Galele said in Gammadian.

"I will," the receptionist answered.

She placed a call to the bland supervisor, then directed me down a hallway to his door. When I entered his tiny office, I found he was an elderly man with a "what-now?" expression, as if nothing surprised him any more—even new blands being dropped on him out of the sky.

He looked me over, human clothes and all, with an expression that seemed to say the world was completely topsy-turvy and there was nothing he could do about it. At last he sighed and said, "Who are you and what are you doing here?"

"I'm Tedla, Magister Galele's Personal. We came from Tapis."

"How did he get a Personal?" the supervisor said, as if it were more evidence of the insanity of the world.

The real story was too complicated, so I stretched the truth and said, "Elector Hornaday assigned me to him."

His face changed, and I realized it was because he had heard Elector Hornaday's name. "Tapis?" he said sharply, as if things had begun falling in place in his mind.

"Yes, sir."

I was afraid he was going to ask more, but he didn't. He just said, "How long will he be here?"

"I don't know, sir."

"We'll have to put him in the guest room, I suppose." He rose slowly and opened the graydoor behind his desk, sticking his head through. "Misery!" he yelled.

"Yes, sir!" said a bright, cheerful voice.

"Come here."

A young bland appeared in the door. The supervisor said, "We've got someone staying in the guest room. This is Tedla, his Personal. Show it around, will you?"

"Yes, sir."

When we were alone in the bland-run I said to my companion, "Why do they call you Misery?"

"Because I love company," it said. The bland must have told the joke a thousand times in its life, but it acted as amused as if it were the first time.

The guest quarters proved to be a luxurious three-room suite. In the sitting room, one whole wall was glass, looking out on the sun-filled plaza on the shaft. We were just above the emissarium's entry door. I put the valise in a closet.

"Is that all his luggage?" Misery asked.

"No, the rest is being delivered."

"Don't expect it today, then."

Since there was no unpacking for me to do, and the room was all ready, Misery took me on a tour of grayspace. The emissarium was a separate building, only four stories high, and unconnected to the rest of the convergence, except at certain points: the front door I had come through, a back door for the humans, and a shipping door into grayspace, where food and supplies came in. The top three floors held the humans' living quarters, dining and entertaining rooms, offices, a library, and a communications room for talking to their ship. The bottom floor was grayspace. I was relieved not to be in a massive, anonymous place again. This building had a cozy, small-house feeling, though much busier than Menoken Lodge. There were only fifteen blands on the staff, and they worked hard. They had their own roundroom, and looked down on the convergence blands outside.

When we got to the kitchen, the blands were just beginning to work on dinner. When they heard I was from Tapis, they gathered around me to ask about the uprising. I was astonished at the story they had already heard: that some of the blands had risen up and murdered their supervisor, then occupied their refectory and held off all human attacks for hours, till the martialists had brought in explosives to blow down the door. Then the humans had gone wild—shocked some to death, and mutilated others with kitchen knives.

I started to deny it all, but realized how little I really knew. I could only say, "I'll tell you what I know tonight in the roundroom."

"Were you there?" the cook, an older bland named Deen, asked.

I nodded; then, to convince them, I unbuttoned my shirt and showed them the burn on my shoulder. "That's where they got me with a shocker," I said.

There were horrified whispers all round. "Were you one of the rebels?" Misery said, round-eyed.

"No, I was trying to help the humans."

"And that's what you got for it?"

"That's right."

I could see that their trust in the basic reason of humans had slipped a notch.

"*Our* humans wouldn't do that," Deen said for the benefit of the younger blands; but somehow, its voice lacked conviction.

Just then the supervisor walked in, and the blands scattered. I shrugged my shirt back on. When I turned around, I saw the supervisor watching me with a wary expression. I had never seen such a look on a human's face before: as if I had given him some terrible foreboding. But all he said was, "You can get a uniform from the laundry."

"Yes, sir," I said.

Contrary to Misery's prediction, the suitcase arrived soon after. I hauled it up to the guest room to begin unpacking. When I came through the graydoor, I found the lights on. Out in the shaft, the sunlight had faded, though the balconies were full of little starlights. Magister Galele was moving restlessly around in front of the window, whispering to himself. I could tell it had not been a pleasant interview. When he looked up at me, he said, "He says we can't grant you a refugee visa."

"Oh," I said. I wasn't terribly sure what a visa was.

"He gave some excuse about not having worked out the legal status of blands," he said. "Never mind, we'll just have to think of something else. I promise you, Tedla, I *will* think of something else."

He looked so agitated, I went up to him and put a hand on his arm to calm him. "Don't worry. You ought to be thinking of yourself, anyway."

"I'm already in so much trouble it doesn't matter any more," he said, laughing edgily. "I don't care. My career's a lost cause. All I care about now is having gotten you involved. I've got to see that nothing happens to you."

I felt a terrible, dangerous warmth for him, then. He looked at me, and must have seen the tenderness in my face, because he said in a whisper, "You understand why, don't you, Tedla? You understand that I—"

We were very close, when I realized that his impulses were taking over and he was going to kiss me right there in front of the window. I flinched away and went to pull the curtains. By the time I turned back, he was grappling to get control of himself.

"I'm sorry, Magister—" I said.

"No, you were right," he said, turning away so he didn't have to look at me. "Please don't . . . I'm terribly ashamed of myself. It won't happen again."

I ached for him. He thought I had rejected him. "Magister, it's not that—"

He gave a shaky laugh. "You'd think there was nothing I could do to make this situation any worse. But trust me to think of something. Thank god one of us has some sense, eh?"

He was back in his old self-mocking mode. I stood there, wanting to ease the terrible strain on him, wanting to let him know I didn't mind. Caution stopped me, even though his self-blame filled the room. The odds of exposure were huge, here; it would only bring him into more danger than he was in already.

I went into the bedroom to unpack his clothes. When my back was turned, he slipped into the bathroom and turned on the shower for a while. When he came out his eyes were bloodshot. I pretended not to notice.

Presently, he turned on the viewscreen in the sitting room. As I hung out his clothes, I listened to the news reports. Absolutely all anyone was talking about was Tapis. Before long, I was irresistibly drawn to the door to watch.

It was then I learned for the first time what had really happened. After Elector Hornaday and I had gone downstairs, the officer of the martialists had decided on her own to lead a party around to the other refectory door—the one into grayspace that I had locked—to prevent any blands from escaping that way and scattering through the blandruns. For some reason, she had decided to put explosives on the door. With a sense of disbelief, I watched an interview in which she said in her cool, metallic voice, "It was an emergency measure, to ensure quick access in case the elector needed our help. At that stage, she had more or less forbidden us to take action. But when the fire alarms went off, and we realized the mutineers were jeopardizing the safety of the convergence, I decided on my own to intervene."

"It sounds like that was a good thing," the interviewer said sympathetically.

"As it turns out, it was. We were able to enter the room and quickly put an end to the whole incident without any loss of life except the one unfortunate woman."

"Was she already dead when you arrived?" the interviewer said.

"No, she died later in the curatory."

Unable to contain myself, I exclaimed, "Of what?" But the interviewer didn't ask.

As the interviewer congratulated the martialist on her decisiveness and heroism, the screen changed to a diagram of the refectory, so everyone could follow the action. I said, "That was a pack of lies!"

Magister Galele looked at me. "What do you mean?"

"We heard the explosion. I didn't know they were blowing the doors down, but all the blands started screaming. It was *after* that the fire alarms went off. It was probably the explosion that set them off."

The Magister thought about it a moment, realized what a difference it made, then turned to me and said, "Are you sure?"

"Absolutely," I said.

"Then the blands hadn't set any fires. That's been the whole excuse for what happened, you know. That they were endangering the convergence."

"It was the damned martialists endangering the convergence," I said angrily.

I went back into the bedroom to finish my job, but couldn't stop listening. A woman began talking, attacking the martialists for their ferocity. Now I learned that seven blands had died. She cataloged them indignantly: one of head trauma, two from internal injuries, and four from repeated electric shock. "Just one shock will incapacitate most blands," the woman said. "Two will paralyze them or induce convulsions. The third, fourth, fifth, and sixth shocks must have been administered to blands lying helplessly on the ground, presenting no threat to anyone."

The rumors about mutilation were also, apparently, true. "I don't need to say a thing," the woman said. "I just ask you to look at these pictures, and ask if this was the work of civilized humans."

I moved to the door, but when I got there, Magister Galele had blanked the screen. He turned to me, looking sickened. "You don't want to see this, Tedla," he said.

"Was there anyone I know?" I asked, dreading the answer.

"I don't know. They didn't show names."

I came out and sat next to him on the couch, the unpacking forgotten. I was terribly afraid again. I had felt safe since leaving Tapis, and now that was gone. There was something volatile in the air, an infectious hysteria, and the viewscreen was spreading it. Magister Galele turned on the picture again, and we watched together, mesmerized by the sight of frenzy feeding on itself.

Everyone was attacking everyone else. A communitarian came on, criticizing Elector Hornaday for her spineless handling of the situation, claiming her delays and vacillation had only escalated the problem till the whole convergence came into danger. "The humanitarians have brought this on all of us, through their laxity," the man said. "We've got to take the warning and crack down. It'll be too late when we're all murdered in our beds."

Then there was the expert who pointed out how vulnerable all the convergences were to an uprising. "You ask, Could it happen here? The answer is, of course it can. The way our cities have been built, they can infiltrate anywhere, through their warrens. We have given them complete access." He argued for riot doors on all the bland-runs, and remote-controlled pipes of knockout gas, and even implanted chips so every bland's movements could be tracked.

"We don't trust each other any more," I said numbly.

"Did you ever?" Magister Galele said.

"It was all built on trust. The humans trusted the blands to be dumb and docile, and the blands trusted the humans to follow their own rules. Even if we didn't like it, we could predict it. Now it's like we're strangers. We don't know each other any more."

"There's only one good thing," Magister Galele said. "No one has said the word 'Capella.'"

The next morning, right after his breakfast, Magister Galele went to the communication room to send a message to his home planet via the orbiting ship. I, meanwhile, dumped out all the data disks we had rescued onto the bed, and began sorting them. When he came back in, he was in a much more cheerful mood. "Let's take all that stuff to the library to work on," he said. "They've got a big table in there. It will be much more convenient."

"Am I allowed in there?" I asked carefully.

"This is a Capellan place, Tedla," he said. "You're allowed anywhere you want to go."

I knew it wasn't as simple as that, but I didn't argue. When we got to the library, it was empty. I spread out the piles of disks and printouts, and he began browsing the shelves, finding assorted Capellan classics he thought I ought to read. Soon he had assembled quite a pile of them, and began telling me what was in each one and why it was important.

After a while he got restless and started pacing, so I said, "Why don't you go out for a walk?"

"That's a good idea," he said; then, "I just wish you could go with me."

"I'm okay," I said.

"I know," he said. "You're always okay." He made it sound like a character flaw.

He left, but was back before ten minutes were up, looking flustered. "They wouldn't let me out," he said. "Emissary's orders. I suppose he's worried I might cause another scandal. You'd think he'd have more trust in me than that."

I didn't say anything. It didn't sound good to me.

Over the next few days we both adjusted to life as virtual prisoners. We read books and cowrote a report on the events at Tapis, and watched the debates on the viewscreen with a growing sense of unreality. On the third day, Magister Galele received a long transmission from Capella Two that cheered him up immeasurably. The next day he announced that he wanted me to take another test. I groaned.

He was always giving me tests, never willing to believe I was no good at them.

"This one is really important," he said. "You have to try hard on this. The original test is in Capellan, so I've gotten permission to translate for you."

By now I was quite good at conversational Capellan—we scarcely spoke anything else between ourselves any more—but academic writing still gave me problems. When I saw the test, though, I realized it wasn't the language that was difficult.

"Answer the ones you're sure of," Magister Galele instructed me. "Then, if you get stuck, I'll help translate."

I started in. Before long he saw me puzzling over something, and, in a wild mix of Gammadian and Capellan, he explained what the question meant in a little mini-lesson that left it perfectly obvious what answer he wanted me to give. A little puzzled, I filled it in. In this collaborative fashion we managed to complete most of the test. At the end, it asked for my name, and I typed in "Tedla."

"You'll need a last name," he said.

"Why?"

"Because I'm sending this to Capella Two."

"What sort of name do they want?"

"It can be any name you like."

He was watching me with anxious expectation. I could tell this was another question he wanted me to get right, but this time he didn't want to prompt me. "Can I—" I started, then fell silent, embarrassed by how presumptuous it sounded. I was only a bland, after all. But he was still watching me, so I gathered my courage and said, "Can I use yours?"

He looked perfectly delighted. "Do you want to?"

"If you don't mind."

"Tedla, I would be honored. Thrilled."

I typed it in and sat looking at it. Tedla Galele. I had a name now, just like a human. My birth name, and the name of my sponsor, the person I wanted to honor by carrying his name for the rest of my life. He was letting me have part of him, as if I were his protégé. "Thank you," I whispered.

"Thank *you*," he said, touching my hand. I wanted to put my arms around him, and knew I didn't dare. Suddenly, I found my eyes were watering. "Tedla, what's the matter?" he said tenderly.

"Nothing. It's just that you're so kind to me."

"My dear child," he said, deeply moved. "My dear, dear child."

We had been in Magnus a little over a week when, one evening, Emissary Ptanka-Ni came to see Magister Galele. When I ushered him in the door, I saw that the emissary was grandly dressed in formal wear. "I can't take long," he said to Magister Galele in Capellan, ignoring me. "I'm on my way to a reception. But I think you ought to know the latest developments."

I went into the bedroom to do some unnecessary task or other to give them the impression of privacy. Of course, I listened sharply.

"Has there been something that's not on screen?" Magister Galele said.

"Everything, Alair. All the real action is happening behind the scenes."

"So tell me."

"Ovide Hornaday's impeachment is a fait accompli. All they've been arguing about for the last three days is the venue for her trial. It will be held here. That's not in her favor. The reformers and atomists have been losing round after round. The climate has really shifted."

"Poor Ovide. She's nothing but a scapegoat. What does it mean for us?"

"It's not good. As you know, Ovide and her allies were quite open to our presence, and we got associated with them in many people's minds. The communitarians are not nearly so welcoming. I've had to send out a communiqué to all the research team, warning them to be extremely cautious. If we can just keep our heads down and our noses clean, we may weather this.''

Magister Galele gave a sigh.

The emissary went on, ''The other thing that's been going on is the investigation. They've been questioning everyone at Tapis, even the blands. I expect there will be some executions before all is said and done.''

Magister Galele exclaimed, ''They execute people here?''

''Not people. Blands.''

''Oh.''

The emissary's voice dropped very low; I strained to hear it. ''I've received a warning from a friend that Tedla's name keeps coming up. Alair, have you told me everything about Tedla's involvement? We can't shelter it if it had a role in the conspiracy.''

Slowly, Magister Galele said, ''Everything Tedla did, it did on my orders.''

''That's not what I wanted to hear.''

''It's what I'll say. No matter who asks me.''

There was an icy silence. Magister Galele went on, ''That's why we've got to prevent them from examining Tedla. It will link us directly to the uprising—or directly enough for the paranoids. You ought to get Tedla out of here, for good.''

''No. I told you, it is too easy for them to trace the bland here. If it disappeared, people would think there was a cover-up. Everyone would say we had something to hide.''

''We *do* have something to hide, damn it!''

The emissary's voice went up a note in pitch; he sounded very angry. ''Alair, I have no idea why you have gotten this Quixotic notion that it's your duty to defend this bland. If we can protect ourselves by handing Tedla over and blaming your mistakes on it, we've got to do that.''

"No."

"Do you want to jeopardize all the years of work establishing a relationship between our planets?"

"Do you want an innocent person executed for helping us?"

"For helping *you*, you mean," the emissary said.

"That's us, Ptanka-Ni. You *can't* cut me loose. I'm Capellan. You're tarred with my brush."

The emissary rose. "You're not rational. I've got to go. I'll talk to you later."

"Oh, one more thing," Magister Galele said, then called out, "Tedla?"

I came to the bedroom door. Magister Galele said, "Tedla speaks fluent Capellan."

The emissary's gaze switched to me, and he flushed scarlet. "Thank you for telling me," he said in a voice the temperature of dry ice, and left.

Everything the emissary had told us became public the next day. We sat together on the couch, watching the reports like addicts. Elector Hornaday was formally impeached by the electors and mattergraves before noon. The vote went through with so little debate it was obviously prearranged. By afternoon, there were pictures of her being brought by aircar to Magnus, looking grim and angry. She asked to make a public statement, but wasn't allowed to.

But the bit of news that made both of us start alert was reported only as an allegation to be investigated by the trial commission. Someone had accused Elector Hornaday of basing her decision to negotiate on the advice of one of the rebel blands. It was a damaging accusation, the way they put it—as if she had been duped by a conspiracy more devious and elaborate than anyone had suspected up to now.

Our Gammadian trials are very different from yours. They are not modeled on war, as yours are—two sides battling to win a confrontation. We do not have hired legal mercenaries to fight in proxy for us. The purpose of our trials is to reach a just reconciliation that serves the best interests of the community. The object is not to decide who wins or loses, but to determine what will benefit everyone most.

But few trials are as politically charged as Ovide Hornaday's.

They wrangled for days over who should sit on the commission of judges. Who, after all, was fit to judge an elector, except other electors? But virtually all were aligned on one side or another. I couldn't follow the maneuvering, not knowing any of them, but when five judges were finally chosen, the emissary told Magister Galele it was a moderate panel, though slightly tilted against her—but then, so was most of the world.

We watched the testimony on screen for days. Everyone told their version—the supervisors, the postulants, the martialists, the investigators, none of them getting close to the truth. "When are they going to ask some blands?" Magister Galele said impatiently.

"We can't testify in court," I said.

"But they've questioned them all. Surely *someone* knows that this so-called rebellion was no such thing."

If they knew, they obviously didn't believe it.

Through all of it, the emissarium received no requests for anyone to come and examine me. I expected it every day. I grew very jumpy whenever the supervisor called me over, or a knock sounded on Magister Galele's door. It was no secret who I had worked for, so it should not have been difficult to track me down. As the days went by, I could only conclude that something was holding them back.

"What should I say, if they question me?" I asked Magister Galele.

"Play dumb," he said. "You know how. I've seen you do it."

"But—"

"They won't ask you, Tedla," he said positively. "Ptanka-Ni will see to it."

Elector Hornaday was the last one scheduled to testify. She was very good at it. She spoke not in the contrite or evasive tone of the guilty, but in a plain, straightforward manner, with a little of the righteous indignation of the unjustly accused. There was more than just her power riding on her testimony. The emissary was right that humans were never executed—those found guilty of major crimes were allowed to choose between ending their own lives and expulsion from human society.

I crouched tensely on the couch, watching, as they got to the crucial part. One of the judges said, "We have heard several people testify that you consulted with a bland before making the decision to talk them out."

"Yes, that's true," she said quite calmly. "It was a bland I was familiar with, and knew to be loyal. I had chosen it myself, from Brice's, and knew it was attached to humans, myself included."

"And what did it say to you?"

"It had escaped from the refectory shortly before the doors were barricaded, and knew the mood of the blands. In its judgment, they were not dangerous."

One of the more hostile judges said, "Was that opinion confirmed by the supervisors?"

"No," the elector said with only the slightest hesitation. "But none of them had actually been down there, and their judgments were influenced by rumor and fear. I thought an eyewitness account was valuable information."

"So you believed the bland over the supervisors?"

"No," the elector said. It was the only thing she could say. "I took their opinion into account. I just decided that negotiation was a viable first option, always keeping the possibility of force in reserve."

She made it sound so well-reasoned, in retrospect. When I thought of the confusion and panic of the actual events, the contrast was almost comic.

"Did it never occur to you that it might be part of the conspiracy to plant a so-called 'loyal' bland to feed you disinformation?" the judge demanded.

"Do you think they are that foresighted?" the elector said in an ironically amused tone. "You give them more credit than I do."

It was a masterful answer, instantly deflating the impression that she was a kindly dupe.

The questioning went on, and I waited for her to challenge the sequence of events surrounding the explosion. But it turned out she had been confused and preoccupied at that point, and didn't remember. I felt a sharp disappointment. Her case would have been so much better.

"I still believe you, Tedla," Magister Galele said.

Even so, by the end of the hearings that day, I felt the worst danger was past. They had seemingly asked all the questions they were going to ask about my role, and had never even mentioned Magister Galele. Elector Hornaday had performed well: slyly ridiculed the conspiracy theories and projected a no-nonsense, feet-on-the-ground demeanor. Acquittal seemed likely to me.

The elector's opponents must have felt the same.

I had just brought some new towels up from the laundry, and was alone in the room, when I heard voices outside the front door, and stepped to the window to look. Emissary Ptanka-Ni was coming across the plaza toward the building. Three vestigators who had apparently been waiting outside the door were rushing toward him, one of them with a handheld recorder. He stopped, clearly surprised, and there was an exchange of questions and answers. I could tell the emissary was growing very tense, from the way he held himself. At last he broke away from the group of vestigators and headed for the emissarium. They pursued him, but he speeded up his pace and finally escaped through the bronze doors below my window.

Less than a minute later, I was in the bathroom when

the door opened and I heard the emissary's voice saying, "Alair!"

I came out to say, "I think he's in the com room."

The emissary turned to go when I said in Capellan, "What's going on, emissary?"

He was startled enough to hear the language that he turned back. "Turn on your viewscreen," he answered in the same tongue, and left.

Quickly, I did. There was a man on it I had never seen before, with a square face and a head shaved like a martialist's. He was talking so fast it took me several minutes to catch on. When I did, my heart started knocking. He was talking about a Capellan conspiracy to provoke insurrection among the blands. The word I kept hearing over and over, till it seemed to be ringing in my ears, was "Galele."

They had found a voicepad in his rooms at Tapis, containing rough notes for a report. Somehow, in my hurry, I had missed it. In a gravelly, ominous voice quite unlike Magister Galele's, the man read passages:

It's not that the blands aren't alienated. They are—profoundly so. The problem is, this hasn't resulted in any sense of solidarity or ideas of collective action. The whole notion of class consciousness was quite alien to Tedla at first. They have no inkling of their own power.

This evening I provided them with some liquor, delivered by Tedla, to act as a social lubricant. We shall see if it jars loose anything beyond mere sorcery. A little experiment in chemical warfare, you might say.

There were other passages, all seemingly quite recent. I groaned aloud. The man on the screen looked up as if he had heard me, and said, "This alien agent infiltrated the very roundrooms that rebelled at Tapis, to infect them with his poisonous notions of 'collective action.' Is this a coincidence? Is it sheer chance that the provocateur Galele was present at the crisis, trying to distract and influence our people? Is it coincidence that his trained proxy was the very bland who deceived Elector Hornaday into thinking the revolt was harmless?''

At that moment Magister Galele came barreling into the room, saying, "What's going on? They told me—''

"Shhh! Be quiet!'' I said.

''. . . And where are these conspirators now? Being sheltered in the Capellan Emissarium at Magnus Convergence, being rewarded for their good work!''

"Good god, does he mean us?'' the Magister said.

"Yes,'' I said. "You're a provocateur, and I'm your proxy.''

"Oh, no.''

I sank onto the couch. I felt like the game was over, and we might as well give up. Whatever happened from now on, there was only one conceivable outcome. The only question was how long it would take.

The man on the viewscreen began repeating the incriminating passages. Magister Galele listened, thunderstruck. "Those are my private notes!'' he said, indignantly.

"I'm sorry I missed them,'' I said.

"They weren't in the studium. They were in my bedroom. I'd been dictating on the little voicepad in bed. It must have gotten hidden in the covers.''

The man got to the part about "chemical warfare,'' and Magister Galele exclaimed, "That was a joke!'' In his accuser's mouth it sounded like anything but.

The emissary came in. He stood in the doorway with his arms crossed, staring at Galele. "Is there any hope we can deny this?'' he said.

The Magister shook his head.

The emissary's gaze was steely, but his voice was controlled. "My god, Alair. How many times had I warned you? How many times did I say, don't pick at the scabs of their culture? What is it that drives you to uncover whatever shames them most?''

He paused, but Magister Galele didn't answer. The emissary's voice changed as he went on, ''Please don't leave this room, either of you. I've already got three factions demanding custody of Tedla, and I've got to work out who has the most legitimate claim. As for you . . .'' He looked at Magister Galele with a mix of despair and contempt. ''. . . I suppose I can't deny you belong to us.''

When we were alone, Magister Galele sat down beside me on the couch. I had turned off the sound, but the man's face was still on the screen, silently mouthing accusations. The Magister said, ''It was my job, Tedla. They sent me here to understand this world. There's no way I can understand them without understanding what shames them. That's what self-knowledge is all about, exposure of those things you least want to know. We can never really know ourselves until we know shame.''

I knew he was talking about more than just my planet. I took his hand and pressed it against my cheek, savoring the feeling of being so close to someone who loved me, and needed me. I would have done anything to take away his shame, but anything I did would only increase it.

''I have hurt you so much, Tedla,'' he said in a thick voice.

''No, you haven't,'' I said. ''You have made me very happy.''

''You can blame everything on me,'' he said. ''Tell them I forced you. Tell them you were afraid to disobey me.''

I didn't say anything. It had already occurred to me that I might do the exact opposite: claim that I had wormed my way into his confidence, manipulated him and deceived him, made use of his naiveté to serve my plans. I could make them believe me, I was sure of it. The thought filled me with a heady terror.

There was a knock on the door, and both of us tensed.

Our eyes met, and I saw he was as frightened as I. Then I got up to answer it.

There were two people outside the door: a Gammadian security guard and the Capellan technician who operated the communications equipment. With a slightly resentful glance at the guard, the technician said, "Alair's message from Capella Two just came in. He's been such a pest about it I thought he'd want to see it."

"Thank you," I said, and took the tablet from her.

When he saw what it was, Magister Galele leaped up and snatched it from my hands, scrolling through the screens and reading eagerly. His whole body had changed: He was animate now with hope. When he reached the part he was looking for he shouted out, "Yes!" then threw his arms around me and hugged me tight. "You did it, Tedla!" he said, stepping back and looking at me with a glowing mix of pride and defiance. "I knew you could."

"Did what?" I said.

"You've been accepted to the Universal Institute, Capella," he said, showing me the screen. "The first Gammadian student accepted to a Capellan university. It's a special program for non-Capellan students, but it's still UIC. Look, your student visa." He pressed a key, and a document appeared with my name, Tedla Galele.

"But I didn't apply," I said, bewildered.

"Yes, you did. Remember that test? That was the entry exam. I filled out a few forms for you, as well. I knew if I told you, you'd just give me some crap about not being able to do it."

"They don't know I'm a bland, do they?" I said. I knew how he operated.

"What difference do you think that makes to UIC?"

He was incorrigible. Insane. I said, "Magister, they'll never let me go. Especially not now."

"We'll see about that!" he said. Energized, he sat down at the terminal and called the com room. The technician who had delivered the message was just coming back in.

"Kirsten, you're a darling!" Magister Galele said.

"Good news, eh?" she said. She had a cynical manner that was obvious only skin deep. I could tell she liked the Magister, though she would rather die than show it.

"Couldn't be better. I only need one more thing now. Can you patch me through to the ship from this terminal?"

"Not without reporting it to His Vindness," she said. "I've been told to tap all communications in and out of your room." She paused. "Alair, do you know what deep shit you're in? They're sending the shuttle down tomorrow. Word is they intend to deport you. Now, do you still want to talk to the ship?"

"No," he said. "Thanks, that's all I need to know."

He cut the connection and turned to me. "Tomorrow," he said. "The shuttle pilot's willing to help. He's a Balavati: sister planet to the Vind, but complete opposites in temperament. They live to subvert power. Nadkarni and I are great buds; we used to drink beer together up in that can they call a questship. All we have to do is get to the shuttle, and Karni will take us. This visa of yours will keep him from getting in trouble, and get you to Capella."

He had obviously been planning it for a long time. I was surprised at how many allies he had—but I shouldn't have been. He could be terribly charming, in a reprobate way.

There were voices in the hall outside. "Quick, hide!" he said, pushing me toward the closet. But I knew hiding there was pointless; instead, I went for the graydoor. As I opened it I saw the cheeky confidence dissolve from his face. "You'll come back?" he said.

"Yes," I promised.

The bland-run was empty. I dashed down it and around a corner, then paused to think of where to go. In Tapis, there would have been a thousand crannies to hide in, but here I didn't know grayspace well enough. Voices were coming toward me from a cross-corridor. I opened the first door I saw, and slipped through.

It was a storage closet, full of brooms and mops and

chemicals. I stood immobile as the voices came nearer, then stopped. Just my luck, the closet was exactly where they were going. When the door opened, Misery looked straight at me, startled. I pressed my finger to my lips and signalled it to be quiet. It recovered its poise and pushed a rolling bucket into the closet. "Let's go, or Deen will have a fit," it said to its companion, who was hidden from my sight behind the door.

I listened to the footsteps receding down the hallway. Before they faded away, there were others, fast and light, coming back again. I blinked at the light as Misery opened the door again.

"Tedla, what's going on?" it whispered.

"You've got to help me, Misery," I said. "The humans want to take me away, and punish me. If I can just keep out of their sight for a day, I can get away. They're going to search grayspace as soon as they find I'm missing. Do you know a place I could hide?"

Misery hesitated. I was asking it to take a terrible risk. "No one will know it was you," I promised.

I could see the arguments pass across its face. "No," it said at last, to someone who wasn't there, "I ought to help. It's what Deen's been saying. You blands stuck together at Tapis. We ought to stick together, too. They wouldn't be able to do these things to us if we stood up for each other."

I was speechless. It was the first hint of solidarity I had heard from a bland's lips. "You're right," I said. "It's what Magister Galele's been saying all along."

"There's a perfect place to hide," Misery said, "if you don't mind being in human space." It remembered who it was talking to then, and said, "*You* won't mind that. Come on."

Misery led the way down the bland-run. We climbed the stairs to the next level up, and into a corridor lined with anonymous, identical graydoors. It stopped at the fourth one on the left and listened at the crack. "There's someone in there right now. We've got to wait."

"Where are we?" I asked, realizing I actually knew the building better from the human side than from the bland side.

"This is the room they're using for their communication equipment. There used to be a graydoor into it, but when they moved the machinery in they blocked it off. They didn't want us to go in there, anyway. But the way they arranged the equipment, there's a crawl space behind. It's not big, and you'll have to keep really quiet."

"It sounds just fine," I said. I glanced nervously down the bland-run, wondering how long it would take them to start the search.

Misery listened again at the door, then said, "Okay, they're gone."

The graydoor opened inward only a couple of feet before it hit the back of a tall metal cabinet. You couldn't see that there was any hide-hole until you slipped in and closed the door behind you. It was absolutely perfect. As I sidled down the narrow space between the machines and the wall, the electricity raised the hairs on my arms. The effect was not so bad down low, so I sat on the dusty floor. There was a crack between two machines where I could actually see into the room: a narrow view of the back of a chair, a coffee cup sitting on some equipment, and the viewscreen high on the wall, showing a picture but no sound.

I had barely settled down when the human door opened and two technicians came back in. I couldn't see them, but I recognized the voice of Kirsten. From his accent, the man with her was Gammadian.

"Look at that. Thirty-two more calls just since I went out," Kirsten said. "That makes one hundred and seventy in the last half hour. Everyone on the planet wants to give us a piece of their mind."

"I'm not surprised," the Gammadian said. He sounded nervous.

"No, not with the crap that regressive pinhead is spouting." Kirsten settled down in the chair. I glimpsed her for a moment before she wheeled out of my line of sight. "Did you hear the latest?" she said.

"No."

"Galele's bland disappeared."

"You mean the one he . . . tampered with?"

"The very same. I'm the last one to have seen it."

"They're looking for it, aren't they?"

She laughed grimly. "You bet they are. With handcuffs and hypodermics. Poor shit, I wouldn't be in its shoes. Did you see the supervisor they sent? No wonder it ran."

"What about the Magister?"

"Oh, he's toast."

"What does that mean?"

"It means they're going to grill him for breakfast. He'll never work again."

"Why did your people send a man like that to us?"

She gave that laugh again. It was the most unamused sound I'd heard in a long time. "You might not believe this, but they didn't have an easy time recruiting for this expedition. The very least we might lose is one hundred and two years out of our lives. Most of us will never make it back. The cream of the crop don't jump for chances like this. WAC had to take what they could get."

They kept on talking for a long time as I sat and listened. After a while they left to get something to eat, and I could move around and stretch. While they were gone, another human came in to look around the room. "Nothing here," she reported to someone in the hall.

It was late when the two technicians came back. They turned on the viewscreen sound, and we all learned that Magister Galele had been subpoenaed to testify before the court the next day. The tenor of the talk had changed. It was no longer a matter of pinning the blame on Elector

Hornaday and her policies. Now, everyone saw the spectre of a far more sinister plot. Elector Hornaday was now a mere dupe of the aliens.

It was so much more plausible than any bland conspiracy. No one could laugh this off, or say the Capellans lacked the intelligence. Listening, there were even moments when I felt a twinge of uncertainty myself. After all, he *had* planted strange new thoughts in my mind. My obedience *had* been corrupted.

When at last they turned out the lights and left, I lay down to sleep. The room was still lit from the screens and dials, flickering, as if machine-thoughts were moving all around me. It was very hot behind the cabinets, and I found it hard to relax. I kept thinking of how far the messages on the screens had traveled to get here, from places that had never heard of supervisors, or blands.

At last a crack of gray light appeared around the door. It opened, then closed. I stayed silent. "Tedla? Are you still here?" Misery whispered.

I crawled toward it. "Did you bring some water?"

"Here. And a meat pie."

I drank gratefully. "What's going on?" I asked, and bit ravenously into the pie.

"They've turned the place upside down looking for you," Misery whispered. "They think now you've escaped into the convergence."

"Good."

"They think you're diabolically clever, Tedla. The humans are really scared of you."

I stopped chewing in surprise. Misery was speaking in a tone of satisfaction, almost pride. "Really?" I said.

"Really."

I couldn't think what to say. Misery stood up. "I've got to get back to the roundroom."

"Wait. Have you told anyone else where I am?"

"They all know. The whole roundroom."

I felt a chill.

"Don't worry, Tedla. You can trust them all."

"I hope so," I said.

It was a long time before I fell asleep, watching the phosphor ghosts from across the galaxy play on the ceiling.

The humans returned early the next morning. The mood was tense and expectant. "Ptanka-Ni's ready to shit bricks," Kirsten told her companion as they came in. "He's been coaching Alair since the wee hours. There's no way we can worm out of letting him testify."

"Why do you want to?" the Gammadian man said. "Do you think he has something to hide?"

"No, it's . . . well, you just never know what's going to come out of his mouth next."

If they had any work to do, it didn't get done that day. They turned on the viewscreen early, and sat drinking coffee while waiting for Magister Galele to start talking. I sat cross-legged with my eye pressed to the crack.

He looked quite spruced up and respectable on screen, and I felt a pang that I hadn't been there to help. At first the gravity of his interrogators kept his answers formal and short. He was constantly glancing toward the place where Emissary Ptanka-Ni sat, listening impassively.

"Yes, I was conducting a study of the group they called blue team," he said in answer to a question. "I wanted to learn more about the culture of blands: the ways they think and behave among themselves, their mental models and communicative techniques."

"Why do the Capellans feel they need to know this?" one of the judges said.

"It wasn't just for me, you see," Magister Galele said. "I thought it would be helpful information for you as well. In old Earth mythology, there is a figure called Janus, who has two faces on either side of his head. That's what this planet is like. You have two faces: one gendered, the other neuter, and you can never tell what the other looks like, because you're really two sides of the same person. You simply can't know the blands, and they can't know you, unless someone comes along with a mirror and shows you what's behind you. Well, I was hoping to be that mirror.''

Often enough I had heard Squire Tellegen make the same sort of analogy; but from his mouth it had been self-analysis. From the mouth of an alien it was unasked-for criticism. I could see the commission stiffen defensively. Quite unaware, Magister Galele went on, ''This whole episode, this so-called rebellion, is a case in point. You have completely misinterpreted it, because you don't understand the worldview of the blands. If you'd had my data, none of this would have happened.''

It was a startling, even arrogant, assertion. Of course, they asked him to explain. He cheerfully embarked on a long, completely new, version of what had happened.

Over the days of testimony up to now, a picture of the events had emerged that was agreed on by all the humans. It was plausible and internally consistent; its only flaw was that it was completely false. Now, as Magister Galele began to talk about sorcery, hexes, and soul-stealing, I could see the disbelief on the humans' faces. There in the bright lights of that hearing room, it sounded wild and improbable, an elaborate evasion.

''Is he out of his mind?'' the Gammadian technician said to Kirsten.

''Don't ask me,'' she said.

''Given the context the blands were functioning in,'' he concluded, ''what was needed to reestablish control was not force but a demonstration of superior magic. That was, in fact, what my assistant was attempting to bring about when your martialists resorted to explosives.''

He stopped speaking then. There was a dead silence for a few seconds; then one of the more moderate judges said in a bemused voice, ''How did you say you knew all this?''

''Primarily through my research assistant.''

''And who was that?''

My name had never been mentioned up to now, though my role had. When Magister Galele said my name, it meant nothing to the judges. He went on, "I had trained Tedla personally in ethnographic techniques and analysis. I'm confident the observations were accurate."

One of the judges was searching the papers in front of her for some previous mention of a Tedla. She said, "This was a questionary?"

"Oh no, a bland," Galele said, as if it were the most ordinary statement in the world.

Slowly, in a tone of disbelief, the judge said, "Your research assistant was a bland?"

"Yes." Glancing at Ptanka-Ni, he said, "We have decided to make all my field notes available to you, holding nothing back. All of Tedla's reports to me, as well as my own notes and interpretations of the reports, will be released to you. Unfortunately, Tedla dictated a number of the most crucial reports in Capellan. I was encouraging it to use the language, you see. We'll be happy to translate them back for you."

He had finally broken the bounds of their credulity. One of the more hostile judges leaned forward and said, "Let me see if I can paraphrase this. You are claiming that some diabolically clever bland convinced you there was nothing going on at Tapis but some harmless superstition, and this same bland was responsible for creating most of the written documents that link you to the uprising, right down to writing your own reports—in Capellan."

I almost groaned aloud. The Gammadian technician exclaimed angrily, "Does he think we're complete idiots? Can't he produce a better cover-up than that?"

"This is the bland who is so conveniently missing from the Capellan Emissarium?" another judge said.

Magister Galele looked utterly taken aback. He said hastily, "I'm not trying to pin anything on Tedla, or claim I was a dupe."

"Really? What *are* you trying to claim?"

"Why, just the truth. Tedla wasn't trying to deceive me. It's clever, yes, but not diabolical." He gave a nervous laugh. "I wish you could see Tedla. You'd know how ridiculous that is."

"Yes, I wish we could see it, as well," one of the judges said pointedly.

Ptanka-Ni rose from his seat and said with unshaken dignity, "We are doing our utmost to locate it."

"I suppose you claim the bland has outwitted you as well, Emissary?" one of the judges challenged.

"So far, Elector. Not forever."

"Oh what a crock," the technician groaned.

With a false jocularity, the judge said, "It seems we have a secret weapon against the mighty Capellans. We simply let our blands lead them around by the nose."

Magister Galele must have been disarmed by the show of levity, and misjudged the hostility it masked. He said, "I'm not trying to make excuses, but you do have a tendency to underestimate your blands."

Every trace of humor vanished. The judges stared at him. Unwarily, he went on, "I haven't been able to do any large-sample testing, but I suspect that what you have is a case of overlapping bell curves. The majority of the bland population may be less intellectually able than the majority of humans, but that doesn't mean an individual bland with talent can't be more intelligent than most of us."

The hiss of my indrawn breath would have been plainly audible, but the technician was exclaiming, "*What*?"

In a dangerous tone, one of the judges said, "I suppose you have proof of your claim."

"As a matter of fact, I do," Magister Galele said.

I knew what was coming then. I wanted to scream at him, "No! Don't say it!" But I could only press my hands over my mouth and squeeze my eyes tight shut, as I heard, "Just recently I had Tedla apply for higher education at the Universal Institute, Capella. UIC has accepted it to the college of humanities. It's quite an honor for your planet.''

I heard nothing but a kind of roaring in my ears. I could not believe he had announced it there on screen, in front of all the world, as if specifically to humiliate every human hearing him. By the time I grew aware again, pandemonium had broken loose, both on screen and in the room. The technician was on his feet, uttering obscenities. I opened my eyes just in time to see the camera rest on Ptanka-Ni's ashen face, then pan the audience, which was in a state of revolt. The president of the commission rang his bell and shouted out, "This hearing will adjourn!" Court guards came forward to flank Magister Galele— whether to protect him or threaten him, I couldn't tell. Then the picture cut off.

"What's the matter?" Kirsten was saying, bewildered. "Why is everyone in such a snit?"

"Didn't you hear how that bastard insulted us?" the Gammadian said.

"What's so insulting about getting a kid admitted to UIC?"

"The first person from Taramond to go to another planet? The one to represent us to all the other worlds— a bland? It should have been some eminent, learned person—or one of our bright young people. The best students on the planet would have competed for the chance to attend an off-world university. We could have sent someone to make us proud. And he wants to send a bland!"

"It's no big deal to go to UIC," Kirsten muttered.

"Not to you, maybe. To us, it's big."

"My god, look at the calls coming in now," Kirsten said.

"You'll be lucky if calls are all that come."

The two of them were forced to turn to their work for a while. I sat there, no longer listening, just watching the faces on screen silently denouncing the Capellan conspiracy.

An hour later, more or less, a disturbance and shouting

in the hall distracted the two technicians. As they went to the door to see what was up, I took my chance and scrambled for the graydoor. Outside it, the bland-run was deserted—not even the normal routine of cleaning carts and laundry deliveries. Listening, I could hear nothing but the hum of ventilation. Walking as silently as I could, I crept down the stairs and to the Magister's room.

When I peered through the peephole, I saw there were three humans in the sitting room. Magister Galele was in a chair, hunched over, while Emissary Ptanka-Ni and one of the Gammadian judges from the hearing stood over him. The judge was dressed in matriculator colors. She looked very angry. Glancing down the empty bland-run, I pressed my ear to the crack of the graydoor. I could barely make out what they were saying.

"I *didn't* fabricate the test!" Magister Galele said defensively. "Tedla answered every question by itself. All I did was translate, and not much of that." He sounded as if he actually believed it.

"If you didn't fabricate the test, then you fabricated the bland," the matriculator said. "What is it, some human posing? Or did you give it hormones to genderize it?"

"Neither," Galele protested. "All I gave it was encouragement."

The matriculator gave an exclamation of disgust.

"Can't you people imagine that you might conceivably be wrong about the blands?" Galele said.

"We're not wrong," the matriculator said.

"How do you know? Have you studied them? Have you tested them? Have you—"

"We're not wrong because we make sure of it!" the matriculator snapped. "Do you think we would allow a child with talent or ability to become a neuter? What a waste of genetic resources that would be!"

There was a short silence. In a very different voice, Magister Galele said, "Neuters are selected?"

"No, *humans* are selected. The neuters are the natural

state. Of course they constitute the least intelligent third. We would be idiots to make it otherwise.''

In a strange tone, Magister Galele said, ''So this planet is a giant eugenics experiment.''

It was a Capellan word he used; even I didn't know what it meant, then. There is no parallel word in our language. Or rather, there is, but it has no pejorative connotations—only positive ones. The matriculator said, ''If you mean we plan our population, of course. Do you see any humans here with epilepsy, or diabetes, or palsy? Do you even see bad teeth or baldness? Do you see a population that overburdens the planet? No. We have eliminated the scourges of humanity, and prevented the scourge of nature.''

Faintly, Magister Galele said, ''And what a handy labor force you've gained in the process.''

''That was never the object,'' the matriculator snapped. ''You don't know our history. There was a time when our population threatened the very existence of life. We had to find a solution. Genetic alteration was the most humane thing we could have done. We have killed no one. There have been no famines or epidemics. As for the neuters, we have provided for their every need. We have integrated them into our communities, given them useful work . . .''

''. . . Until you couldn't do without them,'' Galele said. ''Your population is falling now, isn't it? Every year you need more blands, and that means fewer humans. Your numbers are almost too small to sustain the way you live now. Isn't it time for the experiment to end?''

''You don't know what you are talking about,'' the matriculator said. ''We can't end it.''

There was a sound I couldn't interpret. I looked through the peephole. They were all staring toward the window. Emissary Ptanka-Ni left my line of sight. I heard a loud exclamation, and the other two hurried over to the window. For a moment I could see nothing; then the matriculator and the emissary crossed toward the door.

When I was sure they were gone, I cracked open the graydoor, listened, then slipped through. Magister Galele was peering through the drawn curtains. He looked up, saw me, and came rushing over. He hugged me hard, then said in a whisper, "Thank god you're safe. I just wish you weren't here. I hoped you would be miles away by now."

"I said I'd come back."

"I should never have asked you to. I've gotten us in such trouble, Tedla."

He looked a year older than he had yesterday. He studied my face with a distracted look. "You wouldn't believe what I just learned."

"I know," I said, "I was listening."

"Why didn't you tell me?"

"I didn't know. No one knows. They teach us it's all natural."

"Of course," he said, "they would have to." He touched my cheek lightly. "I wonder what your sin was, that you didn't merit humanity."

Something hit the window hard. Both of us jumped. I started toward the window, to see what was going on. He said, "Careful. Don't let them know you're here."

I pushed the curtains apart a crack and looked out. The plaza outside was filled with people, moving with unfocused energy, like the turbulent surface of a pot about to boil. The cafe tables had been overturned and scattered; one of the sculptures was now the base for a large sign telling the aliens to go away. Just outside the door, a gang of young men scarcely older than me were pelting the building with eggs. Another one hit the window, making me start back.

"We barely managed to get back here from the hearing," Magister Galele said. "We tried to get to the rear door, but the corridors were blocked by a mob. If we'd tried to push through, there would have been violence. So we came around the front way. Those hoodlums attacked us; Ptanka-Ni got roughed up some. The guards were hustling me through so fast I didn't see much."

I saw he finally understood. He had seen the forces that propel us, and he was terrified.

"You thought we were civilized, didn't you?" I said.

He knew his error now.

There was a roar from the plaza outside—not so much a cheer as a vocalization of rage. I quickly looked. Across the plaza, a band of young men was forcing a bland in a gray uniform into the square. They had sticks, and the bland was running to escape their blows. It headed for the other side, but like a membrane forming, a solid wall of humans coalesced to block its way. It tried to climb up onto the awning over one of the shops, but some roughnecks pulled it down. It fell, twisting one leg underneath. The circle of humans closed in, and drove it, limping, toward the emissarium door.

"They'll have to let it in," I said.

"They've got the doors downstairs barricaded," Magister Galele said grimly. "They're not going to open them for anything."

The humans had formed a circle around the bland, and were taunting it. It saw there was no hope and crouched down, trying to shield itself from the inevitable blows. It had blond hair, like me.

"They have to help it!" I said. I knew it was me down there; I was the one they wanted to trap and beat. This poor bland was only my stand-in.

Two young men came out of the crowd and jerked the bland to its feet. There was a table lying nearby; they set it up and forced the bland to lie on it face up, tying its hands and feet to the table legs. Some of the men with sticks came forward to beat the victim, but the others waved them back. Laughing shrilly, a young man brought out a can and began splashing liquid over the bland's body. When the humans smelled it, they surged away into a wider circle, but still shouted, egging the young men on.

The humans vacated the circle, leaving only the bland

lying there, bound helplessly to the table. A perfect silence fell. There was only the bland's voice, sobbing and begging. Then a lit cafe candle arced into the center of the circle, bounced on the bland's stomach, and fell on the floor.

The flames exploded. The fireball was so bright I could barely see the bland's form inside it. At the same time, the crowd let out an animal shriek of vengeance.

"Don't look, Tedla." Magister Galele tried to pull me back from the window. I fought him. I had to see. The flames rose almost to the level of our window, billowing sooty smoke. The faces of the watching humans were contorted like twisted putty, a sweaty yellow in the flames. I strained to hear a scream, but there was nothing.

I didn't see it, but Magister Galele later told me he saw a woman raise a weapon and aim it at the window. The wall of glass exploded in my face. Sheets of it fell like cleavers all around me. The curtains blew into the room on a wind of black smoke.

The roar of the flames was loud now, and I heard what I had been dreading—a scream of unendurable agony. It rose up the scale, penetrating my skin, surrounding me, pursuing me, sharp as glass. It was coming out of my own mouth. I felt myself jerked back from the gaping window that was now a precipice. My feet crunched on glass. Blinded by smoke, choking on the gasoline smell, I felt myself shoved through a door and into silence.

Magister Galele held me in his arms. I was shaking so hard I could barely grasp at him for support. My breath was coming in fast little gasps. "Shh, be quiet, you're safe now," he said in my ear. I knew it was a lie. I wasn't safe. I had seen my own death, and it was more terrible than anything I could have imagined.

We were in the bland-run outside his room. It was as empty as before, and now I knew why. The blands would all be hiding, probably in their roundroom. This was no day to stray into a human's way. I looked up at Magister

Galele, confused by the incongruity of his presence here, and said stupidly, "How did you get here?"

"Through the door," he said.

Of course. He was not Gammadian. No Gammadian human but a supervisor would have passed through a graydoor in any but the direst emergency.

My presence of mind was returning. I said, "We've got to get away. Has your shuttle come down from the ship?"

"I don't know. I suppose so. That was the plan. But it's up on the surface, on the airpad. We can't get to it; the building's under siege."

There was only one choice, and it wasn't a good one. "We've got to go through grayspace," I said.

"Do you know the way?"

"No."

In the next room, the fire alarms went off. Someone would quickly come to investigate, and then the hunt for us would be on. I took the Magister's hand and raced down the bland-run toward the stair.

We met no one till we got to the lowest level. I made Magister Galele wait in the shadows under the stair while I located everyone. There was no one in the laundry, the first place I checked, and after a moment of hesitation I snatched an extra uniform. The next place I checked was the kitchen. They were all there, as near as I could tell— ostensibly working, but really gathered around the table, talking. We would have to pass through to get to the shipping door. There was no help for it; I was going to have to trust them.

I made a hissing sound. Deen looked over. Its eyes widened when it saw me. With a glance over its shoulder at the others, it hurried toward me, drying its hands on a towel. "You should be hiding," it whispered.

"We've got to get away," I said. "My human's with me. They're hunting us both now. Can we get out through the shipping door?"

Deen shook its head. "They locked it, to keep you in.

We've all been trapped here since yesterday."

"Where's the key?"

"Supervisor's office."

"Is he in there?"

"Of course."

I thought of, and discarded, several ideas. We needed something simple. "Will Misery help?" I asked. Deen looked back into the kitchen. They were all watching us edgily. Deen gestured Misery over. It came, looking frightened. I blessed my luck they didn't yet know what was happening outside; none of them would have taken the risk if they had known.

"Misery, I need a decoy," I said to it. "There's no risk to you, as long as you stick to your story. All you have to do is get the supervisor out of his office long enough so I can steal his key."

Misery nodded obediently, as if to a human. I realized my tone of voice was the confident, imperative one humans used to give orders. I had no time to stop and think about it. "Okay, this is what you do. You come rushing to the supervisor's office and say you saw me and Magister Galele in one of the bland-runs upstairs. When he asks you where, you lead him up to the graydoor into the Magister's room. We really were there, so you would have seen us if you'd been there. Keep him up there as long as you can, but don't take any risks. Got it?"

"Yes, sir," Misery said automatically, then blushed.

I turned to Deen. "Warn the others we'll be coming through the kitchen. All they have to do is not see us." Gesturing Misery to follow me, I headed back to the place I had left Magister Galele waiting. When he saw me, he stood up, ready to go. I said, "Magister . . ." and couldn't go any farther. The request I had to make of him was so embarrassing, so insulting, I couldn't bring myself to say it. Instead, not daring to look him in the eye, I held out the uniform.

"What?" he said.

"It might . . . you might . . ."

"Oh. Of course," he said, taking the gray coveralls. No Gammadian would have done it, no matter what the risk. The prospect of being caught dressed as a bland would have been more humiliating than any conceivable punishment. For once, I was grateful for his insanity. In grayspace, he would have been as conspicuous as a brass band, dressed in human clothes.

"I'll be right back," I told him, then dashed up the stairs with Misery close behind me. When we got to the supervisor's graydoor, I said to Misery, "Ready?" It gave me a frightened nod. "You'll do fine," I said, giving its hand a squeeze.

The corridor took a turn a few paces down, giving me a corner to hide around. I listened as Misery first took some deep breaths to gather its courage, then began banging on the supervisor's door. It was several moments before he opened it with an angry, "What's the matter?"

"Supervisor, I saw it. I saw Tedla," Misery said anxiously.

Instead of demanding where, the supervisor said, "Come in here." Misery went into his office, and the door closed.

I waited, wondering what was going on. Was the supervisor going to go search for me through human space? Did he suspect something, and was now interrogating Misery? I shifted from foot to foot, waiting. At last I looked around the corner, then crept toward the door to listen. I had gotten no more than two steps down the hall when the door opened again. I bolted back.

"This way, sir," Misery said, a little too eagerly.

"Yes, I know," the supervisor answered.

I listened as their steps receded, then peeked around the corner. The hall was clear. I dashed down to the graydoor and slipped through it.

His desk terminal was buzzing, and the message light blinking. I was reaching for the desk drawer when I spied a rack of key-cards on the wall. One was labeled Receiving, so I snatched it. Then, only moments after I had slipped in, I was out.

When I came down the stairs, Magister Galele was waiting, dressed in gray coveralls. He looked nothing like a bland up close, but at least he wouldn't attract attention from a distance. I gestured him to follow me, and we burst into the kitchen.

Just then, the building fire alarms went off. Not an individual room alarm this time, but the deafening whole-building alarm. Since earliest childhood we had all been drilled to think one thing at that sound: get out. I saw all the blands in the kitchen freeze as they realized they were trapped.

"This way," I shouted, holding up the key-card and heading for the shipping door. They crowded after me, every thought gone but the one of fire. I shoved the card into the lock. With agonizing slowness, the huge metal door groaned and rose.

"Scatter!" I shouted to the blands. "Spread the alarm!" Then, as the door rose far enough for me to duck under, I shouted "Fire!" at the top of my lungs. The others took up the cry, and pretty soon the word was spreading outward at the speed of panic.

I looked around for Magister Galele, seized his hand, and dragged him after me down a broad bland-run. It was a major thoroughfare, wide enough for pallet-lifters and electric delivery trucks to pass, but today there was very little traffic. We came to a freight elevator, and I dodged inside, pressing the top button. When the door clashed shut and we rose, alone in the huge space, I turned to the Magister. "Keep your head down," I said. "You'll never pass for a bland."

He fingered his mustache self-consciously. "Have you figured out where we're going?"

"No," I said.

"I thought you had. You seemed so confident."

Ten floors up, the mood was much more normal, though in several spots I saw clumps of blands talking with an anxious urgency. Stepping out of the elevator, I spied a supervisor walking away down the hall, so I turned the other direction. Despite my warnings, Magister Galele was looking around in amazement. "It really is a parallel city, isn't it?" he whispered to me.

"Yes," I said. "Now keep your head down."

I stopped to ask directions to the aircar port, but the blands could only tell me the general direction. I headed off down a corridor, trying not to move too fast and risk looking un-blandlike. We had not gotten far when beepers all around us started going off. A supervisor stepped through a graydoor only yards away and announced loudly, "Everyone report to your home base. All blands, return to your supervisors!"

There was a stir among the blands as they realized that something big was happening, something big enough to disturb all the routine life of the convergence. Pretty soon all the corridors would be clear, and two escaping refugees would be very conspicuous.

Down a cross-corridor I spied an electric cart loaded high with luggage, and raced to catch up with it. "Are you going back to the aircar port?" I asked the driver. It had stopped in mid-corridor, confused by the beeper. It was not a very intelligent bland. It said uncertainly, "Is that what I'm supposed to do?"

"Yes," I said. "You're supposed to go back to where the aircars land. You can take us."

I gestured Magister Galele to climb on the pile of suitcases, and pushed into the seat beside the driver. "Let's go," I said.

Obediently, it started off. The bland-runs were clearing out fast. At last we turned through double doors into a big warehouse room full of crates and luggage. I jumped off, saying, "Thanks for the ride!" As the bland drove on, I snatched a leather traveling bag from the back of the cart and dodged behind a shelf unit. Magister Galele was close behind me.

I jerked open the suitcase and pulled out some human clothes. "Put these on," I said. "You've got to be human again."

He stripped off the bland uniform and pulled on the human clothes, while I stuffed the uniform into the suitcase and hefted it. It would be my disguise.

We emerged back into human space in the place where we had left our luggage on arriving at Magnus. I followed Magister Galele, carrying the suitcase and staring at the ground.

All the normal functions of the aircar port had come to a halt. No luggage could get loaded, no cars could get refueled, till the blands were back on the job. Magister Galele headed through the crowd of impatient, stranded travelers toward the nearest set of steps leading up to the glass doors of an aircar pad. Through them, I could see the overcast sky.

"Sorry, sir," a woman said, holding out an arm to stop Magister Galele. "Nothing is taking off right now."

He babbled something like, "That's all right, I'll just wait outside."

Her eyes narrowed. "Aren't you that Capellan that was on screen?"

"No," he said cheerfully. "We just all look alike to you."

"Wait here, both of you," she said, and turned away toward a terminal to make a call.

We exchanged a look. Without a word, I dropped the suitcase and we both dashed up the stairs and out the glass door.

It was a drab and chilly day outside, and rain was coming on. We raced across the pad, under the extended wing of a parked aircar. There was a whole circle of them around us, but Magister Galele didn't seem to recognize any of them. "It's not here," he said.

"Where does it land?" I said.

"There was a runway. There's no runway here."

Shouts broke out behind us. We dashed across a paved area toward a long maintenance shed. When we rounded the end of it, a new part of the landscape came in view. There, down in a slight valley, was the runway. Still there was no sign of a shuttle.

Another aircar was parked nearby, its wings retracted. A group of human pilots was clustered under it, talking. I automatically shied away from them; but Magister Galele stopped dead and shouted, "Nadkarni!"

One of the pilots looked up. I saw he was an alien, though dressed like one of us. Magister Galele hurried over to him. "Where's the shuttle?" he said breathlessly.

"Over there, in its bay," the pilot said.

"Is it ready to leave?"

"Yes. They're just not authorizing—"

"To hell with authorization! I've got to get to the ship."

I saw an eager gleam of mischief in the pilot's eye. He knew something was up, and couldn't resist getting involved. "Alair, are you—"

"Quick! I'll explain later."

Nadkarni turned to one of the other pilots. "Can I borrow your car for a second?"

"Sure," the other pilot said.

Nadkarni waved the Magister toward the door of the aircar. As I started to climb in, the pilot caught my arm. "Hold it. You're not coming."

"Yes, I am!" I said to him furiously, in Capellan. "I'm going to attend UIC, and I've got a visa, so take your hands off me."

Dumbfounded, he backed away. "All right, all right, you're coming." He then jumped into the control seat and started the engine.

I was not even belted in when the car sprang into the air like a cat and twisted round. Seconds later, we were down again, and the pilot threw the door open. Outside stood a much bigger vehicle. I recognized the very alien shuttle I had seen so many years ago on the viewscreen in the creche. It looked a little scorched and worn now, but obviously still in use.

"Your shuttle, Magisters," the pilot said, with a wink at me.

The inside of the shuttle had none of the scuffed-up appearance of the outside. When the automatic airtight door hissed shut behind me, I found myself surrounded by silence and subdued lights. Everywhere gleamed the reflective surfaces of inscrutable control panels. Nothing I looked at seemed familiar, or even recognizable. It came home to me then: These people truly were aliens. And I had just thrown myself into their world.

In the strange, indirect lighting, calculated to a redder spectrum than I was used to, even Magister Galele looked unfamiliar. I watched him settle into a chair that moved and adjusted around him to cushion his body. A musical tone sounded, and a calm voice said in Capellan, "Please take your seat."

Gingerly, I lowered myself into a seat and felt it move sensuously under my weight, like something live. It was even warm, like skin. As a cushioned arm pressed me back, my nerves jangled with claustrophobia. My heart raced; I was trapped.

In the seat beside me, Magister Galele gave a relaxed sigh. "We made it," he said. "Thank god."

For him, it was the end of fear; for me, it was just the beginning.

In the next hour, I watched on screen as the planet of my birth receded beneath us, a bright foam of clouds on a turbulent atmospheric sea. I was pressed back by the kick of acceleration, then drifted in the weightlessness of space. The horizon became a bright hoop against the utter black. Then we saw the ship—a massive thing, despite all Magister Galele's complaints, a cluster of hexagonal crystals, giving off prismatic gleams as it turned in the sun. When we docked and climbed out into the microgravity, the air smelled sterile, and I was surrounded by small brown aliens, talking very fast. I had thought I spoke the language well, but now I learned otherwise. All I managed to gather was that communication with the emissarium had been abruptly cut off, and they were very concerned about their people on the surface. Magister Galele laughed and teased them for worrying, then conducted a number of shrill arguments, then dragged me with him as he bullied and charmed his way into the lightbeam waystation. There, he called up documents and authorizations on a viewscreen till the flustered technicians gave in and led us to the translation cylinder. Magister Galele pushed me forward. "Tedla goes first," he said. "I'll come after."

I clutched at him fearfully. "Do I have to?"

"Yes," he hissed in my ear. "Quick, before they reestablish contact and ask Ptanka-Ni's permission."

If I had known what the machine did—that it would, in fact, kill me by disassembling my body into an information beam—I might have broken down right there. But I didn't know, and my drilled-in obedience took over. At the technician's instructions, I lay down on the slab. When it retracted into the cylinder, and I saw the rings of emitters aimed at me, the claustrophobia came back at double force. I opened my mouth to beg them to let me out again, when

I felt, vaguely, the shock they used to get my heart restarted. I drew in breath to call out, and realized I was no longer in the cylinder. An alien woman bent over me and said, "Tedla?"

"Yes?" I said, groggily.

"Welcome to Capella Two."

Chapter Eleven

৩৩ Val let out a breath and leaned back, the studium chair creaking beneath her. She glanced at Max; he looked like he was still taking it all in. Deedee was fast asleep on Tedla's bed.

"And you wanted to go back?" she said at last.

Tedla hesitated, then said, "If you had left your family on a place like Gammadis, you would want to go back and join them, no matter what. As long as I had a guardian, I belonged with him. But now, my only family—the people I share things with and owe things to—is the other blands. All this education I've gotten—it's pointless unless it's for them."

Max said, "It's also pointless if you waste it in slavery."

Tedla looked away, reddening as if Max had said something too personal.

Val turned to the terminal and hit the time key. It was very late. "We'd better get some sleep. We're going to need our wits tomorrow."

When they were in bed and the room was dark, Val lay staring at the ceiling, thinking. She could tell Max was no more asleep than she. She turned her head toward him and whispered, "Do you think we deserve to be human?"

"God knows what the test is, if Tedla couldn't pass it," Max murmured. "I'm glad we didn't have to take it."

"Me, too," Val said. She turned toward him and put her hand on his chest, feeling the little line of coarse hair down the middle. "I like being human, Max. Even if we couldn't pass the Gammadian test, I'm glad we can have children. I'm so glad I'd be willing to do it all over again."

He looked at her, then raised up on one elbow to study her in the darkness. "You mean it?" he said.

"Yes."

"You always said one was the limit. What if there's an expedition—?"

"To hell with the expedition," Val said, and hooked her leg around his hips to draw him close.

Early the next morning, while Val was struggling to pull on Deedee's purple playsuit against the passive resistance of limp limbs, she heard Max talking to his father on screen. When Val and Deedee came out to the dinery, he said, "Joansie wants to talk to you."

"What did E.G. say?" Val asked.

Max had a smug look. "He knows a good legal consultant. She's coming over this morning to assess the case."

"Some sort of radical?" Val said suspiciously.

"Of course. That's what we need."

Val rolled her eyes and activated the screen. "Hi, Joan," she said. "Deedee, stop standing on the chair."

Joan said, "Val, you remember how we sent a message to C4D when Tedla first showed up? Well, we just got a reply by PPC from a Magister Delgado."

"Tedla's advisor," Val said.

"Right. He talks as if Tedla were one of his star students. Apparently, our friend was on the brink of graduating when it just walked out without a word. Delgado was very concerned, and wants us to send information. Should I?"

"Might as well," Val said. "Tedla can use all the friends it can get right now."

They had barely gotten Deedee settled down and eating her breakfast when Tedla came in, and she asked loudly, "Can we go to the playroom today?"

"We'll see after breakfast," Val said. She turned to Tedla. "When is your hearing?"

Tedla took out the paper and scanned it. "Tomorrow morning."

Val clicked her tongue. "That doesn't give us much time." Which was doubtless what Nasatir wanted. Val studied Tedla across the breakfast table, thinking of all she had learned the night before. "Do you have any idea why they want you back so badly?"

"No," Tedla said. "You'd think they'd want to forget the whole thing. I'm not causing any trouble here. No one even knows who I am. They're the ones stirring it all up again."

"It's your story," Max said, leaning across the table to pour coffee. "They want to gag you, so the Capellan public won't be prejudiced against their planet."

"But I've been quiet for twelve years," Tedla said.

"Yes, it's your damned discretion that's made you such a valuable commodity. You're a secret, and they want to keep you that way." He was on a roll now. "Do you know what your best defense is, Tedla? Expose it all now. Make everything public. Then they'll have no reason to take you back. You'll have no value to them."

He was almost beginning to convince her, Val thought. She said, "There would be a big backlash if people found out about the eugenics part."

"I knew you would react to that," Tedla said. "Capellans always do, as if there is something immoral about it."

Val and Max both stared. "You don't think so?" Val said.

"No. There is no good solution to an overpopulation crisis. My ancestors chose the most humane path open to them. Doing nothing would have destroyed us all."

"But you're the victim of their decision," Max said.

"Don't you have as much right to reproduce as anyone?"

"No," Tedla said stubbornly. "No one has a right to reproduce, any more than they have a right to live. It is a privilege that ought to be earned. Only the best ought to merit it."

Unable to contain himself, Max burst out, "Don't you have any anger, Tedla? Any indignation at what was done to you?"

Tedla gave him a sharp look. "What do you mean, *done* to me? Nothing was done to me. I'm perfectly natural the way I am. Why can't you humans ever understand that I might not *want* to be afflicted with gender?"

Max looked as if he wanted to protest, but apparently he thought better of it.

Val bit into her breakfast pierogie. "I wonder why they petitioned in K-Court," she said. "You'd think that with WAC's resources backing them up, it would be to the delegates' advantage to use Capellan court."

"Isn't K-Court Capellan?" Tedla asked cautiously.

"Not exactly," Val said. "About ten years ago, the enclaves and convocations all rebelled against our system of law—it was astonishing; no one thought they would ever agree on anything. You see, Capellan law is based on precedent and legislation, and our history had gotten so messy and arcane that you could more or less win a case by paying more than the other side to access and sift the records. So they established the Court of a Thousand Peoples to be more sensitive to cultural differences. We call it K-Court for short. Now even native Capellans have begun to use it. But I didn't expect WAC's lawyers to take the Gammadians' case there."

"Maybe they didn't want to wait ten years for a decision," Max said.

When the legal advisor showed up, she had another theory. "They want to use Gammadian law," she said.

She was not Val's picture of a radical lawyer. Dag Sorno was a lanky woman in a hand-knit sweater, with waist-length gray hair braided in a long rope down her back, and a face pebbled with long-gone acne. She shook Tedla's hand with a curious, assessive look, then settled down in the gathering room with a cup of herb tea and a slate for taking notes.

"*Can* they use Gammadian law?" Tedla said, leaning forward nervously.

"In K-Court, you can try a case under any legal system you're willing to pay royalties to use. We can challenge, of course. What's your status under Gammadian law?"

"None at all," Tedla said. "I have no rights, not even to testify."

"Then my guess is, they'll try for it. You've got to argue against it."

"Me?"

"Yes. There are no proxies in K-Court. The participants argue their own cases. I can give you advice, but I can't speak for you."

Tedla blanched. It occurred to Val that this was yet another reason for the delegates' choice of courts. Nasatir doubtless felt no qualms about his ability to out-debate a bland. Val said, "You'll do a terrific job, Tedla. It's no harder than oral exams."

"I was no good at oral exams," Tedla said faintly.

"Don't worry, they're not looking for eloquence," Dag Sorno said. "What they want is good common sense. Now tell me all you know about Gammadian law. Is it based on divination, or oracles, or ordeal?"

"It's based on statutes," Tedla said a little indignantly.

"Too bad. That makes it tricky. Oracles are much more universal. They translate easily. I was at a Xic trial last week where the crucial testimony was given by the sacred lizards of the Psim Principle. When they ate the crickets, the defendant broke down and confessed on the spot. It was very convincing."

"They allowed that in court?" Max said.

"K-Court is universal law," the lawyer shrugged. "If

you're going to be tolerant, you've got to be tolerant.''

Max said, "So K-Court might, for example, accept a legal system that defined Tedla as not human?''

"Sure, if it didn't violate one of the ups—the Universal Principles.'' She embarked then on a long and technical discussion of the ups. Val could see Tedla's eyes glazing over. She tried several times to catch its attention, and finally succeeded, raising her eyebrows in query.

"This is useless,'' Tedla said as the lawyer drew breath. "I appreciate your help, but I just can't do it.''

Dag Sorno studied Tedla's face seriously. "If you don't care enough about the outcome to argue your case, the judges will take it for de facto acquiescence.''

"You've got to do it, Tedla,'' Val said softly. "Otherwise, everything you've been through will go to waste.''

Tedla sat for a moment with its eyes closed, as if trying to draw on some impossibly remote reservoir of courage. At last its jaw tensed, and its eyes came open. "All right,'' it said. "I don't want to let you down.''

The courtroom was laid out in a circle—symbolic, Val supposed, though of what she didn't know. When she and Tedla entered, she found herself looking down on the court arena from the outer edge of a small sunken auditorium. At the center and lowest point of the room was an open circle surrounded by a round counter or desk, divided into three sections. The judges' chairs were ranged behind one section, with the petitioner's and defendant's seats behind the other two, facing the judges on the left and right. Val and Tedla descended the aisle through five tiers of empty seats. A group of Choristers was clearing up from the preceding hearing, which apparently had involved some sort of ritual staged in the open circle before the judges' desk. Two Choristers dressed in feathers were shoveling the remains of a bonfire into some metal pails.

Dag Sorno was waiting, her hair in a ponytail twined with beads so that she rattled softly when she moved. She nodded at the petitioner's desk, where Nasatir already sat waiting, along with his legal advisor and the other Gammadian delegate, a handsome, middle-aged woman. Dag said in a low voice, "WAC isn't one of the petitioners. There must have been a break between them and the Gammadians. They're interceding for the right to give Tedla medical treatment before any other action is taken."

"Medical treatment?" As the words left Val's mouth, a door across the auditorium opened, and her eyes met and clashed with Magister Surin's. "Oh, I understand," she said.

"What's your position on their request?" Dag asked.

"Our position is No," Val said, then caught herself and turned to Tedla. "I'm sorry, I should let you answer that."

"You're right," Tedla said, staring at Magister Surin, looking pale but resolute.

"Epco's also intervening, but it's not clear why," Dag said. "Do you know?"

The door had opened again, and a group headed by Shankar had come through. As Val watched, the Epco representative greeted Surin, shaking hands.

"I thought they were on Tedla's side," Val said.

"Please. They're on their own side."

The two interceders, WAC and Epco, approached down the steps, conversing pleasantly.

Val said, "Epco must want the Gammadian contract pretty badly. Maybe they're here to snatch it up if WAC makes a slip."

"That sounds more likely."

As Tedla took a seat at the defendant's table, Dag Sorno drew Val a few paces down the aisle and whispered, "How's Tedla holding up?"

"All right so far," Val said.

"Two out of three judges are likely to be sympathetic," Dag said. "We've got a good chance, as long as Tedla doesn't lose its nerve."

The Choristers finished clearing up and trooped out,

hauling their equipment with them. A bailiff passed around the room, securing the doors. All hearings were private, to protect the copyright of the participants; but in this case, the petitioners had requested extra security. They hadn't even agreed to allow Max in as an observer.

The last person to enter, just as the bailiff was locking the final door, was Magister Gossup. Val felt a pulse of hope when she saw him, and touched Dag's hand.

"What's he here for?" Dag whispered.

"I don't know. He may be on our side."

"That would be a big advantage." The lawyer looked positively hopeful.

But Gossup didn't look at Val or Tedla. Instead, he skirted the room and took a seat behind the judges' chairs. "He must be advising the court," Dag Sorno said.

"That's good," Val said uncertainly. "He's sympathetic, I'm sure of it."

Skeptically, Dag said, "He's Vind; you can't be sure of anything."

The two women took seats on either side of Tedla. Val noticed that Surin and Shankar did not sit together; each of them chose a place in the auditorium with their own cluster of legal advisors—Surin slightly behind the Gammadians, Shankar square in the middle, facing the judges. There was a moment of silence; then the judges entered in single file. Dag Sorno leaned over to whisper to Tedla, "The judges are called the Judic, the Syndic, and the Logic. Each represents a different aspect of the Universal Principles. You address them by title. Here, they don't have names." Tedla nodded nervously.

K-Court was a chameleon entity; it took on the rituals of whichever culture it represented at the moment, but had few of its own. As a result, the atmosphere was more informal than Val was prepared for. When the judges had settled into their seats and arranged their papers, the Syndic said, "This is the first Gammadian case we have seen. Our briefing on your culture has been very informative.

On behalf of the court, I would like to express my wishes for a long and fruitful association between our peoples. I only regret that your first visit here has brought you to our court. I hope we can resolve your differences equitably.''

Nasatir rose and answered for all Gammadians, "It is most gratifying to find here an institution founded with such respect for differing customs and laws.''

This speech appeared to please the judges. Dag Sorno said in an undertone, "He's smooth.''

They passed quickly through some routine matters: identifying the participants, invoking oaths of truthfulness, explaining the rules of court. The first critical order of business was assignment of the copyright to the trial proceedings. The lawyers got paid from the proceeds for selling the verdict to all the legal databases.

The Judic said, "It is customary to assign joint copyright to the petitioner and defendant. Are there any objections?"

Val gave Tedla a little push; they had discussed this at length. Tedla rose and said in a soft, deferential voice, "Judic, I would prefer to assign my portion of the copyright to Magister Valerie Endrada.''

Nasatir leaped to his feet and said, "I object to that. The person named is hostile to our interests, and might make use of the copyright to injure us." He didn't look at Val, but his animosity radiated across the room.

The Judic turned to Tedla and said kindly, "It's a rather unusual request. What is your reasoning?"

Tedla was trembling, but its voice didn't shake. "If Delegate Nasatir is successful, he will have control of both me and my copyright. He will control both halves.''

Nasatir shot back, "If I am successful, I will have the right to control both halves.''

"It's not unusual to assign copyright to the winner of the case," the Judic pointed out.

Instead of arguing, Tedla said, "If Delegate Nasatir objects to Magister Endrada, then perhaps he would agree to a neutral third party, such as Magister Gossup.''

Gossup looked unmoved, but Val was startled. They had not discussed this. There was a short pause as Nasatir collected his wits; then he said, ''This bland is being influenced to surrender its own rights, so that others can profit.'' This time, he did cast a venomous look at Val. ''It's arguing against its own best interests.''

The Judic turned around to consult Magister Gossup, who leaned forward. The other judges then exchanged some words, and the Judic turned back to the court. ''We don't see a compelling reason to depart from tradition. Copyright will be assigned jointly to petitioner and defendant.''

Tedla sank back into its chair. Val felt deflated by the abrupt, unexplained decision, but she squeezed Tedla's hand and said, ''That was great.''

''I lost,'' Tedla said.

''That doesn't matter. The important thing is, you fought.''

All the same, she and Dag Sorno exchanged a puzzled, apprehensive look.

The next order of business was to determine which legal system applied to the case. This was the crucial argument, as Dag Sorno had drilled them. If Nasatir succeeded in getting Gammadian law accepted, the rest of the case was a foregone conclusion.

The delegate rose and gave a long and eloquent appeal, speaking of the inviolable right of a people to have jurisdiction over their own citizens. When he was done, the Judic said, ''Delegate, how would you reply to the objection that this court cannot adjudicate Gammadian law because of our near-total ignorance of your statutes?''

''I would say, Judic, that no deep knowledge is required in this case. A few simple principles apply, which no one with even a glancing knowledge of Gammadian law would dispute.'' He gave Val a scorching look.

"And those principles would be . . . ?"

"The bland you see before you is a minor who was brought here illegally and against our will over a decade ago. I am now its legal guardian, and therefore entitled to decide what is in its best interest. In Gammadian law, this is equivalent to a custody case."

The Judic turned to Tedla. "Is this true?"

Tedla rose. "Yes, sir. On Gammadis, it would be true. I also would not be permitted to speak for myself, which violates the Universal Principle of free testimony. Gammadian law is at odds with all other known planets on that."

Dag Sorno had wanted that point made.

"That is not strictly true," Nasatir replied smoothly, as if prepared. "In fact, a bland's interests are protected in our courts by its guardian, who speaks on its behalf, much as lawyers do in your native courts. The reason for our law is to protect neuters from betraying their own interests. They are so impressionable and easily influenced that they simply mimic the last person to have coached them. They are quite incapable of reasoning out their own desires. It may appear to you that this bland is testifying. That is not the case. It has been skillfully trained by parties with agendas of their own, and it is those persons' arguments you are hearing. You are not permitting this bland to testify any more than we would."

The Logic, who had been silent up to now, leaned forward, looking from Tedla to Nasatir. "If the defendant cannot express its own true desires, then how are we to determine them?"

"Only someone with a deep historical knowledge of blands, and lifelong experience with them, can know what they truly want."

The Logic turned to Tedla. "What do you say, defendant? Do you know what you truly want?"

It was the moment for a positive affirmation. Instead, Val saw a complicated, introspective look on Tedla's face.

Slowly, it said, "If I'm not entirely sure of my own desires, Logic, it's not because I am a bland, but because I am human. I may not know what my heart truly holds, but who does? I think we're all mysteries, even to ourselves."

Val saw the dismay on Dag Sorno's face, and tried to hide her own.

In a kind, paternal tone, Nasatir said, "It puts a bland at a cruel disadvantage to ask it to articulate a point."

"What is the position of the two interceders on this issue?" the Syndic said.

Shankar rose from her seat in the audience. "Epco favors the use of Gammadian law, Syndic. We believe this dispute to be a purely internal Gammadian matter which is only complicated by the interference of outsiders. In the interest of harmony and cultural relativism, we urge you to turn this matter over to the appropriate Gammadian authority."

Epco was knifing Tedla to get a foot in the door, Val thought.

As Shankar sat down, Surin stood. "Syndic, WAC opposes the use of Gammadian law, because we believe it is not in the defendant's best interest. We have offered Tedla the option of receiving medical treatment for a condition acquired on Capella Two. Tedla has consented to the treatment; we have a recording, if you would like to see it. Delegate Nasatir opposes the treatment, a decision we believe will prove harmful to Tedla. Under Capellan law, Tedla's right to consent would not be abridged."

What strange bedfellows, Val thought.

The Syndic turned to Tedla. "Do you want this medical treatment?"

Tedla paused a moment, caught between self-interest and the truth. Saying yes would make Nasatir look tyrannical and pull in WAC's support. Tedla closed its eyes for a moment, then said, "No, sir."

"Do you deny you consented?"

"No, sir. I've changed my mind."

Surin shot up. "Excuse me, Syndic, but Tedla's mind has been changed for it, by self-interested third parties. The bland will say anything to please the person it perceives as its guardian at the moment. I can give you a technical proof of that trait, if you like. It shows up clearly on the mentation graphs."

"Not right now, thank you, Magister," the Syndic said. He was studying Tedla with an air of perplexity. "I can't remember a case in which so much doubt has been heaped on a participant's ability to represent himself. Everyone claims to have your best interest at heart, Tedla. What do you think? You still have the right to speak."

Visibly gathering its courage, Tedla said, "With respect, sir, I don't think it's possible for any human to know what's best for a bland. No one knows what our lives or our thoughts are like, or when we're well or sick. All my life, humans have told me what ought to make me happy, and they're almost always wrong. I haven't found the answer myself yet, but at least here I have the freedom to search for it."

Tedla paused. Nasatir drew breath to say something, but Tedla said sharply, "I'm not done yet." There was a firmness in its manner now, an urgency to be heard. It turned to the judges. "What people want, by and large, is what they are molded into wanting. When scientists expose laboratory animals to random shocks or loud noises, the animals quickly learn they can do nothing about it. If they are later offered a way to avoid the stress, like pressing a lever, the animals refuse, because they have resigned themselves to discomfort. Do they want it? Perhaps; at least it is familiar.

"People are no different. If we are drilled into accepting inferiority and dependence, we come to want its familiarity. I did, once. But I am different now. I have lived as a Capellan for a dozen years, and I have found what it's like to have control over my own life and thoughts. It is hard, very hard. But at least I can be more than a *thing*, more than the creature of someone else's will. I can construct value from my life, and find the authentic being within myself. Are you prepared to deny me that fundamental right?''

If Val had not been watching Nasatir closely, she would have missed what crossed his face as Tedla spoke. The careful facade of disdain wavered; for the tiniest moment, she glimpsed uncertainty underneath.

There was a short silence when Tedla finished. By its end, Nasatir had recovered his control. He said with exaggerated politeness, "Are you done?"

"Yes, I'm done," Tedla said.

The delegate turned to the judges. "These are Capellan notions it has been taught to mimic, like a parrot. No Gammadian bland has any notion of 'fundamental rights.' " He paused contemptuously, quite unaware of the effect his manner would produce on a Capellan audience—the first slip Val had seen him make. Tedla had obviously rattled him. When he went on, his voice was scornful. "We have seen, actually, the effect of a bland having control over its own life and thoughts. For twelve years now, as it says, Tedla has had the perfect freedom to chart its own course. Look at the results. Given every opportunity to succeed, it instead sank into a depraved life of squalor and whoredom. At last its misery became so great it tried to kill itself in shame. Can you argue that it would not have been better off protected and cared for? Can you say that freedom was to its benefit?"

Tedla's face was flushed and rigid. "I didn't say that being human was easy, or that I got it right the first time."

"Am I lying?" Nasatir demanded. "Can you tell them you didn't sell your body for sexual perversions, or try to blow your brains out?"

Tedla said nothing. Its eyes were on the floor.

After an eloquent pause, Nasatir turned to the judges. "Capellans are very eager to tell us they are concerned for

Tedla's welfare. We have a different definition of kindness, I think."

The judges actually looked uncomfortable. Val had a horrible feeling that the case had just been decided.

The Syndic looked at the other two judges, and said, "We will adjourn to discuss this issue. The court will reconvene in half an hour."

Tedla collapsed into its chair. Its face was still flushed. "I'm sorry," it said softly.

"Don't worry," Val said. "You did well. You almost had him doubting himself."

"Him and his damned ad hominem arguments," Dag Sorno said.

The bailiff had opened the doors, and the others were leaving the room. "I've got to go find some coffee," Val said. "Do you want some?"

"No, thank you," Tedla said. It looked like someone whose last vestige of defense had been stripped away.

When she arrived in the courthouse cafe, Val had to wait just outside the door to avoid meeting Surin in line. When the coast was clear, she bought a cup of coffee and made for an isolated table hedged in by brick partitions. She didn't want to talk to anyone. She sat down and tried to empty her mind of everything.

A voice beyond the wall to her left said, "You really can't help but pity the poor thing."

It was Nasatir. He and his party were completely hidden behind the wall and a screen of plants on top of it. They obviously didn't know that Val was near.

"It did pretty well, actually," a woman with a Gammadian accent said. They were speaking Capellan, so Val assumed they weren't alone. "Are you sure it's really a bland?"

"I've seen its matriculation records. It's a bland all right. Just a devilishly skillful one at manipulating humans. It can wrap kindhearted people around its little finger."

So much for the parrot mimicking human words, Val

thought ironically. She wished the judges could hear this.

"What are you going to do with it?" a woman said. Val wasn't sure of the voice—one of their lawyers, perhaps.

"That's not up to us," Nasatir said. "Our instructions were just to get it back."

A new voice spoke, and Val recognized this one instantly. It was Shankar. "If you don't mind my asking, what's so important about this bland? Why couldn't you just let it sink into obscurity here? Apart from your humanitarian concerns, of course."

"Of course," Nasatir said, giving a little laugh. "It has nothing to do with this bland per se. We just want to draw the line clearly before allowing any more Capellans onto our planet."

"Naturally," Shankar said.

"Actually, it does have a little to do with this bland," the other delegate said.

"Oh, yes," Nasatir said. "The mythology thing."

"What do you mean?" Shankar asked.

"It was the Capellans who taught us to pay attention to the beliefs and superstitions of our blands," Nasatir said. "We learned that even silly stories can cause trouble. Well, Tedla's become the subject of a whole mythology among the blands. You know, the neuter that outsmarted all the humans at their own game and got away. They cherish the belief that the aliens will come back some day and the rest of them will escape. Before any Capellans set foot on Gammadis, we need to demonstrate that no bland gets away. Not even Tedla."

Val stared at the surface of her coffee, watching it quiver slightly, knowing it was growing cold. She didn't touch it. Her mouth already felt bitter.

The woman delegate said, "The judges won't be swayed by this 'fundamental rights' business, will they? I know it's one of your favorite concepts."

There was a silence Val couldn't interpret. Then Shankar said in a low voice, "I wouldn't worry about it. The judges know what's at stake here. We saw to that."

Val left the coffee sitting on her table untouched. As she crossed the cafe, she felt very distant from the noise of conversation around her. She felt very distant from the whole planet. It was like a stage set she had been walking through all her life, mistaking it for truth.

When she came back in the courtroom, Tedla and Dag Sorno were still sitting there, waiting. Val put a hand on Tedla's shoulder and said as quietly as she could, "Tedla, can I talk to you for a second outside?"

She headed for the door farthest from the cafe. Leading the way across a lobby, Val stayed silent till they were in an empty corridor on the other side. Then she stopped.

"What is it?" Tedla said.

"I just learned the verdict."

"How?"

"The judges have been fixed. This whole thing was a charade. Nothing we could have said would have made any difference."

Tedla didn't look nearly as upset, or as surprised, as she felt. Her own disillusion was like bile in her throat. She had trusted the system.

"Who did it?" Tedla said resignedly.

"Epco. Possibly Magister Gossup, though I thought he was working for WAC. I don't know who anyone is working for any more."

"So I'm going back?" Tedla asked.

"No!" Val said fiercely. "Not if I can do anything about it. Damn it, Tedla, I'm not going to let them do this to you. I don't care what it takes."

In a way, it was a relief to be rid of all the constraint, all the inner negotiation, of having to look out for herself. Now there was nothing driving her but the tigress instinct to protect, to fight, to flee. She put her arms around Tedla and hugged it close, as if to claim it for her own. She felt how thin it was, mere bones and muscle, completely yielding against her.

"Come on," she said, taking Tedla's hand. "We've got to find a waystation."

They made three leaps, more or less at random, before stopping in a tile-roofed Gundic market square, where the sun beat down overhead and the air was scented with basil. Val went to a public terminal and called Max.

"Is there a verdict already?" he said as soon as he saw Val's face.

"There was a verdict before the hearing started," she said grimly.

"Why am I not surprised?" he said ironically.

"Listen, Max, we're going to drop out of sight for a while. Don't try to find us."

He looked very alert. "Okay."

"And Max . . . I think you ought to implement your plan. Right away. Before they stop you."

He said, "E.G.'s got the material already. All I need to do is call him, and the story will go out."

"Do it," she said, and cut the transmission. Too late, she remembered she hadn't sent her love to Deedee. Tedla was standing nearby, eyes shifting apprehensively around the crowded enclave. "We've got to disappear now," Val said.

Tedla laid a hand on her arm. It had a determined look. "If you don't mind, Val, I think I know where to go. You don't have to come. I can find my own way around grayspace."

"You're not on Gammadis," Val said. "There isn't any grayspace here to disappear into."

Tedla gave a bitter laugh. "Every planet has grayspace. You Capellans just never see it."

Startled not only by Tedla's words but by its manner, Val stifled her take-charge urge. "All right," she said, "show me." When Tedla hesitated, she said, "I'm not leaving you now."

They took one more wayport leap; then Tedla insisted they switch to public ground transport—cheap and untraceable. It had been years since Val had been on a bus, and she found it even more unsavory and fume-filled than she remembered from her undergraduate days. She and Tedla made their way down the swaying aisle past rows of passengers, toward an empty seat.

They passed the boundary into an enclave that made her own neighborhood seem middle-class. Outside the bus window, everything was the color of dust. Square housing units marched away from the street in monotonous rows. There was not a shred of greenery—just concrete, plasto-ceramic, and people, as far as the eye could see. It was a mass-produced landscape, constructed without a thought for anything but function.

Val wanted to pull out her University scarf to distance herself from her surroundings, but knew it would draw attention. It was not danger she felt, so much as distaste.

"You're on the other side of the glass now," Tedla whispered. When she looked puzzled, it went on, "Power relationships on Capella are all like one-way glass. The people on the power side look at it and see nothing but themselves, reflected. The people on the other side look through and see the whole world outside, beyond their reach."

"These people aren't like blands," Val said.

"Not anatomically," Tedla said. "You have both male and female blands here."

"Not legally, either," Val protested.

"You think you need laws to create blands? Civilization itself creates them. It can't run without them. They're like the waste from manufacturing—impossible to eliminate, impossible to use well. When they build up, they become toxic to your society, just like they did to ours."

Tedla motioned for Val to get out. As the bus pulled away in a cloud of dust, she looked up into the dreary, uniform windows of a tall concrete housing unit across the street. Tedla was staring at it, too.

"You're stereotyping, Tedla," Val said. "Just because these people are poor doesn't mean—"

Tedla gave her an odd, charged look. "I lived here," it said, then turned to point to a window high above. "See there, sixth floor, on the corner? That was my window. Do you want to go in?"

"No," Val said.

"I didn't think you would. It's just as well."

Val felt chastened. "There's a lot about your life you haven't told me."

"Yes," Tedla said.

Tedla led the way down a side street. As they passed further into the enclave, the sidewalk became stained and littered, and the shops began to have barred fronts. Here, the dense life in the housing towers spilled out onto the street; old men lounged in front of shops, idle teenagers clustered on street corners. Tedla moved with a purposeful gait, fast but not fleeing, interacting with no one. At last they came to a sidewalk stand where it bought some bus tokens. When the bus wheezed up, it was even more decrepit than the one that had brought them, but far more crowded. Val and Tedla stood.

Val was afraid she knew where they were bound, but she didn't ask. They transferred two more times on street corners where Val felt acutely conspicuous in her courtroom dress. At last they came to the gate marking the edge of the Worwha Shana enclave.

"I know someone here," Tedla said, its face tense. "He knows how to make people disappear."

The flesh-vendor was an Eclectic, a person living permanently between cultures. His features were Balavati, but his forehead was covered with livid Skor tattoos, and diagonal Worwha scar-ridges ran down his left cheek. A ring of rhinestones belonging to no culture at all was embedded in the skin around his neck. Val disliked him instantly. In her experience, Eclectics adopted the superficial outer trappings of culture, and left all the meaning and morality behind.

"Tedla, darling," Shandurry said, reaching out to stroke the neuter's cheek. Tedla stiffened at the touch. Shandurry gave a vulpine grin, revealing silver-tipped teeth.

They were standing in a wormbore tunnel bar; the only light came from the ever-shifting hairline cracks in the wall as the room breathed. Shandurry's establishment was a vast maze of light-veined tunnels whose only aboveground manifestation was a relatively innocuous druggery. A sinuous barmaid in glittering fishscales brushed past, casting a knowing glance at Tedla.

"I need a room, Shandurry," Tedla said.

"What, are you freelancing now?" the Eclectic said, giving Val a look that left her feeling slimed.

"One of the private ones," Tedla said. "Someone may be looking for me."

"Tell me something I don't know," Shandurry said, crossing his arms. Val noticed that his nails had been replaced by bird claws. "The big man acted like there was a rocket up his ass when you disappeared. He sent some suits to fetch you. They damaged some valuable equipment. You knew they were going to do that, didn't you?"

"No," Tedla said. It was a transparent lie, even to Val, who had no idea what they were talking about.

"How long do you need the room?" Shandurry said.

"Three days. Maybe more."

The flesh-vendor's eyebrows rose. "It'll cost you. Payment in advance."

Val's heart sank. She had almost no cash, and a credit would be traceable. To her surprise, Tedla reached out and touched Shandurry's arm. "Come on, you know I'm good for it."

The flesh-vendor's color changed. "You little tart," he said softly.

Tedla didn't back down. "Well?"

"On one condition. No, not me. You've got to take the big man to heaven one more time."

Tedla hesitated, obviously repelled. At last it forced out the words, "All right. As long as no one finds me for three days."

"Satisfaction guaranteed," Shandurry said, leering at Val.

When he turned to lead them out of the bar, Val whispered to Tedla, "Was that deal what I think it was?"

"I'm sorry if this embarrasses you," Tedla said, its face stiff and unmoving. "You didn't have to come."

They passed the entrance into a lounge where a dancer was undulating under blood-red lights. Ahead, Shandurry placed his palm on the wall, and the plates retracted, momentarily flooding the corridor with lime-colored light. When Val's eyes adjusted, she saw the entrance to a way-port. "Take the rose room," the proprietor said. Tedla nodded and motioned Val through.

On the other side was a short corridor lined with doors. Tedla opened one of the doors with a thumbscan. Val stepped through into a chamber like the inside of an obscenely suggestive flower. The walls were soft velour; the bed erupted from the floor, the shape of a giant orchid. Val stood looking in perplexity at some of the devices with which the room was equipped, quite unable to imagine their use. "Do you know how to operate these?" she said.

Tedla was locking the door. "It's a very high-tech place," it said noncommittally. "This may be offensive to you, but I know it's safe. Shandurry's got clients with reputations, and security is one of the things he charges for. The snoops are constantly poking around, but they've never found these rooms."

Val realized the purpose of the device she was looking at, and turned hastily away. "It's perfect, except for the price," she said.

Tedla looked away. "Don't worry about that. I just

won't do it. I've got three days to think how to get out of it.''

With luck, Val thought, in three days Tedla's name and story would be well enough known that the big man wouldn't want to claim his payment.

"I'm going to take a shower," Tedla said. "Make yourself at home. There's a terminal over there, and you can order food and drink from the dispenser."

When she was alone, Val sat down at the terminal to see whether Max's campaign had commenced. When she tapped one of the big newsnets, there was already a small headline about Gammadis. Not knowing how secure the terminal was, she didn't dare access the story. But checking the other nets, she found two more stories. The info-snowball was just starting. Satisfied, she shut off the terminal and punched up a cup of coffee from the auto-server. She then kicked off her shoes and settled back on the outstretched tongue of the orchid.

Tedla came out of the bathroom wearing only a towel, and opened an armoire where some clothes were hanging. With its back to her, it dropped the towel and took out a silk kimono. Val glimpsed long legs and a hard, adolescent body. She remembered vividly the sensation of holding it pressed against her. Surprised at herself, she suppressed the thought. It was the room. Or was it that simple?

"Do you want something more comfortable to wear?" Tedla asked.

"Later, maybe," Val said.

Tedla finished tying the kimono sash and turned around. There was something both elegant and vulnerable about that ambiguous body; Val was finding it hard to look away. Tedla smiled shyly at her and came to sit on the bed, legs folded under. Its skin was rosy and fragrant from the shower; its hair was slightly damp.

"How long did you work here?" Val said.

"Only a couple months."

"You seem to have made an impression."

Tedla shrugged.

Val said, "Were you good at it?"

Tedla's eyes rose to her face, slightly surprised, slightly knowing. "Yes," it said. "I was very good. I could be anything the client wanted—male, female, adult, child, anything. I changed genders every night. No one could tell what I really was; they were all mystified and attracted, but Shandurry charged a fortune for them to find out. Humans find sexual ambiguity very stimulating."

It was watching her seriously, almost expectant. Very softly, Val said, "Tedla, are you trying to seduce me?"

A look of uncertainty crossed Tedla's face. It watched her intently, poised to jump whatever direction her body language hinted. She realized she could have anything, absolutely anything, from it. The feeling of power was itself seductive.

"What makes you think sex would tie me any more closely to you?" Val said. "Do you think infatuation is your only safety?"

A complex look crossed Tedla's face: part frustration, part unease of being discovered. Val realized that she had hit home. "You're perfectly aware of what you're doing, aren't you?" she said. "All your innocence is just a strategy. Nasatir was right about you. You *are* a master manipulator."

Tedla looked as if it had made a fatal miscalculation. "I've disgusted you," it whispered.

"No, you haven't."

"Yes, I have. You didn't think I was so depraved, so . . ." it drew a shaky breath ". . . sexualized. You think Nasatir's right, that I'm just a piece of filth." Suddenly, there was real panic in its eyes. "Val, please don't leave me here. Even if you hate me now, even if you're repelled, please don't leave me."

The desperation was perfectly genuine. Even aware that she was being handled, Val could barely restrain herself from taking that childlike, unresisting body in her arms.

Instead, she squeezed Tedla's hand between both of hers. "I'm not going to leave you, Tedla. You don't need sex to make me love you. It's not the thing that governs all our thoughts, as you think. You're so much more than your body."

"My body's all I've got," it said, speaking fast. "It's all I've ever had, the only thing you humans want. You can't imagine what it feels like to have no power, no power at all. I have no way to get anything but through humans. You are the ones who cause all things to happen. All the rest of us—plants, animals, whole planets—we are just objects you humans batter around like some cosmic sport, using us in your competition to get ahead. We have no choice about where you're going to hit us, which direction our lives will ricochet—unless somehow we learn a way into your hearts. It's not a game for us, it's survival. It's how we must evolve. You are our natural selection."

This time, Val did take Tedla in her arms. It clung to her, and she stroked its back soothingly. "You're not powerless," she said.

"You don't know anything," Tedla said.

"Yes, I do. I heard you in that courtroom today. You were magnificent." Val took the neuter by the shoulders and pushed it away so she could see its face. She found it hard to believe this was the same person who had stood up to Nasatir, the same who had led her through the city. No wonder Galele had been confused.

"Tedla, you're going to have to tell me how you ended up here. You had a degree from UIC and an Epco scholarship. You didn't need to resort to prostitution. You had a thousand other choices. What happened?"

"It's a terrible story," Tedla said.

"Tell me."

She had no way to record, but that was not what Val wanted any more. This was not professional; it was personal now.

✳️ I knew that Magister Galele was risking something by bringing me to Capella Two. I didn't know how much.

By the time we arrived here, our story was well known in the circles where people's fates are decided. Because of us, WAC's huge investment had come to nothing. Emissary Ptanka-Ni and the rest of the researchers were due to arrive back in disgrace only days after us. There was already a date set for a hearing to investigate Magister Galele's professional ethics.

All their anger was directed at him, none at me. Even so, I quickly learned to trust no one. They tried very hard to seem kind, but their main interest in me was economic. They wanted to tap me for all the information they could get. But they went about it the wrong way.

They tried to separate me from Magister Galele. They put me in a hospital where the alien curators and mentationists could perform their tests and probe my body and my brain, telling me it was for my own good. Never, not even at Brice's, had I felt so dehumanized, so utterly like an object. There was a window in my room that looked out on your strange, barren landscape, all craters and dust. I would watch that ominous orange planet rising in the sky, like an angry ember waiting to incinerate us. I couldn't imagine how such a place could even be habitable, much less home. Whenever I asked to see the Magister, they would answer, "He doesn't want to see you," which I knew was a lie, or "You don't have to see him any more," which made no sense. After a while, I started resisting in the only way I knew how. I stopped responding to them. I stopped even moving. All I would do was sit in bed, staring at the floor. At last they grew concerned enough to consult him, and he persuaded them to let him in. I was so happy to see his funny face that I broke down in tears and begged him to take me away. He said, "If that's what you want, Tedla, you've got to insist on it.

You've got rights here, but you have to exercise them for yourself. I can't do it for you."

"But you're my guardian!" I protested. "That's what guardians are for, to fight for us."

"Not here," he said, a little bitterly.

I couldn't imagine how I was going to survive in this strange land without a guardian. He saw my fear, and said kindly, "You'll do fine, Tedla. Just tell them what you want, and if they don't pay attention, tell them again until they do."

I followed his advice. It took several days, but when they finally realized they weren't going to get another speck of information out of me, they relented. I later found out that Magister Galele had been desperately using the only power he had to achieve the same result.

They only wanted one thing from Magister Galele: silence. WAC had decided to cover the whole thing up and avoid bad publicity. Our silence was the price of staying together.

For Magister Galele, it was a heavy sacrifice. To keep his bargain, he could offer no defense at his hearing, and they stripped him of his degree and credentials. After that, he could no longer work in his own profession. He couldn't teach, he couldn't publish, he couldn't profit in any way from all his knowledge of Gammadis. To keep me out of their hands, he had to accept a life of invisibility.

We moved together into a tiny room in that housing tower I showed you. It was not a very safe area, but we had no money for anything else. After more than a century in travel, he had no friends or family left to help him. He tried to look up the children of some people he had known, but they were not anxious for the friendship of a disgraced and indigent former magister. Facing them was more than he could stand, so he gradually gave up trying to make connections.

He fought through a terrible depression that first year. The hard thing about poverty here is the isolation. This planet is in a constant state of conversation with itself, and to be cut off from that is like being cut off from part of your brain, to be less than aware. He talked constantly about finding enough money to get an infoservice, and I began to realize it was something he needed in order to feel human.

The isolation was not nearly as hard on me. The university had revoked my scholarship, probably under pressure from WAC, but I doubt I would have gone through with it anyway, then. The landscape was unsettling, the customs strange, and the people frightening, and at first I rarely ventured out, instead spending my time making that little room into as much of a home as I could. But I couldn't stay cooped up forever, and when I did go out—that was when I learned about the blands on your planet.

It is not just a matter of poverty, as you seem to think. Here, where people can inherit money, or get it from partners or royalties without earning it, you have many well-to-do blands. But most of them are poor. They live shabby, circumscribed lives—aware of, but never aspiring to, the humanity around them, though they will live off it parasitically if they can. They are the eyes behind all those windows in the housing tower you saw. They take whatever chances others give them. They complain, but not so that you hear them. There are no graydoors here except the ones inside peoples' minds, but those are closed as tight as ever—and locked from both sides.

There were times, that first year, when I was worried Magister Galele himself was turning into a bland. He seemed listless and sad all the time. I tried to get him interested in the world around him—I even suggested he do a study of the people in the building, to compare with my planet. But he was like you—he didn't want to think of his own planet that way, and denied there was any parallel.

"There is only one similarity," he said. "You are no

more free than you were on Gammadis. You are still just a house servant.''

It was hard for me to see him so unhappy, and I would have done anything in my power to cheer him up. Sometimes I would catch him gazing at me as if he dreamed of touching me, and having me touch him in return; but if ever I tried to show him I was willing, through some little gesture or other, he would grow cold and draw away. He insisted we sleep on opposite sides of the room, as if he couldn't trust himself to get any closer. Even so, I more than once woke in the night to find him standing over me, watching me sleep. He always grew very flustered, and tried to make up some excuse.

I think the thing he dreaded more than any other was that I would cease to love him. Every other thing—career, reputation, income—he could give up, but not that. In a strange way, he was utterly dependent on me, as if only my love would justify his life. A thousand ways I tried to show him that he didn't need to worry, but always there was a nagging self-doubt in him.

And so it wasn't until he was truly desperate that he managed to bring himself to suggest how I might earn some money. We were sitting and eating our government-issue rations one night when he said hesitantly, ''I talked to Magister Diabu today.'' I waited for him to go on, but it took a while for him to gather the courage. ''He's a historical linguist, and has been studying the WAC files on the Gammadian language. He wanted to ask me some questions, but of course I couldn't answer because of the agreement with WAC. I told him I wasn't the one to ask, anyway.'' He paused, then said, ''Tedla, you didn't sign any nondisclosure agreements. You could charge him a good price for an interview. We might be able to get a terminal.''

Since I knew a terminal was what he wanted more than anything aside from me, I agreed at once. So the next day he took me to Magister Diabu's office and waited outside in the hall while the linguist asked me questions about Argot, our language. Diabu was surprised and pleased at my cooperation, since WAC had concluded I had nothing of value to say. At the end, he led me out into the hall and paid Magister Galele in cash—more Capellan cash than I had ever seen in one place before—and asked if I could return the next week. Magister Galele was busy hiding the money away under his baggy sweater, so I agreed.

Afterwards, Magister Galele asked me anxiously, "Was it all right? Did you mind doing it?"

"It was fine," I said.

"So if I found someone else willing to pay, would you do some more interviews?"

He didn't want to share me, I could tell; but he desperately needed to. I said, "It doesn't bother me."

It soon proved that there were quite a few researchers eager enough to interview a Gammadian asexual that they were willing to engage in an untraceable financial transaction with Magister Galele to get access to me. He was pressing the boundaries of his agreement with WAC, but he was always careful to abide by its letter. He never dealt with any but the most legitimate scholars—no popularizers or networkers who might start a leak. I expect WAC knew what he was up to, but instead of interfering, they simply bought up all the information and made it proprietary. Naturally, that didn't discourage the magisters, since there was a ready market for their monographs.

Before long, we were able to move into better quarters, and we soon had quite a fine infoservice subscription. Magister Galele had terribly mixed feelings about the situation. On good days he talked about himself as my agent; on bad ones, he bitterly called himself my pimp.

After many return visits, I got to know Magister Diabu rather well, and he became concerned about my welfare. I know he was suspicious of my relationship with Magister Galele, since he often hinted that I could tell him if anything untoward was going on. One day he said, "Tedla, why aren't you enrolled in a university?"

I laughed and told him the story of my brief admission to UIC. "You shouldn't let that stop you," he told me. "If you applied again as a Capellan resident, you could get in."

His words made me very thoughtful. I knew by now that Magister Galele didn't need a Personal here. I felt useless, and he felt gallingly dependent; it was a bad situation. So one day I asked him if he would tutor me so I could get into the university.

"Would you really like that?" he said, quite pleased. I knew then it was the right solution. It put us back on the proper footing, him the sponsor and me the protégé, not this strange reversal of roles we had been struggling with. I really didn't have any ambition to get into the university; what I wanted was to get Magister Galele on his feet again.

It worked. He took my education on as a project, and soon some of his old enthusiasm started coming back. All my earnings started going into access fees for books and databases, and our days were soon quite full of lessons. He began to take me on field trips to the enclaves and convocations, to train and test my observational skills. He made me write reports afterwards, and never let me rest unless I marshalled my evidence and drew conclusions. He taught me the intricacies of your infonets, and drilled me on all the classics.

The second time I applied for entry to UIC, the test took place in a huge hall like a matriculatory. When I saw the hundreds of other applicants, my expectations sank. This time, there was no one to "translate" for me. I was competing against the smartest young people in known space. My only chance was that the university would make allowances for my background.

I don't know if that was what they did, or if Magister Diabu pulled strings for me, but they accepted me. When we got the word, Magister Galele hugged me tight, lifting me right off the ground in his joy. That night we splurged on a fine meal and liquor. After he was rather drunk, he became moody, and I asked him what was wrong. He said, "Will you want to move out?"

"You don't want me to, do you?" I said, alarmed.

"No," he said.

"How could I ever get through university without your help?" This wasn't just for his benefit. I really believed it, and still do.

"Don't worry, I'll get you through," he said with a sad version of his old rapscallion grin. "You'll have the best transcript of any Gammadian who's ever attended UIC."

I laughed, and thought the subject was closed. But later I caught him looking at me, and he blushed and looked away. "Maybe it would be better if you moved out, and had a chance to live a normal life," he said.

"This life is normal for me," I said.

His next words came in a strained, slurred voice. "I'm afraid so much of the time. Afraid of myself, my feelings. Afraid of hurting you."

I couldn't tell what he wanted. He was giving me such contradictory signals, I just sat there confused. He wouldn't look at me, wouldn't give me any hint. At last I said, "I'm going to bed."

I half expected him to follow me, but he just sat there drinking late into the night.

As soon as I was admitted to UIC, Epco offered me a scholarship, on condition that I stop selling information to anyone affiliated with WAC. After that, I could no longer talk to Magister Diabu, except as a student. He was remarkably good-natured about it.

My home life changed very little. Magister Galele helped me with the assignments, often having to read the texts himself, since he was rather out of date. He kept joking about how he was getting a second education free of charge. I attended the classes by myself, of course, but I felt little rapport with the other students. They reminded me of the young humans in the midway house. They seemed to feel it was their right to inherit the universe.

By this time, Magister Galele had begun to pick up some freelance writing and other odd jobs, but his real vocation was still my education. It was the only thing that really touched his inner passions. Watching him, I began to understand something about you Capellans. I had always thought—in fact, you always claim—that you are a perfectly secular society. But that's not true. The feeling you have for knowledge is very close to the awe others feel for the sacred. Faith in knowledge is the principle you will never back away from, the thing you protect when everything else is gone. Creating it is your highest calling. Destroying it, or polluting it, is the unforgivable sin. Learning is your righteousness, research is your sacrament, discovery is your revelation. You believe not in a transcendent God but in a transcendent truth that we all can strive toward through learning. You are profoundly religious people, in your way.

Magister Galele didn't just want me to have a degree. He wanted me to have a soul.

As the years went by my grades improved, and he began talking about getting me into a graduate program in xenology. "Not here, not at UIC," he said, still smarting from the treatment he had gotten. "C4D has a good program."

I never really expected C4D to accept me. The day I got the word, I sat on a bench by the sand fountain in the Court of Induction for a long time, not wanting to have to go home and tell him. I knew that this would mean a parting of our ways.

"I'm going to turn it down," I said to him later that evening. "I don't want to go."

"You can't back down now," he said. "You've got to prove you can do it."

"I don't want to leave you."

He was silent a moment, then said, "Tedla, I'm so damned proud of you it hurts. Everything you accomplish makes my life more worthwhile. It would break my heart to think I had held you back.''

It was as if I had to leave him, to prove that I loved him.

He came with me to the lightbeam waystation, and though he joked bravely, I could tell how badly he was hurting. Neither of us cried when we embraced, though both of us were close. When I lay down on the slab, the last thing I saw was the bittersweet expression on his face.

At C4D I was on my own as I had never been before. The first few months were horrible, and every day I was on the verge of giving up and going back. Magister Galele sent me long, encouraging letters, but we couldn't afford PPC transmission, so they were always four days late. If Magister Delgado hadn't befriended me, I don't think I ever would have made it. I learned later that Magister Galele was in close touch with him, and sent him reams of advice about how to handle me. It was as if he was being my guardian by remote control.

C4D is a tolerant, cosmopolitan place. Even so, it was awkward for me, fitting into a gendered society. There were simple things like which bathroom to use, and more complicated ones like language. I grew accustomed to hearing people stumble in embarrassment over pronouns. I found that they tended to assign me a gender in their minds, so that they could interact, but even so I was excluded from many of the situations where gender pairs are prescribed. Often people took it on themselves to let me know that surgery was available to correct my condition.

I had intended to come back each year to visit Magister Galele, but as it turned out, the money was very scarce, and Epco wouldn't pay for social trips. In four years, I only made it back once. I found that he had relapsed into his old habits of shabbiness and disorder. He seemed unhealthy; his hand had acquired a tremor, and his skin a sallow color. Though he made a great attempt to appear in control, I could tell it was getting hard for him to cope. I felt anxious to finish my business at C4D and get back to him.

Graduate school itself was a terrible disappointment. I had been very naive going into it. I had thought I was going to spend four years learning about other cultures from people who knew a great deal about them. But that's not the purpose of graduate school at all. We didn't study other cultures; we studied the people who had studied other cultures before us. The purpose was to induct new members into the brotherhood of learning by teaching us the history of our predecessors. We learned to offer them honor by citing them in our footnotes, giving them immortality that way. It's an elaborate kind of ancestor-worship, really. The promise was that, if we were good enough, some day future students would immortalize us with their prayer-offering citations.

🙰 "I'm not trying to be disrespectful," Tedla said, glancing at Val nervously.

"I know," Val said, though her laugh sounded uncomfortable even in her own ears. "It's just odd to hear your own culture analyzed by someone who's supposed to be the analyzee."

"That's the risk they took in educating me," Tedla said.

"But you got through it anyway," Val said. "Before you deny it, Joansie talked to Magister Delgado. He said you weren't flunking out, or anything close to it. So what happened? Did you rebel?" As soon as the words were out of her mouth, she felt silly. Rebellion was completely alien to Tedla's nature.

The neuter looked intensely uncomfortable. "I wish I didn't have to tell you the next part."

Val waited in silence.

"Oh well," Tedla said. "You could have found it out yourself by now, if you had just looked up Magister Galele's name."

Tedla had told her a great many things, but had never

looked this reluctant before. "What happened?" she said.

Hesitantly, Tedla said, "I was very close to graduating, as you said. I was preparing for oral exams when I got a message from Capella Two. Magister Galele had been arrested, and was in jail." Tedla closed its eyes, and its voice sank to a whisper. "He had been picked up in a vice raid on a house that specialized in child prostitution."

⇥|↤ I couldn't believe it, at first. I thought it was one more plot to destroy him for what he'd done on my planet. I was outraged. I couldn't think of anything else. I quickly made arrangements to go back to Capella Two. Before I could leave, a peace officer came to interview me. He kept probing, asking leading questions, till I realized they wanted me to supply more evidence. At last he came out and offered to pay my way back if I would just agree to say Magister Galele had molested me, too.

It was like having a tornado in my brain. I was so angry I didn't even tell Magister Delgado where I was going. When I got to Capella Two, I tried to get in to see the magister, but instead they sat me down and showed me the evidence.

It was only then I learned why he was in so much trouble. You see, it was not his first offense. Long before I had known him, before he had even come to my planet, he had been convicted on the same charge, and had taken court-ordered treatments. Now he was a recidivist to the law, one of those rare, incurable people on whom even brain alteration fails. He had used up all his chances.

My entire world shattered around me that day. The person I had known best, the person I had loved and admired with all my heart, had completely hidden his true nature from me. I hadn't known him at all. Everything I had trusted was a complete deception.

I was still angry, but now at him. How well I remember that shabby gray room where they laid it all out before me. I paced up and down between the window and the wall, my mind whirling with outrage and confusion. In that state, they tried again to get me to admit that I also had been his plaything. When I still denied it, they showed me pictures of the children they had picked up in their sweep, children in makeup and grotesquely suggestive costumes, sexualized before their time. There was one, a little girl with curly blond hair and dark eyes, that could have been a picture of myself at that age.

I felt horribly implicated then, dirtied by association, as if I had been an accomplice. But I still wouldn't lie. They put me in a hotel room nearby, where they could keep up the pressure. There they visited me every day, telling me more details, trying to get my cooperation. They needed my testimony because I was an adult now, and all the other witnesses were children.

Any other crime I could have forgiven him. I wouldn't have liked it, but I could have made excuses. This was too personal.

At last his own lawyer came to talk to me, to ask if I would testify on his behalf. He was planning to admit his guilt—he could scarcely do anything else—but hoping that my support might get him clemency.

I refused to say a word in his defense.

I never went to the trial. I stayed in my hotel room through the whole thing, and only learned afterwards what happened. No one defended him, and the judges were very harsh. They sentenced him to prison for twenty years. It might as well have been for the rest of his life.

On the night before he was to be transferred to prison, he sent me a message. When I saw it listed in my mailbox, I returned it, marked Refused. I never found out what was in it.

I had to hire someone to dispose of his belongings. I couldn't have entered his rooms myself, even though they told me any evidence was gone. The woman who did it was discreet and thorough. The only thing she brought me was a sealed envelope addressed to me in Magister Galele's hand. I almost threw it out, but at the last minute I put it away unopened.

I stayed on Capella Two, still living in that hotel, though I couldn't afford it. My mind was in such turmoil I didn't know what else to do. I spent a lot of time wandering around, just walking aimlessly for days on end, porting to other places till I didn't even know where I was, and returning at night so exhausted I didn't even dream.

Magister Galele only lasted two months in prison. He wasn't made for it; the strain was too great, and his heart gave out. It was his lawyer who brought me the news. In his will, he left all his copyrights to me. They were all he had.

That night I sat alone in my room without a light on, utterly wasted with emotion. At last, very late, I turned on a light and took out the envelope he had left me. It was a short note. All I remember of it is:

You are the only beautiful thing in my sordid life. You are the only thing that has ever made me proud of myself. If I am dead by the time you read this, know that I died loving you.

I cried myself to sleep that night, holding the paper pressed against my heart.

What I'd been denying to myself, and could no longer, was that I still loved him. In spite of what he had done, in spite of all my anger, he was the most precious thing in my life. And now it was too late.

For the next few days I sat in my room, barely stirring, barely eating. I had cried so much I felt drained, but I couldn't stop rethinking everything. It was no longer a mystery to me why I had never suspected him. It may sound sentimental, but I think it is true: For a short time, his love had actually redeemed him.

Everything looked different now. I had thought he was my guardian, but he was the one who had needed protection. How badly I had failed him. If only I had read him right, and let him have the kind of relationship he wanted, he might never have turned elsewhere. If only I hadn't left him alone and gone to C4D, he might never have relapsed.

If only I had forgiven him, he might not have died.

They say that blands can never truly love, and the deepest feelings are denied us. I cannot believe that is true. If humans loved or grieved more deeply than I, then the world would be strewn with their empty husks. I *have* loved. I *have* known grief. I know that, if I know anything.

I left my room on the second night, and never returned. I wandered from wayport to wayport till my money ran out, then slept in alleys in the cold. I deserved it, you see. In all my life I'd only truly loved two people, and I had killed them both.

Early one morning I found myself in Shandurry's druggery. He can diagnose a thousand varieties of despair, and he instantly recognized mine. He gave me a drug to blunt the pain and a bed to sleep in, the first true sleep I'd had in days. When he woke me hours later and said I had to get out into the cold again, I broke down and begged him to let me stay. When he told me the price, it only seemed just. After all, I had been trained for it. It seemed like my life had just come full circle.

Everything I earned went back to Shandurry for drugs. The pain was just too intense, I couldn't have survived without them. Shandurry didn't like it; he wants his whores quick in the wits, so they can steal and wheedle higher prices out of the clients. But he kept me on because of the big man, who was very rich and completely obsessed with me. In the end, though, even that wasn't enough. He started withholding the drugs. When I came to my senses and realized what a sink of degradation my life had become, I knew the only solution was to end it. I had already stolen the gun, perhaps sensing what I was going to have

to do. I didn't tell Shandurry anything. I just walked out—
and you know the rest.

❧❧ Tedla's body was rigid with tension. Val
reached out to touch her companion's knee. It flinched
away. She wondered if, all this time, she had been misinterpreting that reaction.

"Tedla, why don't you want me to touch you?" she
said.

"You shouldn't. If you touch me, something horrible
will happen to you. I'm like a carrier."

"But you have let all sorts of people touch you."

"It didn't matter with them. They weren't good people."

Very gently, Val said, "You can't blame yourself,
Tedla. You can't save everyone. Especially not from themselves."

"I don't want to save everyone," Tedla said. "Just the
people I love."

Val thought of Alair Galele. She felt a little betrayed
herself, ashamed that she had actually begun to like the
man. She blamed her own acumen that she had seen nothing of the predator in his writings. Weakness, bad judgment, helpless impulsivity. Not malice.

The brain alteration treatments for pedophilia were severe and rarely failed, the conditioning was so strong. She
looked at Tedla and thought of living year in and year out
within touching distance of the thing you wanted most, the
thing you yearned for more than life. Was it enough to
break down even the strongest conditioning? She looked
away, not wanting Tedla to know what she was thinking.

She suddenly felt an urgent need for a drink. She swung
her legs over the edge of the bed to get up. Tedla caught
her hand. "You're not leaving, are you?"

"I'm not leaving," Val said.

"I'm sorry," Tedla said, its voice shaking. "You don't
know how scared I am. If they catch me, if they take me

back . . . I would be better off if I'd killed myself.''

"They're not going to take you back," Val said. "I'm not going to let them.''

She got up and ordered a double Scotch from the dispenser. When she glanced back, Tedla had collapsed in exhaustion on the bed, its face pressed into the covers. Val sat down at the terminal. She had barely activated it when it buzzed with an incoming call. After a momentary hesitation, she answered.

Shandurry's face was livid with anger. "Put your whore on," he said.

Val scowled at him, but pushed her chair back. Tedla had sat up on the bed. Its eyes looked dark with shadows. "Shandurry?" it said.

"What have you done, you alley cat?" Shandurry demanded.

"What do you mean?"

"Don't try to sell me that innocent crap. Why didn't you tell me you're on the big man's shit list?"

Tedla looked gray with fear. "Did you talk to him? Did you tell him where I am?"

"Oh I see. You were counting on me not following through.''

"Three days! You said I could have three days!" Tedla cried out.

"Save your breath, bitch-boy." Shandurry cut off the call.

Val turned to Tedla. "What was that about?"

"I don't know. I haven't done anything."

"Who is this big man? Is he likely to cause trouble?"

"I don't know anything about him. His real name's Pym.''

Val froze, but her heart was laboring. "Are you kidding, Tedla? You fellated Pym?''

Tedla looked terrified. "What's the matter? Do you know him?''

"He's just the WAC administrator in charge of the

Gammadian project!'' Something struck her. ''No wonder they wanted to wipe your memories! God, do you suppose Surin knew?''

''What do we do?'' Tedla asked.

Val had no chance to answer. There were voices outside the door. She had barely jumped to her feet when the door burst open and Shandurry came in, followed by three men in suits. One of them went straight for her, the other two for Tedla. ''How dare you—'' she began, but got no further. The man grabbed her around the waist, pinning her arms at her sides. She struggled furiously, but her barefoot kicks had little effect.

The second man pinned Tedla back on the bed, while the third took out a transdermal and pressed it against the neuter's neck. They waited a few seconds, then one of them picked up the unconscious body as if it weighed no more than the pillow. One of its arms dangled loosely.

''You fucking bastards!'' Val screamed. She tried to jerk free, but the goon still held her.

The man carrying Tedla left, and the other took out a roll of tape and secured Val's wrists behind her, with another strip over her mouth. They threw her roughly onto the bed, then turned to the door. Shandurry was still holding it open for them. ''Thanks,'' one of them said, the only word they had uttered.

Alone, Val struggled fruitlessly to free her hands. When she was exhausted and sweaty, she lay still a moment. She had to apply her brain to this problem. Looking around the room, her eyes fell on a steel-studded cabinet near the manacles mounted on the wall. She pushed herself upright and went over to it, turning around and groping behind her to unfasten the latch. When she kicked the doors wide, she saw what she had expected: whips, shockers, needles, and other fanciful torture equipment. And, yes, a rack of knives. She wondered if Pym had been stimulated by castration fantasies. She would gladly have given him the real thing at the moment.

Turning around again, she groped for the hilt of one of the knives. When she had maneuvered it out, she took it over to the bed, kicked up the covers, and wedged the handle under the mattress, blade out. Drawing a deep breath to steady herself, she gingerly knelt to saw apart the tape binding her hands.

The knife wasn't very sharp, but it did the trick at last. She ripped the last bits of tape from her wrists, then freed her mouth. No more than ten minutes had passed; they had obviously wanted only to slow her down till they got away. They would be long gone by now; there was no point following. She sat down at the terminal.

"He's not here, Val," Kendra said. "He's at K-Court."

"Page him," Val said grimly. "It's an emergency. Life and death."

"Val, are you okay?"

"Not *my* life and death, Kendra! Someone else's." She gave the number of her terminal and cut off.

She paced up and down in agitation, wondering if she was doing the right thing. It was a choice of evils now, and she needed a big evil to take on WAC. When the message buzzer sounded, she leaped to answer.

She had never seen Magister Gossup look as nearly angry as this. He said, "Valerie, if you expect me to—"

"Never mind!" she cried out. "WAC's got Tedla. You've got to tell Nasatir. If he wants Tedla with an intact brain, he's got to move fast. Pym's the one to call."

"How do you know this?" Gossup said.

"Because I was here when the WAC goons carted Tedla off not ten minutes ago. I would have called sooner, but they left me tied up."

"Where are you?" Gossup said.

"It doesn't matter! What matters is, they're planning to shock Tedla's brain to jelly so it can't expose Pym. He was one of its customers when it sold sex for money. Or maybe you knew that all along."

She had the satisfaction of seeing him look genuinely

shocked. "Can you prove this?" he demanded.

"I know who can," she said. "Anyway, WAC will probably turn Tedla over to Nasatir as soon as they figure it's safe—"

"They have to. The court granted Nasatir custody. And you're in danger of a kidnapping charge."

"—so at this point the only question is, does Tedla go back to Gammadis with a brain or without one?"

At last Gossup seemed to grasp the whole picture. "I'll talk to Delegate Nasatir," he said. The screen went blank.

Val leaned back and closed her eyes, feeling simultaneously exhausted and keyed to fight. She had no idea if she had done the right thing. She thought, with a guilty twinge of empathy, of Magister Galele. No wonder Gossup had called him evil. Gossup probably thought Galele had brought Tedla back solely to serve as his sexual slave. That was what Gossup had been trying to hide. She groaned and put her hand to her forehead. And to think she had denied that humans were complete prisoners of their sexuality.

She got up wearily to leave. When she arrived back in the dark and writhing corridor of Shandurry's entertainment complex, the Eclectic was waiting for her with a long printout. "You racked up some charges," he said.

"You piece of shit," Val said. "As if WAC didn't pay you enough already."

He didn't try to stop her as she walked out.

When she got home, Max and Deedee were out, and her mailbox was crowded with messages—requests for interviews and information, mostly. She skimmed through them with a rising sense of disappointment. They were all from small fringe newsgroups with limited circulation. The major newsnets had picked up on the Gammadian negotiations, but so far they had failed to see any general interest in Tedla's story. It would take work and time to turn them around. Three days might have done it. But she no longer had three days.

She sat staring at her screen. Never before had she felt so completely powerless. There was nothing, absolutely nothing, she could do. It was an alien feeling, and she clenched her fists to deny its validity.

What was it Tedla had said? Something about the powerless having no recourse but through the minds of their masters. At first, her instincts rebelled at the idea. But as she sat there, unable to think of any alternative, her hand moved slowly to pick up her scarf and pack again.

"Please, Magister. I am begging you. You have to do something," Val said, her hoarse voice cracking.

Magister Gossup looked bloodless as a stone god. They were in his office, and the message light on his terminal was blinking furiously, but he was ignoring it. She had just poured out the whole rest of the story to him. His index finger moved against the top of his desk. "I don't know what you expect from me, Valerie," he said.

"Justice," she said. "For Tedla, for all the blands."

"That is not in my power," he said.

Instead of arguing, Val let the silence grow. At last she said, "You know, Tedla kept saying how much easier it was to be powerless. No responsibility. That's what made it attractive to be a bland."

Gossup stirred, frowning at her analogy. "Even if it were in my power, it would be a violation of professional ethics," he said. "We are xenologists, Valerie. Our responsibility is not to change Gammadis, but to observe it as it is."

"Even if we have to collaborate in tyrrany?" Val said.

"It's not our role to make value judgments," he said. "If we did, we would be no better than Alair Galele."

Softly, Val said, "Galele was the only one who did the right thing on Gammadis. With all his flaws, at least he acted with a conscience."

Gossup gave her a sharp look. "I don't condone the system on Gammadis. But we cannot impose change on them. Coercion never works—history has proved that again and again. True change has to come from within. The ultimate solution to injustice is always an influx of information. Our best alternative is to open communication so the Gammadians will gradually grow out of their ways."

"That won't do Tedla any good."

"But if Tedla doesn't return, it will never happen."

Bitterly, she said, "So we sacrifice one bland for the good of the rest?"

"You have an inflammatory way of putting things, Valerie. I thought I'd taught you cultural relativism."

There was a sharp ache in her head. She was too tired to argue with him any more. He had all the standard answers ready, all the answers she had believed herself when they were safely theoretical, before she had had to test them in experience.

In a dull voice she said, "Where is Tedla now?"

"In Nasatir's hands," Gossup said. "We will send it home tomorrow."

"Can I talk to it?"

"Do you really think they are likely to consent to that?"

Val looked down. She felt completely beaten.

Gossup drew in a breath as if to speak, but said nothing. At last, hesitantly, he said, "I might be able to get you into the lightbeam waystation tomorrow. You couldn't say anything, you understand. But you could see it."

She could not tell whether he thought he was being kind, or teaching her a lesson. But it seemed like the only concession she was likely to get. "I guess I'll have to settle for that," she said.

He looked at her thoughtfully. "You need to learn more detachment if you are going to thrive in this profession, Valerie."

Which profession? she wondered. Xenology, or betrayal?

Val had no strategy in mind when she decided to bring Deedee along to the lightbeam waystation the next day. The child's presence attracted no attention, since the facility was regularly open to family members and friends of people departing to other worlds. When she showed Gossup's passcard, the ticket agent directed her to a private viewroom. There were three others waiting when she arrived, none of whom she recognized—witnesses from WAC and Epco, she supposed, there to make sure no mishap occurred.

Beyond a thick glass window lay the translation chamber, silent technicians at work. When a door opened on the other side, Val lifted Deedee up on a chair seat to see. Nasatir entered, followed by Tedla. The neuter wore a loose-fitting gray knit suit, and its eyes were on the ground. If Val had not known otherwise, she would have concluded that WAC had tampered with its brain, its face was so utterly blank of thought or emotion. Val wondered if it was drugged.

"Wave good-bye to Tedla, Deedee," Val said.

She tapped on the window; Tedla glanced up and saw them. No, it wasn't drugged. It was horribly, desperately aware. For a bare second they exchanged a look, and Val tried to pour all of her tangled emotions into her eyes. Deedee leaned forward and pressed a hand against the glass; Tedla reached out as if to press its hand to hers, but Nasatir spoke to it sharply.

Val's eyes met Nasatir's then, and they grappled. *We see you*, Val thought at him. *Even our children see you.*

Deliberately ignoring her, Nasatir drew Tedla over to the translation cylinder. Mechanically, the neuter climbed up on the slab and lay back, staring at the ceiling. The technicians made some last adjustments, then the slab retracted into the disassembler. There was a flash of bright light, and when the slab extruded again, Tedla was gone.

Val laid her forehead against the cold glass. There was nothing more she could do.

"Where has Tedla gone, Mama?" Deedee asked.

"Home," Val answered. "It went home."

"When will it come back?"

"I don't know, Deedee."

She lifted the child to the floor and knelt to hug her tight. This at least, Val thought, was something that she could do right. Here, within the circle of her arms, was a tiny part of the world where an individual had the power to make a difference.

With that thought, her tears began to come.

"You need to get away, Valerie," Magister Gossup said to her a week later.

She saw double meaning in everything now, and this was no exception. He had reasons to want her gone.

She had thought it would get easier as time went on, but her memories were like a dull, chronic ache, as if some poison inside her were digesting in acid, chemically transforming into cynicism.

"I have a contract I could give you," Gossup went on. "It would get you away from Capella Two for a short time."

Now that it was too late, the newsnets had finally discovered Tedla's story, and requests for interviews were flooding in. She was turning down most of them, unable to bring herself to profit from the story. The only satisfaction she got was watching the discomfort in Nasatir's face when he tried to defend his planet on screen. Nasatir doubtless wanted the issue to go away, and getting rid of her would prevent her from stirring the embers.

"How much does it pay?" she asked dully.

"Five thousand."

Hush money, but she could use it. She was going to need help defending her degree before the Magisterium.

They had called her credentials up for review. "Where?" she asked.

"C4D. It's a co-project with the university there."

She sighed. "I'll have to talk to Max."

"We could send him, too. And your daughter. The travel funds are inexplicably generous."

They had clearly pegged Max as a troublemaker, as well. She thought of letting Gossup know she saw through this, but it didn't seem to matter any more. "I'll ask him," she said.

And so, three days later, she was back at the lightbeam waystation, on the other side of the glass this time. She half expected to see someone from WAC witnessing their departure, but no one was there.

Max went first, then Deedee, who acted remarkably good and grown up. When Val's turn came, she lay back on the slab, and her eyes blurred with tears. They were still wet when she got off the receiving couch on C4D.

To Val's surprise, Magister Delgado himself was there to meet them. He proved to be a rotund and voluble assemblage of snow-white, flyaway hair and wispy beard. She instantly saw why Gossup had never gotten along with him, and why Galele had. When Val appeared, the Magister was already teasing Deedee with a grandfatherly air, and she was drinking in the attention. "Welcome, my dear," Delgado said to Val. "I'm delighted to meet someone who's able to fluster that old prig Gossup."

The image of Gossup flustered was so inconceivable it made Val wonder if Delgado had ever met him face to face.

At the baggage desk the Magister got into a loud and polysyllabic argument with a customs agent that seemed likely to result in their luggage being impounded. But just as Val was about to intervene, the Magister and the agent embraced each other warmly, and Val's family was waved through without so much as an inspection.

As they left the waystation, Delgado said, "Gossup tells

me you are probably the leading expert on Gammadis now.''

"Is that why I'm here?" Val said.

With a piercing look, Delgado answered, "You can't seriously think it has nothing to do with it."

No, Val thought ruefully. Gammadis had everything to do with her predicament.

Deedee was excited to be on another planet, and kept pointing at people and asking questions, till Val had to caution her to keep her voice low.

"She's a born xenologist," Delgado said dotingly.

"I wish we could inoculate her against it," Val said.

The hotel had a swimming pool, which sent Deedee into raptures of excitement. All the way up to their room, she begged Val to take her swimming. "As soon as we get settled in," Val said. Max and Delgado were dealing with the luggage, so Val took the key-card. When the door swung open, she saw there was some mix-up; the room was already occupied. A tall figure dressed in black was standing by the window.

"Excuse me, they gave us the wrong room," Val said, and tried to pull the door closed. But Deedee wriggled past her, and dashed across the room toward the stranger.

"Deedee!" Val said sharply, barging into the room to drag Deedee back. "Come back here! I'm sorry, she—"

The stranger had swept Deedee up in a bear hug, and now turned to Val, smiling. Every word left Val's mind, except one. "Tedla!" she shrieked, and then she was across the room. She threw her arms around Tedla and Deedee in a three-way embrace.

"Oh my god, my god, it's really you!" she said, laughing and crying at the same time. Tedla was warm and solid against her. She didn't want to let go, as if Tedla might dissolve into a lost chance if she did.

Tedla set Deedee on the bed, and the child began babbling out news, completely unamazed to find Tedla here.

"How did you get here?" Val said. "What's going on?"

Tedla glanced cautiously at the open door. Max was standing there, staring in amazement; Delgado pushed him on in and closed the door.

"Is this your doing?" Val said.

Delgado raised his hands as if to fend off any credit. "I am only an accomplice," he said.

Conspiracies. They were everywhere. Val felt bewildered. "Who *is* responsible, then?"

"Truth to tell, it was you."

"What?"

"I can't think of any other reason for Kpatksiro Gossup to lay his career on the line for a point of conscience," Delgado said. Then, seeing Val's explosive expression, he explained, "It was simple, really. He arranged with the technicians to divert the lightbeam a little, so instead of going to Gammadis, Tedla ended up here."

"That Vind son of a bitch!" Val said hotly. "He must have been cooking this up while he was lecturing me on objectivity." She turned to Tedla. "Did you know?"

Tedla shook its head. "Not till I got here."

It was ironic: Her moment of greatest helplessness had been the one that had made the difference. Victory didn't feel like she had expected. She had wanted whole planets to stand up and declare that she was right, not this furtive compromise. She looked at Tedla, who was watching her with a cautious expression. And suddenly it didn't matter how small the circle of her success was, as long as Tedla was in it. Even if she had changed only one mind, it was enough.

A thought struck her. "How is Gossup going to explain this to the Gammadians?" she said.

"It's a fifty-one-year bluff," Delgado said. "They won't be expecting Tedla for half a century, and who knows what will have happened by then? They'll have diplomatic relations restored soon, and PPC communications will start. In fifty-one years, there could be a different attitude." He shook his head in wonderment. "Who would have suspected Gossup had the guile? I must remember never to challenge him to poker."

Deedee pulled at Tedla's arm. "Tedla, will you take me swimming?"

Tedla said, "No, Deedee. I'm a secret. No one is supposed to know I'm here. Can you keep a secret?"

Gravely, Deedee nodded.

"That goes for all of you," Delgado said seriously.

After Delgado left they ordered in a meal, and Val took Deedee down for a swim to tire her out. When they had eaten, drunk toasts to Vind duplicity, and gotten Deedee to bed, Val, Max, and Tedla sat in the hotel room before the open window, looking out on the skyline, where C4D University rose in a jumble of geometric shapes against the deep blue sky.

Val couldn't take her eyes off Tedla. It looked svelte and stylish in the new clothes, but something in its eyes seemed older.

"What are you going to do, Tedla?" Val asked. "Will you finish your degree?"

"I suppose I will," Tedla said. A pang crossed its face—a little bit guilt, a little bit longing. "You know, I'm ashamed to say so, but there was a part of me that wanted to go back, even at the end. When I woke up and found I was on C4D, all I could think was, now I'm my own guardian—responsible for making my life work out, and no one to blame if it doesn't. Powerlessness is such a lure, such a poisonous lure."

"Think of the other blands," Val said. "Every day you're free, you give them hope."

Tedla frowned, but didn't deny it. "We'll have to give them more than just hope before the end." Its eyes rose seriously to meet Val's. "I'm going to go back some day. When I can do it on my own terms."

"When you do, I'll be right behind you," Val promised. "But now is not the time."

"I suppose not. Not yet. There are still things in the outside worlds I've never seen, and stories I don't know the end of. Maybe there are even people out here I haven't met, people I may someday love, and who may love me. So it makes sense to finish my degree. It's what Magister Galele would have wanted."

There was an awkward silence.

"Well, you always have a home with us," Val said.

"Thank you," Tedla said. It looked out at the deep sky, the limitless well of free space beyond the planet. "It's so strange. I feel like I don't have any notion of who I am, or even what I am. I half think I might meet myself on the street corner some day, and not even recognize me."

"Welcome to humanity," Val said.

AVON BOOKS PRESENTS
MASTERS OF FANTASY AND ADVENTURE

**THE IRON DRAGON'S
DAUGHTER**   72098-1/$5.99 US/$7.99 CAN
by Michael Swanwick

**THE DRAGONS OF
THE RHINE**   76527-6/$5.99 US/$7.99 CAN
by Diana L. Paxson

TIGER BURNING BRIGHT   77512-3/$6.99 US/$8.99 CAN
*by Marion Zimmer Bradley, Andre Norton
and Mercedes Lackey*

THE LORD OF HORSES   76528-4/$5.99 US/$7.99 CAN
by Diana Paxson

FAIR PERIL   79430-6/$5.99 US/$7.99 CAN
by Nancy Springer

**WHEN THE GODS
ARE SILENT**   78848-9/$5.99 US/$7.99 CAN
by Jane Lindskold

MAGE HEART   78127-1/$5.99 US/$7.99 CAN
by Jane Routley